Wood Magic

Wood Magic

by

RICHARD JEFFERIES

WORDSWORTH CLASSICS

This edition published 1995 by Wordsworth Editions Ltd,
Cumberland House, Crib Street, Ware, Hertfordshire SG12 9ET.

ISBN 1-85326-153-X

Printed and bound in Denmark by Nørhaven.

The paper in this book is produced from pure wood
pulp, without the use of chlorine or any other substance
harmful to the environment. The energy used in its
production consists almost entirely of hydroelectricity
and heat generated from waste materials, thereby
conserving fossil fuels and contributing little to the
greenhouse effect.

VOL. I

CONTENTS.

———◇———

WOOD MAGIC.

CHAPTER I.

SIR BEVIS.

ONE morning as little "Sir" Bevis [such was his pet name] was digging in the farmhouse garden, he saw a daisy, and throwing aside his spade, he sat down on the grass to pick the flower to pieces. He pulled the pink-tipped petals off one by one, and as they dropped they were lost. Next he gathered a bright dandelion, and squeezed the white juice from the hollow stem, which drying presently, left his fingers stained with brown spots. Then he drew forth a bennet from its sheath, and bit and sucked it till his teeth were green from the sap. Lying at full length, he drummed the earth with his toes, while the tall grass blades tickled his cheeks.

Presently, rolling on his back, he drummed again with his heels. He looked up at the blue sky, but only for a moment, because the glare of light was too strong in his eyes. After a minute, he turned on his side, thrust out one arm, placed his head on it, and drew up one knee, as if going to sleep. His little brown wrist, bared by the sleeve shortening as he extended his arm, bent down the grass, and his still browner fingers played with the blades, and every now and then tore one off.

A flutter of wings sounded among the blossom on an apple-tree close by, and instantly Bevis sat up, knowing it must be a goldfinch thinking of building a nest in the branches. If the trunk of the tree had not been so big, he would have tried to climb it at once, but he knew he could not do it, nor could he see the bird for the leaves and bloom. A puff of wind came and showered the petals down upon him; they fell like snowflakes on his face and dotted the grass.

Buzz! A great humble-bee, with a band of red gold across his back, flew up, and hovered near, wavering to and fro in the air as he stayed to look at a flower.

Buzz! Bevis listened, and knew very well what he was saying. It was, "This is a sweet little

garden, my darling; a very pleasant garden; all
grass and daisies, and apple-trees, and narrow patches
with flowers and fruit-trees one side, and a wall
and currant-bushes another side, and a low box-
hedge and a haha, where you can see the high
mowing grass quite underneath you; and a round
summer-house in the corner, painted as blue inside
as a hedge-sparrow's egg is outside; and then
another haha with iron railings, which you are
always climbing up, Bevis, on the fourth side,
with stone steps leading down to a meadow, where
the cows are feeding, and where they have left
all the buttercups standing as tall as your waist,
sir. The gate in the iron railings is not fastened,
and besides, there is a gap in the box-hedge, and
it is easy to drop down the haha wall, but that
is mowing grass there. You know very well you
could not come to any harm in the meadow;
they said you were not to go outside the garden,
but that's all nonsense, and very stupid. *I* am
going outside the garden, Bevis. Good morning,
dear." Buzz! And the great humble-bee flew
slowly between the iron railings, out among the
buttercups, and away up the field.

Bevis went to the railings, and stood on the lowest bar; then he opened the gate a little way, but it squeaked so loud upon its rusty hinges that he let it shut again. He walked round the garden along beside the box-hedge to the patch by the lilac trees; they were single lilacs, which are much more beautiful than the double, and all bowed down with a mass of bloom. Some rhubarb grew there, and to bring it up the faster, they had put a round wooden box on it, hollowed out from the sawn butt of an elm, which was rotten within and easily scooped. The top was covered with an old board, and every time that Bevis passed he lifted up the corner of the board and peeped in, to see if the large red, swelling knobs were yet bursting.

One of these round wooden boxes had been split and spoilt, and half of it was left lying with the hollow part downwards. Under this shelter a Toad had his house. Bevis peered in at him, and touched him with a twig to make him move an inch or two, for he was so lazy, and sat there all day long, except when it rained. Sometimes the Toad told him a story, but not very often, for he was a silent old philosopher, and not very fond of anybody. He had a nephew, quite a lively young fellow, in the cucumber frame on the other side of the lilac bushes, at whom Bevis also peered nearly every day after they had lifted the frame and propped it up with wedges.

The gooseberries were no bigger than beads, but he tasted two, and then a thrush began to sing on an ash-tree in the hedge of the meadow. "Bevis! Bevis!" said the thrush, and he turned round to listen: "My dearest Bevis, have you forgotten the meadow, and the buttercups, and the sorrel? You know the sorrel, don't you, that tastes so pleasant if you nibble the leaf? And I have a nest in the bushes, not very far up the hedge, and you may take just one egg; there are only two yet. But don't tell any more boys about it, or we shall not have one left. That is a very sweet garden, but it is very small. I like all these fields to fly about in, and the swallows fly ever so much farther than I can; so far away and so high, that I cannot tell you how they find their way home to the chimney. But they will tell you, if you ask them. Good morning! *I* am going over the brook."

Bevis went to the iron railings and got up two

bars, and looked over; but he could not yet make
up his mind, so he went inside the summer-house,
which had one small round window. All the lower
part of the blue walls was scribbled and marked
with pencil, where he had written and drawn, and
put down his ideas and notes. The lines were somewhat intermingled, and crossed each other, and some
stretched out long distances, and came back in sharp
angles. But Bevis knew very well what he meant
when he wrote it all. Taking a stump of cedar
pencil from his pocket, one end of it much gnawn,
he added a few scrawls to the inscriptions, and
then stood on the seat to look out of the round
window, which was darkened by an old cob-web.

Once upon a time there was a very cunning
spider—a very cunning spider indeed. The old Toad
by the rhubarb told Bevis there had not been
such a cunning spider for many summers; he knew
almost as much about flies as the old Toad, and
caught such a great number, that the Toad began
to think there would be none left for him. Now
the Toad was extremely fond of flies, and he
watched the spider with envy, and grew more
angry about it every day.

As he sat blinking and winking by the rhubarb in his house all day long, the Toad never left off thinking, thinking, thinking about this spider. And as he kept thinking, thinking, thinking, so he told Bevis, he recollected that he knew a great deal about a good many other things besides flies. So one day, after several weeks of thinking, he crawled out of his house in the sunshine, which he did not like at all, and went across the grass to the iron railings, where the spider had then got his web. The spider saw him coming, and being very proud of his cleverness, began to taunt and tease him.

"Your back is all over warts, and you are an old toad," he said. "You are so old, that I heard the swallows saying their great, great, great grandmothers, when they built in the chimney, did not know when you were born. And you have got foolish, and past doing anything, and so stupid that you hardly know when it is going to rain. Why, the sun is shining bright, you stupid old toad, and there isn't a chance of a single drop falling. You look very ugly down there in the grass. Now, don't you wish that you were me,

and could catch more flies than you could eat?
Why, I can catch wasps and bees, and tie them
up so tight with my threads that they cannot
sting nor even move their wings, nor so much as
wriggle their bodies. I am the very cleverest and
most cunning spider that ever lived."

"Indeed, you are," replied the Toad. "I have
been thinking so all the summer; and so much do
I admire you, that I have come all this way,
across in the hot sun, to tell you something."

"Tell *me* something!" said the spider, much
offended. "*I* know everything."

"Oh, yes, honoured sir," said the Toad; "you
have such wonderful eyes, and such a sharp mind,
it is true that you know everything about the sun,
and the moon, and the earth, and flies. But, as
you have studied all these great and important
things, you could hardly see all the very little
trifles like a poor old toad."

"Oh yes, I can. I know everything — everything!"

"But, sir," went on the Toad so humbly, "this
is such a little—such a very little — thing, and a
spider like you in such a high position of life,

could not mind me telling you such a mere nothing."

"Well, I don't mind," said the spider — "you may go on, and tell me, if you like."

"The fact is," said the Toad, "while I have been sitting in my hole, I have noticed that such a lot of the flies that come into this garden presently go into the summer-house there, and when they are in the summer-house, they always go to that little round window, which is sometimes quite black with them; for it is the nature of flies to buzz over glass."

"I do not know so much about that," said the spider; "for I have never lived in houses, being an independent insect; but it is possible you may be right. At any rate, it is not of much consequence. You had better go up into the window, old toad." Now this was a sneer on the part of the spider.

"But I can't climb up into the window," said the Toad; "all I can do is to crawl about the ground, but you can run up a wall quickly. How I do wish I was a spider, like you. Oh, dear!" And then the Toad turned round, after bowing to the clever spider, and went back to his hole.

Now the spider was secretly very much mortified and angry with himself, because he had not noticed this about the flies going to the window in the summer-house. At first he said to himself that it was not true; but he could not help looking that way now and then, and every time he looked, there was the window crowded with flies. They had all the garden to buzz about in, and all the fields, but instead of wandering under the trees, and over the flowers, they preferred to go into the summer-house and crawl over the glass of the little window, though it was very dirty from so many feet. For a long time, the spider was too proud to go there too; but one day such a splendid blue-bottle fly got in the window and made such a tremendous buzzing, that he could not resist it any more.

So he left his web by the railings, and climbed up the blue-painted wall, over Bevis's writings and marks, and spun such a web in the window as had never before been seen. It was the largest and the finest, and the most beautifully-arranged web

that had ever been made, and it caught such a
number of flies that the spider grew fatter every
day. In a week's time he was so big that he
could no longer hide in the crack he had chosen,
he was quite a giant ; and the Toad came across
the grass one night and looked at him, but the
spider was now so bloated he would not recognise
the Toad.

But one morning a robin came to the iron
railings, and perched on the top, and put his head
a little on one side, to show his black eye the better.
Then he flew inside the summer-house, alighted in
the window, and gobbled up the spider in an
instant. The old Toad shut his eye and opened it
again, and went on thinking, for that was just what
he knew would happen. Ever so many times in
his very long life he had seen spiders go up
there, but no sooner had they got fat than a
robin or a wren came in and ate them. Some of
the clever spider's web was there still when Bevis
looked out of the window, all dusty and draggled,
with the skins and wings of some gnats and a
dead leaf entangled in it.

As he looked, a white butterfly came along the

meadow, and instantly he ran out, flung open the
gate, rushed down the steps, and taking no heed
of the squeak the gate made as it shut behind
him, raced after the butterfly.

The tall buttercups brushed his knees, and bent
on either side as if a wind was rushing through
them. A bennet slipped up his knickerbockers and
tickled his leg. His toes only touched the ground,
neither his heels nor the hollow of his foot; and
from so light a pressure the grass, bowed but not
crushed, rose up, leaving no more mark of his
passage than if a grasshopper had gone by.

Daintily fanning himself with his wings, the
butterfly went before Bevis, not yet knowing that
he was chased, but sauntering along just above
the buttercups. He peeped as he flew under the
lids of the flowers' eyes, to see if any of them
loved him. There was a glossy green leaf which
he thought he should like to feel, it looked so
soft and satin-like. So he alighted on it, and
then saw Bevis coming, his hat on the very back
of his head, and his hand stretched out to catch
him. The butterfly wheeled himself round on the
leaf, shut up his wings, and seemed so innocent,

till Bevis fell on his knee, and then under his fingers there was nothing but the leaf. His cheek flushed, his eye lit up, and away he darted again after the butterfly, which had got several yards ahead before he could recover himself. He ran now faster than ever.

" Race on," said the buttercups; "race on, Bevis; that butterfly disdains us because we are so many, and all alike."

" Be quick," said a great moon-daisy to him; "catch him, dear. I asked him to stay and tell me a story, but he would not."

" Never mind me," said the clover; "you may step on me if you like, love."

" But just look at me for a moment, pet, as you go by," cried the purple vetch by the hedge.

A colt in the field seeing Bevis running so fast, thought he too must join the fun, so he whisked his tail, stretched his long floundering legs, and galloped away. Then the mare whinnied and galloped too, and the ground shook under her heavy hoofs. The cows lifted their heads from gathering the grass close round the slender bennets, and wondered why any one could be so foolish as to rush about, when there was plenty to eat and no hurry.

The cunning deceitful butterfly, so soon as Bevis came near, turned aside and went along a furrow. Bevis running in the furrow, caught his foot in the long creepers of the crowfoot, and fell down bump, and pricked his hand with a thistle. Up he jumped again, red as a peony, and shouting in his rage, ran on so quickly that he nearly overtook the butterfly. But they were now nearer the other hedge. The butterfly, frightened at the shouting and Bevis's resolution, rose over the brambles, and Bevis stopping short flung his hat at him. The hat did not hit the butterfly, but the wind it made puffed him round, and so frightened him, that he flew up half as high as the elms, and went into the next field.

When Bevis looked down, there was his hat, hung on a branch of ash, far beyond his reach. He could not touch the lowest leaf, jump as much as he would. His next thought was a stone to throw, but there were none in the meadow. Then he put his hand in his jacket pocket for his knife, to cut a long stick. It was not in that pocket, nor in the one on the other side, nor in his knickers. Now the knife was Bevis's greatest treasure—his very greatest. He looked all round bewildered, and the tears rose in his eyes.

Just then Pan, the spaniel, who had worked his head loose from the collar and followed him, ran out of the hedge between Bevis's legs with such joyful force, that Bevis was almost overthrown, and burst into a fit of laughter. Pan ran back into the hedge to hunt, and Bevis, with tears rolling down his cheeks into the dimples made by his smiles, dropped on hands and knees and crept in after the dog under the briars. On the bank there was a dead grey stick, a branch that had fallen from the elms. It was heavy, but Bevis heaved it up, and pushed it through the boughs and thrust his hat off.

Creeping out again, he put it on, and remembering his knife, walked out into the field to search for it. When Pan missed him, he followed, and presently catching scent of a rabbit, the spaniel rushed down a furrow, which happened to be the very furrow where Bevis had tumbled. Going after Pan, Bevis found his knife in the grass, where it

had dropped when shaken from his pocket by the
jerk of his fall. He opened the single blade it
contained at once, and went back to the hedge to
cut a stick. As he walked along the hedge, he
thought the briar was too prickly to cut, and the
thorn was too hard, and the ash was too big, and
the willow had no knob, and the elder smelt so
strong, and the sapling oak was across the ditch,
and out of reach, and the maple had such rough
bark. So he wandered along a great way through
that field and the next, and presently saw a nut-
tree stick that promised well, for the sticks grew
straight, and not too big.

He jumped into the ditch, climbed half up the
mound, and began to cut away at one of the rods,
leaning his left arm on the moss-grown stole.
The bark was easily cut through, and he soon
made a notch, but then the wood seemed to grow
harder, and the chips he got out were very small.
The harder the wood, the more determined Bevis
became, and he cut and worked away with such
force that his chest heaved, his brow was set and
frowning, and his jacket all green from rubbing
against the hazel. Suddenly something passed be-

tween him and the light. He looked up, and there was Pan, whom he had forgotten, in the hedge looking down at him. "Pan! Pan!" cried Bevis. Pan wagged his tail, but ran back, and Bevis, forsaking his stick, scrambled up into the stole, then into the mound, and through a gap into the next field. Pan was nowhere to be seen.

There was a large mossy root under a great oak, and, hot with his cutting, Bevis sat down upon it. Along came a house martin, the kind of swallow that has a white band across his back, flying very low, and only just above the grass. The swallow flew to and fro not far from Bevis, who watched it, and presently asked him to come closer. But the swallow said, "I shall not come any nearer, Bevis. Don't you remember what you did last year, sir? Don't you remember Bill, the carters' boy, put a ladder against the wall, and you climbed up the ladder, and put your paw, all brown and dirty, into my nest and took my eggs? And you tried to string them on a bennet, but the bennet was too big, so you went indoors for some thread. And you made my wife and me dreadfully unhappy, and we said we would never come back any more to your house, Bevis."

"But you have come back, swallow."

"Yes, we have come back—just once more; but if you do it again we shall go away for ever."

"But I won't do it again ; no, that I won't ! Do come near."

So the swallow came a little nearer, only two yards away, and flew backwards and forwards, and Bevis could hear the snap of his beak as he caught the flies.

"Just a little bit nearer still," said he. "Let me stroke your lovely white back."

"Oh, no, I can't do that. I don't think you are quite safe, Bevis. Why don't you gather the cowslips?"

Bevis looked up and saw that the field was full of cowslips — yellow with cowslips. "I will pick every one," said he, "and carry them all back to my mother."

"You cannot do that," said the swallow, laughing, "you will not try long enough."

"I *hate* you!" cried Bevis in a passion, and flung his knife, which was in his hand, at the bird.

The swallow rose up, and the knife whizzed by and struck the ground.

"I told you you were not safe," said the swallow over his head; "and I am sure you won't pick half the cowslips."

Bevis picked up his knife and put it in his pocket; then he began to gather the cowslips, and kept on for a quarter of an hour as fast as ever he could, till both hands were full. There was a rustle in the hedge, and looking up he saw Pan come out, all brown with sand sticking to his coat. He shook himself, and sent the sand flying from him in a cloud, just like he did with the water when he came up out of the pond. Then he looked at Bevis, wagged his tail, cried "yowp!" and ran back into the hedge again.

Bevis rushed to the spot, and saw that there was a large rabbits' hole. Into this hole Pan had worked his way so far that there was nothing of him visible but his hind legs and tail. Bevis could hear him panting in the hole, he was working so hard to get at the rabbit, and tearing with his teeth at the roots to make the hole bigger. Bevis clapped his hands, dropping his cowslips, and called "Loo!

Loo!" urging the dog on. The sand came flying out behind Pan, and he worked harder and harder, as if he would tear the mound to pieces.

Bevis sat down on the grass under the shadow of the oak, by a maple bush, and taking a cowslip, began to count the spots inside it. It was always five in all the cowslips—five brown little spots—that he was sure of, because he knew he had five fingers on each hand. He lay down at full length on his back, and looked up at the sky through the boughs of the oak. It was very very blue, and very near down. With a long ladder he knew he could have got up there easily, and it looked so sweet. "Sky," said Bevis, "I love you like I love my mother." He pouted his lips, and kissed at it. Then turning a little on one side to watch Pan, in an instant he fell firm asleep.

Pan put his head out of the hole to breathe two or three times, and looked aside at Bevis, and seeing that he was still, went back to work again. Two butterflies came fluttering along together. The swallow returned, and flew low down along the grass near Bevis. The wind came now and then, and shook down a shower of white and pink petals from a crab-tree in the hedge. By and by a squirrel climbing from tree to tree reached the oak, and stayed to look at Bevis beneath in the shadow. He knew exactly how Bevis felt—just like he did himself when he went to sleep.

CHAPTER II.

AT HOME.

" Yowp, yow ; wow-wow ! " The yelling of Pan
woke Bevis, who jumped up, and seeing the Bailiff
beating the spaniel with a stick, instantly, and without staying the tenth of a second to rub his eyes or
stretch himself, rushed at the man and hit him with
his doubled fists. As if he had seen it in his sleep,
Bevis understood what was taking place immediately
his eye-lids opened. So the Bailiff beat the dog, and
Bevis beat the Bailiff. The noise made quite an
echo against the thick hedges and a high bank
that was near. When the Bailiff thought he had
thrashed Pan sufficiently, he turned round and looked
down at Bevis, whose face was red, and his knuckles
sore with striking the Bailiff's hard coat.

" How fess you be, measter," said the Bailiff
(meaning fierce), " you mind as you don't hurt yourself. Look'ee here, there've bin a fine falarie about
you, zur." He meant that there had been much

excitement when it was found that Bevis was not in the garden, and was nowhere to be found. Everybody was set to hunt for him.

First they thought of the brook, lest he should have walked in among the flags that were coming up so green and strong. Then they thought of the tallet over the stable,—perhaps he had climbed up there again from the manger, over the heads of the great cart-horses, quietly eating their hay, while he put his foot on the manger and then on the projecting steps in the corner, and into the hayrack—and so up. He had done it once before, and could not get down, and so the tallet was searched. One man was sent to the Longpond, with orders to look everywhere, and borrow the punt and push in among the bulrushes.

Another was despatched to the Close, to gruffly enquire where the cottage boys were, and what they had been doing, for Bevis was known to hanker after their company, to go catching loach under the stones in the stream that crossed the road, and creeping under the arch of the bridge, and taking the moorhens' eggs from the banks of the ponds where the rushes were thick. Another was put on the pony,

to gallop up the road after the carter and his
waggon, for he had set off that morning with a load
of hay for the hills that could be seen to the south-
ward.

Running over every possible thing that Bevis
could have done in his mind, his papa remembered
that he had lately taken to asking about the road,
and would not be satisfied till they had taken him
up to the sign-post—a mile beyond the village, and
explained the meaning of it.   Some one had told
him that it was the road to Southampton—the place
where the ships came.   Now, Bevis was full of the
ships, drawing them on the blue wall of the summer-
house, and floating a boat on the trough in the
cow-yard, and looking wistfully up the broad dusty
highway, as if he could see the masts and yards sixty
miles away or more.   Perhaps when the carter went
with the waggon that way, Bevis had slipped up the
footpath that made a short cut across the fields, and
joined the waggon at the cross roads, that he might
ride to the hills thinking to see the sea on the other
side.

And the Bailiff, not to be behindhand, having
just come in for his lunch, ran out again without

so much as wetting his stubbly white beard in the froth of the drawn quart of ale, and made away as fast as his stiff legs could carry him to where there was a steam ploughing engine at work—a mile distant. The sight of the white steam, and the humming of the fly-wheel, always set Bevis "on the jig," as the village folk called it, to get to the machinery, and the smell of the cotton waste and oil wafted on the wind was to him like the scent of battle to the war-horse.

But Bevis was not in the tallet, nor the brook, nor among the bulrushes of the Longpond, nor under the bridge dabbling for loach, nor watching the steam plough, and the cottage boys swore their hardest (and they knew how to swear quite properly) that they had not seen him that morning. But they would look for him, and forthwith eagerly started to scour the fields and hedges. Meantime, Bevis, quite happy, was sleeping under the oak in the shadow, with Pan every now and then coming out of the rabbit-hole to snort out the sand that got into his nostrils.

But, by-and-by, when everything had been done and everybody was scattered over the earth seeking for him, the Bailiff came back from the steam plough, weary with running, and hungry, thirsty, and cross. As he passed through the yard he caught a glimpse of Pan's kennel, which was a tub by the wood pile, and saw that the chain was lying stretched to its full length. Pan was gone. At first the Bailiff thought Bevis had loosed him, and that he had got a clue. But when he came near, he saw that the collar was not unbuckled; Pan had worked his head out, and so escaped.

The Bailiff turned the collar over thoughtfully with his foot, and felt his scanty white beard with his hard hand; and then he went back to the cart-house. Up in the cart-house, on the ledge of the wall beneath the thatch, there were three or four sticks, each about four feet long and as thick as your thumb, with the bark on—some were ground ash, some crab-tree, and one was hazel. This one was straight and as hard as could be. These sticks were put there for the time when the cows were moved, so that the men might find their sticks quick. Each had his stick, and the Bailiff's was the hazel one. With the staff in his hand the Bailiff set out straight across the grass, looking neither to the right nor the left, but walking deliberately and without hesitation.

He got through a gap in one hedge, and then he turned to the corner making towards the rabbit-burrows, for he guessed that Pan had gone there. As he approached he saw Bevis sleeping, and smiled, for looking for the dog he had found the boy. But first stepping softly up to Bevis, and seeing that he was quite right and unhurt, only asleep, the Bailiff went to the hedge and thrust his staff into the hole where Pan was at work.

Out came Pan, and instantly down came the rod. Pan cowered in the grass; he was all over sand, which flew up in a cloud as the rod struck him again. "Yowp! yow—wow—wow!" and this row awoke Bevis.

Bevis battled hard for his dog, but the Bailiff had had his lunch delayed, and his peace of mind upset about the boy, and he was resolutely relieving himself upon the spaniel. Now the hazel rod being dry and stiff, was like a bar of iron, and did not yield or bend in the least, but made the spaniel's ribs rattle. Pan could not get low enough into the grass; he ceased to howl, so great was the pain, but merely whimpered, and the tears filled his brown eyes. At last the Bailiff ceased, and immediately Bevis pulled out his handkerchief, and sat down on the grass and wiped away the spaniel's tears.

" Now, measter, you come along wi' I," said the Bailiff, taking his hand. Bevis would not come, saying he hated him. But when the Bailiff told him about the hunt there had been, and how the people were everywhere looking for him, Bevis began to laugh, thinking it was rare fun.

" Take me ' pick-a-back,' " said he.

So the Bailiff stooped and took him. " Gee-up!" said Bevis, punching his broad back and kicking him to go faster. Pan, now quite forgotten, crept along behind them.

Bevis listened to the lecture they gave him at home with a very bad grace. He sulked and pouted, as if he had himself been the injured party. But no sooner was he released from the dinner-table, than he was down on his knees at his own particular corner cupboard, the one that had been set apart for his toys and things ever since he could walk. It was but a small cupboard, made across the angle of two walls, and with one shelf only, yet it was bottomless, and always contained something new.

There were the last fragments of the great box of wooden bricks, cut and chipped, and notched and splintered by that treasure, his pocket-knife. There was the tin box for the paste, or the worms in moss, when he went fishing. There was the wheel of his old wheelbarrow, long since smashed and numbered with the Noah's arks that have gone the usual way. There was the brazen cylinder of a miniature steam-engine bent out of all shape. There was the hammer-head made specially for him by the blacksmith down in the village, without a handle, for people were tired of putting new handles to it, he broke them so quickly. There was a horse-shoe, and the iron catch of a gate, and besides these a boxwood top, which he could not spin, but which he had paid away half the savings in his money-box for, because he had seen it split the other boys' tops in the road.

In one corner was a brass cannon, the touch-hole blackened by the explosion of gunpowder, and by it the lock of an ancient pistol—the lock only, and neither barrel nor handle. An old hunting crop, some feathers from pheasants' tails, part of a mole-trap, an old brazen bugle, much battered, a wooden fig-box full of rusty nails, several scraps of deal board and stumps of cedar pencil were heaped together in confusion. But these were not all, nor could any written inventory exhaust the contents, and give a perfect list of all that cupboard held. There was always something new in it: Bevis never went there, but he found something.

With the hunting crop he followed the harriers and chased the doubling hare; with the cannon he fought battles, such as he saw in the pictures; the bugle, too, sounded the charge (the Bailiff sometimes blew it in the garden to please him, and the hollow "who-oo!" it made echoed over the fields); with the deal boards and the rusty nails, and the hammer-head, he built houses, and even cities. The jagged and splintered wooden bricks, six inches long, were not bricks, but great beams and baulks of timber; the wheel of the wheelbarrow was the centre of many curious pieces of mechanism. He could see these things easily. So he sat down at his cupboard and forgot the lecture instantly; the pout disappeared from his lips as he plunged his hand into the inexhaustible cupboard.

" Bevis, dear," he heard presently, " you may have an apple."

Instantly, and without staying to shut the door on his treasures, he darted upstairs—up two flights, with a clatter and a bang, burst open the door, and was in the apple-room. It was a large garret or attic, running half the length of the house, and there, in the autumn, the best apples from the orchard were carried, and put on a thin layer of hay, each apple apart from its fellow (for they ought not to touch), and each particular sort, the Blenheim Oranges and the King Pippins, the Creepers and the Grindstone Pippins (which grew nowhere else), divided from the next sort by a little fence of hay.

The most of them were gone now, only a few of the keeping apples remained, and from these Bevis, with great deliberation, chose the biggest, measuring them by the eye and weighing them in his hand. Then down-stairs again with a clatter and a bang, down the second stairs this time, past the gun-room, where the tools were kept, and a carpenter's bench ; then through the whole length of the ground floor from the kitchen to the parlour, slamming

every door behind him, and kicking over the chairs
in front of him.

There he stayed half a minute to look at the
hornet's nest under the glass case on the mantel-
piece. The comb was built round a central pillar or
column, three stories one above the other, and it
had been taken from the willow tree by the brook,
the huge hollow willow which he had twice tried to
chop down, that he might make a boat of it. Then
out of doors, and up the yard, and past the cart-
house, when something moved in the long grass
under the wall. It was a Weasel, caught in a gin.

The trap had been set by the side of a drain for
rats, and the Weasel coming out, or perhaps frightened
by footsteps, and hastening carelessly, had been
trapped. Bevis, biting his apple, looked at the
Weasel, and the Weasel said, "Sir Bevis, please let
me out, this gin hurts me so; the teeth are very
sharp and the spring is very strong, and the tar-
cord is very stout, so that I cannot break it. See
how the iron has skinned my leg and taken off the
fur, and I am in such pain. Do please let me go,
before the ploughboy comes, or he will hit me with
a stick, or smash me with a stone, or put his iron-

shod heel on me; and I have been a very good weasel, Bevis. I have been catching the horrid rats that eat the barley-meal put for the pigs. Oh, let me out, the gin hurts me so!"

Bevis put his foot on the spring, and was pressing it down, and the Weasel thought he was already free, and looked across at the wood pile under which he meant to hide, when Bevis heard a little squeak close to his head, and looked up and saw a Mouse under the eaves of the cart-house, peeping forth from a tiny crevice, where the mortar had fallen from between the stones of the wall.

"Bevis, Bevis!" said the Mouse, "don't you do it—don't you let that Weasel go! He is a most dreadful wicked weasel, and his teeth are ever so much sharper than that gin. He does not kill the rats, because he is afraid of them (unless he can assassinate one in his sleep), but he murdered my wife and sucked her blood, and her body, all dry and withered, is up in the beam there, if you will get a ladder and look. And he killed all my little mouses, and made me very unhappy, and I shall never be able to get another wife to live with me in this cart-house while he is about. There is no

way we can get away from him. If we go out
into the field he follows us there, and if we go into
the sheds he comes after us there, and he is a cruel
beast, that wicked weasel. You know you ate the
partridge's eggs," added the Mouse, speaking to the
Weasel.

"It is all false," said the Weasel. "But it is
true that you ate the wheat out of the ears in the
wheat-rick, and you know what was the consequence.
If that little bit of wheat you ate had been threshed,
and ground, and baked, and made into bread, then
that poor girl would have had a crust to eat, and
would not have jumped into the river, and she would
have had a son, and he would have been a great
man and fought battles, just as Bevis does with his
brazen cannon, and won great victories, and been
the pride of all the nation. But you ate those particular grains of wheat that were meant to do all
this, you wicked little mouse. Besides which, you
ran across the bed one night, and frightened Bevis's
mother."

"But I did not mean to," said the Mouse; "and
you did mean to kill my wife, and you ate the partridge's eggs."

"And a very good thing I did," said the Weasel. "Do you know what would have happened, if I had not taken them? I did it all for good, and with the best intentions. For if I had left the eggs one more day, there was a man who meant to have stolen them all but one, which he meant to have left to deceive the keeper. If he had stolen them, he would have been caught, for the keeper was watching for him all the time, and he would have been put to prison, and his children would have been hungry. So I ate the eggs, and especially I ate every bit of the one the man meant to have left."

"And why were you so particular about eating that egg?" asked Bevis.

"Because," said the Weasel, "if that egg had come to a partridge chick, and the chick had lived till the shooting-time came, then the sportsman and his brother, when they came round, would have started it out of the stubble, and the shot from the gun of the younger would have accidentally killed the elder, and people would have thought it was done to murder him for the sake of the inheritance."

"Now, is this true?" said Bevis.

"Yes, that it is ; and I killed the mouse's wife also for the best of reasons."

"You horrid wretch !" cried the Mouse.

"Oh, you needn't call me a wretch," said the Weasel; "I am sure you ought to be grateful to me, for your wife was very jealous because you paid so much attention to the Miss Mouse you want to marry now, and in the night she meant to have gnawn your throat."

"And you frightened my mother," said Bevis, "by running across her bed in the night;" and he began to press on the spring of the gin.

"Yes, that he did," said the Weasel, overjoyed ; "and he made a hole in the boards of the floor, and it was down that hole that the half-sovereign rolled and was lost, and the poor maid-servant sent away because they thought she had stolen it."

"What do you say to that ?" asked Bevis.

But the Mouse was quite aghast and dumb-founded, and began to think that it was he after all who was in the wrong, so that for the moment he could not speak. Just then Bevis caught sight of the colt that had come up beside his mother, the cart mare, to the fence ; and thinking that he would go and try and stroke the pretty creature, Bevis started forward, forgetting all about the Weasel and the Mouse. As he started, he pressed the spring down, and in an instant the Weasel was out, and had hobbled across to the wood pile. When the Mouse saw this, he gave a little squeak of terror, and ran back to his hiding-place.

But when Bevis put out his hand to stroke the colt, the colt started back, so he picked up a stick and threw at him. Then he took another stick and hunted the hens round and round the ricks to make them lay their eggs faster, as it is well known that is the best way. For he remembered that last year they had shown him three tiny bantam chicks, such darling little things, all cuddled cosily together in the hollow of a silver table-spoon. The hens clucked and raced, and Bevis raced after and shouted, and the cock slipping on one side, for it hurt his dignity to run away like the rest, hopped upon the railings, flapped his wings, crew, and cried, "You'll be glad when I'm dead." That was how Bevis translated his "hurra-ca-roorah."

In the midst of the noise out came Polly, the dairymaid, with a bone for Pan, which Bevis no

sooner saw, than he asked her to let him give Pan
his dinner. "Very well, dear," said Polly, and went
in to finish her work. So Bevis took the bone, and
Pan, all weary and sore from his thrashing, crept
out from his tub to receive it; but Bevis put the
bone on the grass (all the grass was worn bare where
Pan could reach) just where the spaniel could smell
it nicely but could not get it. Pan struggled, and
scratched, and howled, and scratched again, and tugged
till his collar, buckled tightly now, choked him, and
he gasped and panted, while Bevis taking the remnant of his apple from his pocket, nibbled it and
laughed with a face like an angel's for sweetness.

Then a rook went over and cawed, and Bevis, looking up at the bird, caught a glimpse of the swing
over the wall—it stood under the sycamore tree.
Dropping the bit of apple, away he ran to the swing,
and sat in it, and pushed himself off. As he swung
forward he straightened his legs and leant back;
when he swung back he drew his feet under him and
leant forward, and by continuing this the weight of
his body caused the swing to rise like a pendulum
till he went up among the sycamore boughs, nearly
as high as the ivy-grown roof of the summer-house,

just opposite. There he went to and fro, as easily as possible, shutting his eyes and humming to himself.

Presently a cock chaffinch came and perched in the ash close by, and immediately began to sing his war-song: "I am lord of this tree," sang the chaffinch, "I am lord of this tree; every bough is mine, and every leaf, and the wind that comes through it, and the sunshine that falls on it, and the rain that moistens it, and the blue sky over it, and the grass underneath it—all this is mine. My nest is going to be made in the ivy that grows half-way up the trunk, and my wife is very busy to-day bringing home the fibres and the moss, and I have just come back a little while to tell you all that none of you must come into or touch my tree. I like this tree, and therefore it is mine. Be careful that none of you come inside the shadow of it, or I shall peck you with all my might."

Then he paused awhile, and Bevis went on swinging and listening. In a minute or two another chaffinch came to the elm in the hedge just outside the garden, and quite close to the ash. Directly he perched, he ruffled up and began to sing too, "I am lord of this tree, and it is a very high

tree, much higher than the ash, and even above the
oak where that slow fellow the crow is building.
Mine is the very highest tree of all, and I am the
brightest and prettiest of all the chaffinches.   See
my colours how bright they are, so that you would
hardly know me from a bullfinch.   There is not a
feather rumpled in my wing, or my tail, and I have
the most beautiful eyes of all of you."

Hardly had he done singing than another chaffinch came into the crab-tree, a short way up the
hedge, and he began to sing too.   "I have a much
bigger tree than either of you, but as it is at the top
of the field I cannot bring it down here, but I have
come down into this crab-tree, and I say it is mine,
and I am lord of two trees.   I am stronger than
both of you, and neither of you dare come near me."

The two other chaffinches were silent for a
minute, and then one of them, the knight of the
ash-tree, flew down into the hedge under the crab-
tree ; and instantly down flew the third chaffinch,
and they fought a battle, and pecked and buffeted
one another with their wings, till Bevis' tears ran
down with laughing.   Presently they parted, and
the third chaffinch went home to his tree at the top

of the field, leaving one little feather on the ground, which the first chaffinch picked up and carried to his nest in the ash.

But scarcely had he woven it into the nest than down flew the second chaffinch from the elm into the shadow of the ash. Flutter, flutter went the first chaffinch to meet him, and they had such a battle as Bevis had never seen before, and fought till they were tired ; then each flew up into his tree, and sang again about their valour.

Immediately afterwards ten sparrows came from the house-top into the bushes, chattering and struggling all together, scratching, pecking, buffeting, and all talking at once. After they had had a good fight they all went back to the house-top, and began to tell each other what tremendous blows they had given. Then there was such a great cawing from the rook trees, which were a long way off, that it was evident a battle was going on there, and Bevis heard the chaffinch say that one of the rooks had been caught stealing his cousin's sticks.

Next two goldfinches began to fight, and then a blackbird came up from the brook and perched on a rail, and he was such a boaster, for he said he had the yellowest bill of all the blackbirds, and the blackest coat, and the largest eye, and the sweetest whistle, and he was lord over all the blackbirds. In two minutes up came another one from out of the bramble bushes at the corner, and away they went chattering at each other. Presently the starlings on the chimney began to quarrel, and had a terrible set-to. Then a wren came by, and though he was so small, his boast was worse than the blackbirds', for he said he was the sharpest, and the cleverest of all the birds, and knew more than all put together.

Afar off, in the trees, there were six or seven thrushes, all declaring that they were the best singers, and had the most speckled necks; and up in the sky the swallows were saying that they had the whitest bosoms.

"Oo! whoo," cried a wood-pigeon from the very oak under which Bevis had gone to sleep. "There are none who can fly so fast as I can. I am a captain of the wood-pigeons, and in the winter I have three hundred and twenty-two pigeons under me, and they all do exactly as I tell them. They fly when I fly, and settle down when I settle down. If I go to the west, they go to the west; and if I go to the east, then they follow to the east. I have the biggest acorns, and the best of the peas, for they leave them especially for me. And not one of all the three hundred and twenty-two pigeons dares to begin to eat the wheat in August till I say it is ripe and they may, and not one of them dares to take a wife till I say yes. Oo-whoo! Is not my voice sweet and soft, and delicious, far sweeter than that screeching nightingale's in the hawthorn yonder?"

But he had no sooner finished than another one began in the fir copse, and said he was captain of one thousand pigeons, and was ever so much stronger, and could fly ten miles an hour faster. So away went the first pigeon to the fir copse, and there was a great clattering of wings and "oo-whoo"-ing, and how it was settled Bevis could not tell.

So as he went on swinging, he heard all the birds quarrelling, and boasting, and fighting, hundreds of them all round, and he said to the chaffinch on the ash :—

"Chaffinch, it seems to me that you are all very wicked birds, for you think of nothing but fighting all day long."

The chaffinch laughed, and said, "My dear Sir

Bevis, I do not know what you mean by wicked. But fighting is very nice indeed, and we all feel so jolly when fighting time comes. For you must know that the spring is the duelling time, when all the birds go to battle. There is not a tree nor a bush on your papa's farm, nor on all the farms all round, nor in all the country, nor in all this island, but some fighting is going on. I have not time to tell you all about it; but I wish you could read our history, and all about the wars that have been going on these thousand years. Perhaps if you should ever meet the Squirrel he will tell you, for he knows most about history. As we all like it so much, it must be right, and we never hurt one another very much. Sometimes a feather is knocked out, and sometimes one gets a hard peck; but it does not do any harm. And after it is over, in the autumn we are all very good friends, and go hunting together. You may see us, hundreds of us in your papa's stubble-fields, Bevis, all flying together very happy. I think the sky-larks fight the most, for they begin almost in the winter if the sun shines warm for an hour, and they keep on all day in the summer, and till it is quite dark and the stars are out, besides getting up before the cuckoo to go on again. Yet they are the sweetest, and nicest, of all the birds, and the most gentle, and do not mind our coming into their fields. So I am sure, Bevis, that you are wrong, and fighting is not wicked if you love one another. You and Mark are fond of one another, but you hit him sometimes, don't you?"

"Yes, that I do," said Bevis, very eagerly, "I hit him yesterday so hard with my bat that he would not come and play with me. It is very nice to hit any one."

"But you cannot do it like we do it," said the chaffinch, swelling with pride again, "for we sing and you can't, and if you can't sing you have no business to fight, and besides, though you are much older than me you are not married yet. Now I have such a beautiful wife, and to tell you the truth, Bevis, we do the fighting because the ladies love to see it, and kiss us for it afterwards. I am the knight of this tree!"

After which Bevis, being tired of swinging, went to the summer-house to read what he had written with his stump of pencil till he was called to tea. In the evening, when the sun was sinking, he went

out and lay down on the seat—it was a broad plank
grey with lichen—under the russet apple-tree, looking
towards the west, over the brook below. He saw the
bees coming home to the hives close by on the
haha, and they seemed to come high in the air,
flying straight as if from the distant hills where the
sun was. He heard the bees say that there were such
quantities of flowers on the hills, and such pleasant
places, and that the sky was much more blue up
there, and he thought if he could he would go to
the hills soon.

CHAPTER III.

ADVENTURES OF THE WEASEL.

AFTER awhile the mowers came and began to cut the long grass in the Home Field, and the meadow by the brook. Bevis could see them from the garden, and it was impossible to prevent him from straying up the footpath, so eager was he to go nearer. The best thing that could be done, since he could not be altogether stopped, was to make him promise that he would not go beyond a certain limit. He might wander as much as he pleased inside the hedge and the Home Field, in which there was no pond, nor any place where he could very well come to harm. But he must not creep through the hedge, so that he would always be in sight from the garden. If he wished to enter the meadow by the brook he must ask special permission, that some one might be put to watch now and then.

But more expressly he was forbidden to enter the Little Field. The grass there was not yet to be mown

—it was too long to walk in—and they were afraid
lest he should get through the hedge, or climb over
the high pad-locked gate in some way or other, for
the Longpond was on the other side, though it could
not be seen for trees. Nor was he to approach
nearer to the mowers than one swathe; he was always
to keep one swathe between him and the scythes,
which are extremely sharp and dangerous instru-
ments.

Sir Bevis repeated these promises so seriously,
and with so demure and innocent an expression, that
no one could doubt but that he would keep them
strictly, nor, indeed, did any idea of exceeding these
limits occur to him. He was so overjoyed at the
vast extent of territory, almost a new world thrown
open for exploration, that he did not think it possible he could ever want to go any further. He
rushed into the Home Field, jumping over the swathes
till he was tired, and kicking the grass about with
his feet. Then he wanted a prong, and a stout stick
with a fork was cut and pointed for him, and with
this he went eagerly to work for five minutes. Next
he wanted some one to bury under the grass, and
could not be satisfied till the dairy-maid was sent

out and submitted to be completely hidden under a heap of it.

Next he walked all round the field, and back home down the middle. By-and-by he sat down and looked at the mowers, who were just finishing the last corner before they went into the meadow by the brook. While he was sitting there a number of greenfinches, and sparrows, and two or three hasty starlings (for they are always in a hurry), came to the sward where the mowers had just passed, and searched about for food. They seemed so happy and looked so pretty, Bevis thought he should like to shoot one, so away he ran home to the summer-house for his bow and arrow. Hastening back with these, he built a heap of the grass to hide behind, like a breastwork, and then sat down and watched for the birds.

They did not come directly, as they ought to have done, so he kicked up his heels, and rolled over on his back, and looked up at the sky, as was his wont. Every now and then he could hear Pan whining woefully in his tub a long way off. Since the whipping the spaniel had been in disgrace, and no one would let him loose. Bevis, so delighted

with his field to roam about in, quite forgot him,
and left him to sorrow in his tub. Presently he
heard a lark singing so sweetly, though at a great
distance, that he kept quite still to listen. The song
came in verses, now it rose a little louder, and now
it fell till he could hardly hear it, and again returned. Bevis got up on his knees to try and find
where the lark was, but the sky was so blue there,
or the bird so high up, he could not see it, though
he searched and searched. It was somewhere in
the next field, far beyond the great oak where he
once fell asleep.

He then peered round his heap of grass, but
there were no greenfinches near; they had come
out from the hedges, and the starling had come
from the hollow pollard where he had a nest, but
all had settled a long way off from his hiding-
place. Bevis was very angry, so he stood up, and
pulled his bow with all his might, and let the
arrow fly into the air almost straight up. When
it had risen so far, it turned over and came down
among the flock of birds and stuck in the ground.

They flew away in terror, and though he had not
killed any, Bevis was highly delighted at the

fright they were in. He picked up his arrow, and
tried another long shot at a rook on the other side
of the field, but he could not send it so great a distance. As he ran for it, he saw that the rook's back
was towards him, and, thinking that the rook could
not see him, he raced on quietly to try and catch
him, but just as he got close, up rose the rook over
the hedge with a " caw, caw ! " Whizz ! went
Bevis's arrow after him, and fell on the other side of
the hedge, where he was not to go.

In his anger at the rook's behaviour Bevis forgot all about his promise; he jumped into the ditch
regardless of the stinging-nettles, pushed his way
up through the briars, tearing his sleeve, forced his
way across the mound, and went on his hands and
knees through the young green fern on the other
side (just as Pan would have done) under the thick
thorn bushes, and so out into the next field. It was
the very field where he and Pan had wandered before, only another part of it. There was his arrow
ever so far off, sticking upright in the grass among
the cowslips. As he went to pick up his arrow he
saw another flower growing a little further on, and
went to gather that first; it was an orchid, and

when he stood up with it in his hand he heard a mouse rustle in the grass, and stepped quietly to try and see it, but the mouse hid in a hole.

Then there was an enormous humble-bee, so huge that when it stayed to suck a cowslip, the cowslip was bent down with its weight. Bevis walked after the giant humble-bee, and watched it take the honey from several cowslips; then he saw a stone standing in the field, it was not upright, but leaned to one side—yet it was almost as tall as he was. He went to the stone and looked all round it, and got up on it and sat still a minute, and while he was there a cuckoo came by, so close, that he jumped off to run after it. But the cuckoo flew fast, and began to call "cuckoo!" and it was no use to chase him.

When Bevis stopped and looked about he was in a hollow, like a big salad bowl, only all grass, and he could see nothing but the grass and cowslips all round him—no hedges—and the sky overhead. He began to dance and sing with delight at such a curious place, and when he paused the lark was on again, and not very far this time. There he was, rising gradually, singing as he went. Bevis ran

up the side of the hollow towards the lark, and saw
a hedge cut and cropped low, and over it a wheat-
field. He watched the lark sing, sing, sing, up into
the sky, and then he thought he would go and find
his nest, as he remembered the ploughboy had told
him larks made their nests on the ground among the
corn.

He ran to the low hedge, but though it was low
it was very thorny, and while he was trying to find
a place to get through, he looked over and spied a
hare crouched in the rough grass, just under the
hedge between it and the wheat. The hare was lying
on the ground; she did not move, though she saw
Bevis, and when he looked closer he saw that her
big eyes were full of tears. She was crying very
bitterly, all by herself, while the sun was shining
so brightly, and the wind blowing so sweetly, and
the flowers smelling so pleasantly, and the lark sing,
sing, singing overhead.

"Oh! dear," said Bevis, so eager and so sorry,
that he pushed against the hedge, and did not notice
that a thorn was pricking his arm : "What ever is
the matter?" But the Hare was so miserable she
would not answer him at first, till he coaxed her

nicely. Then she said, "Bevis, Bevis, little Sir Bevis, do you know what you have done?"

"No," said Bevis, "I can't think: was it me?"

"Yes, it was you; you let the Weasel loose, when he was caught in the gin."

"Did I?" said Bevis, "I have quite forgotten it."

"But you did it," said the Hare, "and now the Weasel has killed my son, the leveret, while he was sleeping, and sucked his blood, and I am so miserable; I do not care to run away any more." Then the Hare began to weep bitterly again, till Bevis did not know what to do to comfort her.

"Perhaps the Weasel only killed the leveret for your good," he said presently.

"What!" cried the Hare, putting her fore-feet down hard, and stamping with indignation, "That is what the wicked old wretch told you, did he not, about the Mouse and the partridge's eggs. Cannot you see that it is all a pack of lies? But I do not wonder that he deceives you, dear, since he has deceived the world for so long. Let me tell you, Sir Bevis, the Weasel is the wickedest and most dreadful creature that lives, and above all things he is so

cunning he can make people believe anything he
chooses, and he has succeeded in making fools of us
all—every one.

"There is not one of all the animals in the hedge,
nor one of the birds in the trees, that he has not
cheated. He is so very, very, cunning, and his
talk is so soft and smooth. Do you please take
care, Sir Bevis, or perhaps he may deceive you, as
he deceived the Fox. Why, do you know, he has
made the people believe that his crimes are committed by the Fox, who consequently bears all the
disgrace; and not only that, but he has spread it
abroad that the Fox is the most cunning of all, in
order that he may not be suspected of being so clever
as he is. I daresay the Weasel will have me some
day, and I do not care if he does, now my leveret is
dead; and very soon his poor bones will be picked
clean by the ants, and after the corn is carried the
plough will bury them."

Bevis was terribly distressed at the Hare's story,
and showed such indignation against the Weasel, and
stamped his little foot so hard, knitting his brow,
that the Hare was somewhat appeased, and began to
explain all about it.

"Of course you did not know, dear," she said, "when you stepped on the spring of the gin, what trouble we had had to get him into the trap. For we had all suffered so long from his cruelty, that we had all agreed at last to try and put an end to it. The trees could not bear to stand still and see it go on under them, yet they could not move. The earth could not bear to feel him running about on his bloodthirsty business, through the holes the rabbits had made. The grass hated to feel him pushing through, for it had so often been stained with the blood that he had shed. So we all took counsel together, and I carried the messages, dear, from the oak, where you slept, to the ash and the elm, and to the earth in the corner where the rabbits live; and the birds came up into the oak and gave their adherence, every one; and the Fox, too, though he did not come himself, for he is too cunning to commit himself till he knows which way the wind is going to blow, sent word of his high approval.

"Thus we were all prepared to act against that midnight assassin, the Weasel, but we could not begin. The trees could not move, the earth could not wag a step, the grass could do nothing, and so it went

on for some months, during all which time the
Weasel was busy with his wickedness, till at last
the Bailiff set the gin for the Rat by the cart-house.
Then the Fox came out by day—contrary to his custom, for he likes a nap—and went to a spot where
he knew a rabbit sat in the grass; and he hunted
the poor rabbit (it was very good sport to see—I do
not like rabbits), till he had driven him across the
ditch, where the Weasel was. Then the Fox stopped,
and hid himself in the furze; and the Weasel, first
looking round to see that no one was near, stole after
the rabbit. Now the rabbit knew that the Fox was
about, and therefore he was afraid to run across the
open field; all he could do was to go down the
hedge towards the garden.

"Everything was going on well, and we sent word
to the Rat, to warn him against the gin—we did not
like the Rat, but we did not want the gin thrown—
don't you see, dear? But when the rabbit had gone
half-way down the hedge, and was close to the garden,
he became afraid to venture any nearer your house,
Bevis. Still the Weasel crept after him, and presently
drove him almost up to your sycamore-tree. Then
the rabbit did not know what to do; for if he went

forward the people in the house might see him and bring out the gun, and if he turned back the Weasel would have him, and if he ran out into the field the Fox would be there, and he could not climb up a tree. He stopped still, trying to think, till the Weasel came so near he could smell the rabbit's blood, and then, in his terror, the rabbit darted out from the hedge, and into the ditch of your haha wall, under where the bee-hives are. There he saw a dry drain, and hopped into it, forgetting in his fright that he might not be able to get out at the other end.

"The Weasel thought he had now got him safe, and was just going to rush across and follow, when an ant spoke to him from the trunk of a tree it was climbing. The ant said the Fox had asked him yesterday to watch, and if the Weasel came that way, to warn him that there was a plot laid for his life, and not to be too venturesome. This was a piece of the same double-faced ways the Fox has been notorious for these many years past. No one hates the Weasel so much as the Fox, but he said to himself, 'The Weasel is so cunning, that even if he is caught, he is sure to find some way to get free, and then he will perhaps discover that I had a hand in it, and will turn round on me and spoil some of my schemes out of spite. Besides which, I don't see why I should take much interest in the Hare or the Mouse.' So, though he hunted the rabbit for us, yet he sent the Weasel this message, to take care and mind and not be too bold.

"When the Weasel heard this he stopped, and thought to himself that it was rather dangerous to go so near a house, almost under it; and yet he could not help licking his mouth, as he remembered the sweet scent of the rabbit's blood. But he was so very, very cunning, that he thought to himself the rabbit would be obliged to come out again presently, and would be sure to come up the hedge if he did not see the Weasel. So the Weasel turned round to go up the hedge, and we were all in anxiety lest the scheme should miscarry. But as the Weasel was going under the elm, the elm dropped a large dead branch, and as it came crashing down, it fell so near the Weasel as to pinch his foot, and, hearing another branch go crack, he lost his presence of mind, turned back again, and darted across the corner into the drain. There the scent of the rabbit was so strong he could not help but follow it, and in a moment or two he saw the poor creature crouched at the end where he could not pass.

"The Weasel bounded forward, when the earth squeezed out a stone, and the stone fell between the Weasel and the rabbit. Before he could tell what to do, the earth squeezed out another stone behind him, and he was caught, and could neither go forward or backward. Now we thought we had got him, and that he must starve to death. As for the rabbit, when the stone fell down it left a hole above, up which he scrambled into the cow-yard, and there hid himself behind a bunch of nettles till night, when he escaped into the field.

"Meantime the Weasel in a dreadful fright was walking to and fro in his narrow prison, gnashing his teeth with rage and terror, and calling to all the animals and birds and insects and even to the mole (whom he despised most of all) to help him out. He promised to be the nicest, kindest Weasel that ever was known; but it was no use, for they were all in the secret, and overjoyed to see him on the point of perishing. There he had to stay, and though he scratched and scratched, he could not make any hole through the solid stone, and by-and-bye he got weaker, and he began to die. While he was dying the Rat came and peeped down at him through a chink, and laughed and said, ' What is the use of all your cunning, you coward ? If you had been bold like me you would never have got into this scrape, by being afraid of a dead branch of a tree because it pinched your foot. I should have run by quickly. You are a silly, foolish, blind sort of crea-ture ; could you not see that all the things had agreed to deceive you ? '

" At this the Weasel was so wroth it woke him up from his dying, and he returned the taunt and said, ' Rat, you are by far the silliest to help the Hare and the Mouse ; it is true they sent you a message about the gin, but that was not for love of you, I am sure, and I can't think why they should send it ; but you may depend it is some trick, and very likely the gin is not where they said at all, but in another place, and you will walk into it when you are not thinking, and then you will curse the Hare and the Mouse.'

" ' Ah,' said the Rat, ' that sounds like reason ; you are right, the Hare and the Mouse are going to play me a trick. But I will spite them, I will let you out.'

" 'Will you?' said the Weasel, starting up and feeling almost strong again. 'But you can't, these stones are so thick you cannot move them, nor scratch through them, nor raise them; no, you cannot let me out.'

" 'Oh, yes, I can,' said the Rat, 'I know a way to move the biggest stones, and if you can only wait a day or two I will make this chink large enough for you to come up.'

" 'A day or two,' said the Weasel in despair; 'why, I am nearly dead now with hunger.'

" 'Well, then,' said the Rat, 'gnaw your own tail;' and off he went laughing at the joke. The miserable Weasel cried and sniffed, and sniffed and cried, till by-and-bye he heard the Rat come back and begin to scratch outside. Presently the Rat stopped, and was going away again, when the Weasel begged and prayed him not to leave him to die there in the dark.

" 'Very well,' said the Rat, 'I will send the cricket to sing to you. In a day or two you will see the chink get bigger, and meantime you can eat your tail; and as you will get very thin, you will be able to creep through a very small hole and get out all the quicker. Ha! ha! As for me, I am going to have a capital dinner from Pan's dish, for he has fallen asleep in his tub.'

" So the Weasel was left to himself, and though he watched and watched, he could not see the chink open in the least, and he got so dreadfully hungry that at last, after sucking his paws, he was obliged to bring his tail round and begin to gnaw it a little bit. The pain was dreadful, but he could not help himself, he was obliged to do it or die. In the evening the cricket came, as the Rat had promised, to the top of the chink, and at once began to sing. He sang all about the lady cricket with whom he was in love, and then about the beautiful stars that were shining in the sky, and how nice it was to be a cricket, for the crickets were by far the most handsome and clever of all creatures, and everybody would like to be a cricket if they could.

" Next, he went on to praise himself, that his lady might hear what fine limbs he had, and so noble a form, and such a splendid chink to live in. Thus he kept on the livelong night, and all about himself;

and his chirp, chirp, chirp filled the Weasel's prison
with such a noise that the wretched thing could not
sleep. He kept asking the cricket to tell him if the
Rat had really done anything to enlarge the chink;
but the cricket was too busy to answer him till the
dawn, and then, having finished his song, he found
time to attend to the Weasel.

"'You have been very rude,' he said, 'to keep on
talking while I was singing, but I suppose, as you are
only an ignorant Weasel, you do not understand good
manners, and therefore I will condescend so far as to
inform you of the measures taken by my noble friend
the Rat to get you out. If you were not so extremely ignorant and stupid you would guess what
he has done.'

"Now all this was very bitter to the Weasel, who
had always thought he knew everything, to be insulted by a cricket; still he begged to be told what
it was. 'The Rat,' went on the cricket, 'has
brought a little piece from a fungus, and has
scratched a hole beside the stone and put it in there.
Now, when this begins to grow and the fungus
pushes up, it will move the stone and open a chink.
In this way I have seen my lord the Rat heave up

the heaviest paving stones and make a road for himself. Now are you not stupid?' Then the cricket
went home to bed.

"All day long the miserable Weasel lay on the
floor of his prison, driven every now and then to
gnaw his tail till he squeaked with the pain. The
only thing that kept him from despair was the
hope of the revenge he would have, if ever he did
get out, on those who had laid the trap for him.
For hours he lay insensible, and only woke up when
the Rat looked down the chink and asked him,
with a jolly chuckle, how his tail tasted, and then
went off without waiting for an answer. Then the
cricket came again, and taking not the least notice
of the prisoner, sang all night.

"In the morning the Weasel looked up, and saw
that the chink had really opened. He crawled to
it, he was so faint he could not walk, so he had
to crawl over the floor, which was all red with his
own blood. The fungus, a thick, yellowish-green
thing, like a very large and unwholesome mushroom,
was growing fast, so fast he could see it move, and
very slowly it shoved and lifted up the stone. The
chink was now so far open that in his thin, emaciated

state, the Weasel could have got through; but he was so weak he could not climb up. He called to the Rat, and the Rat came and tried to reach him, but it was just a little too far down.

"'If I only had something to drink,' said the Weasel, 'only one drop of water, I think I could do it, but I am faint from thirst.'

"Off ran the Rat to see what he could do, and as he passed the tub where Pan lived he saw a bowl of water just pumped for the spaniel. The bowl was of wood, with a projecting handle—not a ring to put the fingers through, but merely a short straight handle. He went round to the other side of the tub in which Pan was dozing and began to scratch. Directly Pan heard the scratching:—

"'Ho! ho!' said he, 'that's that abominable Rat that steals my food,' and he darted out, and in his tremendous hurry his chain caught the handle of the bowl, just as the Rat had hoped it would. Over went the bowl, and all the water was spilt, but the Rat, the instant he heard Pan coming, had slipped away back to the Weasel.

"When Pan was tired of looking where he had heard the scratching, he went back to take a lap, but found the bowl upset, and that all the water had run down the drain. As he was very thirsty after gnawing a salt bacon-bone, he set up a barking, and the dairy-maid ran out, thinking it was a beggar, and began to abuse him for being so clumsy as to knock over his bowl. Pan barked all the louder, so she hit him with the handle of her broom, and he went howling into his tub. He vowed vengeance against the Rat, but that did not satisfy his thirst.

"Meantime the water had run along the drain, and though the fungus greedily sucked up most of it, the Weasel had a good drink. After that he felt better, and he climbed up the chink, squeezing through and dragging his raw tail behind him, till he nearly reached the top. But there it was still a little tight, and he could not manage to push through, not having strength enough left. He felt himself slipping back again, and called on the Rat to save him. The Rat without ceremony leant down the chink, and caught hold of his ear with his teeth, and snipped it so tight he bit it right through, but he dragged the Weasel out.

"There he lay a long time half dead and exhausted,

under a dock leaf which hid him from view. The Rat began to think that the Weasel would die after all, so he came and said, 'Wake up, coward, and come with me into the cart-house, there is a very nice warm hole there, and I will tell you something; if you stay here very likely the Bailiff may see you, and if Pan should be let loose he will sniff you out in a second.' So the Weasel, with very great difficulty, dragged himself into the cart-house, and found shelter in the hole.

"Now the Rat, though he had helped the Weasel, did not half like him, for he was afraid to go to sleep while the Weasel was about, lest his guest should fasten on his throat, for he knew he was treacherous to the last degree. He cast about in his mind how to get rid of him, and at the same time to serve his own purpose. By-and-by he said that there was a Mouse in the cart-house who had a very plump wife, and two fat little mouses. At this the Weasel pricked up his ears, for he was so terribly hungry, and sat up and asked where they were. The Rat said the wife and the children were up in the beam; the wood had rotted, and they had a hole there, but he was afraid the Mouse himself was away from home just then, most likely in the corn-bin, where the barley-meal for the pigs was kept.

" ' Never mind,' said the Weasel eagerly, ' the wife and the baby mice will do very well,' and up he started and climbed up through the Rat's hole in the wall to the roof, and then into the hole in the beam, where he had a good meal on the mice. Now the Rat hated this Mouse because he lived so near, and helped himself to so much food, and being so much smaller, he could get about inside the house where you live, Bevis, without being seen, and so got very fat, and made the Rat jealous. He thought, too, that when the Weasel had eaten the wife and the babies, that he would be strong enough to go away. Presently the Weasel came down from his meal, and looked so fierce and savage that the Rat, strong as he was, was still more anxious to get rid of him as quickly as possible.

" He told the Weasel that there was a way by which he could get to the corn-bin without the least danger, though it was close to the house, and there he would be certain to find the Mouse himself, and very likely another Miss Mouse whom he used to meet there. At this the Weasel was so excited he could hardly wait to be shown the way, and asked the Rat to put him in the road directly; he was so hungry he did not care what he did. Without delay the Rat took him to the mouth of the hole, and told him to stay there and listen a minute to be sure that no one was coming. If he could not hear any footsteps, all he had to do was to rush across the road there, only two or three yards, to the rough grass, the dandelions, and the docks opposite. Just there there was an iron grating made in the wall of the house to let in the air and keep the rats out; but one of the bars had rusted off and was broken, and that was the Mouse's track to the corn bin.

"The Weasel put out his head, glanced round, saw no one, and without waiting to listen rushed out into the roadway. In an instant the Rat pushed against a small piece of loose stone, which he kept for the purpose, and it fell down and shut up the mouth of his hole. As the Weasel was running across the roadway suddenly one of the labourers came round the corner with a bucket of food for the pigs. Frightened beyond measure, the Weasel hastened back to the Rat's hole, but could not get in because of the stone. Not knowing what to do, he ran round the carthouse, where there was some grass under the wall, with the man coming close behind him. Now it was just there that the Bailiff had set the gin for the Rat, near the mouth of the drain, but the Rat knew all about it, and used the other hole.

"The grass, knowing that we wished to drive the Weasel that way into the gin, had tried to grow faster and hide the trap, but could not get on very well because the weather was so dry. But that morning, when the Rat upset Pan's bowl of water, and it ran down the drain, some part of it reached the roots of the grass and moistened them, then the grass shot up quick and quite hid the trap, except one little piece. Now, seeing the Weasel rushing along in his fright, the grass was greatly excited, but did not know what to do to hide this part, so the grass whispered to his friend the Wind to come to his help.

"This the Wind was very ready to do, for this reason—he hated to smell the decaying carcases of the poor creatures the Weasel killed, and left to rot and to taint the air, so that it quite spoilt his morn-

ing ramble over the fields. With a puff the Wind
came along and blew a dead leaf, one of last year's
leaves, over the trap, and so hid it completely.

"The Weasel saw the mouth of the drain, and
thinking to be safe in a minute darted at it, and
was snapped up by the gin. The sudden shock deprived him of sense or motion, and well for him it
did, for had he squeaked or moved ever so little the
man with the bucket must have seen or heard him.
After a time he came to himself, and again began to
beg the Rat to help him; but the Rat, having had
his revenge on the Mouse, did not much care to
trouble about it, and, besides, he remembered how
very wolfish and fierce the Weasel had looked at him
when in his hole. At least he thought he would have
a night's sleep in comfort first, for he had been
afraid to sleep a wink with the Weasel so near. Now
the Weasel was in the gin he could have a nap.

"All night long the Weasel was in the gin, and
to a certainty he would have been seen—for the
Bailiff would have been sure to come and look at his
trap—but if you remember, Bevis, dear, that was the
very day you were lost (while asleep under the oak),
and everything was confusion, and the gin was for-

gotten. Well, in the morning the Weasel begged so piteously of the Rat to help him again, that the Rat began to think he would, now he had had a good sleep, when just as he was peeping out along you came, Bevis, dear, and found the Weasel in the gin.

"Now, I daresay you remember the talk you had with the Weasel, and what the Mouse said; well, the Rat was listening all the while, and he heard the Weasel say to you that he always killed the rats. 'Aha!' thought the Rat, 'catch me helping you again, sir;' and the Weasel heard him say it. So when you stepped on the spring and loosed the Weasel, he did not dare go into the drain, knowing that the Rat (while awake) was stronger than he, but hobbled as well as he could across to the wood-pile. There he stopped, exhausted, and stiff from his wounds. Meantime the Rat deliberated how best he could drive the treacherous Weasel away from the place.

"At night, accordingly, he cautiously left his hole and went across to the tub where Pan was sleeping, curled up comfortably within. The end of Pan's chain, where it was fastened to the staple outside the tub, was not of iron, but tar-cord. The last link had been broken, and it was therefore tied in this manner. The rat easily gnawed through the tar-cord, and then slipped back to his hole to await events. About the middle of the night, when the Weasel had rested and began to stir out, Pan woke up, and seeing that it was light, stepped out to bay at the moon. He immediately found that his chain was undone, and rushed about to try and find some water, being very thirsty. He had not gone very far before he smelt the Weasel, and instantly began to chase him. The Weasel, however, slipped under a faggot, and so across and under the wood-pile, where he was safe; but he was so alarmed that presently he crept out the other side, and round by the pig-stye, and so past the stable to the rick-yard, and then into the hedge, and he never stopped run-ning, stiff as he was, till he was half-a-mile away in the ash copse, and had crept into a rabbit's hole. He could not have got away from the wood-pile, only Pan, being so thirsty, gave up looking for him, and went down to the brook.

"In the morning, as they thought Pan had broken his chain, they kicked the spaniel howling into his tub again. And now comes the sad part of it, Bevis, dear. You must know that when the Weasel was in the trap we all thought it was quite safe, and that our enemy was done for at last, and so we went off to a dancing-party, on the short grass of the downs by moonlight, leaving our leverets to nibble near the wheat. We stayed at the dancing-party so late that the dawn came and we were afraid to go home in the daylight, and next night we all felt so merry we had another dance, and again danced till it was morning.

"While we were sleeping in the day, the Weasel, having now recovered a good deal, crept out from the rabbit-hole in the copse. We were so far off, you see, the mice could not send us word that he had escaped from the gin in time, and indeed, none of them knew exactly where to find us; they told the swallows, and the swallows searched, but missed us. The Wind, too, blew as many ways as he could to try and reach us, but he had to blow east that day, and could not manage it. If we had only been at home we should have been on the watch; but my poor leveret, and my two friends' poor leverets, were sleeping so comfortably when the wicked Weasel stole on them one by one, and bit their necks

and killed them. He could not eat them, nor half
of them, he only killed them for revenge, and oh!
dear little Sir Bevis, what shall I do? what shall
I do?"

"I will kill the Weasel," said Bevis. "He is
dreadfully wicked. I will shoot him this minute
with my bow and arrow."

But when he looked round he had got neither
of them; he had dropped the bow in the Home Field
when he jumped into the ditch to scramble through
the hedge, and he had wandered so far among the
cowslips that he could not see the arrow. Bevis
looked all round again, and did not recognise any
of the trees, nor the hedges, nor could he see the
house nor the ricks, nor anything that he knew.
His face flushed up, and the tears came into his
eyes; he was lost.

"Don't cry," said the Hare, much pleased at
the eagerness with which he took up the quarrel
against the Weasel; "don't cry, darling, I will
show you the way home and where to find your
arrow. It is not very far, though you cannot see
it because of the ground rising between you and it.
But will you really kill the Weasel next time?"

"Yes, indeed I will," said Bevis, "I will shoot my arrow and kill him quite dead in a minute."

"But I am not sure you can hit him with your arrow; don't you remember that you could not hit the greenfinches nor the rook?"

"Well, then," said Bevis, "if you will wait till I am a man, papa will lend me his gun, and then I can certainly kill him."

"But that will be such a long time, Sir Bevis; did not your papa tell you you would have to eat another peck of salt before you could have a gun?"

"Then I know what I will do," said Bevis, "I will shoot the Weasel with my brass cannon. Ah, that is the way! And I know where papa keeps his gunpowder; it is in a tin canister on the topmost shelf, and I will tell you how I climb up there. First, I bring the big arm-chair, and then I put the stool on that, and then I stand on the lowest shelf, and I can just reach the canister."

"Take care, Sir Bevis," said the Hare, "take care, and do not open the canister where there is a fire in the room, or a candle, because a spark may blow you up just when you are not thinking."

" Oh ! I know all about that; I'll take care," said
Bevis, " and I will shoot the wretch of a Weasel in
no time. Now please show me the way home."

" So I will; you stay there till I come to you,
I will run round by the gateway."

" Why not come straight through the hedge?"
said Bevis, " you could easily creep through, I'm
sure."

" No, dear. I must not come that way, that
road belongs to another hare, and I must not tres-
pass."

" But you can run where you like—can you not ? "

" Oh, dear no; all the hares have different roads,
Sir Bevis, and if I were to run along one of theirs
that did not belong to me, to-night they would bite
me and thump me with their paws till I was all
bruised."

" I can't see any path," said Bevis, " you can
run where you like in the field, I'm sure."

" No, I can't dear; I shall have to go a quarter
of a mile round to .come to you, because there are
three paths between you and me, and I shall have to
turn and twist about not to come on them."

While Bevis was thinking about this, and how

stupid it was of the hares to have roads, the Hare
ran off, and in two or three minutes came to him
through the cowslips. " Oh, you pretty creature ! "
said Sir Bevis, stooping down and stroking her back,
and playing with the tips of her long ears, " Oh, I
do love you so ! " At this the Hare was still more
pleased, and rubbed her head against Bevis's hand.

" Now," she said, " you must come along quickly,
because I dare not stay on this short grass, lest some
dog should see me. Follow me, dear." She went on
before him, and Bevis ran behind, and in a minute or
two they went over the rising ground, past the tall
stone (put there for the cows to rub their sides against),
and then the Hare stopped and showed Bevis the great
oak tree, where he once went to sleep. She told him
to look at it well, and recollect the shape of it, so that
another time he could find his way home by the tree.
Then she told him to walk straight to the tree, and
on his way there he would find the arrow, and close
by the tree was the gap in the hedge, and when he
got through the gap, he would see the house and the
ricks, and if he ' followed the ditch then he would
presently come to the place where he dropped his
bow.

"Thank you," said Bevis, "I will run as fast as I can, for I am sure it must be nearly dinner time. Good-bye, you pretty creature;" and having stroked her ears just once more, off he started. In a few minutes he found his arrow, and looked back to show it to the Hare, but she was gone; so he went on to the oak, got through the gap, and there was the house at the other side of the field. He could hear Pan barking, so he felt quite at home, and walked along the ditch till he picked up his bow. He was very hungry when he got home, and yet he was glad when the dinner was over, that he might go to the cupboard and get his brass cannon.

When he came to examine the cannon, and to think about shooting the Weasel with it, he soon found that it would not do very well, because he could not hold it in his hand and point it straight, and when it went off it would most likely burn his fingers. But looking at his papa's gun he saw that the barrel, where the powder is put in, was fixed in a wooden handle called the stock, so he set to work with his pocket knife to make a handle for his cannon. He cut a long thick willow stick, choosing the willow because it was soft and easiest to cut, and

chipped away till he had made a groove in it at one
end in which he put the cannon, fastening it in with
a piece of thin copper wire twisted round. Next he
cut a ramrod, and then he loaded his gun, and fired
it off with a match to see how it went.

This he did at the bottom of the orchard, a long
way from the house, for he was afraid that if they
saw what he was doing they might take it from him,
so he kept it hidden in the summer-house under an
old sack. The cannon went off with a good bang,
and the shot he had put in it stuck in the bark of
an apple tree. Bevis jumped about with delight,
and thought he could now kill the Weasel. It was
too late to start that day, but the next morning off
he marched with his gun into the Home Field, and
having charged it behind the shelter of a tree out
of sight, began his chase for the Weasel.

All round the field he went, looking carefully into
the ditch and the hedge, and asking at all the rabbits'-holes if they knew where the scoundrel was.
The rabbits knew very well, but they were afraid to
answer, lest the Weasel should hear about it, and
come and kill the one that had betrayed him. Twice
he searched up and down without success, and was

just going to call to the Hare to come and show
him, when suddenly he discovered a thrush sitting
on her nest in a bush. He put down his gun, and
was going to see how many eggs she had got, when
the Weasel (who had no idea he was there) peeped
over the bank, having a fancy for the eggs, but
afraid that the nest was too high for him to reach.

"Ho! Ho!" cried Bevis, "there you are. Now I
have you. Just stand still a minute, while I get
my gun and strike a match."

"Whatever for?" asked the Weasel, very inno-
cently.

"I'm going to shoot you," said Bevis, busy
getting his gun ready.

"Shoot *me*!" said the Weasel, in a tone of the
utmost astonishment; "why ever do you want to
shoot me, Sir Bevis? Did I not tell you that I
spent all my life doing good?"

"Yes, you rascal!" said Bevis, putting a pinch
of powder on the touch-hole, "you know you are a
wicked story-teller; you killed the poor leveret after
I let you loose. Now!" and he went down on one
knee, and put his cannon-stick on the other as a
rest to keep it straight.

"Wait a minute," said the Weasel, "just listen to me a minute. I assure you——"

"No; I sha'n't listen to you," said Bevis, striking his match.

"Oh," said the Weasel, kneeling down, "if you will only wait one second, I will tell you all the wickedness I have committed. Don't, please, kill me before I have got this load of guilt off my mind."

"Well, make haste," said Bevis, aiming along his cannon.

"I will," said the Weasel; "and first of all, if you are going to kill me, why don't you shoot the thrush as well, for she is ever so much more wicked and cruel than I have been?"

"Oh, what a dreadful story!" said the thrush. "How can you say so?"

"Yes, you are," said the Weasel. "Sir Bevis, you remember the two snails you found in the garden path—those you put on a leaf, and watched to see which could crawl the fastest?"

"I remember," said Sir Bevis. "But you must make haste, or my match will burn out."

"And you recollect that the snails had no legs,

and could not walk, and that they had no wings and could not fly, and were very helpless creatures?"

"Yes, I remember; I left them on the path."

"Well, directly you left them, out came this great ugly speckled thrush from the shrubbery—you see how big the thrush is, quite a monster beside the poor snails; and you see what long legs she has, and great wings, and such a strong, sharp beak. This cruel monster of a thrush picked up the snails, one at a time, and smashed them on the stones, and gobbled them up."

"Well," said the thrush, much relieved, "is that all? snails are very nice to eat."

"Was it not brutally cruel?" asked the Weasel.

"Yes, it was," said Bevis.

"Then," said the Weasel, "when you shoot me, shoot the thrush too."

"So I will," said Bevis, "but how can I hit you both?"

"I will show you," said the Weasel. "I will walk along the bank till I am just in a line with the thrush's nest, and then you can take aim at both together."

So he went along the bank and stopped behind the nest, and Bevis moved his cannon-stick and took another aim.

"Dear me!" cried the thrush, dreadfully alarmed, "you surely are not going to shoot me? I never did any harm. Bevis, stop—listen to me!"

Now if the thrush had flown away she might have escaped, but she was very fond of talking, and while she was talking Bevis was busy getting his gun ready.

"It is straight now," said the Weasel; "it is pointed quite straight. Hold it still there, and I will sit so that I shall die quick:—here is my bosom. Tell the Hare to forgive me."

"Oh," said the thrush, "don't shoot!"

"Shoot!" cried the Weasel.

Bevis dropped his match on the touch-hole, puff went the priming, and bang went the cannon. Directly the smoke had cleared away, Bevis looked in the ditch, to see the dead Weasel and the thrush. There was the thrush right enough, quite dead, and fallen out of the nest; the nest, too, was knocked to pieces, and the eggs had fallen out (two were broken), but there was one not a bit smashed, lying on the dead leaves at the bottom of the ditch. But the Weasel was nowhere to be seen.

"Weasel," cried Bevis, "where are you?" But the Weasel did not answer. Bevis looked everywhere, over the bank and round about, but could not find him. At last he saw that under some grass on the bank there was a small rabbit's hole. Now the Weasel had sat up for Bevis to shoot him right over this hole, and when he saw him move the match, just as the priming went puff, the Weasel dropped down into the hole, and the shot went over his head.

Bevis was very angry when he saw how the Weasel had deceived him, and felt so sorry for the poor thrush, whose speckled breast was all pierced by the shot, and who would never sing any more. He did not know what to do, he was so cross; but presently he ran home to fetch Pan, to see if Pan could hunt out the Weasel.

When he had gone a little way the Weasel came out of the hole, and went down into the ditch and feasted on the thrush's egg, which he could not have got had not the shot knocked the nest to pieces, just as he had contrived. He never tasted so sweet an egg as that one, and as he sucked it up he laughed as he thought how cleverly he had deceived them all. When he heard Pan bark he went back into the hole, and so along the hedge till he reached the copse ; and then creeping into another hole, a very small one, where no dog could get at him, he curled himself up very comfortably and went to sleep.

CHAPTER IV.

BROOK-FOLK.

SOME time afterwards it happened one morning that Bevis was sitting on a haycock in the Home Field, eating a very large piece of cake, and thinking how extremely greedy the young rook was yonder across the meadow. For he was as big and as black as his father and mother, who were with him; and yet he kept on cawing to them to stuff his beak with sweets. Bevis, who had another large slice in his pocket, having stolen both of them from the cupboard just after breakfast, felt angry to see such greediness, and was going to get up to holloa at this ill-mannered rook, when he heard a grasshopper making some remarks close by the haycock.

"S——s," said the grasshopper to a friend, "are you going down to the brook? I am, in a minute, so soon as I have hopped round this hay-cock, for there will be a grand show there presently. All the birds are going to bathe, as is their custom on Midsummer Day, and will be sure to appear in their best feathers. It is true some of them have bathed already, as they have to leave early in the morning, having business elsewhere. I spoke to the cricket just now on the subject, but he could not see that it was at all interesting. He is very narrow-minded, as you know, and cannot see anything beyond the mound where he lives. S——s."

" S——s," replied the other grasshopper; "I will certainly jump that way so soon as I have had a chat with my lady-love, who is waiting for me on the other side of the furrow. S——s."

" S——s, we shall meet by the drinking-place," said the first grasshopper; and was just hopping off when Bevis asked him what the birds went down to bathe for.

" I'm sure I do not know," said the grasshopper, speaking fast, for he was rather in a hurry to be gone, he never could stand still long together. " All I can tell you is that on Midsummer Day every one of the birds has to go down to the brook and walk in and bathe; and it has been the law for so many, many years that no one can remember when it began. They like it very much, because they can show off their fine feathers, which are just now in full colour; and if you like to go with me you will be sure to enjoy it."

"So I will," said Bevis, and he followed the grasshopper, who hopped so far at every step that he had to walk fast to keep up with him. "But why do the birds do it?"

"Oh, I don't know why," said the grasshopper; "what is why?"

"I want to know," said Bevis, "why do they do it?"

"Why?" repeated the grasshopper, "I never heard any body say anything about that before. There is always a great deal of talking going on, for the trees have nothing else to do but to gossip with each other; but they never ask why."

After that they went on in silence a good way, except that the grasshopper cried "S—s," to his friends in the grass as he passed, and said good morning also to a mole who peeped out for a moment.

"Why don't you hop straight?" said Bevis presently. "It seems to me that you hop first one side and then the other, and go in such a zig-zag fashion it will take us hours to reach the brook."

"How very stupid you are," said the grasshopper. "If you go straight of course you can only see just what is under your feet, but if you go first this way and then that, then you see everything. You are nearly as silly as the ants, who never see anything beautiful all their lives. Be sure you have nothing to do with the ants, Bevis, they are a mean, wretched, miserly set, quite contemptible and beneath notice. Now I go everywhere all round the field, and spend my time searching for lovely things; sometimes I find flowers, and sometimes the butterflies come down into the grass and tell me the news, and I am so fond of the sunshine, I sing to it all day long. Tell me, now, is there anything so beautiful as the sunshine and the blue sky, and the green grass, and the velvet and blue and spotted butterflies, and the trees which cast such a pleasant shadow and talk so sweetly, and the brook which is always running? I should like to listen to it for a thousand years."

"I like you," said Bevis; "jump into my hand, and I will carry you." He held his hand out flat, and in a second up sprang the grasshopper, and alighted on his palm, and told him the way to go, and thus they went together merrily.

"Are you sure the ants are so very stupid and wicked?" asked Bevis, when the grasshopper had guided him through a gateway into the meadow by the brook.

"Indeed I am. It is true they declare that it is I who am wrong, and never lose a chance of chattering at me, because they are always laying up a store, and I wander about, laughing and singing. But then you see, Bevis, dear, they are quite demented, and so led away by their greedy, selfish wishes that they do not even know that there is a sun. They say they cannot see it, and do not believe there is any sunshine, nor do they believe there are any stars. Now I do not sing at night, but I always go where I can see a star. I slept under a mushroom last night, and he told me he was pushing up as fast as he could before some one came and picked him to put on a gridiron. I do not lay up any store, because I know I shall die when the summer ends, and what is the use of wealth then? My store and my wealth is the sunshine, dear, and the blue sky, and the green grass, and the delicious brook who never ceases sing, sing, singing all day and night. And all the things are fond of me, the grass and the flowers, and the birds, and the animals, all of them love me. So you see I am richer than all the ants put together."

"I would rather be you than an ant," said Bevis, "I think I shall take you home and put you under a glass case on the mantel-piece."

Off jumped the grasshopper in a moment, and fell so lightly on the grass it did not hurt him in the least, though it was as far as if Bevis had tumbled down out of the clouds. Bevis tried to catch him, but he jumped so nimbly this way and that, and hopped to and fro, and lay down in the grass, so that his green coat could not be seen. Bevis got quite hot trying to catch him, and seeing this, the grasshopper, much delighted, cried out, "Are you not the stupid boy everybody is laughing at for letting the Weasel go? You will never catch the Weasel."

"I'll stamp on you," said Bevis, in a great rage.

"S——s," called the grasshopper — who was frightened at this—to his friends, and in a minute there were twenty of them jumping all round in every direction, and as they were all just alike Bevis did not know which to run after. When he looked up there was the brook close by, and the drinking-place where the birds were to meet and bathe. It was a spot where the ground shelved gently down . from the grass to the brook ; the stream was very shallow and flowed over the sandy bottom with a gentle murmur.

He went down to the brook and stood on the bank, where it was high near a bush at the side of the drinking-place. " Ah, dear little Sir Bevis ! " whispered a Reed, bending towards him as the Wind blew, " please do not come any nearer, the bank is steep and treacherous, and hollow underneath where the water-rats run. So do not lean over after the forget-me-nots—they are too far for you. Sit down where you are, behind that little bush, and I will tell you all about the bathing." Bevis sat down and picked a June rose from a briar that trailed over the bush, and asked why the birds bathed.

" I do not know why," said the Reed. " There is no why at all. We have been listening to the Brook, me and my family, for ever so many thousands of years, and though the Brook has been talking and singing all that time, I never heard him ask why about anything. And the great oak, where you went to sleep, has been there, goodness me, nobody can tell how long, and every one of his leaves (he has had millions of them) have all been talking, but not one of them ever asked why; nor does the sun, nor the stars which I see every night shining in the clear water down there, so that I am quite sure there is no why at all.

" But the birds come down to bathe every Midsummer Day, the goldfinches, and the sparrows, and the blackbirds, and the thrushes, and the swallows, and the wrens, and the robins, and almost every one of them, except two or three, whose great grandfathers got into disgrace a long while ago. The rooks do not come because they are thieves, and steal the mussels, nor the crows, who are a very bad lot; the swan does not come either, unless the Brook is muddy after a storm. The swan is so tired of seeing himself in the water that he quite hates it, and that is the reason he holds his neck so high, that he may not see more of himself than he can help.

"It is no use your asking the Brook why they come, because even if he ever knew, he has forgotten. For the Brook, though he sparkles so bright in the sun, and is so clear and sweet, and looks so young, is really so very, very, old that he has quite lost his memory, and cannot remember what was done yesterday. He did not even know which way the moorhen went just now, when I inquired, having a message to send to my relations by the osier-bed yonder.

"But I have heard the heron say—he is talkative sometimes at night when you are asleep, dear, he was down here this morning paddling about— that the birds in the beginning learnt to sing by listening to the Brook, and perhaps that is the reason they pay him such deep respect. Besides, everybody knows that according to an ancient prophecy which was delivered by the Raven before he left this country, if only the birds can all bathe in the Brook on Midsummer Day and hold their tongues, and not abuse one another or quarrel, they will be able to compose their differences, and ever afterwards live happily together.

"Then they could drive away the hawk, for

there is only one hawk to ten thousand finches, and
if they only marched shoulder to shoulder all together they could kill him with ease. They could
smother the cat even, by all coming down at once
upon her, or they could carry up a stone and drop
on her head; and as for the crow, that old coward,
if he saw them coming he would take wing at once.
But as they cannot agree, the hawk, and the cat,
and the crow do as they like. For the chaffinches
all fight one another, you heard them challenging,
and saw them go to battle, and then when at last
they leave off and are good fellows again, they all
flock together and will have nothing to do with
the goldfinches, or the blackbirds. It is true the
wood-pigeons, and the rooks, and the starlings, and
the fieldfares and redwings are often about in the
same field, but that is only because they eat the
same things; if a hawk comes they all fly away
from each other, and do not unite and fight him
as they might do.

"But if once they could come down to the
Brook on Midsummer Day, and never quarrel, then,
according to the prophecy I told you of, all this
diversity would cease, and they would be able to

do just as they pleased, and build three or four nests in the summer instead of one, and drive away and kill all the hawks, and crows, and cats. They tried to do it, I can't tell you how many years, but they could never succeed, for there was always a dispute about something, so at last they gave it up, and it was almost forgotten (for they came to the conclusion that it was no use to try), till last year, when the mole, the one that spoke to the grass-hopper just now, reminded them of it.

"Now the reason the mole reminded them of it was because one day a hawk came down too quick for his wife (who was peeping out of doors), and snapped her up in a minute, so he bore the hawk a grudge, and set about to seek for vengeance. And as he could not fly or get at the hawk he thought he would manage it through the other birds. So one morning when the green woodpecker came down to pick up the ants with his tongue, the mole looked out and promised to show him where there was a capital feast, and to turn up the ground for him, if in return he would fly all round the forest and the fields, and cry shame on the birds for letting the hawk go on as he did when they could so easily prevent it, just by holding their tongues one day.

This the woodpecker promised to do, and after he had feasted off he went, and having tapped on a tree to call attention, he began to cry shame upon them, and having a very loud voice he soon let them know his mind. At which the birds resolved to try again, and, do you know, last year they very nearly succeeded. For it rained hard all Midsummer Day, and when the birds came down to the Brook they were so bedraggled, and benumbed, and cold, and unhappy, that they had nothing to say for themselves, but splashed about in silence, and everything would have happened just right had not a rook, chancing to pass over, accidentally dropped something he was carrying in his bill, which fell into the flags there.

" The starling forgot himself, and remarked he supposed it was an acorn; when the wood-pigeon called him a donkey, as the acorns were not yet ripe, nor large enough to eat; and the usual uproar began again. But afterwards, when they talked it over, they said to each other that, as they had so nearly done it, it must be quite possible, and next year they would all hold their tongues as tight as wax, though the sun should drop out of the sky. Now the Hawk, of course, being so high up, circling round, saw and heard all this, and he was very much alarmed, as they had so nearly succeeded; and he greatly feared lest next year, what he had dreaded so long would come to pass, as the Raven had foretold.

"So he flew down and took counsel of his ancient friend the Weasel. What they said I cannot tell you, nor has it been found out, but I have no doubt they made up something wicked between them, and it is greatly to be regretted that you let the Weasel go, for the Hawk, sharp as he is, is not very clever at anything new, and if he had not got the Weasel to advise him I suspect he would not be much after all. We shall see presently what they have contrived—I am much mistaken if they have not put their heads together for something. Do you keep quite still, Bevis dear, when the birds come, and take care and not frighten them."

"I will," said Bevis; "I will be very quiet."

"It is my turn to tell you a story now," said a green flag waving to and fro in the brook. "The Reed has been talking too much."

"No, it is my turn," said a perch from the water under the bank. Bevis leaned over a little, and could see the bars across his back and sides.

"Hold your tongue," replied the flag; "you ate the roach this morning, whose silvery scales used to flash like a light under the water."

"I will nibble you," said the perch, very angry. "I will teach you to tell tales."

"I will ask the willow, he is a very old friend of mine, not to shake any more insects into the brook for you from his leaves," replied the flag.

"It was not I who ate the roach," said the perch; "it was the pike, Bevis dear."

"Indeed it was not," said the pike, coming forward a little from under some floating weeds, where he had been in hiding, so that Bevis could now see his long body. "The perch says things that are not true."

"You know you hate me," said the perch; "because your great, great grandfather swallowed mine in a rage, and my great, great grandfather's spines stuck in your great, great grandfather's throat and killed him. And ever since then, Bevis dear, they have done nothing but tell tales against me. I did not touch the roach, the pike wanted him, I know, for breakfast."

"I deny it," said the pike; "but if it was not the perch it was the Rat."

"That's false," said the Rat; "I have only this minute come down to the Brook. If it was not the pike nor the perch, depend upon it it was the heron."

"I am sure it was not the heron," said a beautiful drake, who came swimming down the stream. "I was here as early as any one, and I will not have my acquaintance the heron accused in his absence. I assure you it was not the heron."

"Well, who did it then?" said Bevis.

"The fact is," said a frog on the verge of the stream, "they are all as bad as one another; the perch is a rogue and a thief; the pike is a monster of iniquity; the heron never misses a chance of gobbling up somebody; and as for the drake, for all his glossy neck and his innocent look, he is as ready to pick up anything as the rest."

"Quack," cried the drake in a temper; "Quack."

"Hush!" said a tench from the bottom of a deep hole under the bank—he was always a peacemaker. "Hush! do stop the noise you are making. If you would only lie quiet in the mud like me, how pleasant you would find life."

"Bevis," began the Reed; "Bevis dear, Ah, ah!" His voice died away, for as the sun got higher the Wind fell, and the Reed could only speak while the Wind blew. The flag laughed as the Reed was silenced.

"You need not laugh," said the perch; "you can only talk while the water waggles you. The horse will come down to the Brook to-morrow, and bite off your long green tip, and then you will not be able to start any more falsehoods about me."

"The birds are coming," said the frog. "I should like to swim across to the other side, where I can see better, but I am afraid of the pike and the drake. Bevis, dear, fling that piece of dead stick at them."

Bevis picked up the dead stick and flung it at the drake, who hastened off down the stream; the pike, startled at the splash, darted up the brook, and the frog swam over in a minute. Then the birds began to come down to the drinking-place, where

the shore shelved very gently, and the clear shallow
water ran over the sandy bottom. They were all in
their very best and brightest feathers, and as the
sun shone on them and they splashed the water and
strutted about, Bevis thought he had never seen
anything so beautiful.

They did not all bathe, for some of them were
specially permitted only to drink instead, but they
all came, and all in their newest dresses. So bright
was the goldfinch's wing, that the lark, though she
did not dare speak, had no doubt she rouged. The
sparrow, brushed and neat, so quiet and subdued in
his brown velvet, looked quite aristocratic among so
much flaunting colour. As for the blackbird, he had
carefully washed himself in the spring before he
came to bathe in the brook, and he glanced round
with a bold and defiant air, as much as to say,
"There is not one of you who has so yellow a bill,
and so beautiful a black coat as I have." In the
bush the bullfinch, who did not much care to mix
with the crowd, moved restlessly to and fro. The
robin looked all the time at Bevis, so anxious was
he for admiration. The wood-pigeon, very conse-
quential, affected not to see the dove, whom Bevis

longed to stroke, but could not, as he had promised the Reed to keep still.

All this time the birds, though they glanced at one another, and those who were on good terms, like the chaffinch and the greenfinch, exchanged a nod, had not spoken a word, and the Reed, as a puff came, whispered to Bevis that the prophecy would certainly come to pass, and they would all be as happy as ever they could be. Why ever did they not make haste and fly away, now they had all bathed or sipped? The truth was, they liked to be seen in their best feathers, and none of them could make up their minds to be the first to go home; so they strutted to and fro in the sunshine. Bevis, in much excitement, could hardly refrain from telling them to go.

He looked up into the sky and there was the Hawk, almost up among the white clouds, soaring round and round, and watching all that was proceeding. Almost before he could look down again a shadow went by, and a cuckoo flew along very low, just over the drinking-place.

"Cuckoo!" he cried, "Cuckoo! The goldfinch has the prettiest dress," and off he went.

Now the Hawk had bribed the cuckoo, who was his cousin, to do this, and the cuckoo was not at all unwilling, for he had an interest himself in keeping the birds divided, so he said that although he had made up his mind to go on his summer tour, leaving his children to be taken care of by the wagtail, he would stop a day or two longer, to manage this little business. No sooner had the cuckoo said this, than there was a most terrible uproar, and all the birds cried out at once. The blackbird was so disgusted, that he flew straight off, chattering all across the field and up the hedge. The bullfinch tossed his head, and asked the goldfinch to come up in the bush and see which was strongest. The greenfinch and the chaffinch shrieked with derision; the woodpigeon turned his back, and said " Pooh !" and went off with a clatter. The sparrow flew to tell his mates on the house, and you could hear the chatter they made about it, right down at the Brook. But the wren screamed loudest of all, and said that the goldfinch was a painted impostor, and had not got half so much gold as the yellow-hammer. So they were all scattered in a minute, and Bevis stood up.

" Ah !" said the Reed, " I am very sorry. It

was the Hawk's doings, I am sure, and he was put
up to the trick by the Weasel, and now the birds
will never agree, for every year they will remember
this. Is it not a pity they are so vain? Bevis,
dear, you are going, I see. Come down again, dear,
when the wind blows stronger, and I will tell you
another story. Ah! ah!" he sighed; and was silent
as the puff ceased.

Bevis, tired of sitting so long, went wandering
up the Brook, peeping into the hollow willow trees,
wishing he could dive like the rats, and singing to
the Brook, who sang to him again, and taught
him a very old tune. By-and-by he came to the
hatch, where the Brook fell over with a splash, and
a constant bubbling, and churning, and gurgling. A
kingfisher, who had been perched on the rail of the
hatch, flew off when he saw Bevis, whistling, "Weep!
weep!"

"Why do you say, weep, weep," said Bevis; "Is
it because the birds are so foolish?" But the kingfisher did not stay to answer. The water rushing
over the hatch made so pleasant a sound that Bevis,
delighted with its tinkling music, sat down to
listen and to watch the bubbles, and see how far they

would swim before they burst. Then he threw little pieces of stick on the smooth surface above the hatch to see them come floating over and plunge under the bubbles, and presently appear again by the foam on the other side among the willow roots.

Still more sweetly sang the Brook, so that even restless Bevis stayed to hearken, though he could not quite make out what he was saying. A moorhen stole out from the rushes farther up, seeing that Bevis was still enchanted with the singing, and began to feed among the green weeds by the shore. A water-rat came out of his hole and fed in the grass close by. A blue dragon-fly settled on a water-plantain. Up in the ash-tree a dove perched and looked down at Bevis. Only the gnats were busy; they danced and danced till Bevis thought they must be dizzy, just over the water.

"Sing slower," said Bevis presently, "I want to hear what you are saying." So the Brook sang slower, but then it was too low, and he could not catch the words. Then he thought he should like to go over to the other side, and see what there was up the high bank among the brambles. He looked at the hatch, and saw that there was a beam across the

Brook, brown with weeds, which the water only splashed aginst and did not cover deeply. By holding tight to the rail and putting his feet on the beam he thought he could climb over.

He went down nearer and took hold of the rail, and was just going to put his foot on the beam, when the Brook stopped singing, and said, "Bevis, dear, do not do that; it is very deep here, and the beam is very slippery, and if you should fall I would hold you up as long as I could, but I am not very strong, and should you come to harm I should be very unhappy. Do please go back to the field, and if you will come down some day when I am not in such a hurry, I will sing to you very slowly, and tell you everything I know. And if you come very gently, and on tip-toe you will see the kingfisher, or perhaps the heron." Bevis, when he heard this, went back, and followed the hedge a good way, not much thinking where he was going, but strolling along in the shadow, and humming to himself the tune he had learnt from the brook. By-and-by he spied a gap in the hedge under an ash-tree, so he went through in a minute, and there was a high bank with trees like a copse, and bramble-bushes and ferns. He went on up the bank, winding in and out the brambles, and at last it was so steep he had to climb on his hands and knees, and suddenly as he came round a bramble-bush there was the Longpond, such a great piece of water, all gleaming in the sunshine and reaching far away to the woods and the hills, as if it had no end.

Bevis clapped his hands with delight, and was just going to stand up, when something caught him by the ankles; he looked round, and it was the Bailiff, who had had an eye on him all the time from the hayfield. Bevis kicked and struggled, but it was no use, the Bailiff carried him home, and then went back with a bill-hook, and cutting a thorn bush, stopped up the gap in the hedge.

CHAPTER V.

KAPCHACK.

"Q—q—q," Bevis heard a starling say some weeks afterwards on the chimney-top one morning when he woke up. The chimney was very old and big, and the sound came down it to his room. "Q—q—q, my dear, I will tell you a secret"—he was talking to his lady-love.

"Phe-hu," she said, in a flutter. Bevis could hear her wings go plainly. "Whatever is it? Do tell me."

"Look all round first," he said, "and see that no one is about."

"No one is near, dear; the sparrows are out in the corn, and the swallows are very high up; the blackbird is busy in the orchard, and the robin is down at the red currants; there's no one near. Is it a very great secret?"

"It is a very great secret indeed, and you must be very careful not to whistle it out by accident;

now if I tell you will you keep your beak quite shut, darling?"

"Quite."

"Then, listen—Kapchack is in love."

"Phe—hu—u; who is it? Is he going to be married? How old is she? Who told you? When did you hear it? Whatever will people say? Tell me all about it, dear!"

"The tomtit told me just now in the fir-tree; the woodpecker told him on his promising that he would not tell anybody else."

"When is the marriage to come off, dear?" she asked, interrupting him. "Kapchack—Phe—u!"

Somebody came round the house, and away they flew, just as Bevis was going to ask all about it. He went to the window as soon as he was dressed, and as he opened it he saw a fly on the pane; he thought he would ask the fly, but instantly the fly began to fidget, and finding that the top of the window was open out he went, buzzing that Kapchack was in love. At breakfast time a wasp came in—for the fruit was beginning to ripen, and the wasps to get busy—and he went all round the room saying that Kapchack was in love, but he would not listen to anything Bevis asked, he was so full of Kapchack. When Bevis ran out of doors the robin on the palings immediately said, "Kapchack is in love; do you know Kapchack is in love?" and a second afterwards the wren flew up to the top of the wood pile and cried out just the same thing.

Three finches passed him as he went up the garden, telling each other that Kapchack was in love. The mare in the meadow whinnied to her colt that Kapchack was in love, and the cows went "boo" when they heard it, and "booed" it to some more cows ever so far away. The leaves on the apple tree whispered it, and the news went all down the orchard in a moment; and everything repeated it. Bevis got into his swing, and as he swung to and fro he heard it all round him.

A humble-bee went along the grass telling all the flowers that were left, and then up into the elm, and the elm told the ash, and the ash told the oak, and the oak told the hawthorn, and it ran along the hedge till it reached the willow, and the willow told the Brook, and the Brook told the reeds, and the reeds told the kingfisher, and the kingfisher went a mile down the stream and told the heron, and the heron went up into the sky and called it out as loud as he could, and a rabbit heard it and told another rabbit, and he ran across to the copse and told another, and he told a mouse, and he told a butterfly, and the butterfly told a moth, and the moth went into the great wood and told another moth, and a wood-pigeon heard it and told more wood-pigeons, and so everybody said " Kapchack is in love ! "

"But I thought it was a great secret," said Bevis to a thrush, " and that nobody knew it, except the tomtit, and the woodpecker, and the starling; and, besides, who is Kapchack?" The thrush was in the bushes where they came to the haha, and when he heard Bevis ask who Kapchack was, he laughed, and said he should tell everybody that Bevis, who shot his uncle with the cannon-stick, was so very, very stupid he did not know who Kapchack was. Ha! Ha! Could anybody be so ignorant? he should not have believed it if he had not heard it.

Bevis, in a rage at this, jumped out of the swing and threw a stone at the thrush, and so well did he fling it that if the thrush had not slipped

under a briar he would have had a good thump.
Bevis went wandering round the garden, and into his
summer-house, when he heard some sparrows in the
ivy on the roof all chattering about Kapchack, and
out he ran to ask them, but they were off in a
second to go and tell the yellow-hammers. Bevis
stamped his foot, he was so cross because nobody
would tell him about Kapchack, and he could not
think what to do, till as he was looking round the
garden he saw the rhubarb, and remembered the old
Toad. Very likely the Toad would know; he was
so old, and knew almost everything. Away he ran
to the rhubarb and looked under the piece of wood,
and there was the Toad asleep, just as he always
was.

He was so firm asleep, he did not know what
Bevis said, till Bevis got a twig and poked him a
little. Then he yawned and woke up, and asked
Bevis what time it was, and how long it would be
before the moon rose.

"I want to know who Kapchack is, this minute,"
said Bevis, "this *very* minute, mind."

"Well I never!" said the Toad, "well I never!
Don't you know?"

"Tell me directly—this very minute—you horrid old Toad!"

"Don't you really know?" said the Toad.

"I'll have you shovelled up, and flung over to the pigs, if you don't tell me," said Bevis. "No, I'll get my cannon-stick, and shoot you! No, here's a big stone—I'll smash you! I hate you! Who's Kapchack?"

"Kapchack," said the Toad, not in the least frightened, "Kapchack is the Magpie; and he is king over everything and everybody—over the fly and the wasp, and the finches, and the heron, and the horse, and the rabbit, and the flowers, and the trees. Kapchack, the great and mighty Magpie, is the king," and the Toad bumped his chin on the ground, as if he stood before the throne, so humble was he at the very name of Kapchack. Then he shut one eye in a very peculiar manner, and put out his tongue.

"Why, don't you like Kapchack?" said Bevis, who understood him in a minute.

"Hush!" said the Toad, and he repeated out loud, "Kapchack is the great and noble Magpie— Kapchack is the king!" Then he whispered to

Bevis to sit down on the grass very near him, so that he might speak to him better, and not much louder than a whisper. When Bevis had sat down and stooped a little, the Toad came close to the mouth of his hole, and said very quietly, "Bevis, dear, Kapchack is a horrid wretch!"

"Why," said Bevis, "why do you hate him? and where does he live? and why is he king? I suppose he is very beautiful?"

"Oh, dear, no!" said the Toad, hastily, "he is the ugliest creature that ever hopped. The feathers round one eye have all come out and left a bare place, and he is quite blind on the other. Indeed his left eye is gone altogether. His beak is chipped and worn; his wings are so beaten and decayed that he can hardly fly; and there are several feathers out of his tail. He is the most miserable thing you ever saw."

"Then why is he king?" said Bevis.

"Because he is," said the Toad; "and as he is king, nobody else can be. It is true he is very wise—at least everybody says so—wiser than the crow or the rook, or the Weasel (though the Weasel is so cunning). And besides, he is so old, so very old, nobody knows when he was born, and they say that he will always live, and never die. Why, he put my grandfather in prison."

"In prison?" said Bevis. "Where is the prison?"

"In the elm tree, at the top of the Home Field," said the Toad. "My grandfather has been shut up there in a little dungeon so tight, he cannot turn round, or sit, or stand, or lie down, for so long a time that, really Bevis, dear, I cannot tell you; but it was before you were born. And all that time he has had nothing to eat or drink, and he has never seen the sun or felt the air, and I do not suppose he has ever heard anything unless when the thunderbolt fell on the oak, close by. Perhaps he heard the thunder then."

"Well, then, what has he been doing?" asked Bevis, "and why doesn't he get out?"

"He cannot get out, because the tree has grown all round him quite hard, as Kapchack knew it would when he ordered him to be put there in the hole. He has not been doing anything but thinking."

"I should get tired of thinking all that time," said Bevis; "but why was he put there?"

"For reasons of state," said the Toad. "He knows too much. Once upon a time he saw Kapchack do something, I do not know what it was, and Kapchack was very angry, and had him put in there in case he should tell other people. I went and asked him what it was before the tree quite shut him in, while there was just a little chink you could talk through; but he always told me to stop in my hole and mind my own business, else perhaps I should get punished, as he had been. But he did tell me that he could not help it, that he did not mean to see it, only just at the moment it happened he turned round in his bed, and he opened his eyes for a second, and you know the consequences, Bevis, dear. So I advise you always to look the other way, unless you're wanted."

"It was very cruel of Kapchack," said Bevis.

"Kapchack is very cruel," said the Toad, "and very greedy, more greedy even than the ants; and he has such a treasure in his palace as never was heard of. No one can tell how rich he is. And as for cruelty, why he killed his uncle only a week

since, just for not answering him the very instant
he spoke; he pecked him in the forehead and killed
him. Then he killed the poor little wren, whom he
chanced to hear say that the king was not so beautiful as her husband. Next he pecked a thrush to
death, because the thrush dared to come into his
orchard without special permission.

"But it is no use my trying to tell you all the
shameful things he has done in all these years.
There is never a year goes by without his doing
something dreadful; and he has made everybody
miserable at one time or other by killing their
friends or relations, from the snail to the partridge.
He is quite merciless, and spares no one; why, his
own children are afraid of him, and it is believed
that he has pecked several of them to death, though
it is hushed up; but people talk about it all the
same, sometimes. As for the way he has behaved
to the ladies, if I were to tell you you would never
believe it."

"I hate him," said Bevis. "Why ever do they
let him be king? How they must hate him."

"Oh, no they don't, dear," said the Toad. "If
you were to hear how they go on, you would think

he was the nicest and kindest person that ever existed. They sing his praises all day long; that is, in the spring and summer, while the birds have their voices. You must have heard them, only you did not understand them. The finches and the thrushes, and the yellow-hammers and the wrens, and all the birds, every one of them, except Choo Hoo, the great rebel, sing Kapchack's praises all day long, and tell him that they love him more than they love their eggs or their wives, or their nests, and that he is the very best and nicest of all, and that he never did anything wrong, but is always right and always just.

" And they say his eye is brighter than the sun, and that he can see more with his one eye than all the other birds put together; and that his feathers are blacker and whiter and more beautiful than anything else in the world, and his voice sweeter than the nightingale's. Now, if you will stoop a little lower I will whisper to you the reason they do this (Bevis stooped down close); the truth is they are afraid lest he should come himself and peck their eggs, or their children, or their wives, or if not himself that he should send the Hawk, or the Weasel, or the Stoat, or the Rat, or the Crow. Don't you ever listen to the Crow, Bevis; he is a black scoundrel.

"For Kapchack has got all the crows, and hawks, and weasels (especially that very cunning one, that old wretch that cheated you), and rats, to do just as he tells them. They are his soldiers, and they carry out his bidding quicker than you can wink your eye, or than I can shoot out my tongue, which I can do so quickly that you cannot see it. When the spring is over and the birds lose their voices (many of them have already), they each send one or two of their number every day to visit the orchard where Kapchack lives, and to say (as they can no longer sing) that they still think just the same, and they are all his very humble servants. Kapchack takes no notice of them whatever unless they happen to do what he does not like, and then they find out very soon that he has got plenty of spies about.

"My opinion is that the snail is no better than a spy and a common informer. Do you just look round and turn over any leaves that are near, lest any should be here, and tell tales about me. I can tell you, it is a very dangerous thing to talk about Kapchack, somebody or other is sure to hear, and to go and tell him, so as to get into favour. Now, that is what I hate. All the rabbits and hares (and your friend the Hare that lives at the top of the Home Field), and the Squirrel and the Mouse, all of them have to do just the same as the birds, and send messages to Kapchack, praising him and promising to do exactly as he tells them, all except Choo Hoo."

"Who is Choo Hoo?" said Bevis.

"Choo Hoo is the great wood-pigeon," said the Toad. "He is a rebel; but I cannot tell you much about him, for it is only of late years that we have heard anything of him, and I do not know much about the present state of things. Most of the things I can tell you happened, or begun, a long time ago. If you want to know what is going on now, the best person you can go to is the Squirrel. He is a very good fellow; he can tell you. I will give you a recommendation to him, or perhaps he will be afraid to open his mouth too freely; for, as I said before, it is a very dangerous thing to talk about Kapchack, and every-

body is most terribly afraid of him—he is so full
of malice."

"Why ever do they let him be king?" said
Bevis; "I would not, if I were them. Why ever
do they put up with him, and his cruelty and
greediness? I will tell the thrush and the starling
not to endure him any longer."

"Pooh! pooh!" said the Toad. "It is all very
well for you to say so, but you must excuse me
for saying, my dear Sir Bevis, that you really
know very little about it. The thrush and the
starling would not understand what you meant.
The thrush's father always did as Kapchack told
him, and sang his praises, as I told you, and so
did his grandfather, and his great grandfather, and
all his friends and relations, these years and years
past. So that now the thrushes have no idea of
there being no Kapchack. They could not understand you, if you tried to explain to them how nice
it would be without him. If you sat in your
swing and talked to them all day long, for all
the summer through, they would only think you
very stupid even to suppose such a state of things
as no Kapchack. Quite impossible, Bevis, dear!—

excuse me correcting you. Why, instead of liking it, they would say it would be very dreadful to have no Kapchack."

"Well, they are silly!" said Bevis. "But *you* do not like Kapchack!"

"No, I do not," said the Toad; "and if you will stoop down again—— (Bevis stooped still nearer.) No; perhaps you had better lie down on the grass! There—now I can talk to you quite freely. The fact is, do you know, there are other people besides me who do not like Kapchack. The Crow—I can't have anything to do with such an old rogue!—the Crow, I am certain, hates Kapchack, but he dares not say so. Now I am so old, and they think me so stupid and deaf that people say a good deal before me, never imagining that I take any notice. And when I have been out of a dewy evening, I have distinctly heard the Crow grumbling about Kapchack. The Crow thinks he is quite as clever as Kapchack, and would make quite as good a king.

"Nor is the Rat satisfied, nor the Weasel, nor the Hawk. I am sure they are not, but they cannot do anything alone, and they are so suspicious of each other they cannot agree. So that though they are dissatisfied, they can do nothing. I dare say Kapchack knows it very well indeed. He is so wise—so very, very wise—that he can see right into what they think, and he knows that they hate him, and he laughs in his sleeve. I will tell you what he does. He sets the Hawk on against the Rat, and the Rat on against the Crow, and the Crow against the Weasel. He tells them all sorts of things; so that the Weasel thinks the Crow tells tales about him, and the Hawk thinks the Rat has turned tail and betrayed his confidence. The result is, they hate one another as much as they hate him.

"And he told the Rat—it was very clever of him to do so, yes, it was very clever of him, I must admit that Kapchack is extremely clever— that if he was not king somebody else would be, perhaps the Hawk, or the Rat. Now the Rook told his friends at the rookery, and they told everybody else, and when people came to talk about it, they said it was very true. If Kapchack was not king, perhaps the Hawk would be, and he would be as bad, or worse; or the Rat, and he would be very much worse; or perhaps the Weasel, the very worst of all.

"So they agreed that, rather than have these, they would have Kapchack as the least evil. When the Hawk and the Rat heard what the king had said, they hated each other ten times more than before, lest Kapchack—if ever he should give up the crown—should choose one or other of them as his successor, for that was how they understood the hint. Not that there is the least chance of his giving up the crown; not he, my dear, and he will never die, as everybody knows (here the Toad winked slightly), and he will never grow any older, all he does is to grow wiser, and wiser, and wiser, and wiser. All the other birds die, but Kapchack lives for ever. Long live the mighty Kapchack!" said the Toad very loud, that all might hear how loyal he was, and then went on speaking lower. "Yet the Hawk, and the Crow, and the Rook, and the Jay, and all of them, though they hate Kapchack in their hearts, all come round him bowing down, and they peck the ground where he has just walked, and kiss the earth he has stood on, in token of their humility and obedience to him. Each tries to outdo the rest in

servility. They bring all the news to the palace,
and if they find anything very nice in the fields,
they send a message to say where it is, and leave it
for him, so that he eats the very fat of the land."

"And where is his palace?" asked Bevis. "I
should like to go and see him."

"His palace is up in an immense old apple-tree,
dear. It is a long way from here, and it is in an
orchard, where nobody is allowed to go. And this
is the strangest part of it all, and I have often
wondered and thought about it months together,
once I thought about it for a whole year, but I
cannot make out why it is that the owner of the
orchard, who lives in the house close by it, is so
fond of Kapchack. He will not let anybody go
into the orchard unless with him. He keeps it
locked (there is a high wall around), and carries the
key in his pocket.

"As the orchard is very big, and Kapchack's
nest is in the middle, no one can even see it from
the outside, nor can any boys fling a stone and hit
it; nor, indeed, could any one shoot at it, because
the boughs are all round it. Thus Kapchack's palace
is protected with a high wall, by the boughs, by

its distance from the outside, by lock and key, and by the owner of the orchard, who thinks more of him than of all the world besides. He will not let any other big birds go into the orchard at all, unless Kapchack seems to like it; he will bring out his gun and shoot them. He watches over Kapchack as carefully as if Kapchack was his son. As for the cats he has shot for getting into the orchard, there must have been a hundred of them.

"So that Kapchack every year puts a few more sticks on his nest, and brings up his family in perfect safety, which is what no other bird can do, neither the rook, nor the hawk, nor the crow, nor could even the raven, when he lived in this country. This is a very great advantage to Kapchack, for he has thus a fortress to retreat to, into which no one can enter, and he can defy everybody; and this is a great help to him as king. It is also one reason why he lives so long, though perhaps there is another reason, which I cannot, really I dare not, even hint at; it is such a dreadful secret, I should have my head split open with a peck if I even so much as dared to think it. Besides which, perhaps it is not true.

"If it were not so far, and if there was not a wall round the orchard, I would tell you which way to go to find the place. His palace is now so big he can hardly make it any bigger lest it should fall; yet it is so full of treasures that it can barely hold them all. There are many who would like to rob him, I know. The Crow is one; but they dare not attempt it, not only for fear of Kapchack, but because they would certainly be shot.

"Everybody talks about the enormous treasure he has up there, and everybody envies him. But there are very dark corners in his palace, dark and blood-stained, for, as I told you, his family history is full of direful deeds. Besides killing his uncle, and, as is whispered, several of his children, because he suspected them of designs upon his throne, he has made away with a great many of his wives, I should think at least twenty. So soon as they begin to get old and ugly they die—people pretend the palace is not healthy to live in, being so ancient, and that that is the reason. Though doubtless they are very aggravating, and very jealous. Did you hear who it was Kapchack was in love with?"

"No," said Bevis.   "The starling flew away

before I could ask him, and as for the rest they are so busy telling one another they will not answer me."

"One thing is very certain," said the Toad, "if Kapchack is in love you may be sure there will be some terrible tragedy in the palace, for his wife will be jealous, and besides that his eldest son and heir will not like it. Prince Tchack-tchack is not a very good temper—Tchack-tchack is his son, I should tell you—and he is already very tired of waiting for the throne. But it is no use his being tired, for Kapchack does not mean to die. Now Bevis, dear, I have told you everything I can think of, and I am tired of sitting at the mouth of this hole, where the sunshine comes, and must go back to sleep.

"But if you want to know anything about the present state of things (as I can only tell you what happened a long time since) you had better go and call on the Squirrel, and say I sent you, and he will inform you. He is about the best fellow I know; it is true he will sometimes bite when he is very frisky, it is only his play, but you can look sharp and put your hands in your pockets. He is the best of them all, dear; better than the Fox, or the Weasel,

or the Rat, or the Stoat, or the Mouse, or any of
them. He knows all that is going on, because the
starlings, who are extremely talkative, come every
night to sleep in the copse where he lives, and have
a long gossip before they go to sleep; indeed, all
the birds go to the copse to chat, the rooks, the
wood-pigeons, the pheasant, and the thrush, besides
the rabbits and the hares, so that the Squirrel, to
whom the copse belongs, hears everything."

"But I do not know my way to the copse," said
Bevis, "please tell me the way."

"You must go up to the great oak-tree, dear,"
said the Toad, "where you once went to sleep, and
then go across to the wheat-field, and a little farther
you will see a footpath, which will take you to
another field, and you will see the copse on your
right. Now the way into the copse is over a narrow
bridge, it is only a tree put across the ditch, and you
must be careful how you cross it, and hold tight to
the handrail, and look where you put your feet. It
is apt to be slippery, and the ditch beneath is very
deep; there is not much water, but a great deal of
mud. I recollect it very well, though I have not
been there for some time: I slipped off the bridge

one rainy night in the dark, and had rather a heavy fall. The bridge is now dry, and therefore you can pass it easily if you do not leave-go of the handrail. Good morning, dear, I feel so sleepy—come and tell me with whom Kapchack has fallen in love; and remember me to the Squirrel." So saying the Toad went back into his hole and went to sleep.

CHAPTER VI.

THE SQUIRREL.

ALL this talking had passed away the morning, but in the afternoon, when the sun got a little lower, and the heat was not quite so great, Bevis, who had not been allowed to go out at noon, came forth again, and at once started up the Home Field. He easily reached the great oak-tree, and from there he knew his way to the corner of the wheat-field, where he stopped and looked for the Hare, but she was not there, nor did she answer when he called to her. At the sound of his voice a number of sparrows rose from the wheat, which was now ripening, and flew up to the hedge, where they began to chatter about Kapchack's love affair.

Bevis walked on across the field, and presently found a footpath; he followed this, as the Toad had instructed him, and after getting over two stiles there was the copse on the right, though he had to climb over a high gate to get into the meadow next to it.

There was nothing in the meadow except a rabbit, who turned up his white tail and went into his hole, for having seen Bevis with the Hare, whom he did not like, the rabbit did not care to speak to Bevis. When Bevis had crossed the meadow he found, just as the Toad had said, that there was a very deep ditch round the copse, but scarcely any water in it, and that was almost hidden with weeds.

After walking a little way along the ditch he saw the tree which had been cut down and thrown across for a bridge. It was covered with moss, and in the shadow underneath it the hart's-tongue fern was growing. Remembering what the Toad had told him, Bevis put his hand on the rail—it was a willow pole—but found that it was not very safe, for at the end the wasps (a long time ago) had eaten it hollow, carrying away the wood for their nests, and what they had left had become rotten. Still it was enough to steady his footsteps, and taking care that he did not put his foot on a knot, Bevis got across safely. There was a rail to climb over on the other side, and then he was in the copse, and began to walk down a broad green path, a road which wound in among the ash-wood.

Nobody said anything to him, it was quite silent, so silent, that he could hear the snap of the dragon-fly's wing as he stopped in his swift flight and returned again. Bevis pulled a handful of long green rushes, and then he picked some of the burrs from the tall burdocks; they stuck to his fingers when he tried to fling them away, and would not go. The great thistles were ever so far above his head, and the humble-bees on them glanced down at him as he passed. Bevis very carefully looked at the bramble-bushes to see how the black-berries were coming on; but the berries were red and green, and the flowers had not yet all gone. There was such a beautiful piece of woodbine hanging from one of the ash-poles that he was not satisfied till he had gathered some of it; the long brome-grass tickled his face while he was pulling at the honey-suckle.

He clapped his hands when he found some young nuts; he knew they were not ripe, but he picked one and bit it with his teeth, just to feel how soft it was. There were several very nice sticks, some of which he had half a mind to stay and cut, and put his hand in his pocket for his knife, but there were so many things to look at, he thought he would go

on a little farther, and come back and cut them
presently. The ferns were so tall and thick in many
places that he could not see in among the trees.
When he looked back he had left the place, where
he came in, so far behind, that he could not see it,
nor when he looked round could he see any daylight
through the wood; there was only the sky overhead
and the trees and ash-stoles, and bushes, and thistles,
and long grass, and fern all about him.

Bevis liked it very much, and he ran on and
kicked over a bunch of tawny fungus as he went, till
by-and-by he came to a piece of timber lying on the
ground, and sat down upon it. Some finches went
over just then, they were talking about Kapchack
as they flew, they went so fast he could not hear much.
But the Squirrel was nowhere about; he called to
him, but no one answered, and he began to think he
should never find him, when presently, while he sat
on the timber whistling very happily, something came
round the corner, and Bevis saw it was the Hare.

She ran up to him quickly, and sat down at his
feet, and he stroked her very softly. "I called for
you at the wheat-field," he said, "but you were
not there."

"No dear," said the Hare, "the truth is, I have been waiting for ever so long to come into the copse on a visit to an old friend, but you must know that the Weasel lives here."

"Does the Weasel live here?" said Bevis, starting up. "Tell me where, and I will kill him; I will cut off his head with my knife."

"I cannot tell you exactly, where he lives," said the Hare; "but it is somewhere in the copse. It is of no use your looking about; it is in some hole or other, quite hidden, and you would never find it. I am afraid to come into the copse while he is here; but this afternoon the dragon-fly brought me word that the Weasel had gone out. So I made haste to come while he was away, as I had not seen my old friend, the Squirrel, for ever so long, and I wanted to know if the news was true."

"Do you mean about Kapchack?" said Bevis. "I came to see the Squirrel, too, but I cannot find him."

"Yes, I mean about Kapchack," said the Hare. "Is it not silly of him to fall in love at his age? Why, he must be ten times as old as me! Really,

I sometimes think that the older people get the sillier they are. But it is not much use your looking for the Squirrel, dear. He may be up in the fir tree, or he may be in the beech, or he may have gone along the hedge. If you were by yourself, the best thing you could do would be to sit still where you are, and he would be nearly sure to come by, sooner or later. He is so restless, he goes all over the copse, and is never very long in one place. Since, however, you and I have met, I will find him for you, and send him to you."

"How long shall you be?" said Bevis. "I am tired of sitting here now, and I shall go on along the path."

"Oh, then," said the Hare, "I shall not know where to find you, and that will not do. Now, I know what I will do. I will take you to the raspberries, and there you can eat the fruit till I send the Squirrel."

The Hare leapt into the fern, and Bevis went after her. She led him in and out, and round the ash-stoles and bushes, till he had not the least idea which way he was going. After a time, they came

to an immense thicket of bramble and thorn, and
fern growing up in it, and honeysuckle climbing
over it.

" It is inside this thicket," said the Hare.
" Let us go all round, and see if we can find a
way in."

There was a place under an ash-stole, where
Bevis could just creep beneath the boughs (the
boughs held up the brambles), and after going on
his hands and knees after the Hare a good way,
he found himself inside the thicket, where there
was an open space grown over with raspberry canes.
Bevis shouted with delight as he saw the raspberries were ripe, and began to eat them at
once.

" How ever did they get here?" he asked.

" I think it was the thrush," said the Hare.
" It was one of the birds, no doubt. They take
the fruit out of the orchards and gardens, and that
was how it came here, I dare say. Now, don't
you go outside the thicket till the Squirrel comes.
And when you have quite done talking to the
Squirrel, ask him to show you the way back to
the timber, and there I will meet you, and lead you

to the wheat-field, where you can see the oak tree, and know your way home. Mind you do not go outside the thicket without the Squirrel, or you will lose your way, and wander about among the trees till it is night."

Off went the Hare to find the Squirrel, and Bevis set to work to eat as many of the raspberries as he could.

Among the raspberry canes he found three or four rabbit-holes, and hearing the rabbits talking to each other, he stooped down to listen. They were talking scandal about the Hare, and saying that she was very naughty, and rambled about too much. At this Bevis was very angry, and stamped his foot above the hole, and told them they ought to be ashamed of themselves for saying such things. The rabbits very much frightened, went down farther into their holes. After which Bevis ate a great many more raspberries, and presently, feeling very lazy, he lay down on some moss at the foot of an oak-tree, and kicked his heels on the ground, and looked up at the blue sky, as he always did when he wanted some one to speak to. He did not know how long he had been gazing at the sky, when he heard some one say, "Bevis, dear!" and turning that way he saw the Squirrel, who had come up very quietly, and was sitting on one of the lower branches of the oak, close to him.

"Well, Squirrel," said Bevis, sitting up; "the Toad said I was to remember him to you. And now be very quick, and tell me all you know about Kapchack, and who it is he is in love with, and all about the rebel, Choo Hoo, and everything else, in a minute."

"Well, you are in a hurry," said the Squirrel, laughing; "and so am I, generally; but this afternoon I have nothing to do, and I am very glad you have come, dear. Now, first——"

"First," said Bevis, interrupting, "why did the starling say it was a great secret, when everybody knew it?"

"It was a great secret," said the Squirrel, "till Prince Tchack-tchack came down here (he is the heir, you know) in a dreadful fit of temper, and told the tomtit whom he met in the fir-tree, and the tomtit told the woodpecker, and the woodpecker told the starling, who told his lady-love on the chimney, and the fly heard him, and when you opened the

window the fly went out and buzzed it to everybody
while you were at breakfast. By this time it is
all over the world; and I daresay even the sea-gulls,
though they live such a long way off, have heard
it. Kapchack is beside himself with rage that it
should be known, and Tchack-tchack is afraid to go
near him. He made a great peck at Tchack-tchack
just now."

"But why should there be so much trouble about
it?" said Bevis.

"Oh," said the Squirrel, "it is a very serious
business, let me tell you. It is not an ordinary
falling in love, it is nothing less than a complete
revolution of everything, and it will upset all the
rules and laws that have been handed down ever
since the world began."

"Dear me!" said Bevis. "And who is it Kapchack is in love with? I have asked twenty people,
but no one will tell me."

"Why, I am telling you," said the Squirrel.
"Don't you see, if it had been an ordinary affair—
only a young magpie—it would not have mattered
much, though I daresay the queen would have been
jealous, but this——"

"Who is it?" said Bevis, in a rage. "Why don't you tell me who it is?"

"I am telling you," said the Squirrel, sharply.

"No, you're not. You're telling me a lot of things, but not what I want to know."

"Oh, well," said the Squirrel, tossing his head and swishing his tail, "of course, if you know more about it than I do it is no use my staying." So off he went in a pet.

Up jumped Bevis. "You're a stupid donkey," he shouted, and ran across to the other side, and threw a piece of stick up into an elm-tree after the Squirrel. But the Squirrel was so quick he could not see which way he had gone, and in half-a-minute he heard the Squirrel say very softly, "Bevis, dear," behind him, and looked back, and there he was sitting on the oak bough again.

The Squirrel, as the Toad had said, was really a very good fellow; he was very quick to take offence, but his temper only lasted a minute. "Bevis, dear," he said; "come back and sit down again on the moss, and I will tell you."

"I shan't come back," said Bevis, rather sulkily. "I shall sit here."

"No, no; don't stop there," said the Squirrel, very anxiously. "Don't stop there, dear; can't you see that great bough above you; that elm-tree is very wicked, and full of malice, do not stop there, he may hurt you."

"Pooh! what rubbish!" said Bevis; "I don't believe you. It is a very nice elm, I am sure. Besides, how can he hurt me? He has got no legs, and he can't run after me, and he has no hands and he can't catch me. I'm not a bit afraid of him;" and he kicked the elm with all his might. Without waiting a second, the Squirrel jumped down out of the oak and ran across and caught hold of Bevis by his stocking—he could not catch hold of his jacket—and tried to drag him away. Seeing the Squirrel in such an excited state, Bevis went with him to please him, and sat down on the moss under the oak. The Squirrel went up on the bough, and Bevis laughed at him for being so silly.

"Ah, but my dear Sir Bevis," said the Squirrel, "you do not know all, or you would not say what you did. You think because the elm has no legs, and cannot run after you, and because he has no hands, and cannot catch you, that therefore he cannot do you any harm. You are very much mistaken; that is a very malicious elm, and of a very wicked disposition. Elms, indeed, are very treacherous, and I recommend you to have nothing to do with them, dear."

"But how could he hurt me?" said Bevis.

"He can wait till you go under him," said the Squirrel, "and then drop that big bough on you. He has had that bough waiting to drop on somebody for quite ten years. Just look up and see how thick it is, and heavy, why, it would smash a man out flat. Now, the reason the elms are so dangerous is because they will wait so long till somebody passes. Trees can do a great deal, I can tell you; why I have known a tree when it could not drop a bough, fall down altogether when there was not a breath of wind, nor any lightning, just to kill a cow or a sheep, out of sheer bad temper."

"But oaks do not fall, do they?" asked Bevis; looking up in some alarm at the oak above him.

"Oh, no," said the Squirrel; "the oak is a very good tree, and so is the beech and the ash, and many more (though I am not quite certain of the horse-chestnut, I have heard of his playing tricks), but the elm is not; if he can he will do something spiteful. I never go up an elm if I can help it, not unless I am frightened by a dog or somebody coming along. The only fall I ever had was out of an elm.

"I ran up one in a hurry, away from that wretch, the Weasel (you know him), and put my foot on a dried branch, and the elm, like a treacherous thing as he is, let it go, and down I went crash, and should have hurt myself very much if my old friend the ivy had not put out a piece for me to catch hold of, and so just saved me. As for you, dear, don't you ever sit under an elm, for you are very likely to take cold there, there is always a draught under an elm on the warmest day.

"If it should come on to rain while you are out for a walk, be sure and not go under an elm for shelter if the wind is blowing, for the elm, if he possibly can, will take advantage of the storm to smash you.

"And elms are so patient, they will wait sixty or seventy years to do somebody an injury; if they cannot get a branch ready to fall they will let the rain in at a knot-hole, and so make it rotten inside, though it looks green without, or ask some fungus to come up and grow there, and so get the bough ready for them. That elm across there is quite rotten inside—there is a hole inside so big you could stand up, and yet if anybody went by they would say what a splendid tree.

"But if you asked Kauhaha, the rook, he would shake his head, and decline to have anything to do with that tree. So my dear Sir Bevis, do not you think any more that because a thing has no legs, nor arms, nor eyes, nor ears, that therefore it cannot hurt you. There is the earth for instance; you may stamp on the earth with your feet and she will not say anything, she will put up with anything, but she is always lying in wait all the same, and if you could only find all the money she has buried you would be the richest man in the world; I could tell you something about that. The flints even—"

"Now I do not believe what you are going to say," said Bevis, "I am sure the flints cannot do anything, for I have picked up hundreds of them and flung them splash into the brook."

"But I assure you they can," said the Squirrel. "I will tell you a story about a flint that happened

only a short time since, and then you will believe.
Once upon a time a waggon was sent upon the hills
to fetch a load of flints, it was a very old waggon,
and it wanted mending, for it belonged to a man
who never would mend anything."

"Who was that?" said Bevis. "What a curious
man."

"It was the same old gentleman (he is a farmer,
only he is like your papa, Sir Bevis, and his land is
his own), the same old gentleman who is so fond
of Kapchack, whose palace is in his orchard. Well,
the waggon went up on the hills, where the men
had dug up some flints which had been lying quite
motionless in the ground for so many thousand
years that nobody could count them. There were at
least five thousand flints, and the waggon went
jolting down the hill and on to the road, and as
it went the flints tried to get out, but they could
not manage it, none but one flint, which was smaller
than the rest.

"This one flint, of all the five thousand, squeezed
out of a hole in the bottom of the waggon, and
fell on the dust in the road, and was left there.
There was not much traffic on the road (it is the

same, dear, that goes to Southampton, where the ships are), so that it remained where it fell. Only one waggon came by with a load of hay, and had the wheel gone over the flint of course it would have been crushed to pieces. But the waggoner, instead of walking by his horses, was on the grass at the side of the road talking to a labourer in the field, and his team did not pass on their right side of the road, but more in the middle, and so the flint was not crushed.

"In the evening, when it was dark, a very old and very wealthy gentleman came along in his dog-cart, and his horse, which was a valuable one, chanced to slip on the flint, which, being sharp and jagged, hurt its hoof, and down the horse fell. The elderly gentleman and his groom, who was driving, were thrown out, the groom was not hurt, but his master broke his arm, and the horse broke his knees. The gentleman was so angry that no sooner did he get home than he dismissed the groom, though it was no fault of his, for how could he see the flint in the night? Nor would he give the man a character, and the consequence was he could not find another place. He soon began to starve, and then he was obliged to steal, and after a while he became a burglar.

" One night he entered a house in London, and was getting on well, and stealing gold watches and such things, when somebody opened the door and tried to seize him. Pulling out his pistol, he shot his assailant dead on the spot, and at once escaped, and has not since been heard of, though you may be sure if he is caught he will be hung, and they are looking very sharp after him, because he stole a box with some papers in it which are said to be of great value. And the person he shot was the same gentleman who had discharged him because the horse fell down. Now all this happened through the flint, and as I told you, Bevis dear, about the elm, the danger with such things is that they will wait so long to do mischief.

" This flint, you see, waited so many years that nobody could count them, till the waggon came to fetch it. They are never tired of waiting. Be very careful, Bevis dear, how you climb up a tree, or how you put your head out of window, for there is a thing that is always lying in wait, and will pull you down in a minute, if you do not take care. It has been waiting there to make something fall ever since the beginning of the world, long before your house was built, dear, or before any of the trees grew. You cannot see it, but it is there, as you may prove by putting your cap out of window, which in a second will begin to fall down, as you would if you were tilted out.

"And I daresay you have seen people swimming, which is a very pleasant thing, I hear from the wild ducks; but all the time the water is lying in wait, and if they stop swimming a minute they will be drowned, and although a man very soon gets tired of swimming, the water never gets tired of waiting, but is always ready to drown him.

"Also, it is the same with your candle, Bevis dear, and this the bat told me, for he once saw it happen: looking in at a window as he flew by, and he shrieked as loud as he could, but his voice is so very shrill that it is not everybody can hear him, and all his efforts were in vain. For a lady had gone to sleep in bed and left her candle burning on the dressing-table, just where she had left it fifty times before, and found it burnt down to the socket in the morning, and no harm done. But that night she had had a new pair of gloves, which were wrapped up in a piece of paper, and she undid these gloves and left the piece of paper underneath the candlestick, and yet it would not have hurt had the candle been put up properly, but instead of that a match had been stuck in at the side, like a wedge, to keep it up. When the flame came down to the match the match caught fire, and when it had burnt a little way down, that piece fell off, and dropped on the paper in which the gloves had been wrapped. The paper being very thin was alight in an instant, and from the paper the flame travelled to some gauze things hung on the looking-glass, and from that to the window curtains, and from the window curtains to the bed curtains, till the room was in a blaze, and though the bat shrieked his loudest the lady did not wake till she was very much burnt.

"Also with the sea; for the cod-fish told the sea-gull, who told the heron, who related the fact to the kingfisher, who informed me. The cod-fish was swimming about in the sea and saw a ship at anchor, and coming by the chain-cable the fish saw that one of the links of the chain was nearly eaten through with rust; but as the wind was calm it did

not matter.   Next time the ship came there to anchor
the cod-fish looked again; and the rust had gone still
further into the link.   A third time the ship came
back to anchor there, and the sailors went to sleep
thinking it was all right, but the cod-fish swam by
and saw that the link only just held.   In the night
there came a storm, and the sailors woke up to find
the vessel drifting on the rocks, where she was
broken to pieces, and hardly any of them escaped.

"Also, with Living Things, Bevis dear; for there
was once a little creeping thing (the sun-beetle told
me he heard it from his grandfather) which bored
a hole into a beam under the floor of a room—the hole
was so tiny you could scarcely see it, and the beam
was so big twenty men could not lift it.   After the
creeping thing had bored this little hole it died,
but it left ten children, and they bored ten more
little holes, and when they died they left ten each,
and they bored a hundred holes, and left a thousand,
and they bored a thousand holes, and they left a
thousand tens, who bored ten thousand holes, and
left ten thousand tens, and they bored one hundred
thousand holes, and left one hundred thousand tens,
and they bored a million holes; and when a great

number of people met in the room to hear a man speak, down the beam fell crash, and they were all dreadfully injured.

" Now, therefore, Bevis, my dear little Sir Bevis, do you take great care and never think any more that a thing cannot hurt you, because it has not got any legs, and cannot run after you, or because it has no hands, and cannot catch you, or because it is very tiny, and you cannot see it, but could kill a thousand with the heel of your boot. For as I told you about the malice-minded elm, all these things are so terribly dangerous, because they can wait so long, and because they never forget.

"Therefore, if you climb up a tree, be sure and remember to hold tight, and not forget, for the earth will not forget, but will pull you down to it thump, and hurt you very much. And remember if you walk by the water that it is water, and do not forget, for the water will not forget, and if you should fall in, will let you sink and drown you. And if you take a candle be careful what you are doing, and do not forget that fire will burn, for the fire will not forget, but will always be on the look out and ready, and will burn you without mercy. And be sure to see that no little unseen creeping thing is at work, for they are everywhere boring holes into the beam of life till it cracks unexpectedly; but you must stay till you are older, and have eaten the peck of salt your papa tells you about before you can understand all that. Now,"——

"But," said Bevis, who had been listening to the story very carefully, "you have not told me about the wind. You have told me about the earth, and the water, and the fire, but you have not said anything about the wind."

"No more I have," said the Squirrel. "You see I forget, though the earth does not, neither does the water, nor the fire. Well, the Wind is the nicest of all of them, and you need never be afraid of the Wind, for he blows so sweetly, and brings the odour of flowers, and fills you with life, and joy, and happiness. And oh, Bevis dear, you should listen to the delicious songs he sings, and the stories he tells as he goes through the fir-tree and the oak. Of course if you are on the ground, so far below, you can only hear a sound of whispering, unless your ears are very sharp; but if you were up in the boughs with me, you would be enchanted with the beauty of his voice.

"No, dear, never be afraid of the Wind, but put your doors open and let him come in, and throw your window open and let him wander round the room, and take your cap off sometimes, and let him stroke your hair. The Wind is a darling —I love the Wind, and so do you, dear, for I have seen you racing about when the Wind was rough, chasing the leaves and shouting with delight. Now with the Wind it is just the reverse to what it is with all the others. If you fall on the earth it thumps you ; into the water, it drowns you ; into the fire, it burns you ; but you cannot do without wind.

"Always remember that you must have wind, dear, and do not get into a drawer, as I have heard of boys doing, from the Mouse, who goes about a good deal indoors, and being suffocated for want of wind ; or into a box, or a hole, or any-where where there is no wind. It is true he some-times comes along with a most tremendous push, and the trees go cracking over. That is only be-cause they are malice-minded, and are rotten at the heart; and the boughs break off, that is only because they have invited the fungus to grow on them; and the thatch on your papa's ricks is lifted up at the corner just as if the Wind had chucked them under the chin.

"But that is nothing. Everybody loses his temper now and then, and why not the Wind? You should see the nuts he knocks down for me where I could not very well reach them, and the showers of acorns, and the apples! I take an apple out of your orchard, dear, sometimes, but I do not mean any harm—it is only one or two. I love the Wind! But do not go near an elm, dear, when the wind blows, for the elm, as I told you, is a malicious tree, and will seize any pretence, or a mere puff, to do mischief."

"I love the Wind, too!" said Bevis. "He sings to me down the chimney, and hums to me through the door, and whistles up in the attic, and shouts at me from the trees. Oh, yes, I will do as you say; I will always have plenty of the Wind. You are a very nice Squirrel. I like you very much; and you have a lovely silky tail. But you have not told me yet who it is Kapchack is in love with."

"I have been telling you all the time," said the Squirrel; "but you are in such a hurry; and, as I was saying, if it was only a young magpie, now—only an ordinary affair—very likely the queen would be jealous, indeed, and there would be a fight in the palace, which would be nothing at all new, but this is much more serious, a very serious matter, and none can tell how it will end. As Kauc, the crow, was saying to Cloctaw, the jackdaw, this morning——"

"But who is it?" asked Bevis, jumping up again in a rage.

"Why, everybody knows who it is," said the Squirrel; "from the ladybird to the heron; from the horse to the mouse; and everybody is talking of it, and as since the Raven went away, there is no judge to settle any dispute—"

"I hate you!" said Bevis, "you do talk so much; but you do not tell me what I want to know. You are a regular donkey, and I will pull your tail."

He snatched at the Squirrel's tail, but the Squirrel was too quick; he jumped up the boughs and showed his white teeth, and ran away in a temper.

Bevis looked all round, but could not see him, and as he was looking, a dragon-fly came and said that the Squirrel had sent him to say that he was very much hurt, and thought Bevis was extremely rude to him, but he had told the dragon-fly to show him the way to the piece of timber, and if he would come back to-morrow, and not be so rude, he should hear all about it. So the dragon-fly led Bevis to the piece of timber, where the Hare was waiting, and the Hare led him to the wheat-field, and showed him the top of the great oak-tree, and from there he easily found his way home to tea.

CHAPTER VII.

THE COURTIERS.

THE next morning passed quickly, Bevis having so much to do. Hur-hur, the pig, asked him to dig up some earth-nuts for him with his knife, for the ground was hard from the heat of the sun, and he could not thrust his snout in. Then Pan, the spaniel, had to be whipped very severely because he would not climb a tree; and so the morning was taken up. After the noontide heat had decreased, Bevis again started, and found his way by the aid of the oak to the corner of the wheat-field. The dragon-fly was waiting for him with a message from the Hare, saying that she had been invited to a party on the hills, so the dragon-fly would guide him into the copse.

Flying before him, the dragon-fly led the way, often going a long distance ahead, and coming back in a minute, for he moved so rapidly it was not possible for Bevis to keep pace with him, and he was

too restless to stand still. Bevis walked carefully
over the bridge, holding to the rail, as the Toad had
told him; and passing the thistles, and the grass,
and the ferns, came to the piece of timber. There
he sat down to rest, while the dragon-fly played
to and fro, now rising to the top of the trees, and
now darting down again, to show off his dexterity.
While he was sitting there a crow came along and
looked at him hard, but said nothing; and immediately afterwards a jackdaw went over, remarking
what a lovely day it was.

"Now take me to the raspberries," said Bevis;
and the dragon-fly, winding in and out the trees,
brought him to the thicket, showed him the place
to creep in, and left, promising to return by-and-by
and fetch him when it was time to go home. Bevis,
warm with walking in the sunshine, after he had
crept into the raspberries, went across and sat down
on the moss under the oak; and he had hardly
leant his back against the tree than the Squirrel
came along on the ground and sat beside him.

"You are just in time, my dear," he said, speaking low and rapidly, and glancing round to see that
no one was near; "for there is going to be a

secret council of the courtiers this afternoon, while
Kapchack takes his nap; and in order that none of the
little birds may play the spy and carry information
to the police, Kauc, the crow, has been flying round
and driving them away, so that there is not so much
as a robin left in the copse. This is an employment
that suits him very well, for he loves to play the
tyrant. Perhaps you saw him coming in. And
this council is about Kapchack's love affair, and to
decide what is to be done, and whether it can be
put up with, or whether they must refuse to receive
her."

"And who is she?" said Bevis; "you keep on
talking, but you do not tell me." The Squirrel
pricked up his ears and looked cross, but he heard
the people coming to the council, and knew there
was no time to be lost in quarrelling, so he did not go
off in a pet this time. "The lady is the youngest
jay, dear, in the wood; La Schach is her name; she
is sweetly pretty, and dresses charmingly in blue and
brown. She is sweetly pretty, though they say
rather a flirt, and flighty in her ways. She has
captivated a great many with her bright colour, and
now this toothless old Kapchack—but hush! It is a

terrible scandal. I hear them coming; slip this way, Bevis dear."

Bevis went after him under the brambles and the ferns till he found a place in a hollow ash-stole, where it was hung all round with honeysuckle, and then, doing as the Squirrel told him, he sat down, and was quite concealed from sight; while the Squirrel stopped on a bough just over his head, where he could whisper and explain things. Though Bevis was himself hidden, he could see very well; and he had not been there a minute before he heard a rustling, and saw the Fox come stealthily out from the fern, and sit under an ancient hollow pollard close by.

The Stoat came close behind him; he was something like the Weasel, and they say a near relation; he is much bolder than the Weasel, but not one quarter so cunning. He is very jealous, too, of the power the Weasel has got on account of his cunning, and if he could he would strangle his kinsman. The Rat could not attend, having very important business at the brook that day, but he had sent the Mouse to listen and tell him all that was said. The Fox looked at the Mouse askance from the corner of his eye; and the Stoat could not refrain from licking his lips, though it was well understood that at these assemblies all private feelings were to be rigidly suppressed. So that the Mouse was quite safe; still, seeing the Fox's glance, and the Stoat's teeth glistening, he kept very near a little hole under a stole, where he could rush in if alarmed.

"I understood Prince Tchack-tchack was coming," said the Fox, "but I don't see him."

"I heard the same thing," said the Stoat. "He's very much upset about this business."

"Ah," said the Fox, "perhaps he had an eye himself to this beautiful young creature. Depend upon it there's more under the surface than we have heard of yet." Just then a message came from the Weasel regretting very much that he could not be present, owing to indisposition, but saying that he quite agreed with all that was going to be said, and that he would act as the others decided, and follow them in all things. This message was delivered by a humble-bee, who having repeated all the Weasel had told him to, went buzzing on among the thistles.

"I do not quite like this," said a deep hollow voice; and looking up, Bevis saw the face of the Owl at the mouth of a hole in the pollard-tree. He was winking in the light, and could not persuade himself to come out, which was the reason the council was held at the foot of his house, as it was necessary he should take part in it. "I do not quite like this," said the Owl, very solemnly. "Is the Weasel sincere in all he says? Is he really unwell, or does he keep away in order that if Kapchack hears of this meeting he may say, 'I was not there. I did not take any part in it?'"

"That is very likely," said the Stoat. "He is capable of anything—I say it with sorrow, as he is so near a relation, but the fact is, gentlemen, the Weasel is not what he ought to be, and has, I am afraid, much disgraced our family."

"Let us send for the Weasel," said the Hawk, who just then came and alighted on the tree above the Owl. "Perhaps the Squirrel, who knows the copse so well, will go and fetch him."

"I really do not know where he lives," said the Squirrel. "I have not seen him lately, and I am afraid he is keeping his bed." Then the Squirrel whispered down to Bevis, "That is not all true, but you see I am obliged not to know too much, else I should offend somebody and do myself no good."

"Well, then," said the Rook, who had just arrived, "send the Mouse; he looks as if he wanted something to do."

"I cannot agree to that," said the Owl, "the Mouse is very clever, and his opinion worthy of attention; we cannot spare him." The truth was, the Owl, squinting down, had seen what a plump Mouse it was, and he reflected that if the Weasel saw him he would never rest till he had tasted him, whereas he thought he should like to meet the Mouse by moonlight shortly. "Upon the whole, I really don't know that we need send for the Weasel," he went on; thinking that if the Weasel came he would fasten his affections upon the Mouse.

"But I do," said the Stoat.

"And so do I," said the Fox.

"And I," said Kauc, the crow; settling down on a branch of the pollard.

"For my part," said Cloctaw, the old jackdaw, taking his seat on a branch of horse-chestnut, "I think it very disrespectful of the Weasel."

"True," said the wood-pigeon. "True-whoo," as he settled on the ash.

"Quite true-oo," repeated the dove; perching in the hawthorn.

"Send for the Weasel, then," said a missel-thrush, also perching in the hawthorn. "Why all this delay? I am for action. Send for the Weasel immediately."

"Really, gentlemen," said the Mouse, not at all liking the prospect of a private interview with the Weasel, "you must remember that I have had a long journey here, and I am not quite sure where the Weasel lives at present."

"The council is not complete without the Weasel," screamed a Jay, coming up; he was in a terrible temper, for the lady jay whom Kapchack was in love with had promised him her hand, till the opportunity of so much grandeur turned her head, and she jilted him like a true daughter of the family, as she was. For the jays are famous for jilting their lovers. "If the Mouse is afraid," said the Jay, "I'll fetch the Humble-bee back, and if he wont come I'll speak a word to my friend the shrike, and have him spitted on a thorn in a minute." Off he flew, and the

Humble-bee, dreadfully frightened, came buzzing back directly.

"It falls upon you, as the oldest of the party, to give him his commands," said Tchink, the chaffinch, addressing the Owl. The Owl looked at the Crow, and the Crow scowled at the chaffinch, who turned his back on him, being very saucy. He had watched his opportunity while the Crow went round the copse to drive away the small birds, and slipped in to appear at the council. He was determined to assert his presence, and take as much part as the others in these important events. If the goldfinches, and the thrushes, and blackbirds, and robins, and greenfinches, and sparrows, and so on, were so meek as to submit to be excluded, and were content to have no voice in the matter till they were called upon to obey orders, that was their affair. They were a bevy of poor-spirited, mean things. He was not going to be put down like that. Tchink was, indeed, a very impudent fellow: Bevis liked him directly, and determined to have a chat with him by-and-by.

"If I am the oldest of the party, it is scarcely competent for you to say so," said the Owl with great dignity, opening his eyes to their full extent, and glaring at Tchink.

" All right, old spectacles," said Tchink, " you're not a bad sort of fellow by daylight, though I have heard tales of your not behaving quite so properly at night." Then catching sight of Bevis (for Tchink was very quick) he flew over and settled near the Squirrel, intending, if any violence was offered to him, to ask Bevis for protection.

The Owl, seeing the Fox tittering, and the Crow secretly pleased at this remark, thought it best to take no notice, but ordered the Humble-bee, in the name of the council, to at once proceed to the Weasel, and inform him that the council was unable to accept his excuses, but was waiting his arrival.

" Is Tchack-tchack coming? " asked the Mouse, recovering his spirits now.

" I too-whoo should like to know if Tchack-tchack is coming," said the wood-pigeon.

" And I so, too-oo," added the dove. " It seems to me a most important matter."

" In my opinion," said Cloctaw, speaking rather huskily, for he was very old, " Tchack-tchack will not come. I know him well—I can see through him—

he is a double-faced rascal like—like (he was going to say the Fox, but recollected himself in time) his —well, never matter; like all his race then. My opinion is he started the rumour that he was coming just to get us together, and encourage us to conspire against his father, in the belief that the heir was with us and approved of our proceedings. But he never really meant to come."

"The jackdaw is very old," said the Crow, with a sneer. "He is not what he used to be, gentlemen; you must make allowance for his infirmities."

"It seems to me," said the missel-thrush, interrupting, "that we are wasting a great deal of time. I propose that we at once begin the discussion, and then if the Weasel and Tchack-tchack come they can join in. I regret to say that my kinsman, the missel-thrush, who frequents the orchard (by special permission of Kapchack, as you know) is not here. The pampered fawning wretch!—I hate such favourites—they disgrace a court. Why all the rest of our family are driven forth like rogues, and are not permitted to come near! If the tyrant kills his children in his wanton freaks even then this minion remains loyal: despicable being! But now without further delay let us ask the Owl to state the case plainly, so that we can all understand what we are talking about."

"Hear, hear," said Tchink.

"I agree too," said the wood-pigeon.

"I too," said the dove.

"It is no use waiting for Tchack-tchack," said the Hawk.

"Hum! haw! caw!" said the Rook, "I do not know about that."

"Let us go on to business," said the Stoat, "the Weasel knows no more than we do. His reputation is much greater than he deserves."

"I have heard the same thing," said the Fox. "Indeed I think so myself."

"I am sure the Owl will put the case quite fairly," said the Mouse, much pleased that the Owl had saved him from carrying the message to the Weasel.

"*We* are all waiting, Owl," said Tchink.

"*We*, indeed," said the Hawk, very sharply.

"Hush! hush!" said the Squirrel. "This is a privileged place, gentlemen; no personal remarks, if you please."

"I think, think, the Owl is very stupid not to begin," said the Chaffinch.

"If you please," said the Fox, bowing most politely to the Owl, "we are listening."

"Well then, gentlemen, since you all wish it," said the Owl, ruffling out his frills and swelling up his feathers, "since you all wish it, I will endeavour to put the case as plainly as possible, and in as few words as I can. You must understand, gentlemen, indeed you all understand already, that from time immemorial, ever since the oak bore acorns, and the bramble blackberries, it has been the established custom for each particular bird and each particular animal to fall in love with, and to marry some other bird or animal of the same kind.

"To explain more fully, so that there cannot by any possibility be the least chance of any one mistaking my meaning, I should illustrate the position in this way, that it has always been the invariable custom for owls to marry owls; for crows to marry crows; for rooks to fall in love with rooks; for woodpigeons to woo wood-pigeons; doves to love doves; missel-thrushes to court lady missel-thrushes; jackdaws, jackdaws; hawks, hawks; rats, rats; foxes,

foxes; stoats, stoats; weasels, weasels; squirrels, squirrels; for jays, to marry jays (' Just so,' screamed the Jay); and magpies to marry magpies."

"And chaffinches to kiss chaffinches," added Tchink; determined not to be left out.

"This custom," continued the Owl, "has now existed so long, that upon looking into the archives of my house, and turning over the dusty records, not without inconvenience to myself, I can't discover one single instance of a departure from it since history began. There is no record, gentlemen, of any such event having taken place. I may say, without fear of contradiction, that no precedent exists. We may, therefore, regard it as a fixed principle of common law, from which no departure can be legal, without the special and express sanction of all the nation, or of its representatives assembled. We may even go farther, and hazard the opinion, not without some authority, that even with such sanction, such departure from constitutional usage could not be sustained were an appeal to be lodged.

"Even the high court of representatives of all the nation, assembled in the fulness of their

power, could not legalise what is in itself and
of its own nature, illegal. Customs of this kind,
which are founded upon the innate sense and feeling
of every individual, cannot, in short, be abolished
by Act of Parliament. Upon this all the authorities
I have consulted are perfectly agreed. What has
grown up during the process of so many generations, cannot be now put on one side. This, gentlemen, is rather an abstruse part of the question,
being one which recommends itself for consideration to the purely legal intellect. It is a matter,
too, of high state policy which rises above the
knowledge of the common herd. We may take it
for granted, and pass on from the general to the
special aspect of this most remarkable case.

" What do we see? We see a proposed alliance
between an august magpie and a beautiful jay.
Now we know by experience that what the palace
does one day, the world at large will do to-morrow.
It is the instinct of nature to follow the example
of those set so high above us. We may therefore conclude, without fear of contradiction, that this
alliance will be followed by others equally opposed
to tradition. We shall have hundreds of other

equally ill-assorted unions. If it could be confined to this one instance, a dispensation might doubtless be arranged. I, for one, should not oppose it. ('I hate you!' shouted the Jay.) But no one can for a moment shut his eye to what must happen. We shall have, as I before remarked, hundreds of these ill-assorted unions.

"Now I need not enlarge upon the unhappy state of affairs which would thus be caused: the family jars, the shock to your feelings, the pain that must be inflicted upon loving hearts. With that I have nothing to do. It may safely be left to your imagination. But what I, as a statesman and a lawyer, have to deal with, is the legal, that is the common sense view of the situation, and my first question is this: I ask myself, and I beg you, each of you, to ask yourselves—I ask myself what effect would these ill-assorted unions produce upon the inheritance of property?"

"True—whoo!" said the wood-pigeon.

"Hum! Haw!" said the Rook.

"Law-daw!" said Cloctaw.

"Very important, very!" said the Fox. "The sacred laws of property cannot with safety be interfered with."

"No intrusion can be thought of for a moment," said the Stoat.

"Most absurd!" said the Jay.

"The very point!" said the missel-thrush.

"Very clear, indeed!" said the Mouse; "I am sure the Rat will echo the sentiment."

"Every one will agree with you," said Ki Ki, the Hawk.

"I think the same," said the chaffinch.

"The question is undoubtedly very important," continued the Owl, when the buzz had subsided, and much pleased at the sensation he had caused. "You all agree that the question is not one to be lightly decided or passed over. In order to fully estimate the threatened alteration in our present system, let us for a moment survey the existing condition of affairs. I, myself, to begin with, I and my ancestors, for many generations, have held undisputed possession of this pollard. Not the slightest flaw has ever been discovered in our title-deeds; and no claimant has ever arisen. The Rook has had, I believe, once or twice some little difficulty respecting his own particular tenancy, which is not a freehold; but his townsmen, as a body, possess their trees in peace. The Crow holds an oak; the wood-pigeon has an ash; the missel-thrush a birch; our respected friend the Fox here, has a burrow which he inherited from a deceased rabbit, and he has also contingent claims on the withey-bed, and other property in the country; the Stoat has a charter of free warren."

"And I have an elm," said Tchink, "let anybody come near it, that's all."

"The Squirrel," continued the Owl, "has an acknowledged authority over this copse; and the Jay has three or four firs of his own."

"And St. Paul belongs to me," said Cloctaw, the jackdaw.

"Well, now," said the Owl, raising his voice and overpowering the husky Cloctaw, "about these various properties little or no dispute can take place; the son succeeds to the father, and the nephew to the uncle. Occasional litigation, of course, occurs, which I have often had the pleasure of conducting to an amicable and satisfactory termination. But, upon the whole, there is very little difficulty; and the principle of inheritance is accepted by all. Your approval, indeed, has just been signified in the most unanimous manner. But what shall we see if the example set by the palace spreads among society? The ash at the present moment is owned by the wood-pigeon; were the wood-pigeon's heir to marry the missel-thrush's heiress, just imagine the conflicting claims which would arise?

"The family would be divided amongst itself; all the relations upon the paternal side, and the relations upon the maternal side, would join the contest, and peace would be utterly at an end. And so in all other instances. The crow would no longer have a fee-simple of the oak, the jackdaw of the steeple, the rook of the elm, the fox of the burrow, or I of my pollard. We might even see the rook claiming the— But I will not follow the illustration farther, lest I be charged with descending to personalities. I will only add, in conclusion, that if this ill-fated union takes place, we must look forward to seeing every home broken up, our private settlements, our laws of hereditary succession set upon one side, our property divided among a miscellaneous horde of people, who will not know their own grandfathers, and our most cherished sentiments cast to the winds of heaven." With which words the Owl concluded, and was greeted with marks of approval from all parts of the circle.

"We are all very much indebted to the Owl," said the Fox, "for putting the true aspect of the case so clearly before us. His learned discourse— not more learned than lucid—has convinced us all of the extreme inexpediency of this alliance."

"If this course is persisted in," said the Crow, "it can only end, in my opinion, in a way disastrous to the state. The king cannot decline to listen to our representations, if we are united."

"Haw!" said the Rook; "I'm not so sure of that. Kapchack likes his own way."

"Kapchack is very self-willed," said the Hawk. "It is almost our turn to have our way once now."

"So I should say," screamed the Jay; who could never open his beak without getting into a temper. "So I should say; Kapchack is a wicked old—"

"Hush, hush," said the Squirrel; "you can't tell who may be listening."

"I don't care," said the Jay, ruffling up his feathers; "Kapchack is a wicked old fellow, and Tchack-tchack is as bad."

"Capital!" said Tchink, the chaffinch; "I like

outspoken people. But I have heard that you (to the Jay) are very fond of flirting." At this there would have been a disturbance, had not the Fox interfered.

"We shall never do anything, unless we agree amongst ourselves," he said. "Now, the question is, are we going to do anything?"

"Yes, that is it," said the missel-thrush, who hated talking, and liked to be doing; "what is it we are going to do?"

"Something must be done," said the Owl, very solemnly.

"Yes; something must be done," said Cloctaw.

"Something must be done," said Ki Ki.

"I think, think so," said Tchink.

"I, too," said the dove.

"Quite true," said the wood-pigeon.

"Something must be done," said the Stoat.

"Let us tell Kapchack what we think," said the Mouse, getting bold, as he was not eaten.

"A good idea," said the Crow; "a very good idea. We will send the Mouse with a message."

"Dear me! No, no," cried the Mouse, terribly frightened; "Kapchack is awful in a rage—my life would not be worth a minute's purchase. Let the Stoat go."

"Not I," said the Stoat; "I have had to suffer enough already, on account of my relation to that rascal the Weasel, whom Kapchack suspects of designs upon his throne. I will not go."

"Nor I," said the Fox; "Kapchack has looked angrily at me for a long time—he cannot forget my royal descent. Let the Hawk go."

"I! I!" said Ki Ki. "Nonsense; Kapchack does not much like me now; he gave me a hint the other day not to soar too high. I suppose he did not like to think of my overlooking him kissing pretty La Schach."

"Wretch! horrid wretch!" screamed the Jay, at the mention of the kissing, in a paroxysm of jealousy. "Pecking is too good for him!"

"Send the Jackdaw or the Crow," said Ki Ki.

"No, no," said Kauc and Cloctaw together. "Try the wood-pigeon."

"I go?—whoo," said the pigeon. "Impossible. Kapchack told me to my face the other day that he more than half suspected me of plotting to go over to Choo Hoo. I dare not say such a thing to him."

"Nor I," said the dove. "Why not the Owl?"

"The fact is," said the Owl, "my relations with Kapchack are of a peculiar and delicate nature. Although I occupy the position of a trusted counsellor, and have the honour to be chief secretary of state, that very position forbids my taking liberties, and it is clear if I did, and were in consequence banished from the court, that I could not plead your cause. Now, the Rat——"

"I am sure the Rat will not go," said the Mouse. "My friend the Rat is very particularly engaged, and could not possibly stir from home at this juncture. There is the missel-thrush."

"Ridiculous," said the missel-thrush. "Everybody knows I had to leave my hawthorn-tree because Prince Tchack-tchack took a fancy to it. He would very likely accuse me to his father of high treason, for he hates me more than poison ever since he did me that injury, and would lose no chance of compassing my destruction. Besides which my relative—the favourite—would effectually prevent me from obtaining an audience. Now, there's the Squirrel."

"My dear sir," said the Squirrel, "it is well known

I never meddle with politics. I am most happy to see you all here, and you can have the use of my copse at any time, and I may say further that I sympathise with your views in a general way. But on no account could I depart from my principles."

"His principles," muttered the Crow, always a cynical fellow. "His principles are his own beech-trees. If anybody touched them he would not object to politics then."

"This is rather awkward," said the Owl. "There seems an embarrassment on the part of all of us, and we must own that to venture into the presence of a despotic monarch with such unpleasant advice requires no slight courage. Now, I propose that since the Weasel has attained so high a reputation for address, that he be called upon to deliver our message."

"Hear, hear," said the Fox.

"Hear, hear," said the Stoat.

"Capital," said the Chaffinch. "Old Spectacles can always see a way out of a difficulty."

"Haw!" said the Rook. "I'm doubtful. Perhaps the Weasel will not see it in this light."

"Buzz," said the Humble-bee, just then returning. "Gentlemen, I have seen the Weasel. His lordship was lying on a bank in the sun—he is very ill indeed. His limbs are almost powerless; he has taken a chill from sleeping in a damp hole. He sends his humble apology, and regrets he cannot move. I left him licking his helpless paw. Buzz, buzz."

"Hark! hark!" said the Woodpecker; bursting into the circle with such a shout and clatter that the dove flew a little way in alarm. "Kapchack is waking up. I have been watching all the time to let you know. And there is no chance of Prince Tchack-tchack coming, for he told me that Kapchack ordered him not to leave the orchard while he was asleep."

"I do not believe it," said the Jay. "He is a false scoundrel, and I dare say Kapchack never gave any such order, and never thought about it. However, there is no help for it, we must break up this meeting, or we shall be missed. But it is clear that something must be done."

"Something must be done," said the wood-pigeon, as he flew off.

"Something must be done," repeated the dove.

"Something must be done," said the Owl, as he
went down into the pollard to sleep the rest of the
day. Off went the Mouse as fast as he could go,
anxious to get away from the neighbourhood of the
Weasel. The missel-thrush had started directly he
heard what the Woodpecker said, disgusted that there
was no action, and nothing but talk. The Jay went
off with the Hawk, remarking as he went that he
had expected better things of the Fox, whose royal
ancestors had so great a reputation, and could contrive
a scheme to achieve anything, while their ignoble
descendant was so quiet, and scarce spoke a word.
It seemed as if the Weasel would soon outdo him
altogether. The Rook flew straight away to the flock
to which he belonged, to tell them all that had been
said. The Chaffinch left at the same time; the Fox
and the Stoat went away together; the Crow and the
Jackdaw accompanied each other a little way. When
they had gone a short distance the Crow said he
wanted to say something very particular, so they
perched together on a lonely branch.

"What is it?" said Cloctaw.

"The fact is," said the Crow, "my belief is—
come a little nearer—my belief is that Kapchack's

reign is coming to an end. People won't put up with this."

"Ah," said the Jackdaw, "if that is the case who is to be king?"

"Well," said the Crow, "let me whisper to you; come a little nearer." He hopped towards Cloctaw. Cloctaw hopped the other way. The Crow hopped towards him again, till Cloctaw came to the end of the branch, and could go no further without flying, which would look odd under the circumstances. So he kept a very sharp eye on Kauc, for the fact was they had had many a quarrel when they were younger, and Cloctaw was not at all sure that he should not have a beak suddenly driven through his head.

"The truth is," said the Crow, in a hoarse whisper, "there's a chance for you and me. Can't you see the Fox is very stupid, quite abject, and without the least spirit; the Stoat is very fierce, but has no mind; everybody suspects the Weasel, and will not trust him; as for the Rat, he is no favourite; the Hawk is—well, the Hawk is dangerous, but might be disposed of ('You black assassin,' thought Cloctaw to himself); the Rook has

not a chance, for his friends would be too jealous
to let one of their number become a king; and for
the rest, they are too weak. There's only you and
me left."

"I see," said Cloctaw; "but we could not both
be king."

"Why not?" said the Crow; "you wear the
crown and live in the palace; you are old, and it
would be nice and comfortable; you have all the
state and dignity, and I will do the work."

"It is very kind of you to propose it," said
Cloctaw, as if considering. In his heart he thought,
"Oh, yes, very convenient indeed; I am to wear
the crown, and be pecked at by everybody, and *you*
to do all the work—that is, to go about and collect
the revenue, and be rich, and have all the power,
while I have all the danger."

"It is quite feasible, I am sure," said the Crow;
"especially if Prince Tchack-tchack continues his
undutiful course, and if Choo Hoo should come up
with his army."

"I must think about it," said Cloctaw; "we must
not be too hasty."

"Oh, dear no," said the Crow, delighted to have

won over one important politician to his cause so easily; "we must wait and watch events. Of course this little conversation is quite private?"

"Perfectly private," said Cloctaw; and they parted.

The Crow had an appointment, and Cloctaw flew direct to the steeple. His nest was in the highest niche, just behind the image of St. Paul; and it was not only the highest, but the safest from intrusion, for there was no window near, and on account of some projections below, even a ladder could not be put up, so that it was quite inaccessible without scaffolding. This niche he discovered in his hot youth, when he won renown by his strength and courage: he chose it for his home, and defended it against all comers. He was now old and feeble, but his reputation as a leading politician, and his influence at the court of king Kapchack was too great for any to think of ousting him by force.

But the members of his family, in their extreme solicitude for his personal safety, frequently represented to him the danger he incurred in ascending so high. Should a wing fail him, how terrible the consequences! more especially for the race of which he was so distinguished an ornament. Nor was there the least reason for his labouring to that elevation; with his reputation and influence, none would dare to meddle with him. There were many pleasant places not so exposed, as the gurgoyle, the leads, the angle of the roof, where he could rest without such an effort; and upon their part they would willingly assist him by collecting twigs for a new nest.

But Cloctaw turned a deaf ear to these kindly proposals, and could not be made to see the advantages so benevolently suggested. He would in no degree abate his dignity, his right, power, or position. He adhered to St. Paul. There he had built all his days, and there he meant to stay to the last, for having seen so much of the world, well he knew that possession is ten points of the law, and well he understood the envy and jealousy which dictated these friendly counsels.

At the same time, as the Fox and the Stoat were going though the fern, the Stoat said, "It appears to me that this is a very favourable opportunity for ruining the Weasel. Could we not make up some tale, and tell Kapchack how the Weasel asked us to a secret meeting, or something?"

Now the Fox had his own ideas, and he wanted to get rid of the Stoat. "Another time," he said, "another time, we will consider of it; but why waste such a capital chance as you have to-day?"

"Capital chance to-day?" said the Stoat; "what is it you mean?"

"Did you not see the Mouse?" said the Fox. "Did you not see how fat he was? And just think, he has a long and lonely road home; and it would be very easy to make a short cut (for he will not leave the hedges which are round about), and get in front of, and so intercept him. I should go myself, but I was out last night, and feel tired this afternoon."

"Oh, thank you," said the Stoat; "I'll run that way directly." And off he started, thinking to himself, "How silly the Fox has got, and how much he has fallen off from the ancient wisdom for which his ancestors were famous. Why ever did he not hold his tongue, and I should never have thought of the Mouse, and the Fox could have had him another day?"

But the fact was the Fox recollected that the Mouse had had a long start, and it was very doubtful if the Stoat could overtake him, and if he did, most likely the Rat would come to meet his friend, and the Stoat would get the worst of the encounter.

However ill the Rat served the Mouse, however much he abused his superior strength, wreaking his temper on his weaker companion, still the Mouse clung to him all the more. On the other hand the Rat, ready enough to injure the Mouse himself, would allow no one else (unless with his permission) to touch his follower, wishing to reserve to himself a monopoly of tyranny.

So soon as the Stoat was out of sight, the Fox looked round to see that no one was near, and he said to a fly, "Fly, will you carry a message for me?"

"I am very busy," said the fly, "very busy indeed."

So the Fox went a little farther, and said to a humble-bee, "Humble-bee, will you carry a message for me?"

"I am just going home," said the humble-bee, and buzzed along.

So the Fox went a little farther, and said to a butterfly, "Beautiful butterfly, will you carry a message for me?" But the disdainful butterfly did not even answer.

The Fox went a little farther, and met a tomtit. "Te-te," said he, addressing the tomtit by name, "will you carry a message for me?"

"What impudence!" said Te-te. "Mind your own business, and do not speak to gentlemen."

"I see how it is," said the Fox to himself, "the fortunes of my family are fallen, and I am disregarded. When we were rich, and had a great reputation, and were the first of all the people in the wood, then we had messengers enough, and they flew to do our bidding. But now, they turn aside. This is very bitter. When I get home, I must curl round and think about it; I cannot endure this state of things. How dreadful it is to be poor! I wish we had not dissipated our wealth so freely. However, there is a little left still in a secret corner. As I said, I must see about it. Here is a gnat. 'Gnat, will you carry a message for me?'"

"Well, I don't know," said the gnat; "I must think about it. Will to-morrow do?"

"No," said the Fox quickly, before the gnat

flew off. "Go for me to Kapchack, and say there has been a secret——"

"A secret?" said the gnat; "that's another matter." And he went down closer to the Fox.

"Yes," said the Fox, "you fly as fast as you can, and whisper to Kapchack—you have free admittance, I know, to the palace—that there has been a secret meeting in the copse about his love affair, and that the courtiers are all against it, and are bent on his destruction, especially the Owl, the Hawk, the Crow, the Rook, the Weasel (the Weasel worst of all, for they would have chosen him as their deputy), the Stoat, and the Jackdaw, and that he has only one true friend, the Fox, who sends the message."

"All right!" said the gnat; "all right, I'll go!" And off he flew, delighted to be entrusted with so great a secret.

While the courtiers were thus intriguing, not only against Kapchack, but against each other, Bevis and the Squirrel went back into the raspberries, and Bevis helped himself to the fruit that had ripened since yesterday.

"It seems to me," said Bevis, after he had

eaten as much as he could, "that they are all very wicked."

"So they are," said the Squirrel. "I am sorry to say they are rather treacherous, and I warned you not to believe all they said to you. I would not let them use my copse, but the fact is, if they are wicked, Kapchack is a hundred times more so. Besides, it is very hard on the Jay, who is an old acquaintance of mine—we often have a chat in the fir-trees—to have his dear, sweet, pretty lady stolen away from him by such a horrid old wretch, whose riches and crown have quite turned her head!"

"What a business it all is," said Bevis. "Everybody seems mixed up in it. And so it is true that Prince Tchack-tchack is also in love with the pretty jay?"

"Yes, that it is," said the Squirrel; "and, between you and me, I have seen her flirt with him desperately, in that very hawthorn bush he forced the missel-thrush to give up to him. And that is the reason he will not let Kapchack peck his eye out, as he is so vain, and likes to look nice."

"Let Kapchack peck his eye out! But Kapchack is his father. Surely his papa would not peck his eye out?"

"Oh, dear me!" said the Squirrel, "I almost let the secret out. Goodness! I hope nobody heard me. And pray Bevis, dear, don't repeat it — oh, pray don't!—or it will be sure to be traced to me. I wish I had never heard it. If I had not listened to that vile old Crow; if I had not been so curious, and overheard him muttering to himself, and suggesting doubts at night! Bevis, dear, don't you ever be curious, and don't you say a word."

The Squirrel was in a terrible fright, till Bevis promised not to repeat anything.

"But," said he, "you have not told me the secret."

"No," said the Squirrel, "but I very nearly did, and only just stopped in time. Why, if the trees heard it, they would pass it from one to the other in a moment. Dear, dear!" He sat down, he was so frightened he could not frisk about. But Bevis stroked him down, and soothed him, and said he had the most lovely silky tail in the world, and this brought him to himself again.

"All this comes," said the Squirrel, "of my having run up the wrong side of the tree first this morning. Take care, Bevis dear, that you too do not make a mistake, and put the wrong foot first out of bed when you get up." Bevis laughed at this, and asked which was his wrong foot. "Well," said the Squirrel, "the fact is, it depends : sometimes it is one, and sometimes it is the other, and that is the difficulty, to know which it is, and makes all the difference in life. The very best woman I ever knew (and she was a farmer's wife) always, when she was out walking, put one foot before the other, and so was always right."

"Nonsense," said Bevis, "how could she walk without putting one foot before the other ?"

"Oh, yes," said the Squirrel, "many people, though they think they put one foot before the other, really keep the wrong foot foremost all the time. But do you remember to-morrow morning when you get up."

"I do not see what difference it can make," said Bevis.

"If you put one foot out first," said the Squirrel, "it will very likely lead you to the looking-glass, where you will see yourself and forget all the rest, and you will do one sort of thing that day; and if you put the other out first it will lead you to the window, and then you will see something, and you will think about that, and do another sort of thing; and if you put both feet out of bed together they will take you to the door, and there you will meet somebody, who will say something, and you will do another kind of thing. So you see it is a very important matter, and this woman, as I said, was the best that ever lived."

"No she wasn't," said Bevis, " she was not half so good as my mother is."

"That is true dear," said the Squirrel, "your mother is the very best of all. But don't forget about your feet to-morrow morning, dear."

"Look up," said Bevis, "and tell me what bird that is."

The Squirrel looked up, and saw a bird going over at a great height. "That is a peewit," he said. " He is a messenger; you can see how fast and straight he is flying. He is bringing some news, I feel sure, about Choo Hoo. Kapchack sent an out-post of peewits over the hills to watch Choo Hoo's movements, and to let him know directly if he began to gather his army together. Depend upon it dear, there is some very important news. I must tell the Woodpecker, and he will find out; he is very clever at that." The Squirrel began to get restless, though he did not like to tell Bevis to go.

"You promised to tell me about Choo Hoo," said Bevis.

"So I did," said the Squirrel, "and if you will come to-morrow I will do so; I am rather in a hurry just now."

"Very well," said Bevis, "I will come to-morrow. Now show me the way to the felled tree." As they were going Bevis recollected the Weasel, and asked if he was really so ill he could not move, but was obliged to lick his paw to cure the pain.

The Squirrel laughed. "No," he whispered, "Don't you say I said so: the truth is the Weasel is as well as you or I, and now the council is broken up I daresay he is running about as quickly as he likes. And, Bevis dear, stoop down and I'll tell you (Bevis stooped) the fact is he was at the council all the time."

"But I never saw him," said Bevis, "and he never said anything."

"No," whispered the Squirrel very quietly, "he wanted to hear what they said without being present; he was in the elm all the time; you know dear, that malice-minded elm on the other side of the raspberries, which I told you was rotten inside. He lives there in that hole; there is a way into it level with the ground; that is his secret hiding place."

"I will bring my cannon-stick to-morrow," said Bevis, delighted to have discovered where the Weasel lived at last, "and I will shoot into the hole and kill him."

"I could not let you do that," said the Squirrel. "I do not allow any fighting, or killing, in my copse, and that is the reason all the birds and animals come here to hold their meetings, because they know it is a sanctuary. If you shoot off your cannon the birds are sure to hear it, and you will not be present at any more of their meetings, and you will not hear any more of the story. Therefore it would be very foolish of you to shoot off your cannon; you must wait, Bevis dear, till you can catch the Weasel outside my copse, and then you may shoot him as much as you like."

"Very well," said Bevis, rather sulkily, "I will not shoot him in the hole if you do not want me to. But how could the Weasel have been in the elm all the time, when the Humble-bee said he found him lying in the sunshine on a bank licking his paw?"

"Why, of course he told the Humble-bee to say that."

"What a cheater he is, isn't he?" said Bevis. "And how did you find out where he lived? I looked everywhere for him, and so did Pan—Pan sniffed and sniffed, but could not find him."

"Nor could I," said the Squirrel. "After you shot the—I mean after the unfortunate business with the thrush, he kept out of the way, knowing that you had vowed vengeance against him, and although I go about a good deal, and peep into so many odd corners, I could not discover his where-abouts, till the little tree-climber told me. You know the tree-climber, dear, you have seen him in your orchard at home; he goes all round and round the trees, and listens at every chink, and so he learns almost all the secrets. He heard the Weasel in the elm, and came at once and told me. Here is the timber, and there is the dragon-fly. Good afternoon, Bevis dear, come to-morrow, and you shall hear the peewit's news, and be sure and not forget to put the right foot out of bed first in the morning." Bevis kissed his hand to the Squirrel, and went home with the dragon-fly.

CHAPTER VIII.

THE EMPEROR CHOO HOO.

When he woke next morning, Bevis quite forgot
what the Squirrel had told him; he jumped out of bed
without thinking, and his right foot touched the floor
first, and led him to the window. From the window
he saw the Brook, and recollected that the Brook had
promised to tell him what he was singing, so as
soon as ever he could get out of doors away he went
through the gateway the grasshopper had shown
him, and down to the hatch. Instead of coming
quietly on tip-toe, as the Brook had told him, he
danced up, and the kingfisher heard him, and went
off as before, whistling "weep, weep." Bevis stood
on the brink and said, "Brook, Brook, what are you
singing? You promised to tell me what you were
saying."

The Brook did not answer, but went on singing.
Bevis listened a minute, and then he picked a willow
leaf and threw it into the bubbles, and watched it

go whirling round and round in the eddies, and back up under the fall, where it dived down, and presently came up again, and the stream took it and carried it away past the flags. "Brook, Brook," said Bevis, stamping his foot, "tell me what you are singing."

And the Brook, having now finished that part of his song, said, "Bevis dear, sit down in the shadow of the willow, for it is very hot to-day, and the reapers are at work; sit down under the willow, and I will tell you as much as I can remember."

"But the Reed said you could not remember anything," said Bevis, leaning back against the willow.

"The Reed did not tell you the truth, dear; indeed, he does not know all; the fact is, the reeds are so fond of talking that I scarcely ever answer them now, or they would keep on all day long, and I should never hear the sound of my own voice, which I like best. So I do not encourage them, and that is why the reeds think I do not recollect."

"And what is it that you sing about?" said Bevis, impatiently.

"My darling," said the Brook, "I do not know

myself always what I am singing about. I am so
happy I sing, sing, and never think about what it
means ; it does not matter what you mean as long as
you sing. Sometimes I sing about the sun, who
loves me dearly, and tries all day to get at me through
the leaves and the green flags that hide me; he
sparkles on me everywhere he can, and does not like
me to be in the shadow. Sometimes I sing to the
Wind, who loves me next most dearly, and will come
to me everywhere, in places where the sun cannot get.
He plays with me whenever he can, and strokes me
softly, and tells me the things he has heard in the
woods and on the hills, and sends down the leaves
to float along, for he knows I like something to carry.
Fling me in some leaves, Bevis, dear.

"Sometimes I sing to the earth and the grass;
they are fond of me, too, and listen the best of all.
I sing loudest at night, to the stars, for they are so
far away they would not otherwise hear me."

"But what do you say?" said Bevis; but the
Brook was too occupied now to heed him, and went
on.

"Sometimes I sing to the trees; they, too, are
fond of me, and come as near as they can; they

would all come down close to me if they could.
They love me like the rest, because I am so happy,
and never cease my chaunting. If I am broken to
pieces against a stone, I do not mind in the least;
I laugh just the same, and even louder. When I
come over the hatch, I dash myself to fragments;
and sometimes a rainbow comes and stays a little
while with me. The trees drink me, and the grass
drinks me, the birds come down and drink me; they
splash me, and are happy. The fishes swim about,
and some of them hide in deep corners. Round the
bend I go, and the osiers say they never have enough
of me. The long grass waves and welcomes me;
the moorhens float with me; the kingfisher is always
with me somewhere, and sits on the bough to see his
ruddy breast in the water. And you come, too,
Bevis, now and then to listen to me; and it is all
because I am so happy."

"Why are you so happy?" said Bevis.

"I do not know," said the Brook. "Perhaps it
is because all I think of is this minute; I do not
know anything about the minute just gone by, and
I do not care one bit about the minute that is just
coming; all I care about is this minute, this very

minute now. Fling me in some more leaves, Bevis. Why do you go about asking questions, dear? Why don't you sing, and do nothing else?"

"Oh, but I want to know all about everything," said Bevis. "Where did you come from, and where are you going, and why don't you go on and let the ground be dry—why don't you run on, and run all away? Why are you always here?"

The Brook laughed, and said, "My dear, I do not know where I came from, and I do not care at all where I am going. What does it matter, my love? All I know is I shall come back again; yes, I shall come back again." The Brook sang very low, and rather sadly now, "I shall go into the sea, and shall be lost; and even you would not know me—ask your father, love, he has sailed over the sea in the ships that come to Southampton, and l was close to him, but he did not know me. But by-and-by, when I am in the sea, the sun will lift me up, and the clouds will float along—look towards the hills, Bevis dear, every morning, and you will see the clouds coming and bringing me with them; and the rain and the dew, and sometimes the thunder and the lightning, will put me down again, and I shall run along here and sing to you, my sweet, if you will come and listen. Fling in some little twigs, my dear, and some bits of bark from the tree."

Then the Brook sang very low and very sad, and said, "I shall come back again, Bevis; I always come back, and I am always happy; and yet I do not know either if I am really happy when I am singing so joyously. Bevis, dear, try and think and tell me. Am I really happy, Bevis? Tell me, dear; you can see the sun sparkling on me, and the Wind stroking me, just as he strokes your hair (he told me he was very fond of you, and meant to tell you a story some day), and the reeds whispering, and the willows drooping over me, and the bright king-fisher; you can hear me singing, Bevis, now am I happy?"

"I do not know," said Bevis; "sometimes you sound very happy, but just now you sound very sad. Stop a little while and think about it."

"Oh, no, Bevis; I cannot stop, I must keep running. Nothing can stop, dear: the trees cannot stop growing, they must keep on growing till they die; and then they cannot stop decaying, till they are all quite gone; but they come back again. Nor can you stop, Bevis, dear."

"I will stop," said Bevis.

"You cannot," said the Brook.

"But I will."

"You cannot. You are a very clever boy, Bevis, but you cannot stop; nor can your papa, nor anybody, you must keep on. Let me see, let me think. I remember, I have seen you before; it was so many, many thousand years ago, but I am almost sure it was you. Now I begin to think about it, I believe I have seen you two or three times, Bevis; but it was before the hippopotamus used to come and splash about in me. I cannot be quite certain, for it is a long time to remember your face, dear."

"I do not believe it," said Bevis; "you are babbling, Brook. My mamma says you babble—it is because you are so old. I am sure I was not born then."

"Yes, you were, dear; and I daresay you will come back again, when all the hills are changed and the roads are covered with woods, and the houses gone. I daresay you will come back and splash in me, like the blackbirds."

"Now you are talking nonsense; you silly Brook," said Bevis, "the hills will never change; and the roads will always be here, and the houses will not be gone; but why are you sighing, you dear old Brook?"

"I am sighing, my love, because I remember."

"What do you remember?"

"I remember, before the hills were like they are now; I remember when I was a broad deep river; I remember the stars that used to shine in me, and they are all gone, you cannot see them now, Bevis ("Pooh," said Bevis); I remember the stories the lions used to tell me when they came down to drink; I remember the people dancing on the grass by me, and sing, singing, they used to sing like me, Bevis, without knowing what it was they sung, and without any words (not stupid songs, Bevis, like your people sing now) but I understood them very well. I cannot understand the songs the folk sing now, the folk that live now have gone away so far from me."

"What nonsense you say, old Brook; why we live quite close, and the waggons go over your bridge every day."

"I remember" (the Brook took no notice, but went on) "I remember them very well, and they loved me dearly too; they had boats, Bevis, made out of trees, and they floated about on me."

"I will have a boat," said Bevis, "and float about on you."

"And they played music, which was just like my singing, and they were very happy, because as I told you about myself, they did not think about the minute that was coming, or the minute that had gone by, they only thought about This Minute."

"How long was that ago?" said Bevis.

"Oh," said the Brook, "I daresay your papa would tell you it was thousands upon thousands of years, but that is not true, dear; it was only a second or two since."

"I shall not stay to listen much longer, silly Brook, if you talk like that; why it must be longer than that, or I should have seen it."

"My dear," said the Brook, "That which has gone by, whether it happened a second since, or a thousand thousand years since, is just the same; there is no real division betwixt you and the past. You people who live now have made up all sorts of stupid, very stupid stories, dear; I hope you will not believe them; they tell you about time and all that.

Now there is no such thing as time, Bevis my love; there never was any time, and there never will be; the sun laughs at it, even when he marks it on the sun-dial. Yesterday was just a second ago, and so was ten thousand years since, and there is nothing between you and then; there is no wall between you and then—nothing at all, dear,"—and the Brook sang so low and thoughtfully that Bevis could not catch what he said, but the tune was so sweet, and soft, and sad that it made him keep quite still. While he was listening the kingfisher came back and perched on the hatch, and Bevis saw his ruddy neck and his blue wings.

"There is nothing between you and then," the Brook began again, "nothing at all dear, only some stories which are not true; if you will not believe me, look at the sun, but you cannot look at the sun, darling; it shines so bright. It shines just the same, as bright and beautiful; and the Wind blows as sweet as ever, and I sparkle and sing just the same, and you may drink me if you like; and the grass is just as green; and the stars shine at night. Oh, yes, Bevis dear, *we* are all here just the same, my love, and all things are as bright and beautiful as ten thousand times ten thousand years ago, which is no longer since than a second.

"But your people have gone away from us—that is their own fault. I cannot think why they should do so; they have gone away from us, and they are no longer happy, Bevis; they cannot understand our songs,—they sing stupid songs they have made up themselves, and which they did not learn of us, and then because they are not happy, they say "The world is growing old." But it is not true, Bevis, the world is not old, it is as young as ever it was. Fling me a leaf—and now another. Do not you forget me, Bevis; come and see me now and then, and throw twigs to me and splash me."

"That I will," said Bevis; and he picked up a stone and flung it into the water with such a splash that the kingfisher flew away, but the Brook only laughed, and told him to throw another, and to make haste and eat the peck of salt, and grow bigger and jump over him. "That I will," said Bevis, "I am very hungry now—good morning, I am going home to dinner."

"Good morning dear," said the Brook, "you will always find me here when you want to hear a song." Bevis went home to dinner humming the tune the Brook had taught him, and by-and-by, when the hot sun had begun to sink a little, he started again for the copse, and as before, the dragon-fly met him, and led him to the timber, and from there to the raspberries.

The Squirrel was waiting for him on a bough of the oak, and while Bevis picked the fruit that had ripened since yesterday, told him the news the peewits had brought about the great rebel Choo Hoo. A party of the peewits, who had been watching ever so far away, thought they saw a stir and a movement in the woods; and presently, out came one of the captains of the wood-pigeons with two hundred of his soldiers, and they flew over the border into king Kapchack's country, and began to forage in one of his wheat-fields, where the corn was ripe. When they saw this, the peewits held a council on the hill, and they sent a messenger to Kapchack with the news. While they were waiting for him to return, some of the wood-pigeons having foraged enough, went home to the woods, so that there was not much more than half of them left.

Seeing this—for his soldiers who were wheeling

about in the air came and told him—the captain of the peewits thought, "Now is my time! This is a most lucky and fortunate circumstance, and I can now win the high approval of king Kapchack, and obtain promotion. The captain of the wood-pigeons has no idea how many of us are watching his proceedings, for I have kept my peewits behind the cover of the hill so that he could not count them, and he has allowed half of the wood-pigeons to go home. We will rush down upon the rest, and so win an easy victory."

So saying he flew up, and all the peewits followed him in the expectation of an easy conquest. But, just as they were descending upon the wheat-field, up flew the wood-pigeons with such a terrible clangour of their strong wings, and facing towards them, showed such a determination to fight to the last breath, that the peewits, who were never very celebrated for their courage, turned tail, and began to retreat.

They would still have reached the hills in good order, and would have suffered no great disgrace (for they were but a small party, and not so numerous as the wood-pigeons), but in the midst of these

manœuvres, the lieutenant of the pigeons, who had
gone home with those who had done foraging, flew
out from the wood with his men, and tried by a
flank movement to cut off the peewits' retreat. At
this they were so alarmed they separated and broke
up their ranks, each flying to save himself as best
he might. Nor did they stop till long after the
wood-pigeons, being cautious and under complete
control, had ceased to pursue ; not till they had
flown back two or three miles into the fastnesses
of Kapchack's hills. Then some of them collecting
again, held a hurried council, and sent off messengers with the news of this affray.

About the same time, it happened that a missel-
thrush arrived at the court, a son of the favourite
missel-thrush, the only bird whom Kapchack (and
the farmer) allowed to build in the orchard. The
missel-thrush had just travelled through part of the
country which once belonged to Kapchack, but which
Choo Hoo had over-run the year before, and he
brought Kapchack such a terrible account of the
mighty armies that he saw assembling, that the
king was beside himself with terror. Next came a
crow, one of Kauc's warriors, who had been that

way, and he said that two captains of the wood-pigeons, hearing of the peewits' defeat, had already, and without staying for instructions from Choo Hoo, entered the country and taken possession of a copse on the slope of the hill from which the peewits had descended.

"And," said the Squirrel, as Bevis having eaten all the raspberries, came and sat down on the moss under the oak, "the upshot of it is that king Kapchack has called a general council of war, which is to be held almost directly at the Owl's castle, in the pollard hard by. For you must understand that the farmer who lives near Kapchack's palace is so fierce, he will not let any of the large birds (except the favourite missel-thrush) enter the orchard, and there-fore Kapchack has to hold these great councils in the copse. What will be the result I cannot think, and I am not without serious apprehensions myself, for I have hitherto held undisputed possession of this domain. But Choo Hoo is so despotic, and has such an immense army at his back, that I am not at all certain he will respect my neutrality. As for Kapchack, he shivers in his claws at the very name of the mighty rebel."

"Why does Choo Hoo want king Kapchack's country?" said Bevis. "Why cannot he stop where he is?"

"There is no reason, dear; but you know that all the birds and animals would like to be king if they could, and when Choo Hoo found that the wood-pigeons (for he was nothing but an adventurer at first, without any title or property except the ancestral ash) were growing so numerous that the woods would hardly hold them, and were continually being increased both by their own populousness and by the arrival of fresh bands, it occurred to him that this enormous horde of people, if they could only be persuaded to follow him, could easily over-run the entire country. Hitherto, it was true, they had been easily kept in subjection, notwithstanding their immense numbers, first, because they had no leaders among them, nor even any nobles or rich people to govern their movements and tell them what to do; and next, because they were barbarians, and totally destitute of art or refinement, knowledge, or science, neither had they any skill in diplomacy or politics, but were utterly outside the civilized nations.

"Even their language, as you yourself have heard, is very contracted and poor, without inflection or expression, being nothing but the repetition of the same sounds, by which means—that is simply by the number and the depth or hollowness of the same monosyllables—they convey their wishes to each other. It is, indeed, wonderful how they can do so, and our learned men, from this circumstance, have held that the language of the wood-pigeon is the most difficult to acquire, so much so that it is scarce possible for one who has not been born among the barbarians to attain to any facility in the use of these gutturals. This is the reason why little or no intercourse has ever taken place between us who are civilised and these hordes; that which has gone on has been entirely conducted by the aid of interpreters, being those few wood-pigeons who have come away from the main body, and dwell peaceably in our midst.

"Now, Choo Hoo, as I said, being an adventurer, with no more property than the ancestral ash, but a pigeon of very extraordinary genius, considered within himself, that if any one could but persuade these mighty and incredible myriads to follow him he could overrun the entire country. The very absence of any nobles or rich pigeons among them would make his sway the more absolute if he once got power, for there would be none to dispute it, or to put any check upon him. Ignorant and barbarous as they were, the common pigeons would worship such a captain as a hero and a demi-god, and would fly to certain destruction in obedience to his orders.

" He was the more encouraged to the enterprise because it was on record that in olden times great bodies of pigeons had passed across the country sweeping everything before them. Nothing could resist their onward march, and it is owing to these barbarian invasions that so many of our most precious chronicles have been destroyed, and our early history, Bevis dear, involved in obscurity. Their dominion—destructive as it was—had, however, always passed away as rapidly as it arose, on account of the lack of cohesion in their countless armies. They marched without a leader, and without order, obeying for a time a common impulse; when that impulse ceased they retired tumultuously, suffering grievous losses from the armies which gathered behind and hung upon their rear. Their bones whitened the fields, and the sun, it is said, was darkened at noonday by their hastening crowds fleeing in dense columns, and struck down as they fled by hawks and crows.

" Had they possessed a leader in whom they felt confidence the result might have been very different; indeed, our wisest historians express no doubt that civilisation must have been entirely extinguished, and these lovely fields and delicious woods have been wholly occupied by the barbarians. Fortunately it was not so. But, as I said, Choo Hoo, retiring to the top of a lofty fir-tree, and filled with these ideas, surveyed from thence the masses of his countrymen returning to the woods to roost as the sun declined, and resolved to lose no time in endeavouring to win them to his will, and to persuade them to embark upon the extraordinary enterprise which he had conceived.

" Without delay he proceeded to promulgate his plans, flying from tribe to tribe, and from flock to flock, ceaselessly proclaiming that the kingdom was the wood-pigeons' by right, by reason of their numbers, and because of the wickedness of Kapchack and his court, which wickedness was notorious, and must end in disaster. As you may imagine, he met with little or no response—for the most part the pigeons, being of a stolid nature, went on with their feeding and talking, and took no notice whatever of his orations. After a while the elder ones, indeed, began to say to each other that this agitator had better be put down and debarred from freedom of speech, for such seditious language must ultimately be reported to Kapchack, who would send his body-guards of hawks among them and exact a sanguinary vengeance.

"Finding himself in danger, Choo Hoo, not one whit abashed, instead of fleeing, came before the elders and openly reproached them with misgovernment, cowardice, and the concealment or loss of certain ancient prophecies, which foretold the future power of the wood-pigeons, and which he accused them of holding back out of jealousy, lest they should lose the miserable petty authority they enjoyed on account of their age. Now, whether there were really any such prophecies, I cannot tell you, or whether it was one of Choo Hoo's clever artifices, it is a moot point among our most learned antiquaries; the Owl, who has the best means of information, told me once that he believed there was some ground for the assertion.

"At any rate it suited Choo Hoo's purpose very well; for although the elders and the heads of the

tribes forthwith proceeded to subject him to every
species of persecution, and attacked him so violently
that he lost nearly all his feathers, the common pigeons
sympathised with him, and hid him from their pursuit. They were the more led to sympathise with him
because, on account of their ever-increasing numbers,
the territory allotted to them by Kapchack was daily
becoming less and less suited to their wants, and
in short, there were some signs of a famine. They,
therefore, looked with longing eyes at the fertile
country, teeming with wheat and acorns around
them, and listened with greedy ears to the tempting
prospect so graphically described by Choo Hoo.

" Above all, the young pigeons attached themselves
to his fortunes and followed him everywhere in con-
continually increasing bands, for he promised them
wives in plenty and trees for their nests without
number; for all the trees in their woods were already
occupied by the older families, who would not moreover, part with their daughters to young pigeons who
had not a branch to roost on. Some say that the
Fox, who has long been deeply discontented at the
loss of his ancestors' kingdom and of his own wealth
which he dissipated so carelessly, did not scruple to

advise Choo Hoo how to proceed. Be that as it may, I should be the last to accuse any one of disloyalty without evident proof; be that as it may, the stir and commotion grew so great among the wood-pigeons, that presently the news of it reached king Kapchack.

"His spies, of whom he has so many (the chief of them is Te-te, the tomtit of whom I bid you beware) brought him full intelligence of what was going on. Kapchack lost no time in calling his principal advisers around him; they met close by here (where the council is to take place this afternoon) for he well knew the importance of the news. It was not only you see, the immense numbers of the wood-pigeons and the impossibility of resisting their march, were they once set in motion, but he had to consider that there was a considerable population of pigeons in our midst who might turn traitors, and he was by no means sure of the allegiance of various other tribes, who were only held down by terror.

"The council fully acknowledged the gravity of the situation, and upon the advice of the Hawk it was resolved that Choo Hoo, as the prime mover

of the trouble, and as the only one capable of bringing matters to a crisis, should be forthwith despatched. But when the executioners proceeded to
seize him he eluded their clutches with the greatest
ease; for his followers (such was their infatuation)
devoted their lives to his, and threw themselves in
the way of Kapchack's emissaries, the hawks, submitting to be torn in pieces rather than see their
beloved hero lose a feather. Thus baffled, the enraged Kapchack next tried to get him assassinated,
but as before, his friends watched about him with
such solicitude, that no one could enter the wood
where he slept at night without their raising such
a disturbance that their evil purpose was defeated.

"In his rage Kapchack ordered a decimation of
the wood-pigeons, which I myself think was a great
mistake; but as I have told you before, I do not
meddle with politics. Still I cannot help thinking that if he had, instead, of his royal bounty and
benevolence, given the wood-pigeons an increase of
territory, seeing how near they sometimes came to
a famine, that they would have been disarmed and
their discontent turned to gratitude; but he ordered
in his rage and terror that they should be decimated,

and let loose the whole army of his hawks upon
them, so that the slaughter was awful to behold,
and the ground was strewn with their torn and
mangled bodies. Yet they remained faithful to Choo
Hoo, and not one traitor was found amongst these
loyal barbarians.

"But Choo Hoo, deeply distressed in mind, said
that he would relieve them from the burden of his
presence rather than thus be the cause of their
sorrow. He therefore left those provinces and flew
out of the country, leaving word behind him that he
would never return till he had seen the Raven, and
recovered from him those ancient prophecies that had
so long been lost. He flew away, and disappeared
in the distance; the days and weeks passed, but he
did not return, and at last Kapchack, relieved of
his apprehensions, recalled his murderous troops, and
the pigeons were left in peace to lament their Choo
Hoo.

"A twelvemonth passed, and still Choo Hoo did
not come; the people said he had been called to the
happy Forest of the Heroes, and averred that sometimes they heard his voice calling to them when no
one was near. There was no doubt that he had gone

with the Raven. The Raven you must know, my dear Sir Bevis, was once the principal judge and arbiter of justice amongst us,- so much so that he was above kings, and it is certain that had he been here we should not have had to submit to the sanguinary tyranny of Kapchack, nor condemned to witness the scandalous behaviour of his court, or the still greater scandal of his own private life. But for some reason the Raven mysteriously left this country about a hundred years ago, leaving behind him certain prophecies, some of which no doubt you have heard, especially that upon his return there will be no more famine, nor frost, nor slaughter, nor conflict, but we shall all live together in peace.

"However that may be, the Raven has never come back; the learned hold that he must have died long since, for he was so aged when he went away no one knew his years, hinting in their disbelief that he went away to die, and so surround his death with a halo of mystery; but the common people are quite of a different opinion, and strenuously uphold the belief that he will some day return. Well, as I told you, a twelvemonth went by, and Choo Hoo did not come, when suddenly in the spring (when

Kapchack himself was much occupied in his palace, and most of his spies were busy with their nests, and the matter had almost been forgotten) Choo Hoo re-appeared, bringing with him the most beautiful young bride that was ever beheld, as he himself was, on the other hand, the strongest and swiftest of the wood-pigeons.

"When this was known (and the news spread in a minute) the enthusiasm of the barbarians knew no bounds. Notwithstanding it was nesting-time, they collected in such vast numbers that the boughs cracked with their weight; they unanimously proclaimed Choo Hoo emperor (for they disdained the title of king as not sufficiently exalted) and declared their intention, as soon as the nesting-time was over, and the proper season—the autumn—for campaigning arrived, of following him, and invading the kingdom of Kapchack.

"Choo Hoo told them that, after many months of wandering, he had at last succeeded in finding the Raven; at least he had not seen the Raven himself, but the Raven had sent a special messenger, the hawfinch, to tell him to be of good cheer, and to return to the wood-pigeons, and to lead them forth against

Kapchack, who tottered upon his throne; and that he (the Raven) would send the night-jar, or goat-sucker, with crooked and evil counsels to confound Kapchack's wisdom. And indeed, Bevis, my dear, I have myself seen several night-jars about here, and I am rather inclined to think that there is some truth in this part at least of what Choo Hoo says; for it is an old proverb, which I daresay you have heard, that when the gods design the destruction of a monarch they first make him mad, and what can be more mad than Kapchack's proposed marriage with the jay, to which he was doubtless instigated by the night-jars, who, like genii of the air, have been floating in the dusky summer twilight round about his palace.

"And they have, I really believe, confounded his council and turned his wisdom to folly; for Kapchack has been so cunning for so many many years, and all his family have been so cunning, and all his councillors, that now I do believe (only I do not meddle with politics) that this extreme cunning is too clever, and that they will overreach themselves. However, we shall see what is said at the council by-and-by.

"Choo Hoo having told the pigeons this, added that he had further been instructed by the Raven to give them a sacred and mystic pass-word and rallying cry; he did not himself know what it meant, it was, however something very powerful, and by it they would be led to victory. So saying, he called 'Koos-takke!' and at once the vast assembly seized the signal and responded 'Koos-takke!' which mystic syllables are now their war-cry, their call of defiance, and their welcome to their friends. You may often hear them shouting these words in the depths of the woods; Choo Hoo learnt them in the enchanted Forest of Savernake, where, as everyone knows, there are many mighty magicians, and where, perhaps, the Raven is still living in its deep recesses. Now this war-cry supplied, as doubtless the Raven had foreseen, the very link that was wanting to bind the immense crowd of wood-pigeons together. Thenceforward they had a common sign and pass-word, and were no longer scattered.

"In the autumn Choo Hoo crossed the border with a vast horde, and although Kapchack sent his generals, who inflicted enormous losses, such as no other nation but the barbarians could have sustained, nothing could stay the advance of such incredible numbers. After a whole autumn and winter of severe and continued fighting, Choo Hoo, early in the next year found that he had advanced some ten (and in places fifteen) miles, giving his people room to feed and move. He had really pushed much further than that, but he could not hold all the ground he had taken for the following reason: In the spring, as the soft warm weather came, and the sun began to shine, and the rain to fall, and the brook to sing more sweetly, and the wind to breathe gently with delicious perfume, and the green leaves to come forth, the barbarians began to feel the influence of love.

"They could no longer endure to fly in the dense column, they no longer obeyed the voice of their captain. They fell in love, and each marrying set about to build a nest, free and unmolested in those trees that Choo Hoo had promised them. Choo Hoo himself retired with his lovely bride to the ancestral ash, and passed the summer in happy dalliance. With the autumn the campaign recommenced, and with exactly the same result. After a second autumn and winter of fighting, Choo Hoo had pushed his fron-

tier another fifteen miles further into Kapchack's
kingdom. Another summer of love followed, and
so it went on year after year, Choo Hoo's forces
meantime continually increasing in numbers, since
there were now no restrictions as to nest trees, but
one and all could marry.

"Till at last he has under his sway a horde of
trained warriors, whose numbers defy calculation,
and he has year by year pushed into Kapchack's
territory till now it seems as if he must utterly
overwhelm and destroy that monarch. This he would
doubtless have achieved ere now, but there is one
difficulty which has considerably impeded his advance,
as he came farther and farther from his native province. This difficulty is water.

"For in the winter, when the Longpond is frozen,
and the brook nearly covered with ice, and all the
ponds and ditches likewise, so vast a horde cannot find
enough to satisfy their thirst, and must consequently
disperse. Were it not for this Choo Hoo must ere
now have overwhelmed us. As it is, Kapchack shivers
in his claws, and we all dread the approaching
autumn, for Choo Hoo has now approached so near
as to be at our very doors. If he only knew one

thing he would have no difficulty in remaining here and utterly destroying us."

" What is that ? " said Bevis.

" Will you promise faithfully not to tell anyone ? " said the Squirrel, " for my own existence depends upon this horde of barbarians being kept at bay; for you see should they pass over they will devour every thing in the land, and there will certainly be a famine—the most dreadful that has ever been seen."

" I will promise," said Bevis, " I promise you faithfully."

" Then I will tell you," went on the Squirrel:

" In this copse of mine there is a spring of the clearest and sweetest water (you shall see it, I will take you to it some day) which is a great secret, for it is so hidden by ferns and fir-trees over-hanging it, that no one knows anything about it except Kapchack, myself, the Weasel, and the Fox; I wish the Weasel did not know, for he is so gluttonous for blood, which makes him thirsty, that he is continually dipping his murderous snout into the delicious water.

" Now this spring being so warm in the fern,

and coming out of ground which is, in a manner,
warm too, of all the springs in this province does
not freeze, but always runs clear all the winter. If
Choo Hoo only knew it, don't you see, he could
stay in Kapchack's country, no matter how hard the
frost, and his enormous army, whose main object is
plunder, would soon starve us altogether. But he
does not know of it.

" He has sent several of his spies, the wood-
cocks, to search the country for such a spring, but
although they are the most cunning of birds at
that trick, they have not yet succeeded in finding
my spring and thrusting their long bills into it. They
dare not come openly, but fly by night, for Kapchack's
hawks are always hovering about; well enough he
knows the importance of this secret, and they would
pay for their temerity with their lives if they were
seen. All I am afraid of is lest the Weasel or the
Fox, in their eagerness for empire, should betray
the secret to Choo Hoo.

" The Fox, though full of duplicity, and not to be
depended upon, is at least brave and bold, and so far
as I can judge his character would not, for his own
sake (hoping some day to regain the kingdom) let

out this secret. But of the Weasel I am not so sure; he is so very wicked, and so cunning, no one can tell what he may do. Thus it is that in the highest of my beech trees I do not feel secure, but am in continual fear lest a wood-cock should steal in, or the Weasel play the traitor, for if so a famine is imminent, and that is why I support, so far as I can without meddling with politics, the throne of Kapchack, as the last barrier against this terrible fate.

"Even now could he but be brought to reform his present life something might be hoped for, for he has a powerful army; but, as you have seen, this affair with the jay has caused ambitious ideas to spring up in the minds of his chief courtiers, some of whom (especially I think the Crow and the Weasel) are capable of destroying a country for their private and personal advantage. Therefore it is that I look forward to this council, now about to be held, with intense anxiety, for upon it will depend our future, the throne of Kapchack, our existence or destruction. And here comes the Rook; the first as usual."

VOL. II

CONTENTS.

— ◆◆ —

WOOD MAGIC.

CHAPTER I.

THE COUNCIL.

BEFORE Bevis could ask any questions, the Squirrel went off to speak to the Rook, and to show him a good bough to perch on near the Owl's castle. He then came back and conducted Bevis to the seat in the ash-stole, where he was hidden by the honey-suckle, but could see well about him. Hardly had Bevis comfortably seated himself than the councillors began to arrive. They were all there; even the Rat did not dare stay away, lest his loyalty should be suspected, but took up his station at the foot of the pollard-tree, and the Mouse sat beside him. The Rook sat on the oak, no great way from the Squirrel; Kauc, the crow, chose a branch of ash which projected close to the pollard. So envious was he of the crown that he could not stay far from it.

Cloctaw, the jackdaw, who had flown to the
council with him, upon arrival, left his side, and
perched rather in the rear. Reynard, the fox, and
Sec, the stoat, his friend, waited the approach of
the king by some fern near the foot of the pollard.
The Owl every now and then appeared at the window
of his castle, sometimes to see who had arrived,
and sometimes to look for the king, who was not
yet in sight. Having glanced round, the Owl retreated to his study, doubtless to prepare his speech
for this important occasion. The heaving up of the
leaves and earth, as if an underground plough was
at work, showed that the mole had not forgotten his
duty; he had come to show his loyalty, and he
brought a message from the badger, who had long
since been left outside the concert of the animals
and birds, humbly begging king Kapchack to accept
his homage.

It is true that neither the Hare nor the rabbit
were present, but that signified nothing, for they
had no influence whatever. But the pheasant, who
often stood aloof from the court, in his pride
of lineage despising Kapchack though he was
king, came on this occasion, for he too, like the

Squirrel, was alarmed at the progress of Choo Hoo, and dreaded a scarcity of the berries of the earth. Tchink, the chaffinch, one of the first to come, could not perch still, but restlessly passed round the circle, now talking to one and now to another, and sometimes peering in at the Owl's window. But merry as he was, he turned his back upon Te-te, the tomtit, and chief of the spies, disdaining the acquaintance of a common informer. Te-te, not one whit abashed, sat on a willow, and lifted his voice from time to time.

The Jay came presently, and for some reason or other he was in high good spirits, and dressed in his gayest feathers. He chaffed the Owl, and joked with Tchink; then he laughed to himself, and tried to upset the grave old Cloctaw from his seat, and in short, played all sorts of pranks to the astonishment of everybody, who had hitherto seen him in such distress for the loss of his lady-love. Everybody thought he had lost his senses. Eric, the favourite missel-thrush (not the conspirator) took his station very high up on the ash above Kauc, whom he hated and suspected of treason, not hesitating even to say so aloud. Kauc, indeed, was not now quite comfort-

able in his position, but kept slyly glancing up at
the missel-thrush, and would have gone elsewhere had
it not been that everybody was looking.

The wood-pigeon came to the hawthorn, some little
way from the castle; he represented, and was the chief
of those pigeons who dwelt peacefully in Kapchack's
kingdom, although aliens by race. His position was
difficult in the extreme, for upon the one hand he
knew full well that Kapchack was suspicious of him
lest he should go over to Choo Hoo, and might at any
moment order his destruction, and upon the other
hand he had had several messages from Choo Hoo
calling upon him to join his brethren, the invaders,
on pain of severe punishment. Uncertain as to his
fate, the wood-pigeon perched on the hawthorn at
the skirt of the council place, hoping from thence to
get some start if obliged to flee for his life. The
dove, his friend, constant in misfortune, sat near him
to keep him in countenance.

The humble-bee, the bee, the butterfly, the cricket,
the grasshopper, the beetle, and many others arrived
as the hour drew on. Last of all came Ki Ki, lord
of all the hawks, attended with his retinue, and
heralding the approach of the king. Ki Ki perched

on a tree at the side of the pollard, and his warriors
ranged themselves around him: a terrible show,
at which the Mouse verily shrank into the ground.
Immediately afterwards a noise of wings and talking
announced the arrival of Kapchack, who came in
full state, with eight of his finest guards. The
king perched on the top of the pollard, just over
the Owl's window, and the eight magpies sat above
and around, but always behind him.

"What an ugly old fellow he is!" whispered
Bevis, who had never before seen him. "Look at
his ragged tail!"

"Hush!" said the Squirrel, "Te-te is too
near."

"Are they all here?" asked the king, after he
had looked round and received the bows and lowly
obeisance of his subjects.

"They are all here," said the Owl, sitting in
his porch. "They are all here—at least, I think:
no, they are not, your majesty."

"Who is absent?" said Kapchack, frowning,
and all the assembly cowered.

"It is the Weasel," said the Owl. "The Weasel
is not here."

Kapchack frowned and looked as black as thunder, and a dead silence fell upon the council.

"If it please your majesty," said the Humble-bee, presently coming to the front. "If it please your majesty, the Weasel——"

"It does *not* please me," said Kapchack.

But the Humble-bee began again, "If it please your majesty——"

"His majesty is *not* pleased," repeated the Owl severely.

But the Humble-bee, who could sing but one tune, began again, "If it please your majesty, the Weasel asked me to say——"

"What?" said the king in a terrible rage, "What did he say?"

"If it please your majesty," said the Humble-bee, who must begin over again every time he was interrupted, "the Weasel asked me to say that he sent his humble, his most humble, loyal, and devoted obedience, and begged that you would forgive his absence from the council, as he has just met with a severe accident in the hunting field, and cannot put one paw before the other."

"I do not • believe it," said king Kapchack. "Where is he?"

"If it please your majesty," said the Humble-bee, "he is lying on a bank beyond the copse, stretched out in the sunshine, licking his paw, and hoping that rest and sunshine will cure him."

"Oh, what a story!" said Bevis.

"Hush," said the Squirrel.

"Somebody said it was a story," said the Owl.

"So it is," said Te-te. "I have made it my business to search out the goings-on of the Weasel, who has kept himself in the background of late, suspecting that he was up to no good, and with the aid of my lieutenant, the tree-climber, I have succeeded in discovering his retreat, which he has concealed even from your majesty."

"Where is it?" said Kapchack.

"It is in the elm, just there," said Te-te, "just by those raspberries."

"The rascal," said the Owl, in a great fright. "Then he has been close by all the time listening."

"Yes, he has been listening," said Te-te, meaningly.

The Owl became pale, remembering the secret meeting of the birds, and what was said there, all of which the treacherous Weasel must have overheard. He passed it off by exclaiming, "This is really intolerable."

"It *is* intolerable," said Kapchack; "and you," addressing the Humble-bee, "wretch that you are to bring me a false message——"

"If it please your majesty," began the Humble-bee, but he was seized upon by the bee (who was always jealous of him) and the butterfly, and the beetle, and hustled away from the precinct of the council.

"Bring the Weasel here, this instant," shouted Kapchack. "Drag him here by the ears."

Everybody stood up, but everybody hesitated, for though they all hated the Weasel they all feared him. Ki Ki, the hawk, bold as he was, could not do much in the bushes, nor enter a hole; Kauc, the crow, was in the like fix, and he intended if he was called upon to take refuge in the pretence of his age; the Stoat, fierce as he was, shrank from facing the Weasel, being afraid of his relation's tricks and stratagems. Even the Fox, though he was the biggest of all, hesitated, for he recollected once when Pan, the spaniel, snapped at the Weasel, the Weasel made his teeth meet in Pan's nostrils.

Thus they all hesitated, when the Rat suddenly stood out and said, " I will fetch the Weasel, your majesty; I will bring that hateful traitor to your feet."

" Do so, good and loyal Rat," said the king, well pleased. And the Rat ran off to compel the Weasel to come.

As the elm was so close, they all looked that way, expecting to hear sounds of fighting; but in less than half a minute the Rat appeared, with the Weasel limping on three legs in his rear. For when the Weasel heard what the Rat said, he knew it was of no use to stay away any longer; but in his heart he vowed that he would, sooner or later, make the Rat smart for his officious interference.

When he came near, the Weasel fell down and bowed himself before the king, who said nothing, but eyed him scornfully.

" I am guilty," said the Weasel, in a very humble voice; " I am guilty of disobedience to your majesty's commands, and I am guilty of sending you a deceitful message, for which my poor friend the Humble-bee has been cruelly hustled from your presence; but I am not guilty of the treason of which I am accused. I hid in the elm, your majesty, because I went in terror of my life, and I feigned to be ill, in order to stay away from the council, because there is not one of all these (he pointed to the circle of councillors) who has not sworn to destroy me, and I feared to venture forth. They have all banded together to compass my destruction, because I alone of all of them have remained faithful to your throne, and have not secretly conspired."

At these words, there was such an outcry on the part of all the birds and animals, that the wood echoed with their cries; for the Stoat snapped his teeth, and the Fox snarled, and the Jay screamed, and the Hawk flapped his wings, and the Crow said "Caw!" and the Rook "Haw!" and all so eagerly denied the imputation, that it was some minutes before even king Kapchack could make himself heard.

When the noise in some degree subsided, however, he said, "Weasel, you are so false of tongue, and you have so many shifts and contrivances ('That he has!' said Bevis, who was delighted at the downfall of the Weasel), that it is no longer possible for any of us to believe anything you say. We have now such important business before us, that we cannot stop to proceed to your trial and execution, and we therefore order that in the meantime you remain where you are, and that you maintain complete silence—for you are degraded from your rank—until such time as we can attend to your contemptible body, which will shortly dangle from a tree, as a warning to traitors for all time to come. My lords, we will now proceed with our business, and, first of all, the Secretary will read the roll-call of our forces."

The Owl then read the list of the army, and said, "First, your Majesty's devoted body-guard, with —with Prince Tchack-tchack (the King frowned, and the Jay laughed outright) at their head; Ki Ki, lord of hawks, one thousand beaks; the Rooks, five thousand beaks; Kauc, the crow, two hundred beaks;" and so on, enumerating the numbers which all the tribes could bring to battle.

In the buzz of conversation that arose while the Owl was reading (as it usually does), the Squirrel told Bevis that he believed the Crow had not returned the number of his warriors correctly, but that there were really many more, whom he purposely kept in the background. As for Prince Tchack-tchack, his absence from the council evidently disturbed his majesty, though he was too proud to show how he felt the defection of his eldest son and heir.

The number of the rooks, too, was not accurate, and did not give a true idea of their power, for it was the original estimate furnished many years ago, when Kapchack first organised his army, and although the rooks had greatly increased since then, the same return was always made. But it was well understood that the nation of the rooks could send, and doubtless would send, quite ten thousand beaks into the field.

"It is not a little curious," said the Squirrel, "that the rooks, who, as you know, belong to a limited monarchy—so limited that they have no real king—should form the main support of so despotic a monarch as Kapchack, who obtains even more de-

cisive assistance from them than from the ferocious
and wily Ki Ki. It is an illustration of the singular
complexity and paradoxical positions of politics that
those who are naturally so opposed, should thus form
the closest friends and allies. I do not understand
why it is so myself, for as you know, dear, I do
not attempt to meddle with politics, but the Owl
has several times very learnedly discoursed to me
upon this subject, and I gather from him that one
principal reason why the rooks support the tyrant
Kapchack, is because they well know if he is not
king some one else will be. Now Kapchack, in
return for their valuable services, has for one thing
ordered Ki Ki on no account to interfere with them
(which is the reason they have become so populous),
and under the nominal rule of Kapchack they really
enjoy greater liberty than they otherwise could.

"But the beginning of the alliance, it seems,
was in this way. Many years ago, when Kapchack was a young monarch, and by no means
firmly established upon his throne, he sought about
for some means of gaining the assistance of the
rooks. He observed that in the spring, when the
rooks repaired their dwellings, they did so in a

very inferior manner, doing indeed just as their
forefathers had done before them, and repeating the
traditional architecture handed down through innumerable generations. So ill-constructed were their
buildings, that if, as often chanced, the March
winds blew with fury, it was a common thing to
see the grass strewn with the wreck of their houses.
Now Kapchack and all his race are excellent archi-
tects, and it occurred to him to do the rooks
a service, by instructing them how to bind their
lower courses, so that they should withstand the
wind.

"With some difficulty, for the older rooks, though
they would loudly deny it, are eminently con-
servative (a thing I do not profess to understand),
he succeeded in persuading the younger builders to
adopt his design; and the result was that in the
end they all took to it, and now it is quite the exception to hear of an accident. Besides the pre-
servation of life, Kapchack's invention also saved
them an immense amount in timber for re-building.
The consequence has been that the rooks have flourished
above all other birds. They at once concluded an
alliance with Kapchack, and as they increased in

numbers, so they became more firmly attached to his throne.

"It is not that they feel any gratitude—far from it, they are a selfish race—but they are very keen after their own interest, which is, perhaps, the strongest tie. For, as I observed, the rooks live under a limited monarchy; they had real kings of their own centuries since, but now their own king is only a name, a state fiction. Every single rook has a voice in the affairs of the nation (hence the tremendous clamour you may hear in their woods towards sunset when their assemblies are held), but the practical direction of their policy is entrusted to a circle or council of about ten of the older rooks, distinguished for their oratorical powers. These depute, again, one of their own number to Kapchack's court; you see him yonder, his name is Kauhaha. The council considers, I have no doubt, that by supporting Kapchack they retain their own supremacy, for very likely if they did not have a foreigner to reign over them, some clever genius of their own race would arise and overturn these mighty talkers.

"On the other hand Kapchack fully appreciates

their services, and if he dared he would give the
chief command of his forces to the generalissimo of
the rooks—not the one who sits yonder—the commander's name is Ah Kurroo. But he dreads the
jealousy of Ki Ki, who is extremely off-handed
and high in his ways, and might go off with his
contingent. I am curious to see who will have
the command. As for the starlings, I dare say you
will notice their absence, they are under the juris-
diction of the rooks, and loyal as their masters; the
reason they are not here is because they are already
mobilised and have taken the field; they were
despatched in all haste very early this morning,
before you were awake, Bevis dear, to occupy the
slope from whence the peewits fled. Now they are
discussing the doubtful allies."

"The larks," the Owl was saying as the Squirrel
finished, "have sent a message which I consider
extremely impertinent. They have dared to say
that they have nothing whatever to do with the
approaching contest, and decline to join either party.
They say that from time immemorial they have been
free mountaineers, owing allegiance to no one, and
if they have attended your court it has been from

courtesy, and not from any necessity that they were under."

"They are despicable creatures," said the king, who was secretly annoyed, but would not show it. "Ki Ki, I deliver them over to you; let your men plunder them as they like."

"The finches," went on the Owl. "I hardly know——"

"We are loyal to the last feather," said Tchink, the chaffinch, bold as brass, and coming to the front, to save his friends from the fate of the larks. "Your majesty, we are perfectly loyal—why our troops, whom you know are only lightly armed, have already gone forward, and have occupied the furze on the summits of the hills."

"I am much pleased," said the king, who had been a little doubtful. "Tell your friends to continue in that spirit."

"With all my heart," said Tchink, laughing in Ki Ki's face; he actually flew close by the terrible hawk, and made a face at him, for he knew that he was disappointed, having hoped for permission to tear and rend the finches as the larks.

"The thrushes," began the Owl again.

"Pooh," said the king, "they are feeble things; we can easily keep the whole nation of them in subjection by knocking out some of their brains now and then, can't we, Ki Ki?"

"It is a capital way," said Ki Ki. "There is no better."

"They are fit for nothing but ambassadors and couriers," said Kapchack. "We will not waste any more time over such folk whose opinions are nothing to us. Now I call upon you all to express your views as to the best means of conducting the campaign, and what measures had better be taken for the defence of our dominions. Ki Ki, speak first."

"I am for immediate action," said Ki Ki. "Let us advance and attack at once, for every day swells the ranks of Choo Hoo's army, and should there be early frosts it would be so largely increased that the mere numbers must push us back. Besides which in a short time he will receive large reinforcements, for his allies, the fieldfares and redwings, are preparing to set sail across the sea hither. But now, before his host becomes irresistible, is our opportunity; I counsel instant attack. War to the beak is my motto!"

"War to the beak," said the Crow.

"War to the beak," said the Jay, carefully adjusting his brightest feathers, "and our ladies will view our deeds."

"I agree," said the Rook, "with what Ki Ki says." The Rook was not so noisy and impetuous as the Hawk, but he was even more warlike, and by far the better statesman. "I think," Kauhaha went on, "that we should not delay one hour, but advance and occupy the plain where Choo Hoo is already diminishing our supplies of food. If our supplies are consumed or cut off our condition will become critical."

"Hear, hear," said everybody except the Crow, who hated the Rook. "Hear! hear! the Rook speaks well."

"All are then for immediately advancing?" said Kapchack, much pleased.

"May it please your majesty," said the Fox, thus humbling himself, he who was the descendant of kings, "May it please your majesty, I am not certain that the proposed course is the wisest. For, if I may be permitted to say so, it appears to me that the facts are exactly opposite to what Ki Ki

and the Rook have put forward as the reason for
battle. My experience convinces me that the very
vastness of Choo Hoo's host is really its weakness.
The larger his numbers the less he can effect. It
is clear that they must soon, if they continue to
draw together in these enormous bodies, destroy all
the forage of the country, and unless they are prepared to die of starvation they must perforce
retire.

"If, therefore, your majesty could be prevailed
upon to listen to my counsels, I would the rather
suggest, most humbly suggest, that the defensive
is your best course. Here in the copse you have an
enclosure capable with a little trouble of being con-
verted into an impregnable fortress. Already the
ditches are deep, the curtain wall of hawthorn high
and impenetrable, the approaches narrow. By retiring hither with your forces, occupying every twig,
and opposing a beak in every direction, you would
be absolutely safe, and it is easy to foresee what
would happen.

"Choo Hoo, boastful and vainglorious, would approach with his enormous horde, he would taunt us,
no doubt, with his absurd 'Koos-takke,' which I verily

believe has no meaning at all, and of which we need take no heed. In a few days, having exhausted the supplies, he would have to retire, and then sallying forth we could fall upon his rear and utterly destroy his unwieldy army."

This advice made some impression upon Kapchack, notwithstanding that he was much prejudiced against the Fox, for it was evidently founded upon facts, and the Fox was known to have had great experience. Kapchack appeared thoughtful, and leaning his head upon one side was silent, when Kauc, the crow (who had his own reasons for wishing Kapchack to run as much risk as possible), cried out that the Fox was a coward, and wanted to sneak into a hole. Ki Ki shouted applaudingly; the Rook said he for one could not shut himself up while the country was ravaged; and the Jay said the ladies would despise them. Kapchack remembered that the Fox had always had a character for duplicity, and perhaps had some secret motive for his advice, and just then, in the midst of the uproar, a starling flew into the circle with part of his tail gone and his feathers greatly ruffled.

It was evident that he had brought news from

the seat of war, and they all crowded about him. So
soon as he had recovered breath the starling told
them that half an hour since Choo Hoo had himself
crossed the border, and driving in the outposts
of the starlings, despite the most desperate resistance,
had passed the front line of the hills. At this news
the uproar was tremendous, and for some time not
a word could be heard. By-and-by the Owl obtained
something like order, when the Rook said he for
one could not stay in council any longer, he must
proceed to assemble the forces of his nation, as while
they were talking his city might be seized. Ki Ki,
too, flapping his wings, announced his intention of
attacking; the Jay uttered a sneer about one-eyed
people not being able to see what was straight before
them, and thus goaded on against his better judg-
ment, Kapchack declared his intention of sending his
army to the front.

He then proceeded to distribute the commands.
Ki Ki was proclaimed commander-in-chief (the Rook
did not like this, but he said nothing, as he knew
Kapchack could not help himself), the Rooks had
the right wing, the Crow the left wing (the Crow
was surprised at this, for his usual post was to guard

the rear, but he guessed at once that Kapchack suspected him, and would not leave him near the palace), and the Owl had the reserve. As they received their orders each flew off; even the Owl, though it was daylight, started forth to summon his men, and though he blundered against the branches, did not stay a second on that account. The Squirrel had charge of the stores, and jumped down to see after them. Not one was forgotten, but each had an office assigned, and went to execute it, all except the Fox and the Weasel. The Weasel, obedient to orders, lay still at the foot of the pollard, humbly hiding his head.

The Fox, presently finding that he had been overlooked, crept under Kapchack, and, bowing to the earth, asked if there was no command and no employment for him.

"Begone," said Kapchack, who was not going to entrust power to one of royal descent. "Begone, sir; you have not shown any ability lately."

"But did not the gnat tell you," began the Fox, humbly.

"The gnat told me a great deal," said Kapchack.

"But did he not say I sent him?"

"No, indeed," said Kapchack, for the gnat, not to be outdone, had indeed delivered the Fox's message, but had taken the credit of it for himself. "Begone, sir (the Fox slunk away); and do you (to his guards) go to the firs and wait for me there." The eight magpies immediately departed, and there was no one left but the Weasel.

The king looked down at the guilty traitor; the traitor hung his head. Presently the king said: "Weasel, false and double-tongued Weasel, did I not choose you to be my chiefest and most secret counsellor? Did you not know everything? Did I not consult you on every occasion, and were you not promoted to high honour and dignity? And you have repaid me by plotting against my throne, and against my life; the gnat has told me everything, and it is of no avail for you to deny it. You double traitor, false to me and false to those other traitors who met in this very place to conspire against me. It is true you were not among them in person, but why were you not among them? Do you suppose that I am to be deceived for a moment? Wretch that you are. You set them on to plot against me while you kept out of it with clean paws, that you might seize the throne so soon as I was slain. Wretch that you are."

Here the Weasel could not endure it any longer, but crawling to the foot of the tree, besought the king with tears in his eyes, to do what he would —to order him to instant execution, but not to reproach him with these enormities, which cut him to the very soul. But the more he pleaded, the more angry Kapchack became, and heaped such epithets upon the crouching wretch, and so bitterly upbraided him that at last the Weasel could bear it no more, but driven as it were into a corner, turned to bay, and faced the enraged monarch.

He sat up, and looking Kapchack straight in the face, as none but so hardened a reprobate could have done, he said, in a low but very distinct voice—"You have no right to say these things to me, any more than you have to wear the crown! I do not believe you are Kapchack at all—you are an impostor!"

At these words Kapchack became as pale as death, and could not keep his perch upon the pollard, but fluttered down to the ground beside the Weasel. He was so overcome that for a moment or two he could not speak. When he found breath, he turned to the Weasel and asked him what he meant. The Weasel, who had now regained his spirits, said boldly enough that he meant what he said; he did not believe that the king was really Kapchack.

"But I am Kapchack," said the king, trembling, and not knowing how much the Weasel knew.

In truth the Weasel knew very little, but had only shot a bolt at random from the bow of his suspicions, but he had still a sharper shaft to shoot, and he said, "You are an impostor, for you told La Schach, who has jilted you, that you were not so old as you looked."

"The false creature!" said Kapchack, quite beside himself with rage. In his jealousy of Prince Tchack-tchack, who was so much younger, and had two eyes, he had said this, and now he bitterly repented his vanity. "The false creature!" he screamed, "where is she? I will have her torn to pieces! She shall be pecked limb from limb! Where is she?" he shrieked. "She left the palace yesterday evening, and I have not seen her since."

"She went to the firs with the Jay," said the Weasel. "He is her old lover, you know. Did you not see how merry he was just now, at the council?"

Then Kapchack pecked up the ground with his beak, and tore at it with his claws, and gave way to his impotent anger.

"There shall not be a feather of her left!" he said. "I will have her utterly destroyed! She shall be nailed to a tree!"

"Nothing of the kind," said the Weasel, with a sneer. "She is too beautiful. As soon as you see her, you will kiss her and forgive her."

"It is true," said Kapchack, becoming calmer. "She is so beautiful, she must be forgiven. Weasel, in consideration of important services rendered to the state in former days, upon this one occasion you shall be pardoned. Of course the condition is that what has passed between us this day is kept strictly private, and that you do not breathe a word of it."

"Not a word of it," said the Weasel.

"And you must disabuse your mind of that extraordinary illusion as to my identity of which

you spoke just now. You must dismiss so absurd
an idea from your mind."

"Certainly," said the Weasel, "it is dismissed
entirely. But, your majesty, with your permission,
I would go further. I would endeavour to explain
to you, that although my conduct was indiscreet,
and so far open to misconstruction, there was really
nothing more in it than an ill-directed zeal in
your service. It is really true, your majesty, that
all the birds and animals are leagued against me,
and that is why I have been afraid to stir abroad.
I was invited to the secret council, of which you
have heard from the gnat, and because I did not
attend it, they have one and all agreed to vilify
me to your majesty.

"But in fact I, for once, with the service of
your majesty in view, descended (repugnant as it
was to my feelings) to play the eavesdropper, and
I overheard all that was said, and I can convince
your majesty that there are far greater traitors in
your dominions than you ever supposed me to be.
The gnat does not know half that took place at
the council, for he only had it second-hand from
that villain, the Fox, who is, I believe, secretly

bent on your destruction. But I can tell you not only all that went on—I can also relate to you the designs of Kauc, the crow, who conferred with Cloctaw in private, after the meeting was over. And I can also give you good reasons for suspecting Ki Ki, the hawk, whom you have just nominated to the command of your forces, of the intention of making a bargain with Choo Hoo, and of handing you over to him a prisoner."

Now this last was a pure invention of the Weasel's out of envy, since Ki Ki had obtained such distinction. Kapchack, much alarmed at these words, ordered him to relate everything in order, and the Weasel told him all that had been said at the council, all that Kauc, the crow, had said to Cloctaw, and a hundred other matters which he made up himself. When Kapchack heard these things he was quite confounded, and exclaimed that he was surrounded with traitors, and that he did not see which way to turn. He hopped a little way off, in order the better to consider by himself, and leant his head upon one side.

First he thought to himself, " I must take the command from Ki Ki, but I cannot do that

suddenly, lest he should go over to Choo Hoo. I
will therefore do it gradually. I will countermand
the order for an immediate attack; that will give
me time to arrange. Who is to take Ki Ki's place?
Clearly the Weasel, for though he is an arch-
traitor, yet he is in the same boat with me; for
I know it to be perfectly true that all of them
are bitter against him."

So he went back to the Weasel, and told him
that he should give him the chief command of the
forces, on the third day following, and meantime
told him to come early in the evening to the drain
which passed under the orchard, where his palace
was, so that he could concert the details of this
great state business in secret with him.

The Weasel, beyond measure delighted at the
turn things had taken, and rejoicing extremely at
the impending fall of Ki Ki, whom he hated,
thanked Kapchack with all his might, till Kapchack, enjoining on him the necessity of secrecy,
said "Good afternoon;" and flew away towards the
firs, where his guard was waiting for him. Then
the Weasel puffed up, and treading the ground
proudly, went back to his cave in the elm, and

Bevis, seeing that there was nothing more going on that day, stole back to the raspberry canes.

None of them had noticed, not even the cunning Weasel, that the mole, when the council broke up, had not left with the rest: indeed, being under the surface of the earth they easily overlooked him. Now the mole, who hated the Weasel beyond all, had waited to have the pleasure of hearing king Kapchack upbraid the traitor, and presently consign him to execution. Fancy then his feelings when, after all, the Weasel was received into the highest favour, and promised the supreme command of the army, while he himself was not even noticed, though he was a clever engineer, and could mine and countermine, and carry on siege operations better than any of them.

He listened to all that was said attentively, and then, so soon as Kapchack had flown away, and the Weasel had gone to his hole, and Bevis to the raspberries, he drove a tunnel to the edge of the copse, and there calling a fly, sent him with a message to the hawk, asking Ki Ki to meet him beside the leaning stone in the field (which Bevis had once passed), because he had a

secret to communicate which would brook no delay.
At the same time, as Kapchack was flying to
the firs where his guards were waiting, it occurred
to him that, although he had no alternative, it was
dangerous in the extreme to trust the army to the
Weasel, who, perhaps, just as there was an opportunity of victory would retire, and leave him to be
destroyed. Thinking about this, he perched on a
low hawthorn bush, and asked himself whether it
was worth while to attempt to defend a kingdom
held under such precarious tenure? Would it not
be better to make terms with Choo Hoo, who was
not unreasonable, and to divide the territory, and
thus reign in peace and safety over half at least,
—making it, of course, a condition of the compact
that Choo Hoo should help him to put down all
domestic traitors.

The idea seemed so good that, first glancing
round to see that he was not observed, he called
a thrush, who had been coming to the hawthorn,
but dared not enter it while the king was there.
The thrush, much frightened, came as he was bid,
and Kapchack carefully instructed him in what he
was to do. Having learnt his message by heart,

the thrush, delighted beyond expression at so high
a negotiation being entrusted to him, flew straight
away towards Choo Hoo's camp. But not unob-
served; for just then Ki Ki, wheeling in the air at
an immense height, whither he had gone to survey
the scene of war, chanced to look down and saw
him quit the king, and marked the course he took.
Kapchack, unaware that Ki Ki had detected this
manœuvre, now returned to his guards, and flew
to his palace.

Meantime the Weasel, curled up on his divan in
the elm, was thinking over the extraordinary good
fortune that had befallen him. Yet such was his
sagacity that even when thus about to attain almost
the topmost pinnacle of his ambition, he did not
forget the instability of affairs, but sought to confirm
his position, or even to advance it. He reflected
that Kapchack was not only cunning beyond everything ever known, but he was just now a prey to
anxieties, and consumed with jealousy, which upset
the tenour of his mind, so that his course could not
be depended upon, but might be changed in a moment.
The favour of a despotic monarch was never a firm
staff to lean upon; when that monarch was on the

brink of a crisis which threatened both his throne and his life, his smile might become a frown before any one was aware that a change was impending.

Impressed with these ideas, the Weasel asked himself how he could at once secure his position and advance himself to further dignity. He considered that up to the present the forces of Kapchack had always been compelled to retreat before the over-whelming masses thrown against them by Choo Hoo. He could scarcely hope under the most favourable circumstances to do more than defend the frontier, and should Choo Hoo win the battle, Kapchack would either be taken prisoner, or, what was not at all unlikely, fall a victim during the confusion, and be assassinated, perhaps, by the villanous Crow. Where, then, would be his own high command? But by making terms with Choo Hoo he might himself obtain the throne, and reign perfectly secure as Choo Hoo's regent.

On coming to this conclusion, he called to his old friend, the Humble-bee, and said he desired to send a message to Choo Hoo, the purport of which must not be divulged to any flower upon the route. The Humble-bee instantly guessed that this message must

be something to the injury of Kapchack, and resenting
the manner in which he had been hustled from the
council, declared that he would carry it without a
moment's delay.

"Go then, my friend," said the Weasel. "Go
straight to Choo Hoo, and say—'The Weasel is
appointed to the command of king Kapchack's army,
and will supersede Ki Ki, the hawk, upon the third
day. On that day he will lead forth the army to
the south, professing to go upon a flank march,
and to take you in the rear. Be not deceived by this
movement, but so soon as you see that the guards
are withdrawn from the frontier, cross the border in
force, and proceed straight towards the palace. When
Kapchack's army finds you between it and its base
of supplies it will disperse, and you will obtain an
easy victory.

"And in proof of his good will towards you, the
Weasel, furthermore, bade me inform you of the
great secret which has hitherto been preserved with
such care, and which will enable your army to remain
in this place all the winter. In the Squirrel's copse
there is a spring, which is never frozen, but always
affords excellent drinking water, and moistens a con-

siderable extent of ground." This was the Weasel's
message, and without a moment's delay the Humble-
bee buzzed away direct to Choo Hoo's camp.

At the same time the fly with the mole's message
reached Ki Ki, the hawk, as he was soaring among the
clouds. Ki Ki having finished his observations, and
full of suspicions as to the object with which the
king had despatched the thrush to Choo Hoo, decided
to keep the mole's appointment at once, so down he
flew direct to the leaning stone in the meadow, where
Bevis had gathered the cowslips, and found the mole
already waiting for him.

Now, the mole hated Ki Ki exceedingly, because,
as previously related, he had killed his wife, but he
hated the Weasel, who had persecuted him all his
life, even more, and by thus betraying the Weasel
to the Hawk he hoped to set the two traitors by the
ears, and to gratify his own vengeance by seeing
them tear each other to pieces. Accordingly he now
informed Ki Ki of everything—how the Weasel had
disclosed the names of all those who attended the
secret meeting (exeept one, *i.e.*, the Owl, which, for
reasons of his own, the Weasel had suppressed), particularly stating that Ki Ki had taken a foremost part,

that Kapchack was enraged against the Hawk, and had already promised the Weasel the chief command, so that in three days Ki Ki would be superseded.

Ki Ki, suppressing his agitation, thanked the mole very cordially for his trouble, and soared towards the sky, but he had scarce gone a hundred yards before one of Kapchack's bodyguard met him with a message from the king countermanding the advance of the army which had been decided upon. Ki Ki replied that his majesty's orders should be implicitly obeyed, and continued his upward flight. He had now no doubt that what the mole had told him was correct in every particular, since it had been so immediately confirmed, and as for the thrush, it seemed clear that Kapchack had some design of saving himself by the sacrifice of his friends. That must be his reason for countermanding the advance— to give time for negotiation. Angry beyond measure, Ki Ki flew to his own clump of trees, and calling to him a keen young hawk—one of his guard, and who was only too delighted to be selected for confidential employment—sent him with a flag of truce to Choo Hoo.

He was to say that Ki Ki, being disgusted with

the treachery of king Kapchack, had determined
to abandon his cause, and that on the day of
battle in the midst of the confusion, if Choo Hoo
would push forward rapidly, Ki Ki would draw off
his contingent and expose the centre, when Kapchack must inevitably be destroyed. Away flew
the hawk, and thus in one hour Choo Hoo received
three messengers.

CHAPTER II.

TRAITORS.

THE first that arrived was the thrush, bearing the message from the king. Choo Hoo, delighted beyond expression at so pleasant a solution of the business, which he knew must, if it came to battle, entail great slaughter of his friends, received the thrush with the highest honours, called his principal counsellors around him, and acceded to everything king Kapchack had proposed. The territory should be equally divided: Choo Hoo to have the plains, and Kapchack the woods and hills, and peace should be proclaimed, Choo Hoo engaging to support Kapchack against all domestic enemies and traitors. This treaty having been completed, the thrush made as if about to depart, but Choo Hoo would in no wise permit this. "Remain with us," he said, "my dear thrush, till the evening, feast and make merry."

So the thrush was surrounded with a guard of honour, and conducted to the choicest feeding places, and regaled upon the fat of the land. Thus enjoying himself, he thought it was the happiest day of his life, and was not at all desirous of seeing the shadows lengthen.

Hardly had the thrush gone with his guard to the banquet, than the Humble-bee was announced, bearing the message from the Weasel. To this the assembled counsellors listened attentively, but Choo Hoo, being only a barbarian, could on no account break faith, but was resolved to carry out his compact with king Kapchack. Nevertheless, he reflected that the king was extremely cunning, and not altogether to be relied upon (the Humble-bee, for aught he knew, might have been in reality sent by Kapchack to try him), and therefore he would go so far as this, he would encourage the Weasel without committing himself. " Return," he said to the Humble-bee, " Return to him who sent you, and say, ' Do you do your part, and Choo Hoo will certainly do his part.' " With which ambiguous sentence (which of course the Weasel read in his own sense), he dismissed the Humble-bee, who had scarce departed from the camp, than the flag of truce arrived from Ki Ki, and the young hawk, bright and defiant in his bearing, was admitted to the great emperor Choo Hoo.

When the council heard his message they all cried with one accord, "Koos-takke! koos-takke! the enemy are confounded; they are divided against each other. They are delivered over to us. Koos-takke!"

So soon as there was silence, Choo Hoo said, "Young sir, tell your master that we do not need his assistance," and he waved the messenger to depart.

But the hawk said, "Mighty emperor, consider that I am young, and that if I go to my master with so curt a message, you know that he is fierce beyond reason, and I shall infallibly be torn to pieces."

"Very well," said Choo Hoo, speaking in a harsh tone of voice, for he hated the whole race of hawks, and could scarce respect the flag of truce, "Very well, tell your master the reason I do not want his assistance is, first, because Kapchack and I have concluded a treaty; secondly, because the

Weasel has been before him, and has told me where the secret spring is in the Squirrel's copse—the spring that does not freeze in winter."

The hawk, not daring to parley further with the emperor, bowed his way out, and went direct to Ki Ki with this reply.

All the council of Choo Hoo rejoiced exceedingly, both at the treaty which assured so peaceful and pleasant a conclusion to their arduous labours, and to a sanguinary war which had lasted so many years, and in which they had lost so many of their bravest, and also at the treachery which prevailed in Kapchack's palace and confounded his efforts. They cried, " Koos-takke ! " and the shout was caught up throughout the camp with such vehemence, that the woods echoed to the mysterious sound.

Now the young hawk, winging his way swiftly through the air, soon arrived at the trees where Ki Ki was waiting for him, and delivered the answer in fear and trembling, expecting every moment to be dashed to the ground and despatched. Ki Ki, however, said nothing, but listened in silence, and then sat a long time thinking.

Presently he said, " You have done ill, and have

not given much promise of your future success; you should not have taken Choo Hoo's answer so quickly. You should have argued with him, and used your persuasive powers. Moreover, being thus admitted to the very presence of our greatest enemy, and standing face to face with him, and within a few inches of his breast, you should have known what it was your business to do. I could not tell you beforehand, because it would have been against my dignity to seem to participate before the deed in things of that kind. To you the opportunity was afforded, but you had not the ready wit either to see, or to seize it.

"While Choo Hoo was deliberating you should have flown at his breast, and despatched the arch-rebel with one blow of your beak. In the confusion you could have escaped with ease. Upon such a catastrophe becoming known, the whole of Choo Hoo's army would have retreated, and hanging upon their rear we could have wreaked our wills upon them. As for you, you would have obtained fame and power; as for me, I should have retained the chief command; as for Kapchack, he would have rewarded you with untold wealth. But you missed—you did not even see—this golden opportunity, and you will never have another such a chance."

At this, the young hawk hung his head, and could have beaten himself to death against the tree, in shame and sorrow at his folly.

"But," continued Ki Ki, "as I see you are unfeignedly sorry, I will even yet entrust you with one more commission (the hawk began to brighten up a little). You know that at the end of the Longpond there is a very large wood which grows upon a slope; at the foot of the slope there is an open space or glade, which is a very convenient spot for an ambush. Now when the thrush comes home in the evening, bringing the treaty to Kapchack, he is certain to pass that way, because it is the nearest, and the most pleasant. Go there and stay in ambush till you hear him coming, then swoop down and kill him, and tear his heart from his breast. Do not fail, or never return to my presence.

"And stay—you may be sure of the place I mean, because there is an old oak in the midst of the glade, it is old and dead, and the route of the thrush will be under it. Strike him there."

Without waiting a moment, the hawk, knowing

that his master liked instant obedience, flew off swift
as the wind, determined this time to succeed. He
found the glade without trouble, and noted the old
oak with its dead gaunt boughs, and then took up
his station on an ash, where he watched eagerly for
the shadows to lengthen. Ki Ki, after sitting a little
longer, soared up into the sky to reflect upon further
measures. By destroying the thrush he knew that
the war must continue, for Choo Hoo would never
believe but that it had been done by Kapchack's
order, and could not forgive so brutal an affront to
an ambassador charged with a solemn treaty. Choo
Hoo must then accept his (Ki Ki's) offer; the Weasel,
it was true, had been before him, but he should be
able to destroy the Weasel's influence by revealing
his treachery to Kapchack, and how he had told
Choo Hoo the secret of the spring which was never
frozen. He felt certain that he should be able to
make his own terms, both with Kapchack and Choo
Hoo.

Thus soaring up he saw his messenger, the young
hawk, swiftly speeding to the ambush, and smiled
grimly as he noted the eager haste with which the
youthful warrior went to fulfil his orders. Still soar-

ing, with out-stretched wings, he sought the upper sky.

Meantime Bevis had grown tired of waiting for the Squirrel, who had gone off to see about the stores, and flung himself at full length on the moss under the oak. He hardly stopped there a minute before he got up again and called and shouted for the Squirrel, but no one answered him; nor did the dragon-fly appear. Bevis, weary of waiting, determined to try and find his way home by himself, but when he came to look round he could not discover the passage through the thicket. As he was searching for it he passed the elm, which was hollow inside, where the Weasel lay curled up on his divan, and the Weasel, hearing Bevis go by, was so puffed up with pride, that he actually called to him, having conceived a design of using Bevis for his own purposes.

"Sir Bevis! Sir Bevis!" he said, coming to the mouth of his hole, "Sir Bevis, I want to speak to you!"

"You are the Weasel," said Bevis, "I know your hateful voice—I hate you, and if ever I find you outside the copse I will smash you into twenty pieces. If it was not for the Squirrel, whom I love (and I

have promised not to hurt anything in his copse) I
would bring my papa's hatchet and chop your tree
down and cut your head off; so there."

"If you did that," said the Weasel, "then you
would not know what the Rat is going to do in your
house to-night."

"Why should I not know?" said Bevis.

"Because if you cut my head off I could not tell
you."

"Well, tell me what it is," said Bevis; who was
always very curious, "and make haste about it, for
I want to go home."

"I will," said the Weasel, "and first of all, you
know the fine large cake that your mamma is making
for you?"

"No," said Bevis, excitedly, "Is she making me
a cake? I did not know it."

"Yes, that she is, but she did not tell you, because she wished it to be a surprise to you to-morrow
morning at lunch, and it is no use for you to ask her
about it, for she would not tell you. But if you are
not very sharp it is certain that you will never touch
a mouthful of it."

"Why not?" said Bevis.

"Because," said the Weasel, "the Mouse has found out where your mamma has put it in the cupboard, and there is a little chink through which he can smell it, but he cannot quite get through, nor is he strong enough to gnaw such very hard wood, else you may depend he would have kept the secret to himself. But as he could not creep through he has gone and told Raoul, the Rat, who has such strong teeth he can bite a way through anything, and to-night, when you are all in bed and firm asleep, and everything is quiet, Yish, the Mouse, is going to show the Rat where the chink is, the Rat is going to gnaw a hole, and in the morning there will be very little left of your cake."

"I will tell the Bailiff," said Bevis in a rage, "and the Bailiff shall set a trap for the Rat."

"Well, that was what I was going to suggest," said the Weasel; "but upon consideration I am not so sure that it is much use telling the Bailiff, because, as I daresay you recollect, the Bailiff has often tried his hand setting up a trap for the Rat, but has never yet caught him, from which I conclude that the Rat knows all the places where the Bailiff sets the trap, and takes good care not to go that way without previous examination."

"I'll set up the trap," said Bevis, "I'll set it up myself in a new place. Let me see, where can I put it?"

"I think it would be a very good plan if you did put it up yourself," said the Weasel, "because there is no doubt you understand more about these things than the Bailiff, who is getting old."

"Yes," said Bevis, "I know all about it—I can do it very well indeed."

"Just what I thought," said the Weasel, "I thought to myself, Bevis knows all about it—Bevis can do it. Now, as the Bailiff has set up the trap by the drain or grating beside the carthouse, and under the wood-pile, and by the pump, and has never caught the Rat, it is clear that the Rat knows these places as well as the Bailiff, and if you remember there is a good deal of grass grows there, so that the Rat no doubt says to himself, 'Aha! They are sure to put the trap here, because they think I shall not see it in the grass—as if I was so silly.' So that, depend upon it, he is always very careful how he goes through the grass there.

"Therefore I think the best place you could select to set up the trap would be somewhere where there is no kind of cover, no grass, nor anything, where it is quite bare and open, and where the Rat would run along quickly and never think of any danger. And he would be sure to run much faster and not stay to look under his feet in crossing such places, lest Pan should see him and give chase, or your papa should come round the corner with a gun. Now I know there is one such place the Rat passes every evening; it is a favourite path of his, because it is a short cut to the stable—it is under the wall of the pigstye. I know this, because I once lived with the Rat a little while, and saw all his habits.

"Well, under this wall it is quite open, and he always runs by extremely fast, and that is the best place to put the trap. Now when you have set the trap, in order to hide it from view do you get your little spade with which your dig in your garden, and take a spadeful of the dust that lies about there (as it is so dry there is plenty of dust) and throw it over the trap. The dust will hide the trap, and will also prevent the Rat (for he has a wonderful sharp nose of his own) from scenting where your fingers touched it. In the morning you are sure to find him caught.

"By-the-by, you had better not say anything to your mamma that you know of the cake, else perhaps she will move it from the cupboard, and then the Rat may go on some other moonlit ramble instead. As I said, in the morning you are sure to find him in the trap, and then do not listen to anything he has to say, for he has a lying tongue, but let Pan loose, who will instantly worry him to death."

"I will do as you say," said Bevis, "for I see that it is a very clever way to catch the Rat, but Sir Weasel, you have told me so many false stories that I can scarce believe you now it is plain you are telling me the truth; nor shall I feel certain that you are this time (for once in your wicked life) saying the truth, unless I know why you are so anxious for the Rat to be caught."

"Why," said the Weasel, "I will tell you the reason; this afternoon the Rat played me a very mean and scurvy trick; he disgraced me before the king, and made me a common laughing-stock to all the council, for which I swore to have his life. Besides upon one occasion he bit his teeth right through my

ear—the marks of it are there still. See for yourself."
So the Weasel thrust his head out of his hole, and
Bevis saw the marks left by the Rat's teeth, and
was convinced that the Weasel, out of malice, had
at last been able for once to tell the truth.

"You are a horrid wretch," said Bevis, "still you
know how to catch the Rat, and I will go home and
do it; but I cannot find my way out of this thicket
—the Squirrel ought to come."

"The way is under the ash bough there," said
the Weasel, "and when you are outside the thicket
turn to your left and go down hill, and you will come
to the timber—and meantime I will send for the
dragon-fly, who will overtake you."

"All right, horrid wretch," said Bevis, and away
he went. Now all this that the Weasel had said
really was true, except about the cake; it was true
that the Rat was very careful going through the grass,
and that he knew where the Bailiff set the gin, and
that he used to run very quickly across the exposed
place under the wall of the pigstye. But the story
about the cake he had made up out of his cunning
head just to set Bevis at work to put up the
trap; and he hoped too, that while Bevis was setting

up the gin, the spring would slip and pinch his fingers.

By thus catching the Rat, the Weasel meant in the first place to gratify his own personal malice, and next to get rid of a very formidable competitor. For the Rat was very large and very strong, and brave and bold beyond all the others; so much so that the Weasel would even have preferred to have a struggle with the Fox (though he was so much bigger) whose nostril he could bite, than to meet the Rat in fair and equal combat. Besides, he hated the Rat beyond measure, because the Rat had helped him out of the drain, which was when his ear was bitten through. He intended to go down to the farmyard very early next morning when the Rat was caught, and to go as near as he dared and taunt the Rat, and tell him how Pan would presently come and crunch up his ribs. To see the Rat twist, and hear him groan, would be rare sport; it made his eyes glisten to think of it. He was very desirous that Bevis should find his way home all right, so he at once sent a wasp for the dragon-fly, and the dragon-fly at once started after Bevis.

Just after the Weasel had sent the wasp, the

Humble-bee returned from Choo Hoo, and delivered
the emperor's message, which the Weasel saw at once
was intended to encourage him in his proposed
treachery. He thanked the Humble-bee for the care
and speed with which his errand had been accomplished, and then curled himself up on his divan to
go to sleep, so as to be ready to go down early in the
morning and torment the Rat. As he was very
happy since his schemes were prospering, he went
to sleep in a minute as comfortable as could be.

Bevis crept through the thicket, and turned to the
left, and went down the hill, and found the timber,
and then went along the green track till he came to
the stile. He got over the bridge and followed the
footpath, when the dragon-fly overtook him, and
apologised most sincerely for his neglect. "For,"
said he, "we are so busy making ready for the army,
and I have had so much to do going to and fro with
messages, that my dear Sir Bevis, you must forgive
me for forgetting you. Next time I will send a moth
to stay close by you, so that the moment you want
me the moth can go and fetch me."

"I will forgive you just this once," said Bevis;
and the dragon-fly took him all the way home. After

tea Bevis went and found the gin, and tried to set it up under the pigstye wall, just as the Weasel had told him; but at first he could not quite manage it, being as usual in such a hurry.

Now there was a snail on the wall, and the snail looked out of his shell and said, " Sir Bevis, do not be too quick. Believe me, if you are too quick to-day you are sure to be sorry to-morrow."

" You are a stupid snail," said Bevis. Just then, as the Weasel had hoped, he pinched his fingers with the spring so hard that tears almost came into his eyes.

" That was your fault," he said to the snail; and snatching the poor thing off the wall, he flung him ever so far; fortunately the snail fell on the grass, and was not hurt, but he said to himself that in future, no matter what he saw going on, he would never interfere, but let people hurt themselves as much as they liked. But Bevis, though he was so hasty, was also very persevering, and presently he succeeded in setting up the trap, and then taking his spade he spread the dust over it and so hid it as the Weasel had told him to. He then went and put his spade back in the summer-house, and having told Pan that in the morning there would be a fine big rat for him to worry, went in-doors.

Now it is most probable that what the Weasel had arranged so well would all have happened just as he foresaw, and that the trap so cleverly set up would have caught the Rat, had not the Bailiff, when he came home from the fields, chanced to see Bevis doing it. He had to attend to something else then, but by-and-by, when he had finished, he went and looked at the place where Bevis had set the gin, and said to himself, " Well, it is a very good plan to set up the gin, for the Rat is always taking the pig's food, and even had a gnaw at my luncheon, which was tied up in my handkerchief, and which I—like a stupid—left on the ground in my hurry instead of hanging it up. But it is a pity Sir Bevis should have set it here, for there is no grass or cover, and the Rat is certain to see it, and Bevis will be disappointed in the morning, and will not find the Rat. Now I will just move the gin to a place where the Rat always comes, and where it will be hidden by the grass, that is, just at the mouth of the drain by the carthouse ; it will catch the Rat there, and Sir Bevis will be pleased."

So the Bailiff, having thought this to himself, as he

leant against the wall, and listened to the pigs snoring, carefully took up the gin and moved it down to the mouth of the drain by the carthouse, and there set it up in the grass.

The Rat was in the drain, and when he heard the Bailiff's heavy footsteps, and the noise he made fumbling about with the trap, he laughed, and said to himself, " Fumble away, you old stupid—I know what you are doing. You are setting up a gin in the same place you have set it twenty times before. Twenty times you have set the gin up there and never caught anything, and yet you cannot see, and you cannot understand, and you never learn anything, and you are the biggest dolt and idiot that ever walked, or rather, you would be, only I thank Heaven everybody else is just like you! As if I could not hear what you are doing; as if I did not look very carefully before I come out of my hole, and before I put my foot down on grass or leaves, and as if I could not smell your great clumsy fingers : really I feel insulted that you should treat me as if I was so foolish. However, upon the whole, this is rather nice and considerate of you. Ha ! Ha ! " and the Rat laughed so loud that if the Bailiff had been sharp he must have heard this unusual

chuckling in the drain. But he heard nothing, but
went off down the road very contented with himself,
whistling a bar from Madame Angôt which he had
learnt from Bevis.

When Bevis went to bed he just peeped out of the
window to look at the moon, but the sky was now
overcast, and the clouds were hurrying by, and the
wind rising—which the snail had expected, or he would
not have ventured out along the wall. While Bevis
was peeping out he saw the Owl go by over the
orchard and up beside the hedge.

The very same evening the young hawk, as
has been previously related, had gone to the glade in
the wood, and sat there in ambush waiting for the
thrush. Like Sir Bevis, the hawk was extremely
impatient, and the time as he sat on the ash passed
very slowly, till at last he observed with much delight
that the sun was declining, and that the shadow of
the dead oak tree would soon reach across towards
him.

The thrush, having sat at the banquet the whole of
the afternoon, and tasted every dainty that the camp of
Choo Hoo afforded, surrounded all the time by crowds
of pleasant companions, on the other hand, saw the

shadows lengthening with regret. He knew that it was time for him to depart and convey the intelligence to king Kapchack that Choo Hoo had fully agreed to his proposal. Still loth to leave he lingered, and it was not until dusk that he quitted the camp, accompanied a little way over the frontier by some of Choo Hoo's chief counsellors, who sought in every way to do him honour. Then wishing him good-night, with many invitations to return shortly, they left him to pursue his journey.

Knowing that he ought to have returned to the king before this, the thrush put forth his best speed, and thought to himself as he flew what a long account he should have to give his wife and his children (who were now grown up) of the high and important negotiation with which he had been entrusted, and of the attentions that had been paid to him by the emperor. Happy in these anticipations, he passed rapidly over the fields and the woods, when just as he flew beneath the old dead oak in the glade down swooped the hawk and bore him to the ground. In an instant a sharp beak was driven into his head, and then, while yet his body quivered, the feathers were plucked from his breast and his

heart laid bare. Hungry from his fast, for he had
touched nothing that day, being so occupied with
his master's business, the hawk picked the bones,
and then, after the manner of his kind, wishing
to clean his beak, flew up and perched on a large
dead bough of the oak just overhead.

The moment he perched, a steel trap which had
been set there by the keeper, flew up and caught him,
with such force that his limbs were broken. With
a shriek the hawk flapped his wings to fly, but this
only pulled his torn and bleeding legs, and overcome
with the agony, he fainted, and hung head downwards
from the bough, suspended by his sinews. Now this
was exactly what Ki Ki had foreseen would happen.
There were a hundred places along the thrush's route
where an ambush might have been placed, as well as
in the glade, but Ki Ki had observed that a trap was
set upon the old dead oak, and ordered his servant to
strike the thrush there, so that he might step into
it afterwards, thus killing two birds with one stone.

He desired the death of his servant lest he should
tell tales, and let out the secret mission upon which
he had been employed, or lest he should boast, in the
vain glory of youth, of having slain the ambassador.

Cruel as he was, Ki Ki, too, thought of the torture
the young hawk would endure with delight, and said
to himself that it was hardly an adequate punishment for having neglected so golden an opportunity
for assassinating Choo Hoo. From the fate of the thrush
and the youthful hawk, it would indeed appear that
it is not always safe to be employed upon secret business of state. Yet Ki Ki, with all his cruel cunning,
was not wholly successful.

For the Owl, as he went his evening rounds, after
he had flown over the orchard where Bevis saw him,
went on up the hedge by the meadow, and skirting
the shore of the Longpond, presently entered the
wood and glided across the glade towards the dead
oak tree, which was one of his favourite haunts. As
he came near he was horrified to hear miserable groans
and moans, and incoherent talking, and directly afterwards saw the poor hawk hanging head downwards.
He had recovered his consciousness only to feel again
the pressure of the steel, and the sharp pain of his
broken limbs, which presently sent him into a delirium.

The Owl circling round the tree was so overcome
by the spectacle that he too nearly fainted, and said
to himself, " It is clear that my lucky star rose to

night, for without a doubt the trap was intended for
me. I have perched on that very bough every evening
for weeks, and I should have alighted there to-night
had not the hawk been before me. I have escaped
from the most terrible fate which ever befel any
one, to which indeed crucifixion, with an iron nail
through the brain, is mercy itself, for that is over in
a minute, but this miserable creature will linger till
the morning."

So saying, he felt so faint that (first looking very
carefully to see that there were no more traps) he perched
on a bough a little way above the hawk. The hawk,
in his delirium, was talking of all that he had done
and heard that day, reviling Ki Ki and Choo Hoo,
imploring destruction upon his master's head, and
then flapping his wings and so tearing his sinews and
grinding his broken bones together, he shrieked with
pain. Then again he went on talking about the treaty,
and the Weasel's treason, and the assassination of
the ambassador. The Owl, sitting close by, heard all
these things, and after a time came to understand
what the hawk meant; at first he could not
believe that his master, the king, would conclude a
treaty without first consulting him, but looking

underneath him he saw the feathers of the thrush scattered on the grass, and could no longer doubt that what the hawk said was true.

But when he heard the story of Ki Ki's promised treason on the day of battle, when he heard that the Weasel had betrayed the secret of the spring, which did not freeze in winter, he lifted up his claw and opened his eyes still wider in amazement and terror. "Wretched creature!" he said, "what is this you have been saying." But the hawk, quite mad with agony, did not know him, but mistook him for Ki Ki, and poured out such terrible denunciations that the Owl, shocked beyond measure, flew away.

As he went, after he had gone some distance under the trees, and could no longer hear the ravings of the tortured hawk, he began to ask himself what he had better do. At first he thought that he would say nothing, but take measures to defeat these traitors. But presently it occurred to him that it was dangerous even to know such things, and he wished that he had never heard what the hawk had said. He reflected, too, that the bats had been flying about some time, and might have heard the hawk's confessions, and although they were not admitted at court, as they belonged to the lower orders, still under such circumstances they might obtain an audience. They had always borne him ill-will, they must have seen him, and it was not unlikely they might say that the Owl knew all about it, and kept it from the king. On the other hand he thought that Kapchack's rage would be terrible to face.

Upon the whole, however, the Owl came to the conclusion that his safest, as well as his most honourable course, was to go straight to the king, late as it was, and communicate all that had thus come to his knowledge. He set out at once, and upon his way again passed the glade, taking care not to go too near the dead oak, nor to look towards the suspended hawk. He saw a nightjar, like a ghost wheeling to and fro not far from the scaffold, and anxious to get from the ill-omened spot, flew yet more swiftly. Round the wood he went, and along the hedges, so occupied with his thoughts that he did not notice how the sky was covered with clouds, and once or twice narrowly escaping a branch blown off by the wind which had risen to a gale. Nor did he see the Fox with his brush touching the ground, creeping unhappily along the mound, but never looked to the right nor left, hastening as fast as he could glide to king Kapchack.

Now the king had waited up that night as long as ever he could, wondering why the thrush did not return, and growing more and more anxious about the ambassador every moment. Yet he was unable to imagine what could delay him, nor could he see how any ill could befall him, protected as he was by the privileges of his office. As the night came on, and the ambassador did not come, Kapchack, worn out with anxieties, snapped at his attendants, who retired to a little distance, for they feared the monarch in these fits of temper.

Kapchack had just fallen asleep when the Owl arrived, and the attendants objected to letting him see the king. But the Owl insisted, saying that it was his particular privilege as chief secretary of state to be admitted to audience at any moment. With some difficulty, therefore, he at last got to the king, who woke up in a rage, and stormed at his faithful counsellor with such fury that the attendants again retired in affright. But the Owl stood his ground and told his tale.

When King Kapchack heard that his ambassador had been foully assassinated, and that, therefore, the treaty was at an end—for Choo Hoo would never brook such an affront; when he heard that Ki Ki, his trusted Ki Ki, who had the command, had offered to retreat in the hour of battle, and expose him to be taken prisoner; when he heard that the Weasel, the Weasel whom that very afternoon he had restored to his highest favour, had revealed to the enemy the existence of the spring, he lost all his spirit, and he knew not what to do. He waved the Owl from his presence, and sat alone hanging his head, utterly overcome.

The clouds grew darker, the wind howled, the trees creaked, and the branches cracked (the snail had foreseen the storm and had ventured forth on the wall), a few spots of rain came driving along. Kapchack heard nothing. He was deserted by all: all had turned traitors against him, every one. He who had himself deceived all was now deceived by all, and suffered the keenest pangs. Thus, in dolour and despair the darkness increased, and the tempest howled about him.

CHAPTER III.

THE STORM IN THE NIGHT.

WHEN the fox, after humbling himself in the dust, was rudely dismissed by king Kapchack, he was so mortified, that as he slunk away his brush touched the ground, and the tip of his nostrils turned almost white. That he, whose ancestors had once held regal dignity, should thus be contemned by one who in comparison was a mere upstart, and that, too, after doing him a service by means of the gnat, and after bowing himself, as it were, to the ground, hurt him to his soul. He went away through the fern and the bushes to his lair in the long grass which grew in a corner of the copse, and having curled himself up, tried to forget the insult in slumber.

But he could not shut his eyes, and after a while he went off again down the hedgerow to another place where he sometimes stayed, under thick brambles on a broad mound. But he could not rest there, nor in the osier-bed, nor in the furze,

but he kept moving from place to place all day,
contrary to his custom, and not without running
great danger. The sting lingered in him, and the
more so because he felt that it was true—he knew
himself that he had not shown any ability lately.
Slowly the long day passed, the shadows lengthened
and it became night. Still restlessly and aimlessly
wandering he went about the fields noticing nothing
but miserable to the last degree. The Owl flew
by on his errand to king Kapchack: the bats
fluttered overhead; the wind blew and the trees
creaked, but the Fox neither saw, nor heard, nor
thought of anything except his own degradation.
He had been cast forth as unworthy—even the very
Mouse had received some instructions, but he, the
descendant of illustrious ancestors, was pointedly told
that the wit for which they had been famous did not
exist in him.

As the night drew on, the wind rose higher, the
clouds became thicker and darker, the branches crashed
to the earth, the tempest rushed along bearing everything before it. The owls, alarmed for their safety,
hid in the hollow trees, or retired to their barns;
the bats retreated into the crevices of the tiles;

nothing was abroad but the wildfowl, whose cries occasionally resounded overhead. Now and then, the fall of some branch into a hawthorn bush frightened the sleeping thrushes and blackbirds, who flew forth into the darkness, not knowing whither they were going. The rabbits crouched on the sheltered side of the hedges, and then went back into their holes. The larks cowered closer to the earth.

Ruin and destruction raged around: in Choo Hoo's camp the ash poles beat against each other, oaks were rent, and his vast army knew no sleep that night. Whirled about by the fearful gusts, the dying hawk, suspended from the trap, no longer fluttered, but swung unconscious to and fro. The feathers of the murdered thrush were scattered afar, and the leaves torn from the boughs went sweeping after them. Alone in the scene the Fox raced along, something of the wildness of the night entered into him; he tried, by putting forth his utmost speed, to throw off the sense of ignominy.

In the darkness, and in his distress of mind, he neither knew nor cared whither he was going. He passed the shore of the Longpond, and heard the waves dashing on the stones, and felt the spray driven far up on the sward. He passed the miserable hawk. He ran like the wind by the camp of Choo Hoo, and heard the hum of the army, unable to sleep. Weary, at last, he sought for some spot into which to drag his limbs, and crept along a mound which, although he did not recognise it in his stupefied state of mind, was really not far from where he had started. As he was creeping along he fancied he heard a voice which came from the ground beneath his feet; it sounded so strange in the darkness that he started and stayed to listen.

He heard it again, but though he thought he knew the voices of all the residents in the field, he could not tell who it was, nor whence it came. But after a time he found that it proceeded from the lower part or butt of an elm tree. This tree was very large, and seemed perfectly sound, but it seems there was a crack in it, whether caused by lightning or not he did not know, which did not show at ordinary times. But when the wind blew extremely strong as it did to-night, the tree leant over before the blast, and thus opened the crack. The Fox, listening at the crack, heard the voice lamenting the long years that had passed, the darkness and the dreary time, and imploring every species of vengeance upon the head of the cruel king Kapchack.

After a while the Fox came to the conclusion that this must be the toad who, very many years ago, for some offence committed against the state, was imprisoned by Kapchack's orders in the butt of an elm, there to remain till the end of the world. Curious to know why the toad had been punished in this terrible manner, the Fox resolved to speak to the prisoner, from whom perhaps he might learn something to Kapchack's disadvantage. Waiting, therefore, till the crack opened as the gust came, the Fox spoke into it, and the toad, only too delighted to get some one to talk to at last, replied directly.

But the chink was so small that his voice was scarcely audible; the chink, too, only opened for a second or two during the savage puffs of the gale, and then closed again, so that connected conversation was not possible, and all the Fox heard was that the toad had some very important things to say. Anxious to learn these things, the Fox tried his hardest to discover some way of communicating with the toad, and at last he hit upon a plan. He looked round till he found a little bit of flint, which he picked up, and when the elm bent over before the gale, and the chink opened, he pushed the splinter of flint into the crevice.

Then he found another piece of flint just a trifle larger, and, watching his opportunity, thrust it in. This he did three or four times, each time putting in a larger wedge, till there was a crack sufficiently open to allow him to talk to the toad easily. The toad said that this was the first time he had spoken to anybody since his grandson, who lived in the rhubarb patch, came to exchange a word with him before the butt of the tree grew quite round him.

But though the Fox plied him with questions, and persuaded him in every way, he would not reveal the reason why he was imprisoned, except that he had unluckily seen Kapchack do something. He dared not say what it was, because if he did he had no doubt he would be immediately put to death, and although life in the tree was no more than a living death, still it was life, and he had this consolation, that through being debarred from

all exercise and work, and compelled to exist without
eating or drinking, notwithstanding the time passed
and the years went by, still he did not grow any
older. He was as young now as when he was first
put into the dungeon, and if he could once get out,
he felt that he should soon recover the use of his
limbs, and should crawl about and enjoy himself
when his grandson who lived in the rhubarb patch,
and who was already very old and warty, was
dead.

Indeed by being thus shut up he should survive
every other toad, and he hoped some day to get out,
because although he had been condemned to im-
prisonment till the end of the world, that was only
Kapchack's vain-glorious way of pronouncing sentence,
as if his (Kapchack's) authority was going to endure
for ever, which was quite contrary to history and the
teachings of philosophy. So far from that he did
not believe himself that Kapchack's dynasty was
fated to endure very long, for since he had been
a prisoner immured in the earth, he had heard many
strange things whispered along underground, and
among them a saying about Kapchack. Besides
which he knew that the elm tree could not exist for

ever; already there was a crack in it, which in time would split further up; the elm had reached its prime, and was beginning to decay within. By-and-by it would be blown over, and then the farmer would have the butt grubbed up, and split for firewood, and he should escape. It was true it might be many years hence, perhaps a century, but that did not matter in the least—time was nothing to him now—and he knew he should emerge as young as when he went in.

This was the reason why he so carefully kept the secret of what he had seen, so as to preserve his life; nor could the Fox by any persuasion prevail upon him to disclose the matter.

"But at least," said the Fox, " at least tell me the saying you have heard underground about king Kapchack."

" I am afraid to do so," said the toad; "for having already suffered so much I dread the infliction of further misery."

"If you will tell me," said the Fox, "I will do my very best to get you out. I will keep putting in wedges till the tree splits wide open, so that you may crawl up the chink."

"Will you," said the toad, excited at the hope of liberty, "will you really do that?"

"Yes, that I will," said the Fox, "wait an instant, and I will fetch another flint."

So he brought another flint, which split the tree so much, that the toad felt the fresh air come down to him. "And you really will do it?" he said.

"Yes," repeated the Fox, "I will certainly let you out."

"Then," said the toad, "the saying I have heard underground is this: 'When the hare hunts the hunter in the dead day, the hours of king Kapchack are numbered.' It is a curious and a difficult saying, for I cannot myself understand how the day could be dead, nor how the hare could chase the sportsman; but you, who have so high a reputation for sagacity, can no doubt in time interpret it. Now put in some more wedges and help me out."

But the Fox having learnt all that the toad could tell him, went away, and finding the osiers, curled himself up to sleep.

The same night, the Weasel, having had a very pleasant nap upon his divan in the elm in the Squirrel's copse, woke up soon after midnight, and started for

the farm, in order to enjoy the pleasure of seeing the
Rat in the gin, which he had instructed Bevis how to
set up. Had it not been for this he would not have
faced so terrible a tempest, but to see the Rat in torture he would have gone through anything. As he
crept along a furrow, not far outside the copse, choosing
that route that he might be somewhat sheltered in the
hollow from the wind, he saw a wire which a poacher
had set up, and stayed to consider how he could turn
it to his advantage.

"There is Ulu, the Hare," he said to himself,
"who lives in the wheat-field; I had her son, he was
very sweet and tender, and also her nephew, who was
not so juicy, and I have noticed that she has got very
plump of late. She is up on the hill to-night I have
no doubt, notwithstanding the tempest, dancing and
flirting with her disreputable companions, for vice has
such an attraction for some minds that they cannot
forego its pleasures, even at the utmost personal inconvenience. Such revels, at such a time of tempest, while
the wrath of Heaven is wreaked upon the trees, are
nothing short of sacrilege, and I for one have always
set my mind against irreverence. I shall do the
world a service if I rid it of such an abandoned

creature." So he called to a moorhen, who was flying over from the Longpond at a tremendous pace, being carried before the wind, and the moorhen, not without a great deal of trouble, managed to wheel round (she was never very clever with her wings) to receive his commands, for she did not dare to pass over, or slight so high a personage.

"Moorhen," said the Weasel; "do you go dirèct to the hills and find Ulu, the Hare, and tell her that little Sir Bevis, of whom she is so fond, is lost in the copse, and that he is crying bitterly because of the darkness and the wind, and what will become of him I do not know. I have done my very best to show him the way home, but he cherishes an unfortunate prejudice against me, and will not listen to what I say. Therefore if the Hare does not come immediately and show him the way I greatly fear that he will be knocked down by the branches, or cry his dear pretty darling heart out; and tell her that he is at this minute close to the birches. Go quickly, moorhen."

"I will, my lord," said the moorhen, and away she flew.

Then the Weasel proceeded on his way, and shortly afterwards arrived at the farm. As he came

quietly down from the rick-yard, he said to himself, "I will keep a good way from the wall, as
it is so dark, and I do not know the exact place
where Bevis has put the trap. Besides, it is just
possible that the Rat may not yet have passed that
way, for he does most of his business in the early
morning, and it is not yet dawn."

So he crossed over to the wood-pile and listened
carefully, but could hear no groans, as he had expected; but on consideration, he put this down to
the wind, which he observed blew the sound away
from him. He then slipped over to the grass by
the cart-house wall, intending to listen at the mouth
of the drain to hear if the Rat was within, and
then if that was not the case, to go on along
towards the wall of the pigstye, for he began to
think the Rat must have been stunned by the trap,
and so could not squeak.

If that was the case, he thought he would just
bite off the end of the Rat's tail, in revenge for
the terrible meal he had once been obliged to make
upon his own, and also to wake up the Rat to the
misery of his position. But just as he approached
the mouth of the drain, sniffing and listening with

the utmost caution, it happened that a drop of
rain fell through a chink in the top of Pan's tub,
and woke him from his slumber. Pan shook himself and turned round, and the Weasel, hearing the
disturbance, dreaded lest Pan was loose, and had
caught scent of him. He darted forwards to get
into the drain, when the trap, which the Bailiff had
so carefully removed from where Bevis had set
it, snapped him up in a second. The shock and
the pain made him faint; he turned over and lay
still.

About the same time the moorhen, borne swiftly
along by the wind on her way to the river, reached
the hills, and seeing the Hare, flew low down and
delivered the Weasel's message as well as she could.
The Hare was dreadfully alarmed about Sir Bevis,
and anxious to relieve him from his fright in the
dark copse, raced down the hill, and over the fields
as fast as she could go, making towards that part
of the copse where the birches stood, as the Weasel
had directed, knowing that in running there she
would find her neck in a noose.

It happened just as he had foreseen. She came
along as fast as the wind, and could already see

the copse like a thicker darkness before her, when the loop of the wire drew up around her neck, and over she rolled in the furrow.

Now the Weasel had hoped that the wire would not hang her at once. He intended to have come back from the farm, and from taunting the Rat in the trap, in time to put his teeth into her veins, before, in her convulsive efforts to get free, she tightened the noose and died.

And this, too, happened exactly as the Weasel had intended, but in a different manner, and with a different result; for it had chanced that the wind, in the course of its ravages among the trees, snapped off a twig of ash, which rolling over and over before the blast along the sward, came against the stick which upheld the wire, and the end of the twig where it had broken from the tree lodged in the loop. Thus, when Ulu kicked, and struggled, and screamed, in her fear, the noose indeed drew up tight and half-strangled her, but not quite, because the little piece of wood prevented it. But, exhausted with pain and terror, and partially choked, the poor Hare at last could do nothing else but crouch down in the furrow, where the rain fell on and soaked her warm coat of fur. For as the dawn came on the wind sunk, and the rain fell.

In this unhappy plight she passed the rest of the night, dreading every moment lest the Fox should come along (as she could not run away), and not less afraid of the daybreak, when some one would certainly find her.

After many weary hours, the Bailiff coming to his work in the morning with a sack over his shoulders to keep out the rain, saw something on the grass, and pounced upon the wretched Hare. Already his great thumb was against the back of her neck—already she was thrown across his knee —already she felt her sinews stretch, as he proceeded to break her neck, regardless of her shrieks —when suddenly it occurred to him how delighted Bevis would be with a living Hare. For the Bailiff was very fond of Bevis, and would have done anything to please him. So he took the Hare in his arms, and carried her down to the farm.

When Bevis got up and came to breakfast, the Bailiff came in and brought him the Hare, expecting that he would be highly pleased. But Bevis in an

instant recognised his friend who had shown him
his way in the cowslips, and flew into a rage, and
beat the Bailiff with his fist for his cruelty. Nothing
would satisfy him but he must let the Hare go
free before he touched his breakfast. He would not
sit down, he stamped and made such a to-do that
at last they let him have his own way.

He would not even allow the Bailiff to carry
the Hare for him; he took her in his arms and
went with her up the footpath into the field. He
would not even permit them to follow him. Now,
the Hare knew him very well but could not speak
when any one else was near, for it is very well
known to be a law among hares and birds, and
such creatures, that they can only talk to one
human being, and are dumb when more than one
are present. But when Bevis had taken her out
into the footpath, and set her down, and stroked
her back, and her long ears, black at the tip, and
had told her to go straight up the footpath, and
not through the long grass, because it was wet with
the rain, the Hare told him how she came in the
wire through the wicked Weasel telling her that he
was lost in the copse.

"I was not lost," said Bevis; "I went to bed, and saw the Owl go by. The Weasel told another of his stories—now, I remember, he told me to set the trap for the Rat."

"Did he?" said the Hare, "then you may depend it is some more of his dreadful wickedness; there will be no peace in the world while he is allowed to go roaming about."

"No," said Bevis, "that there will not: but as sure as my papa's gun, which is the best gun in the country, as sure as my papa's gun I will kill him the next time I see him. I will not listen to the Squirrel, I will cut the Weasel's tree down, and chop off his head."

"I hope you will, dear," said the Hare. "But now I must be gone, for I can hear Pan barking, and no doubt he can smell me, besides which, it is broad daylight, and I must go and hide; good-bye, my dear Sir Bevis." And away went the Hare up the footpath till Bevis lost sight of her through the gateway.

Then he went to his breakfast, and directly afterwards, putting on his great coat, for it still rained a little, he went up to the wall by the pigstye expecting to find the Rat in the trap. But the trap was gone.

"There now," said he, falling into another rage, twice already that morning; "I do believe that stupid Bailiff has moved it," and so the Bailiff trying to please him fell twice into disgrace in an hour.

Looking about to see where the Bailiff had put the trap, he remembered what the Weasel had told him, and going to the carthouse-wall by the drain, found the trap and the Weasel in it: "Oh! you false and treacherous creature!" said Bevis, picking up a stone, "now I will smash you into seventy thousand little pieces," and he flung the stone with all his might, but being in too much of a hurry (as the snail had warned him) it missed the mark, and only knocked a bit of mortar out of the wall. He looked round for a bigger one, so that he might crush the wretch this time, when the Weasel feebly lifted his head, and said, "Bevis! Bevis! It is not generous of you to bear such malice towards me now I am dying; you should rather —— "

"Hold your tongue, horrid thing," said Bevis, "I will not listen to anything you have to say. Here is a brick, this will do, first-rate, to pound you

with, and now I think of it, I will come a little
nearer so as to make quite sure."

"Oh, Bevis!" said the Weasel with a gasp,
"I shall be dead in a minute," and Bevis saw his
head fall back.

"Tell the Hare I repented," said the Weasel.
"I have been very wicked, Bevis—oh!—But I shall
never, never do it any more—oh!"—

"Are you dead?" said Bevis. "Are you quite
dead?" putting down the brick, for he could not
bear to see anything in such distress, and his rage
was over in a minute.

"I am," said the Weasel, "at least I shall be
in half-a-minute, for I must be particular to tell
the exact truth in this extremity. Oh! there is
one thing I should like to say—"

"What is it?" said Bevis.

"But if you smash me I can't," said the Weasel,
"and what is the use of smashing me, for all my
bones are broken."

"I will not smash you," said Bevis, "I will
only have you nailed up to the stable door so that
everybody may see what a wretch you were."

"Thank you," said the Weasel very gratefully,

"will you please tell the Hare and all of them that if I could only live I would do everything I could to make up to them for all the wickedness I have committed—Oh!—I have not got time to say all I would. Oh! Bevis, Bevis!"

"Yes, poor thing," said Bevis, now quite melted and sorry for the wretched criminal, whose life was ebbing so fast, "what is it you want? I will be sure to do it."

"Then, dear Sir Bevis—how kind it is of you to forgive me, dear Sir Bevis; when I am dead do not nail me to the door—only think how terrible that would be—bury me dear."

"So I will," said Bevis; "but perhaps you needn't die. Stay a little while, and let us see if you cannot live."

"Oh, no," said the Weasel, "my time is come. But when I am dead, dear, please take me out of this cruel trap in which I am so justly caught, as I set it for another; take me out of this cruel trap which has broken my ribs, and lay me flat on the grass, and pull my limbs out straight, so that I may not stiffen all in a heap and crooked. Then get your spade, my dear Sir Bevis, and dig a hole and bury me, and put a stone on top of me, so that Pan cannot scratch me up—Oh! Oh!—will you—Oh!"

"Yes, indeed I will. I will dig the hole—I have a capital spade," said Bevis; "stay a minute."

But the Weasel gave three gasps and fell back quite dead. Bevis looked at him a little while, and then put his foot on the spring and pressed it down and took the Weasel out. He stroked down his fur where the trap had ruffled it, and rubbed the earth from his poor paws with which he had struggled to get free, and then having chosen a spot close by the woodpile, where the ground was soft, to dig the hole, he put the Weasel down there, and pulled his limbs out straight, and so disposed him for the last sad ceremony. He then ran to the summer-house, which was not far, and having found the spade came back with it to the wood-pile. But the Weasel was gone.

There was the trap; there was the place he had chosen—all the little twigs and leaves brushed away ready for digging—but no Weasel. He was bewildered, when a robin perched on the top of the wood-pile, put his head on one side, and said so softly and sadly—"Bevis, Bevis, little Sir Bevis, what have you done?" For the Weasel was not dead, and was not even very

seriously injured; the trap was old, and the spring
not very strong, and the teeth did not quite meet. If
the Rat, who was fat, had got in, it would have pinched
him dreadfully, but the Weasel was extremely thin,
and so he escaped with a broken rib—the only true
thing he had said.

So soon as ever Sir Bevis's back was turned, the
Weasel crawled under the wood-pile, just as he had
done once before, and from there made his way as
quickly as he could up the field sheltered by the after-
math, which had now grown long again. When
Bevis understood that the Weasel had only shammed
dying, and had really got away, he burst into tears,
for he could not bear to be cheated, and then threw
his spade at the robin.

CHAPTER IV.

THE OLD OAK.—THE KING'S DESPAIR.

THE very same morning, after the rain had ceased, the keeper who looked after the great woods at the other end of the Longpond, set out with his gun and his dogs to walk round the preserves. Now the dogs he took with him were the very best dogs he had, for that night a young gentleman, who had just succeeded to the estate, was coming down from London, and on the following morning would be sure to go out shooting. This young gentleman had unexpectedly come into the property through the death of the owner, who was shot in his bedroom by a burglar. The robber had once been his groom, and the Squirrel told Bevis how it all happened through a flint falling out of the hole in the bottom of the waggon which belonged to the old farmer in whose orchard Kapchack had his palace.

The heir had been kept at a distance during the old gentleman's lifetime, for the old gentleman always

meant to marry and have a son, but did not do so,
and also always meant to make a will and leave the
best part of his estate to somebody else, but he did
not do so, and as the old Toad in the rhubarb patch
told Bevis afterwards when he heard the story, if you
are only going to do a thing, it would be no use if
you lived a thousand years, it would always be just
the same. So the young fellow who had been poor
all his life, when he thus suddenly jumped into such
a property, was not a little elated, and wrote to the
keeper that he should come down and have some
shooting.

The keeper was rather alarmed at this, for the
former owner was not a sporting man, and did not
look strictly after such things, so that the game had
been neglected and had got scarce, and what was
worse the dogs were out of training. He therefore
got up early that morning, intending to go his rounds
quickly, and then take the dogs out into the stubble,
and try and thrash them into some use. Presently, as
he walked along, he came to the glade in the woods,
and saw the dead hawk hanging from the trap up
in the old oak tree. Pleased to find that his trap, so
cunningly placed, had not been prepared in vain, he

went up to the oak, leaned his gun against the trunk,
ordered the dogs to lie down (which they did with
some reluctance), and then climbed up into the tree
to re-set the gin.

He took the hawk from the trap (his feathers were
all draggled and wet from the rain), and threw the dead
bird down; and, whether it was that the act of
throwing it caused an extra strain upon the bough,
or whether the storm had cracked it in the night,
or whether it had rotted away more than appeared
on the surface, or whether it was all of these
things together, certain it is the bough broke, and
down came the keeper thud on the sward. The
bough fell down with him, and as it fell it struck
the gun, and the gun exploded, and although the
dogs scampered aside when they heard the crack,
they did not scamper so quick but one of them
was shot dead, and the other two were mortally
wounded.

For a while the keeper lay there stunned, with
the wet grass against his face. But by-and-by,
coming to himself, he sat up with difficulty, and
called for assistance, for he could not move, having
sprained one ankle, and broken the small bone of

the other leg. There he sat and shouted, but no
one came for some time, till presently a slouching
labourer (it was the very same who put up the
wire by the copse in which the Hare was caught)
chanced to pass by outside the wood. The keeper
saw him, but hoarse with shouting, and feeling
faint too (for a sprained ankle is extremely painful),
he could not make him hear. But he bethought
him of his gun, and dragging it to him, hastily
put in a cartridge and fired.

The report drew the labourer's attention, and
peering into the wood, he saw some one on the
ground waving a white handkerchief. After looking
a long time, he made up his mind to go and see
what it was ; but then he recollected that if he
put his foot inside the wood he should be tres-
passing, and as he had got a wire in his pocket that
would be a serious matter. So he altered his mind,
and went on.

Very likely the keeper was angry, but there
was no one to hear what he said except the dead
hawk. He would have fired off fifty cartridges if
he had had them, but as he did not like a weight
to carry he had only two or three, and these did

not attract attention. As for the labourer, about midday, when he sat down to lunch in the cart-house at the farm where he worked with the other men, he did just mention that he thought he had seen something white waving in the wood, and they said it was odd, but very likely nothing to speak of.

One of the wounded dogs ran home, bleeding all the way, and there crept into his kennel and died; the other could not get so far, but dropped in a hedge. The keeper's wife wondered why he did not come home to dinner, but supposed, with a sigh, that he had looked in at the alehouse, and went on with her work.

The keeper shouted again when his throat got less hoarse, but all the answer he obtained was the echo from the wood. He tried to crawl, but the pain was so exquisite he got but a very little way, and there he had to lie. The sun rose higher and shone out as the clouds rolled away, and the rain-drops on the grass glistened bright till presently they dried up.

With the gleaming of the sun there was motion in the woods : blackbirds came forth and crossed

the glades; thrushes flew past; a jay fluttered round
the tops of the firs; after a while a pheasant came
along the verge of the underwood, now stepping
out into the grass, and now back again into the
bushes. There was a pleasant cawing of rooks, and
several small parties of wood-pigeons (doubtless from
Choo Hoo's camp) went over. Two or three rabbits
hopped out and fed; humble-bees went buzzing by;
a green woodpecker flashed across the glade and disappeared among the trees as if an arrow had been
shot into the wood.

The slow hours went on, and as the sun grew
hotter the keeper, unable to move, began to suffer
from the fierceness of the rays, for anything still
finds out the heat more than that which is in
movement. First he lifted his hat from time to
time above his head, but it was not much relief,
as the wind had fallen. Next he tried placing his
handkerchief inside his hat. At last he took off
his coat, stuck the barrels of his gun into the
ground (soft from the rain), and hung the coat
upon it. This gave him a little shadow. The dead
oak-tree having no leaves cast but a narrow shade,
and that fell on the opposite side to where he was.

In the afternoon, when the heat was very great, and all the other birds appeared to have gone, a crow came (one of Kauc's retainers) and perched low down on an ash-tree not more than fifty yards away. Perhaps it was the dead dog; perhaps it was the knowledge that the man was helpless, that brought him. There he perched, and the keeper reviled him, wishing that he had but saved one of his cartridges, and forgetting that even then the barrels of his gun were too full of earth. After a while the crow flew idly across to the other side of the glade, and went out of sight; but it was only for a short time, and presently he came back again. This the crow did several times, always returning to the ash.

The keeper ran over in his mind the people who would probably miss him, and cause a search to be made. First there was his wife; but once, when he had been a long time from home, and she in a great alarm had sought for him, she found him drunk at the alehouse, and he beat her for her trouble. It was not likely that she would come. The lad who acted as his assistant (he had but one, for as previously stated, the former owner did not shoot)

was not likely to look for him either, for not long
since, bringing a message to his superior, he discovered him selling some game, and was knocked
down for his pains. As for his companions at the
alehouse, they would be all out in the fields, and
would not assemble till night: several of them he
knew were poachers, and though glad enough to
share his beer would not have looked towards him if
in distress.

The slow hours wore on, and the sun declining
a little, the shadow of the dead oak moved round,
and together with his coat, sheltered him fairly well.
Weary with the unwonted labour of thinking, the
tension of his mind began to yield, and by and by
he dropped asleep, lying at full length upon his
back. The crow returned once more to the ash, and
looked at the sleeping man and the dead dog, cleaned
his beak against the bough, and uttered a low croak.
Once he flew a little way out towards them, but
there was the gun: it was true he knew very well
there was no powder (for, in the first place, he could
not smell any, and secondly, if there had been any,
he knew he should have had the shot singing about his
ears long before this; you see, he could put two and

two together), still there was the gun. The dog does not like the corner where the walking-stick stands. The crow did not like the gun, though it was stuck in the ground: he went back to the ash, cleaned his bill, and waited.

Something came stealthily through the grass, now stopping, now advancing with a creeping evil motion. It was the Weasel. When he stole away from the wood-pile, after escaping from the trap, he made up the field towards the copse, but upon reflection he determined to abandon his lair in the hollow elm, for he had so abused Bevis's good-nature that he doubted whether Bevis might not attack him even there despite the Squirrel. He did not know exactly where to go, knowing that every creature was in secret his enemy, and in his wounded state, unable to move quickly or properly defend himself, he dreaded to trust himself near them. After a while he remembered the old dead oak, which was also hollow within, and which was so far from the copse it was not probable Bevis would find it.

Thither he bent his painful steps, for his broken rib hurt him very much, and after many pauses to rest, presently, in the afternoon, he came near.

Lifting his head above the grass he saw the dead dog, and the sleeping keeper; he watched them a long time, and seeing that neither of them moved he advanced closer. As he approached he saw the dead hawk, and recognised one of Ki Ki's retainers; then coming to the dog the blood from the shot wounds excited his terrible thirst. But it had ceased to flow; he sniffed at it and then went towards the man.

The crow envious, but afraid to join the venture, watched him from the ash. Every few inches the Weasel stayed, lifted his head; looked, and listened. Then he advanced again, paused, and again approached. In five minutes he had reached the keeper's feet; two minutes more and he was by his waist. He listened again; he sniffed, he knew it was dangerous, but he could not check the resistless prompting of his appetite.

He crept up on the keeper's chest; the crow fidgetted on the ash. He crept up to the necktie; the crow came down on a lower bough. He moved yet another inch to the collar; the crow flew out ten yards and settled on the ground. The collar was stiff, and partly covered that part of the neck which fascinated the Weasel's gaze. He put his foot softly on the collar; the crow hopped thrice towards them. He brought up his other foot, he sniffed—the breath came warm from the man's half-open lips—he adventured the risk, and placed his paw on the keeper's neck.

Instantly—as if he had received an electric shock—the keeper started to his knees, shuddering; the Weasel dropped from his neck upon the ground, the crow hastened back to the ash. With a blow of his open hand the keeper knocked the Weasel yards away; then, in his rage and fear, with whitened face, he wished instead he had beaten the creature down upon the earth, for, the Weasel, despite the grinding of his broken rib, began to crawl off, and he could not reach him.

He looked round for a stick or stone, there was none; he put his hand in his pocket, but his knife had slipped out when he fell from the tree. He passed his hands over his waistcoat seeking for something, felt his watch—a heavy silver one—and in his fury snatched it from the swivel, and hurled it at the Weasel. The watch thrown with such force missed the Weasel, struck the sward, and

bounded up against the oak: the glass shivered and
flew sparkling a second in the sunshine; the watch
glanced aside, and dropped in the grass. When
he looked again the Weasel had gone. It was
an hour before the keeper recovered himself—the
shuddering terror with which he woke up haunted him
in the broad daylight.

An intolerable thirst now tormented him, but
the furrow was dry. In the morning, he remembered it had contained a little water from the rain,
which during the day had sunk into the earth.
He picked a bennet from the grass and bit it, but
it was sapless, dried by the summer heat. He
looked for a leaf of sorrel, but there was none.
The slow hours wore on; the sun sank below the
wood, and the long shadows stretched out. By-and-
by the grass became cooler to the touch; dew
was forming upon it. Overhead the rooks streamed
homewards to their roosting trees. They cawed incessantly as they flew; they were talking about
Kapchack and Choo Hoo, but he did not understand them.

The shadows reached across the glade, and yonder
the rabbits appeared again from among the bushes

where their burrows were. He began now to seriously think that he should have to pass the night
there. His ankle was swollen, and the pain almost
beyond endurance. The slightest attempt at motion
caused intense agony. His one hope now was that
the same slouching labourer who had passed in the
morning would go back that way at night; but
as the shadows deepened that hope departed, and he
doubted too whether any one could see him through
the underwood in the dark. The slouching labourer
purposely avoided that route home. He did not
want to see anything, if anything there was.

He went round by the high road, and having
had his supper, and given his wife a clout in the
head, he sauntered down to the alehouse. After he
had taken three quarts of beer, he mentioned the
curious incident of the white handkerchief in the
wood to his mates, who congratulated him on his
sense in refraining from going near it, as most
likely it was one of that keeper's tricks, just to
get somebody into the wood. More talk, and more
beer. By-and-by the keeper's wife began to feel
alarmed. She had already found the dead dog in
the kennel; but that did not surprise her in the

least, knowing her husband's temper, and that if a dog disobeyed, it was not at all unusual for a cartridge to go whistling after him.

But when the evening came, and the darkness fell; when she had gone down to the alehouse, braving his wrath, and found that he was not there, the woman began to get hysterical. The lad who acted as assistant had gone home, so she went out into the nearest stubble herself, thinking that her husband must have finished his round before lunch, and was somewhere in the newly-reaped fields. But after walking about the rustling stubble till she was weary, she came back to the alehouse, and begged the men to tell her if they had seen anything of him. Then they told her about the white handkerchief which the slouching poacher had seen in the wood that morning. She turned on him like a tiger, and fiercely upbraided him; then rushed from the house. The sloucher took up his quart, and said that he saw "no call" to hurry.

But some of the men went after the wife. The keeper was found, and brought home on a cart, but not before he had seen the owl go by, and the dark speck of the bat passing to and fro over head.

All that day Bevis did not go to the copse, being much upset with the cheat the Weasel had played him, and also because they said the grass and the hedges would be so wet after the storm. Nor did anything take place in the copse, for king Kapchack moped in his fortress, the orchard, the whole day long, so greatly was he depressed by the wide-spread treason of which the Owl had informed him.

Choo Hoo, thinking that the treaty was concluded, relaxed the strictness of discipline, and permitted his army to spread abroad from the camp and forage for themselves. He expected the return of the ambassador with further communications, and ordered search to be made for every dainty for his entertainment; while the thrush, for whom this care was taken, had not only ceased to exist, but it would have been impossible to collect his feathers, blown away to every quarter.

The vast horde of barbarians were the more pleased with the liberty accorded to them, because they had spent so ill a night while the gale raged through their camp. So soon as the sun began to gleam through the retreating clouds, they went forth in small parties, many of which the keeper saw go over him while lying helpless by the dead oak-tree.

King Kapchack, after the Owl had informed him of the bewildering maze of treason with which he was surrounded, moped, as has been said before, upon his perch. In the morning, wet and draggled from the storm, his feathers out of place, and without the spirit to arrange them, he seemed to have grown twenty years older in one night, so pitiable did he appear. Nor did the glowing sun, which filled all other hearts with joy, reach his gloomy soul. He saw no resource ; no enterprise suggested itself to him ; all was dark at noonday.

An ominous accident which had befallen the aged apple-tree in which his palace stood contributed to this depression of mind. The gale had cracked a very large bough, which, having shown signs of weakness, had for many years been supported by a prop carefully put up by the farmer. But whether the prop in course of time had decayed at the line where the air and earth exercise their corroding influence upon wood; or whether the bough had stiffened with age, and could not swing easily to

the wind; or whether, as seems most likely, the
event occurred at that juncture in order to indicate
the course of fate, it is certain that the huge
bough was torn partly away from the trunk, leaving
a gaping cavity.

Kapchack viewed this injury to the tree, which
had so long sustained his family and fortune, with
the utmost concern; it seemed an omen of approaching destruction so plain and unmistakeable that he
could not look at it; he turned his mournful gaze
in the opposite direction. The day passed slowly,
as slowly as it did to the keeper lying beneath the
oak, and the king, though he would have resented
intrusion with the sharpest language, noticed with
an increasing sense of wrong that the court was
deserted, and, with one exception, none called to
pay their respects.

The exception was Eric, the favourite missel-
thrush, who alone of all the larger birds was allowed
to frequent the same orchard. The missel-thrush,
loyal to the last, came, but seeing Kapchack's condition, did not endeavour to enter into conversation.
As for the rest, they did not venture from fear of
the king's violent temper, and because their unquiet

consciences made them suspect that this unusual depression was caused by the discovery of their treachery. They remained away from dread of his anger. Kapchack, on the other hand, put their absence down to the mean and contemptible desire to avoid a falling house. He observed that even the little Te-te, the tomtit, and chief of the secret police, who invariably came twice or thrice a day with an account of some gossip he had overheard, did not arrive. How low he must have fallen, since the common informers disdained to associate with him!

Towards the evening he sent for his son, Prince Tchack-tchack, with the intention of abdicating in his favour, but what were his feelings when the messenger returned without him! Tchack-tchack refused to come. He, too, had turned away. Thus, deserted by the lovely La Schach, for whom he had risked his throne; deserted by the whole court and even by his own son; the monarch welcomed the darkness of the night, the second of his misery, which hid his disgrace from the world.

The Owl came, faithful by night as the Missel-thrush by day, but Kapchack, in the deepest despondency, could not reply to his remarks. Twice the Owl came back, hoping to find his master somewhat more open to consolation, and twice had to depart unsuccessful. At last, about midnight, the king, worn out with grief, fell asleep.

Now the same evening the Hare, who was upon the hills as usual, as she came by a barn overheard some bats who lived there conversing about the news which they had learnt from their relations who resided in the woods of the vale. This was nothing less than the revelations the dying hawk had made of the treacherous designs of Ki Ki and the Weasel, which, as the Owl had suspected, had been partly overheard by the bats. The Hare, in other circumstances, would have rejoiced at the overthrow of king Kapchack, who was no favourite with her race, for he had, once or twice, out of wanton cruelty, pecked weakly leverets to death, just to try the temper of his bill. But she dreaded lest if he were thrust down the Weasel should seize the sovereignty, the Weasel, who had already done her so much injury, and was capable of ruining not only herself but her whole nation if once he got the supreme power.

Not knowing what to do herself for the best, away she went down the valley and over the steep ridges in search of a very old hare, quite hoar with age—an astrologer of great reputation in those parts. For the hares have always been good star-gazers, and the whole race of them, one and all, are not without skill in the mystic sciences, while some are highly charged with knowledge of futurity, and have decided the fate of mighty battles by the mere direction in which they scampered. The old hare no sooner heard her information than he proceeded to consult the stars, which shone with exceeding brilliance that night, as they often do when the air has been cleared by a storm, and finding, upon taking accurate observations, that the house of Jupiter was threatened by the approach of Saturn to the meridian, he had no difficulty in pronouncing the present time as full of danger and big with fate.

The planets were clearly in combination against king Kapchack, who must, if he desired to avoid extinction, avoid all risks, and hide his head, as it were, in a corner till the aspect of the heavens changed. Above all things let him not make war or go forth himself into the combat; let him conclude peace, or at least enter into a truce, no matter at what loss of dignity, or how much territory he had to concede to conciliate Choo Hoo. His person was threatened, the knife was pointed at his heart, could he but wait awhile, and tide as it were over the shallows, he might yet resume the full sway of power; but if he exposed his life at this crisis the whole fabric of his kingdom might crumble beneath his feet.

Having thus spoken, the hoary astrologer went off in the direction of Stonehenge, whose stones formed his astrolabe, and the Hare, much excited with the communication she had received (confirmed as it was to by the facts of the case) resolved to at once warn the monarch of his danger. Calling a beetle, she charged him with a message to the king:—That he should listen to the voice of the stars, and conclude peace at no matter what cost, or at least a truce, submitting to be deprived of territory, or treasure to any amount or extent, and that above all things he should not venture forth personally to the combat. If he hearkened he would yet reign; if he closed his ears the evil influence which then threatened him must have its way. Strictly enjoining the beetle to make haste, and turn neither to the right nor the left, but to speed straight away for the palace, she dismissed him.

The beetle, much pleased to be employed upon so important a business, opened his wing-cases, began to hum, and increasing his pace as he went, flew off at his utmost velocity. He passed safely over the hills, descended into the valley, sped across the fields and woods, and in an incredibly short space of time, approached the goal of his journey. The wall of the orchard was in sight, he began to repeat his message to himself, so as to be sure and not miss a word of it, when going at this tremendous pace, and as usual, without looking in front, but blundering onwards, he flew with his whole force against a post. His body, crushed by the impetus of its own weight, rebounded with a snop, and he fell disabled and insensible to the earth.

CHAPTER V.

THE COURTSHIP IN THE ORCHARD.

THE next morning Bevis's papa looking at the almanac found there was going to be an eclipse of the sun, so Bevis took a piece of glass (part of one of the many window panes he had broken) and smoked it over a candle, so as to be able to watch the phenomenon without injury to his eyes. When the obscuration began too, the dairymaid brought him a bucket of clear water in which the sun was reflected and could be distinctly seen. But before the eclipse had proceeded beyond the mere edge of the sun, Bevis heard the champing of a bit, and the impatient pawing of hoofs, and running up to the stable to see who it was, found that his papa was just on the point of driving over in the dog-cart to see another farmer (the very old gentleman in whose orchard Kapchack's palace was situated) about a load of straw.

Bevis of course insisted upon going too, the smoked glass was thrown aside, he clambered up and held the reins, and away they went, the eclipse now counting for nothing. After a while, however, as they went swiftly along the road, they came to a hill, and from the summit saw a long way off a vast shadow like that cast by some immense cloud which came towards them over the earth, and in a second or two arrived, and as it were, put out the light. They looked up and the sun was almost gone. In its place was a dark body with a rim of light round it, and flames shooting forth.

As they came slowly down the hill a pheasant crowed as he flew up to roost, the little birds retired to the thickets, and at the farmyards they passed the fowls went up to their perches. Presently they left the highway and drove along a lane across the fields, which had once been divided from each other by gates. Of these there was nothing now standing but the posts, some of which could hardly be said to stand, but declining from the perpendicular, were only kept from falling by the bushes. The lane was so rough and so bad from want of mending that they could only walk the impatient horse, and at times the jolting was extremely unpleasant.

Sometimes they had to stoop down in the trap

to pass under the drooping boughs of elms and other trees, which not having been cut for years, hung over and almost blocked the track. From the hedges the brambles and briars extended out into the road, so that the wheels of the dog-cart brushed them, and they would evidently have entirely shut up the way had not waggons occasionally gone through and crushed their runners. The meadows on either hand were brown with grass that had not been mown, though the time for mowing had long since gone by, while the pastures were thick with rushes and thistles. Though so extensive there were only two or three cows in them, and these old and poor, and as it were, broken-down. No horses were visible, nor any men at work.

There were other fields which had once grown wheat, but were now so choked with weeds as to be nothing but a wilderness. As they approached the farmhouse where the old gentleman dwelt, the signs of desolation became more numerous. There were walls that had fallen, and never been repaired, around whose ruins the nettles flourished. There were holes in the roofs of the sheds exposing the rafters.

Trees had fallen and lay as they fell, rotting

away, and not even cut up for firewood. Railings
had decayed till there was nothing left but a few
stumps; gates had dropped from their hinges, and
nothing of them remained but small bits of rotten
board attached to rusty irons. In the garden all was
confusion, the thistles rose higher than the gooseberry
bushes, and burdocks looked in at the windows.
From the wall of the house a pear that had been
trained there had fallen away, and hung suspended,
swinging with every puff; the boughs, driven against
the windows, had broken the panes in the adjacent
casement; other panes which had been broken were
stuffed up with wisps of hay.

Tiles had slipped from the roof, and the birds
went in and out as they listed. The remnants of
the tiles lay cracked upon the ground beneath the
eaves just as they had fallen. No hand had touched
them; the hand of man indeed had touched nothing.
Bevis, whose eyes were everywhere, saw all these
things in a minute. "Why," said he, "there's the
knocker; it has tumbled down." It had dropped
from the door as the screws rusted; the door itself
was propped up with a log of wood. But one thing
only appeared to have been attended to, and that

was the wall about the orchard, which showed traces of recent mortar, and the road leading towards it, which had not long since been mended with flints.

Now Bevis, as I say, noting all these things as they came near with his eyes, which, like gimlets, went through everything, was continually asking his papa questions about them, and why everything was in such a state, till at last his papa, overwhelmed with his enquiries, promised to tell him the whole story when they got home. This he did, but while they are now fastening up the horse (for there was no one to help them or mind it), and while Bevis is picking up the rusty knocker, the story may come in here very well :—

Once upon a time, many, many years ago, when the old gentleman was young, and lived with his mother at the farmhouse, it happened that he fell in love. The lady he loved was very young, very beautiful, very proud, very capricious, and very poor. She lived in a house in the village little better than a cottage, with an old woman who was said to be her aunt. As the young farmer was well off, for the land was his own, and he had no one to keep but his old mother, and as the young lady dearly loved him, there seemed no possible obstacle in their way. But it is well known that a brook can never run straight, and thus, though all looked so smooth, there were, in reality, two difficulties.

The first of these was the farmer's old mother, who having been mistress in the farmhouse for very nearly fifty years, did not like, after half a century, to give place to a mere girl. She could not refrain from uttering disparaging remarks about her, to which her son, being fond of his mother, could not reply, though it angered him to the heart, and at such times he used to take down his long single-barrelled gun with brass fittings, and go out shooting. More than once the jealous mother had insulted the young lady openly in the village street, which conduct, of course, as things fly from roof to roof with the sparrows, was known all over the place, and caused the lady to toss her head like a filly in spring to show that she did not care for such an old harridan, though in secret it hurt her pride beyond expression.

So great was the difficulty this caused, that the young lady, notwithstanding she was so fond of the handsome young farmer, who rode so well and shot so straight, and could carry her in his arms as if she were no more than a lamb, would never put her dainty foot, which looked so little and pretty even in the rude shoes made for her by the village cobbler, over the threshold of his house. She would never come in, she said, except as a wife, while he on his part, anxious as he was to marry her, could not, from affection for his mother, summon up courage to bring her in, as it were, rough-shod over his mother's feelings.

Their meetings, therefore, as she would not come indoors, were always held in the farmer's orchard, where was a seat in an arbour, a few yards in front of which stood the ancient apple-tree in which Kapchack, who was also very young in those days, had built his nest. At this arbour they met every day, and often twice a day, and even once again in the evening, and could there chat and make love as sweetly as they pleased, because the orchard was enclosed by a high wall which quite shut out all spying eyes, and had a gate with lock and key. The young lady had a duplicate key, and came straight to the orchard from the cottage where she lived by a footpath which crossed the lane along which Bevis had been driven.

It happened that the footpath just by the lane, on coming near the orchard, passed a moist place, which in rainy weather was liable to be flooded, and as this was inconvenient for her, her lover had a waggon-load of flints brought down from the hills where the hares held their revels, and placed in the hollow so as to fill it up, and over these he placed faggots of nut-tree wood, so that she could step across perfectly clean and dry. In this orchard, then, they had their constant rendezvous; they were there every day when the nightingale first began to sing in the spring, and when the apple-trees were hidden with their pink blossom, when the haymakers were at work in the meadow, when the reapers cut the corn, and when the call of the first fieldfare sounded overhead. The golden and rosy apples dropped at their feet, they laughed and ate them, and taking out the brown pips she pressed them between her thumb and finger to see how far they would shoot.

Though they had begun to talk about their affairs in the spring, and had kept on all the summer and autumn, and though they kept on as often as the weather was dry (when they walked up and down the long orchard for warmth, sheltered by the wall), yet when the spring came again they had not half finished. Thus they were very happy, and the lady used particularly to laugh at the antics of the magpie, who became so accustomed to their presence as to go on with the repairs to his nest without the least shyness. Kapchack, being then very young and full of spirits, and only just married, and in the honeymoon of prosperity played such freaks, and behaved in so amusing a manner that the lady became quite attached to him, and in order to protect her favourite, her lover drove away all the other large birds that came near the orchard, and would not permit any one whatever to get up into Kapchack's apple-tree, nor even to gather the fruit, which hung on the boughs till the wind pushed it off.

Thus, having a fortress to retreat to, and being so highly honoured of men, Kapchack gave the reins to his natural audacity, and succeeded in obtaining the sovereignty. When the spring came again they had still a great deal of talking to do; but whether the young lady was weary of waiting for the marriage-ring, or whether she was jealous of the farmer's mother, or whether she thought they might continue like this for the next ten years if she did not make some effort, or whether it was the worldly counsels of her aunt, or what it was— perhaps her own capricious nature, it is certain that they now began to quarrel a little about another gentleman.

This gentleman was very rich, and the owner of a large estate in the neighbourhood; he did not often reside there, for he did not care for sport or country life, but once when he came down he happened to see the young lady, and was much attracted towards her. Doubtless she did not mean any harm, but she could not help liking people to admire her, and, not to go into every little particular, in the course of time (and not very long either) she and the gentleman became acquainted. Now, when her own true lover was aware of this, he was so jealous that he swore if ever he saw them together he would shoot his rival with his long-barrelled gun, though he were hung for it the next day.

The lady was not a little pleased at this frantic passion, and secretly liked him ten times better for it, though she immediately resorted to every artifice

to calm his anger, for she knew his violent nature,
and that he was quite capable of doing as he had said.
But the delight of two strings to her bow was not
easily to be foregone, and thus, though she really
loved the farmer, she did not discourage the gentleman. He, on his part, finding after a while that
although she allowed him to talk to her, and even
to visit her at the cottage, and sometimes (when
she knew the young farmer was at market) go for
a walk with him, and once even came and went over
his grand mansion, still finding that it was all
talk, and that his suit got no further, he presently
bethought him of diamonds.

He gave her a most beautiful diamond locket,
which he had had down all fresh and brilliant from
London. Now this was the beginning of the mischief. She accepted it in a moment of folly, and
wished afterwards ten times that she had refused,
but having once put it on, it looked so lovely she
could not send it back. She could not openly wear
it, lest her lover should see it, but every morning
she put it on indoors, and frequently glanced in
the glass.

Nor is it any use to find fault with her; for

in the first place she has been dead many years, and in the second she was then very young, very beautiful, and living quite alone in the world with an old woman. Now her lover, notwithstanding the sweet assurances she gave him of her faithful-fulness, and despite the soft kisses he had in abundance every day in the orchard, soft as the bloom of the apple-trees, could not quite recover his peace of mind. He did not laugh as he used to do. He was restless, and the oneness of his mind was gone. Oneness of mind does not often last long into life, but while it lasts everything is bright. He had now always a second thought, a doubt behind, which clouded his face and brought a line into his forehead.

After a time his mother observing his depres-sion, began to accuse herself of unkindness, and at last resolved to stand no longer in the way of the marriage. She determined to quit the house in which she had lived ever since she came to it a happy bride half-a-century before. Having made up her mind, that very morning she walked along the footpath to the young lady's cottage, intending to atone for her former unkindness, and to bring the girl back to lunch, and thus surprise her son when he came in from the field.

She had even made up her mind to put up with the cold reception she would probably meet with, nor to reply if any hard words were used towards her. Thus thinking, she lifted the latch, as country people do not use much ceremony, and stepped into the cottage, when what was her surprise to find the girl she had come to see with a beautiful diamond locket about her neck, gleaming in the sunshine from the open door! She instantly understood what it meant, and upbraiding the girl with her falseness, quitted the place, and lost no time in telling her son, but first she took the precaution of hiding his gun. As he could not find that weapon, after the first storm of his jealous anger had gone over he shut himself up in his room.

The lady came the same evening to the rendezvous in the orchard, but her lover did not meet her. She came again next day, and in the evening; and again the third day, and so all through the week, and for nearly a month doing all she could without actually entering the house to get access to him. But he sullenly avoided her; once seeing her in the road, he leaped his horse over the hedge rather than pass her. For the diamond locket looked so like a price—as if she valued a glittering bauble far above true love.

At last one day she surprised him at the corner of the village street, and notwithstanding that the people (who knew all the story) were looking on, she would speak to him. She walked by his side, and said : "George, I have put the locket in the arbour, with a letter for you. If you will not speak to me, read the letter, and throw the locket in the brook."

More she could not say, for he walked as fast as he could, and soon left her behind.

He would not go near the orchard all day, but at last in the evening, something prompted him to go. He went and looked, but the locket and the letter were not there.

Either she had not left them as she had said, or else some one had taken them. No one could enter the orchard without a key, unless they went to the trouble of bringing a ladder from the rick-yard, and as it was spring, there were no apples to tempt them to do that. He thought, perhaps, his mother might have taken his key and gone to the arbour, and there was a terrible scene and bitter words between them—the first time he had ever replied to her. The consequence was that she packed a chest that very day, took a bag of money, which in old-fashioned style she kept under her bed, and left her home for ever; but not before she had been to the cottage, and reviled the girl with her duplicity and her falseness, declaring that if she had not got the locket, she had not put it in the orchard, but had sold it, like the hussy she was! Fortunately, however, she added, George could now see through her.

The farmer himself, much agitated at his mother's departure, made another search for the locket, and mowed the grass in the orchard himself, thinking that perhaps the lady had dropped it, or that it had caught in her dress and dragged along, and he also took the rake, and turned over every heap of dead leaves which the wind had blown into the corners. But there was no locket and no letter. At last he thought that perhaps the magpie, Kapchack—as magpies were always famous for their fondness for glittering things, such as silver spoons—might have picked up the locket, attracted by the gleaming diamonds. He got a ladder and searched the nest, even pulling part of it to pieces, despite Kapchack's angry remonstrances, but the locket was not there.

As he came down the ladder there was the young lady who had stolen into the orchard, and watched his operations. They stood and faced each other for a minute : at least, she looked at him, *his* sullen gaze was bent upon the ground. As for her, the colour came and went in her cheek, and her breast heaved so that, for a while, she could not speak. At last she said very low, " So you do not believe me, but some day you will know that you have judged me wrongly." Then she turned, and without another word went swiftly from the orchard.

He did not follow her, and he never saw her again. The same evening she left the village, she and the old woman, her aunt, quietly and without any stir, and where they went (beyond the market town) no one knew, or even heard. And the very same evening, too, the rich gentleman who had given her the locket, and who had made an unwonted stay in his country home because of her, also left the place, and went, as was said, to London. Of course people easily put two and two together, and said no doubt the girl had arranged to meet her wealthy admirer, but no one ever saw them together. Not even the coachman, when the gentleman once more returned home years afterwards, though the great authority in those days, could say what had become of her; if she had met his master it was indeed in some secret and mysterious manner. But the folk, when he had done speaking, and had denied these things, after he had quaffed his ale and departed, nudged each other, and said that no doubt his master, foreseeing the inquiries that would be made, had bribed him with a pocketful of guineas to hold his tongue.

So the farmer, in one day, found himself alone; his dear lady, his mother, and his rival were gone. He alone remained, and alone he remained for the rest of his days. His rival, indeed, came back once now and then for short periods to his mansion; but his mother never returned, and died in a few years' time. Then indeed deserted, the farmer had nothing left but to cultivate, and dwell on the memory of the past. He neglected his business, and his farm; he left his

house to take care of itself; the cows wandered away,
the horses leaped the hedges, other people's cattle
entered his corn, trampled his wheat, and fattened
on his clover. He did nothing. The hand of man
was removed, and the fields, and the house, and the
owner himself, fell to decay.

Years past, and still it was the same, and thus
it was, that when Bevis and his papa drove up, Bevis
was so interested and so inquisitive about the knocker,
which had fallen from the front door. One thing,
and one place only, received the owner's care, and
that was the orchard, the arbour, the magpie's nest,
and the footpath that led to the orchard gate.
Everything else fell to ruin, but these were very
nearly in the same state as when the young lady
used to come to the orchard daily. For the old
gentleman, as he grew old, and continued to dwell
yet more and more upon the happy days so long
gone by, could not believe that she could be dead,
though he himself had outlived the usual span of
life.

He was quite certain that she would some day
come back, for she had said so herself; she had said
that some day he would know that he had judged

her wrongly, and unless she came back it was not possible for him to understand. He was, therefore, positively certain that some day she would come along the old footpath to the gate in the orchard wall, open it with her duplicate key, walk to the arbour and sit down, and smile at the magpie's ways. The woodwork of the arbour had of course decayed long since, but it had been carefully replaced, so that it appeared exactly the same as when she last sat within it. The coping fell from the orchard wall, but it was put back; the gate came to pieces, but a new one was hung in its place.

Kapchack, thus protected, still came to his palace, which had reached an enormous size from successive additions and annual repairs. As the time went on people began to talk about Kapchack, and the extraordinary age to which he had now attained, till, by-and-by, he became the wonder of the place, and in order to see how long he would live, the gentlemen who had gamekeepers in the neighbourhood, instructed them to be careful not to shoot him. His reputation extended with his years, and those curious in such things came to see him from a distance, but could never obtain entrance to the

orchard, nor approach near his tree, for neither
money nor persuasion could induce the owner to
admit them.

In and about the village itself Kapchack was
viewed by the superstitious with something like awe.
His great age, his singular fortune, his peculiar
appearance—having but one eye—gave him a wonderful prestige, and his chattering was firmly believed
to portend a change of the weather or the wind, or
even the dissolution of village personages. The knowledge that he was looked upon in this light rendered
the other birds and animals still more obedient than
they would have been. Kapchack was a marvel, and
it gradually became a belief with them that he would
never die.

Outside the orchard-gate, the footpath which
crossed the lane, and along which the lady used to
come, was also carefully kept in its former condition.
By degrees the nut-tree faggots rotted away—they
were supplanted by others; in the process of time
the flints sunk into the earth, and then another waggon
load was sent for. But the waggons had all dropped
to pieces except one which chanced to have been
under cover; this, too, was much decayed, still it

held together enough for the purpose. It was while this very waggon was jolting down from the hills with a load of flints to fill this hollow that the one particular flint, out of five thousand, worked its way through a hole in the bottom and fell on the road. And the rich old gentleman, whose horse stepped on it the same evening, who was thrown from the dog-cart, and whose discharged groom shot him in his house in London, was the very same man, who, years and years before had given the diamond locket to the young lady.

In the orchard the old farmer pottered about every day, now picking up the dead wood which fell from the trees, now raking up the leaves, and gathering the fruit (except that on Kapchack's tree) now mowing the grass, according to the season, now weeding the long gravel path at the side under the sheltering wall, up and down which the happy pair had walked in the winters so long ago. The butterflies flew over, the swallows alighted on the topmost twigs of the tall pear and twittered sweetly, the spiders spun their webs, or came floating down on gossamer year after year, but he did not notice that they were not the same butterflies or the same swallows which had

been there in his youth. Everything was the same
to him within the orchard, however much the world
might change without its walls.

Why the very houses in the village close by had
many of them fallen and been rebuilt; there was
scarcely a resident left who dwelt there then; even
the ancient and unchangeable church was not the
same—it had been renovated; why even the ever-
lasting hills were different, for the slopes were now
in many places ploughed, and grew oats where nothing
but sheep had fed. But all within the orchard was
the same; his lady, too, was the same without doubt,
and her light step would sooner or later come down
the footpath to her lover. This was the story Bevis's
papa told him afterwards.

They had some difficulty in fastening up the
horse, until they pulled some hay from a hayrick, and
spread it before him, for like Bevis he had to be
bribed with cake, as it were, before he would be
good. They then knocked at the front door, which
was propped up with a beam of timber, but no
one answered, nor did even a dog bark at the
noise; indeed, the dog's kennel had entirely disappeared, and only a piece of the staple to which his

chain had been fastened remained, a mere rusty stump in the wall. It was not possible to look into this room, because the broken windows were blocked with old sacks to keep out the draught and rain; but the window of the parlour was open, the panes all broken, and the casement loose, so that it must have swung and banged with the wind.

Within, the ceiling had fallen upon the table, and the chairs had mouldered away; the looking-glass on the mantelpiece was hidden with cobwebs, the cobwebs themselves disused; for as they collected the dust, the spiders at last left them to spin new ones elsewhere. The carpet, if it remained, was concealed by the dead leaves which had been carried in by the gales. On these lay one or two picture frames, the back part upwards, the cords had rotted from the nails, and as they dropped so they stayed. In a punch bowl of ancient ware, which stood upon the old piano untouched all these years, a robin had had his nest. After Bevis had been lifted up to the window ledge to look in at this desolation, they went on down towards the orchard, as if the old gentleman was not within he was certain to be there.

They found the gate of the orchard open—rather

an unusual thing, as he generally kept it locked, even when at work inside—and as they stepped in, they saw a modern double-barrel gun leant against a tree. A little farther, and Bevis caught sight of Kapchack's nest, like a wooden castle in the boughs, and clapped his hands with delight. But there was a ladder against Kapchack's tree, a thing which had not been seen there these years and years, and underneath the tree was the old farmer himself, pale as his own white beard, and only kept from falling to the ground by the strong arms of a young gentleman who upheld him. They immediately ran forward to see what was the matter.

Now it had happened in this way. It will be recollected that when the keeper fell from the dead oak-tree, he not only disabled himself, but his gun going off shot the dogs. Thus when the heir to the estate came down the same evening, he found that there was neither dog nor keeper to go round with him the next day. But when the morning came, not to be deprived of his sport, he took his gun and went forth alone into the fields. He did not find much game, but he shot two or three par- tridges and a rabbit, and he was so tempted by the crowds of wood-pigeons that were about (parties from Choo Hoo's army out foraging), that he fired away the remaining cartridges in his pocket at them.

So he found himself early in the day without a cartridge, and was just thinking of walking back to the house for some more, when the shadow of the eclipse came over. He stayed leaning against a gate to watch the sun, and presently as he was looking up at it a hare ran between his legs—so near, that had he seen her coming he could have caught her with his hands.

She only went a short way down the hedge, and he ran there, when she jumped out of the ditch, slipped by him, and went out fifty or sixty yards into the field, and sat up. How he now wished that he had not shot away all his ammunition at the wood-pigeons! While he looked at the hare she went on, crossed the field, and entered the hedge on the other side; he marked the spot, and hastened to get over the gate, with the intention of running home for cartridges. Hardly had he got over, than the hare came back again on that side of the hedge, passed close to him, and again leaped into

the ditch. He turned to go after her, when out
she came again, and crouched in a furrow only some
twenty yards distant.

Puzzled at this singular behaviour (for he had
never seen a hare act like it before), he ran after
her; and the curious part of it was, that although
she did indeed run away, she did not go far—she
kept only a few yards in front, just evading him. If
she went into a hedge for shelter, she quickly came
out again, and thus this singular chase continued
for some time. He got quite hot running, for
though he had not much hope of catching the creature, still he wanted to understand the cause of this
conduct.

By-and-by the zig-zag and uncertain line they
took led them close to the wall of the old gentleman's orchard, when suddenly a fox started out
from the hedge, and rushed after the hare. The
hare, alarmed to the last degree, darted into a large
drain which went under the orchard, and the fox
went in after her. The young gentleman ran to
the spot, but could not of course see far up the
drain. Much excited, he ran round the orchard
wall till he came to the gate, which chanced to

be open, because the farmer that day, having discovered that the great bough of Kapchack's tree
had been almost torn from the trunk by the gale,
had just carried a fresh piece of timber in for a
new prop, and having his hands full, what with
the prop and the ladder to fix it, he could not shut
the gate behind him. So the sportsman entered
the orchard, left his gun leaning against a tree, and
running down to see if he could find which way
the drain went, came upon the old gentleman, and
caught sight of the extraordinary nest of old king
Kapchack.

Now the reason Ulu (for it was the very
hare Bevis was so fond of) played these fantastic
freaks, and ran almost into the very hands of the
sportsman, was because the cunning Fox had driven
her to do so for his own purposes.

After he learnt the mysterious underground saying
from the toad imprisoned in the elm, he kept on
thinking, and thinking, what it could mean; but
he could not make it out. He was the only fox
who had a grandfather living, and he applied to
his grandfather, who after pondering on the matter
all day, advised him to keep his eyes open. The

Fox turned up his nostrils at this advice, which seemed to him quite superfluous. However, next day instead of going to sleep as usual he did keep his eyes open, and by-and-by saw a notch on the edge of the sun, which notch grew bigger, until the shadow of the eclipse came over the ground.

At this he leaped up, recognising in a moment the dead day of the underground saying. He knew where Bevis' hare had her form, and immediately he raced across to her, though not clearly knowing what he was going to do; but as he crossed the fields he saw the sportsman without any dogs, and an empty gun leaning over the gate and gazing at the eclipse. With a snarl the Fox drove Ulu from her form, and so worried her that she was obliged to run (to escape his teeth) right under the sportman's legs, and thus to fulfil the saying, "The hare hunted the hunter."

Even yet the Fox did not know what was going to happen, or why he was doing this, for such is commonly the case during the progress of great events. The actors do not recognise the importance of the part they are playing. The age does not know what it is doing; posterity alone can appreciate it. But after a while, as the Fox drove the Hare out of the hedges, and met and faced her, and bewildered the poor creature, he observed that her ziz-zag course, entirely unpremeditated, was leading them closer and closer to the orchard where Kapchack (whom he wished to overthrow) had his palace.

Then beginning to see whither fate was carrying them, suddenly he darted out and drove the Hare into the drain, and for safety followed her himself. He knew the drain very well, and that there was an outlet on the other side, having frequently visited the spot in secret in order to listen to what Kapchack was talking about. Ulu, quite beside herself with terror, rushed through the drain, leaving pieces of her fur against the projections of the stones, and escaped into the lane on the other side, and so into the fields there. The Fox remained in the drain to hear what would happen.

The sportsman ran round, entered the gate, and saw the old farmer trimming the prop, the ladder just placed against the tree, and caught sight of the palace of king Kapchack. As he approached a missel-thrush flew off—it was Eric; the farmer looked up at this, and saw the stranger, and was

at first inclined to be very angry, for he had never
been intruded upon before, but as the young gentleman at once began to apologise for the liberty, he
overlooked it, and listened with interest to the story
the sportsman told him of the vagaries of the Hare.
While they were talking the sportsman looked up
several times at the nest above him, and felt an
increasing curiosity to examine it. At last he expressed his wish; the farmer demurred, but the
young gentleman pressed him so hard, and promised
so faithfully not to touch anything, that at last the
farmer let him go up the ladder, which he had
only just put there, and which he had not himself as
yet ascended.

The young gentleman accordingly went up the
ladder, being the first who had been in that tree
for years, and having examined and admired the
nest, he was just going to descend, when he stayed
a moment to look at the fractured bough. The
great bough had not broken right off, but as the
prop gave way beneath it had split at the part
where it joined the trunk, leaving an open space,
and revealing a hollow in the tree. In this hollow
something caught his eye; he put in his hand and

drew forth a locket, to which an old and faded
letter was attached by a mouldy ribbon twisted
round it. He cast this down to the aged farmer,
who caught it in his hand, and instantly knew the
locket which had disappeared so long ago.

The gold was tarnished, but the diamonds were
as bright as ever, and glittered in the light as the
sun just then began to emerge from the eclipse.
He opened the letter, scarce knowing what he did;
the ink was faded and pale, but perfectly legible,
for it had been in a dry place. The letter said that
having tried in vain to get speech with him, and
having faced all the vile slander and bitter remarks
of the village for his sake, she had at last resolved
to write and tell him that she was really and truly
his own. In a moment of folly she had, indeed,
accepted the locket, but that was all, and since the
discovery she had twice sent it back, and it had
twice been put on her dressing-table, so that she
found it there in the morning (doubtless by the
old woman, her aunt, bribed for the purpose).

Then she thought that perhaps it would be
better to give it to him (the farmer), else he might
doubt that she had returned it; so she said, as he

would not speak to her, she should leave it in the
arbour, twisting the ribbon round her letter, and
she begged him to throw the locket in the brook,
and to believe her once again, or she should be
miserable for life. But if after this he still refused to
speak to her, she would still stay a while and endeavour to obtain access to him; and if even then he
remained so cruel, there was nothing left for her
but to quit the village, and go to some distant
relations in France. She would wait, she added,
till the new moon shone in the sky, and then she
must go, for she could no longer endure the insinu-
ations which were circulated about her. Lest there
should be any mistake she enclosed a copy of a
note she had sent to the other gentleman, telling
him that she should never speak to him again.
Finally, she put the address of the village in France
to which she was going, and begged and prayed
him to write to her.

When the poor old man had read these words,
and saw that after all the playful magpie must have
taken the glittering locket and placed it, not in his
nest, but a chink of the tree; when he learned that
all these years and years the girl he had so dearly

loved must have been waiting with aching heart for a letter of forgiveness from him, the orchard swam round, as it were, before his eyes, he heard a rushing sound like a waterfall in his ears, the returning light of the sun went out again, and he fainted. Had it not been for the young gentleman, who caught him, he would have fallen to the ground, and it was just at this moment that Bevis and his papa arrived at the spot.

CHAPTER VI.

THE GREAT BATTLE.

EARLY the same morning when Kapchack awoke, he was so much refreshed by the sound slumber he had enjoyed, that much of his depression—the sharp edge of his pain as it were—had passed away. The natural vivacity of his disposition asserted itself, and seemed to respond to the glory of the sunshine. Hungry from his long fast, away he flew to well-known places reserved for his own especial feeding-ground, and having satisfied his appetite went up into a hawthorn, trimmed his feathers, and began to think things over.

He at once decided that something of an exceptional character must be attempted in order to regain his authority. Half measures, delays, and intrigues were now in vain; some grand blow must be struck, such as would fill all hearts with admiration or dismay. Another treaty with Choo Hoo was out of the question, for the over-bearing rebel would throw in his face the assassination of the envoy, and even could it be thought of, who could he entrust with the mission? His throne was completely surrounded with traitors. He ground his beak as he thought of them, and resolved that terrible indeed should be the vengeance he would take if once he got them again into his power. The hope of revenge was the keenest spur of all to him to adventure something bold and unexpected; the hope of revenge, and the determination that the house of Kapchack should not fall without an effort worthy of a monarch.

He resolved to at once attack the mighty horde Choo Hoo commanded with the only troops he could get quickly together in this emergency. These were the rooks, the prætorian guard of his state, the faithful, courageous, and warlike tenth legion of his empire. No sooner did he thus finally resolve than his whole appearance seemed to change. His outward form in some degree reflected the spirit within. His feathers ruffled up, and their black and white shone with new colour. The glossy green of his tail gleamed in the sunshine. One eye indeed was gone, but the other sparkled with the fire of war; he scented the battle, and sharpened his bill against the bough.

He only regretted that he had not taken this course before, instead of idling in the palace, and leaving his kingdom to the wiles of traitorous courtiers and delegates. If he had only bestirred himself like the ancient Kapchack of former days this extremity would not have arisen. Even yet it was not too late; war was a desperate and uncertain game, and it was not always the greatest army, in point of numbers, that rejoiced in the victory. He would trust in his fortune, and swoop down upon the enemy. Calling to his body guard, he flew at once straight towards the plain, where, at that time in the morning, he knew the main body of the rooks would be foraging. Full of these resolutions he did not observe the maimed beetle lying helpless in the grass, but looking neither to the right nor the left, taking counsel of no one—for to whom could he apply for honest advice?—he winged his way swiftly onward.

In about half-an-hour he reached the plain, and saw the rooks scattered over the ground; he rested here upon the lower branch of an elm, and sent forward a messenger, one of the eight magpies who attended him, to tell the commander-in-chief to wait upon him. Upon receiving the message, the general, hoping that at last the king had decided upon action, since so abrupt a summons to his side was somewhat unusual, flew hastily to the elm and saluted the monarch. Kapchack, without any preamble, announced his intention of forming the rooks into column, and falling at once upon the horde of barbarians. In the rooks, he said, and their loyal commander, lay the last hope of the state—he placed himself in their midst and relied upon them solely and alone.

Ah Kurroo Khan, the commander-in-chief, could scarcely refrain from shouting with delight. He was not only wild with the joy of coming combat, but this straightforward speech and conduct went to his heart, and never in all his long, long reign, had Kapchack so complete and autocratic an empire as at that moment over the rooks.

Ah Kurroo, when he had in some degree expressed his pleasure at these commands, and the readiness with which he placed himself and his army at Kapchack's orders, proceeded first to pass the

word to the legions to fall into their ranks, and
next to inform the monarch of the position held by
the enemy.

They were, he said, dispersed in all directions
foraging, and discipline was much relaxed, insomuch
that several bands of them had even fallen to blows
amongst themselves. To attack these scattered positions, which could individually be easily overwhelmed,
would be a mistake, for these reasons. The advantage of destroying one or two such bands of ma-
rauders would be practically nothing, and while it
was being accomplished the rest would carry the
information to Choo Hoo, and he would assemble
his enormous horde. Thus the chance of surprising
and annihilating his army would be lost.

But it appeared that Choo Hoo's son, Tu Kiu,
who was also the second in command of the barbarians, finding that already the country was becoming denuded of supplies close to the camp, had
during the previous day, at his father's orders,
marched a large division—in itself an immense army
—into a plain at a few miles distance, which was
surrounded with the hills, and out of sight from
the camp. The best strategy therefore open to

Kapchack, was either to assail Choo Hoo's camp, or else to fall upon the divisions of Tu Kiu.

The difficulty in the case of the camp was that amidst the trees the assailants would suffer as much loss from crushing and confusion as would be inflicted upon the enemy. It was impossible, when once involved in a forest conflict, to know which way the issue was tending. The battle became split up into a thousand individual combats, discipline was of no avail, no officer could survey the scene or direct the movements, and a panic at any moment was only too probable. On the other hand, the division of Tu Kiu offered itself for annihilation. It was not only several miles distant from the main body, but a range of hills between prevented all view, and obstructed communication. There was a route by which the plain could be approached, through a narrow valley well sheltered with woods, which would screen the advancing troops from sight, and enable them to debouch at once into the midst of the invaders. Without doubt, thus suddenly attacked, Tu Kiu must give way; should victory declare for them decisively, it was easy to foretell what would happen. Tu Kiu falling back in disorder would confuse the regiments of Choo Hoo coming to his assistance, a panic would arise, and the incredible host of the barbarians would encumber each other's flight.

Kapchack listened to the Khan with the deepest attention, approved of all he had put forward, and gave the order to attack Tu Kiu.

Without a sound—for Ah Kurroo had strictly enjoined silence, lest the unusual noise should betray that something was intended—the legions fell into rank, and at the word of command, suppressing even the shout of joy which they wished so much to utter, moved in a dense column to the southwards. Kapchack, with his guards behind him, and Ah Kurroo Khan at his side led the van.

The Khan secretly congratulated himself as he flew upon his extraordinary good fortune, that he should thus enter the field of battle unhampered with any restrictions, and without the useless and unpleasant companionship of a political officer, appointed by the council of his nation. Well he knew that had Kapchack given the least notice of his intention, the rook council would have assembled and held interminable discussions upon the best method of carrying out the proposed object, ending, as usual, with a vote in which mere numbers prevailed, without any reference to reason or experience, and with the appointment of a state official to overlook the conduct of the general, and to see that he did not arrogate too much to himself.

Thus in fact the rooks were accustomed to act, lest a commander should become too victorious. They liked indeed to win, and to destroy the enemy, and to occupy his territory, but they did not like all this to be accomplished by one man, but the rather, at the very zenith of his fame, provided him with an opportunity for disgracing himself, so that another might take his place and divide the glory. Ah Kurroo knew all this; imagine, then, his joy that Kapchack without calling parliament together had come direct to the camp, and ordered an immediate advance. Himself choosing the route, trusting to no guides, not even to his own intelligence department, Ah Kurroo pointed the way, and the legions with steady and unvarying flight followed their renowned commander.

The noise of their wings resounded, the air was oppressed with their weight and the mighty mass in

motion. Then did Kapchack indeed feel himself
every feather a king. He glanced back—he could
not see the rear-guard, so far did the host extend.
His heart swelled with pride and eagerness for the fight.
Now quitting the plain, they wound by a devious
route through the hills—the general's object being
to so manage the march that none of them should
appear above the ridges. The woods upon the slopes
concealed their motions, and the advance was executed
without the least delay, though so great was their
length in this extended order that when the head of
the column entered the plain beyond, the rear-guard
had not reached the hills behind. This rendered their
front extremely narrow, but Ah Kurroo, pausing when
he had gone half-a-mile into the plain, and when
the enemy were already in sight, and actually beneath
them, ordered the leading ranks to beat time with
their wings, while their comrades came up.

Thus, in a few minutes, the place where the narrow
valley debouched into the hill-surrounded plain, was
darkened with the deploying rooks. Kapchack, while
waiting, saw beneath him the hurrying squadrons
of Tu Kiu. From the cut corn, from the stubble,
from the furrows (where already the plough had begun

its work), from the green roots and second crops of clover, from the slopes of the hills around, and the distant ridges, the alarmed warriors were crowding to their standards.

While peacefully foraging happy in the sunshine and the abundance of food, without a thought of war and war's hazards, they suddenly found themselves exposed, all unprepared to the fell assault of their black and mortal enemies. The sky above them seemed darkened with the legions, the hoarse shouts of command as the officers deployed their ranks, the beating of the air, struck them with terror. Some, indeed, overwhelmed with affright, cowered on the earth; a few of the outlying bands, who had wandered farthest turned tail and fled over the ridges. But the majority, veterans in fight, though taken aback, and fully recognising the desperate circumstances under which they found themselves, hastened with all speed towards Tu Kiu, whose post was in a hedge, in which stood three low ash trees by a barn. This was about the centre of the plain, and thither the squadrons and companies hurried, hoarsely shouting for their general.

Tu Kiu, undismayed, and brave as became the son

and heir of the mighty emperor Choo Hoo, made the
greatest efforts to get them into some kind of array
and order. Most fell into rank of their own accord
from long use and habit, but the misfortune was that
no sooner had one regiment formed than fresh arrivals
coming up threw all into disorder again. The crowd,
the countless multitude overwhelmed itself; the air
was filled, the earth covered, they struck against each
other, and Tu Kiu, hoarse with shouting, was borne
down, and the branch of ash upon which he stood
broken with the weight of his own men. He struggled, he called, he cried; his voice was lost in the
din and clangour.

Ah Kurroo Khan, soaring with Kapchack, while the
legions deployed, marked the immense confusion of the
enemy's centre. He seized the moment, gave the
command, and in one grand charge the whole army
bore swiftly down upon Tu Kiu. Kapchack himself
could scarce keep pace with the increasing velocity of
the charge; he was wrapped, as it were, around with
the dense and serried ranks, and found himself hurled
in a moment into the heart of the fight. Fight,
indeed it could not be called.

The solid phalanx of the rooks swept through the

confused multitude before them, by their mere momentum cutting it completely in two, and crushing innumerable combatants underneath. In a minute, in less than a minute, the mighty host of Tu Kiu, the flower of Choo Hoo's army, was swept from the earth. He himself wounded, and half-stunned by the shock, was assisted from the scene by the unwearied efforts of his personal attendants.

Each tried to save himself regardless of the rest; the oldest veteran, appalled by such utter defeat, could not force himself to turn again and gather about the leaders. One mass of fugitives filled the air; the slopes of the hills were covered with them. Still the solid phalanx of Kapchack pressed their rear, pushing them before it.

Tu Kiu, who weary and faint, had alighted for a moment upon an ancient grass-grown earthwork—a memorial of former wars—which crowned a hill, found it necessary to again flee with his utmost speed, lest he should be taken captive.

It was now that the genius of Ah Kurroo Khan showed itself in its most brilliant aspect. Kapchack, intoxicated with battle, hurried the legions on to the slaughter—it was only by personal interference

that the Khan could restrain the excited king.
Ah Kurroo, calm and far-seeing in the very moment
of victory, restrained the legions, held them in, and
not without immense exertion succeeded in checking
the pursuit, and retaining the phalanx in good order.
To follow a host so completely routed was merely
to slay the slain, and to waste the strength that
might profitably be employed elsewhere. He con-
jectured that so soon as ever the news reached
Choo Hoo, the emperor, burning with indignation,
would arouse his camp, call his army together, and
without waiting to rally Tu Kiu's division, fly immediately to retrieve this unexpected disaster. Thus,
the victors must yet face a second enemy, far more
numerous than the first, under better generalship,
and prepared for the conflict.

Ah Kurroo was, even now, by no means certain
of the ultimate result. The rooks, indeed, were flushed
with success, and impelled with all the vigour of
victory; their opponents, however brave, must in some
degree feel the depression attendant upon serious loss.
But the veterans with Choo Hoo not only outnumbered
them, and could easily outflank or entirely surround,
but would also be under the influence of his personal

leadership. They looked upon Choo Hoo, not as their king, or their general only, but as their prophet, and thus the desperate valour of fanaticism must be reckoned in addition to their natural courage. Instead, therefore, of relying simply upon force, Ah Kurroo, even in the excitement of the battle, formed new schemes, and aimed to out-general the emperor.

He foresaw that Choo Hoo would at once march to the attack, and would come straight as a line to the battle-field. His plan was to wheel round, and, making a detour, escape the shock of Choo Hoo's army for the moment, and while Choo Hoo was looking for the legions that had overthrown his son, to fall upon and occupy his undefended camp. He was in hopes that when the barbarians found their rear threatened, and their camp in possession of the enemy, a panic would seize upon them.

Kapchack, when he had a little recovered from the frenzy of the fray, fully concurred, and without a minute's delay, Ah Kurroo proceeded to carry out this strategical operation. He drew off the legions for some distance by the same route they had come, and then, considering that he had gone far enough to avoid Choo Hoo, turned sharp to the left, and

flew straight for the emperor's camp, sheltered from
view on the side towards it by a wood, and in front
by an isolated hill, also crowned with trees. Once
over that hill, and Choo Hoo's camp must inevitably
fall into their hands. With swift, steady flight, the
dark legions approached the hill, and were now
within half a mile of it, when to Ah Kurroo's surprise
and mortification the van-guard of Choo Hoo
appeared above it, advancing directly upon them.

When the fugitives from the field of battle
reached Choo Hoo, he could at first scarce restrain
his indignation, for he had deemed the treaty in full
force; he exclaimed against the perfidy of a Power
which called itself civilised and reproached his host
as barbarians, yet thus violated its solemn compacts.
But recognising the gravity of the situation, and
that there was no time to waste in words, he gave
orders for the immediate assembly of his army, and
while the officers carried out his command flew to
a lofty fir to consider a few moments alone upon
the course he should take.

He quickly decided that to attempt to rally
Tu Kiu's division would be in vain, he did not even
care to protect its retreat, for as it had been taken

so unawares, it must suffer the penalty of indiscretion.
To march straight to the field of battle, and to
encounter a solid phalanx of the best troops in the
world, elated with victory, and led by a general like
Ah Kurroo, and inspired, too, by the presence of
their king, while his own army was dispirited at
this unwonted reverse, would be courting defeat.
He resolved to march at once, but to make a wide
detour, and so to fall upon the rooks in their rear
while they were pursuing Tu Kiu. The signal was
given, and the vast host set out.

Thus the two generals, striving to out-wit each
other, suddenly found themselves coming into direct
collision. While fancying that they had arranged
to avoid each other, they came, as it were, face to
face, and so near, that Choo Hoo, flying at the head
of his army, easily distinguished king Kapchack and
the Khan. It seemed now inevitable that sheer force
must decide between them.

But Choo Hoo, the born soldier, no sooner cast
his keen glance over the fields which still inter-
vened, than he detected a fatal defect in Kapchack's position. The rooks, not expecting attack,
were advancing in a long dense column, parallel

with, and close to, a rising ground, all along the
summit of which stood a row of fine beech-trees.
Quick as thought, Choo Hoo commanded his centre
to slacken their speed while facing across the line
the rooks were pursuing.   At the same time he
sent for his left to come up at the double in extended order, so as to outflank Ah Kurroo's column,
and then to push it, before it could deploy, bodily,
and by mere force of numbers, against the beeches,
where their wings entangled and their ranks broken
by the boughs they must become confused.   Then
his right coming up swiftly, would pass over, and
sweep the Khan's disordered army before it.

This manœuvre, so well-conceived, was at once
begun.   The barbarian centre slackened over the hill,
and their left rushing forward, enclosed Ah Kurroo's
column, and already bore down towards it, while
the noise of their right could be heard advancing towards the beeches above, and on the other
side of which it would pass.   Ah Kurroo saw
his danger—he could discover no possible escape
from the trap in which he was caught, except in
the desperate valour of his warriors.   He shouted
to them to increase their speed, and slightly swerv-

ing to his right, directed his course straight towards
Choo Hoo himself. Seeing his design—to bear down
the rebel emperor, or destroy him before the battle
could well begin—Kapchack shouted with joy, and
hurried forward to be the first to assail his rival.

Already the advancing hosts seemed to feel the
shock of the combat, when a shadow fell upon
them, and they observed the eclipse of the sun.
Till that moment, absorbed in the terrible work
they were about, neither the rank and file, nor the
leaders had noticed the gradual progress of the
dark semi-circle over the sun's disk. The ominous
shadow fell upon them still more awful from its
suddenness. A great horror seized the serried hosts.
The prodigy in the heavens struck the conscience
of each individual; with one consent, they hesitated
to engage in carnage with so terrible a sign above
them.

In the silence of the pause they heard the
pheasants crow, and the fowls fly up to roost, the
lesser birds hastened to the thickets. A strange
dulness stole over their senses, they drooped, as it
were; the barbarians sank to the lower atmosphere;
the rooks, likewise overcome with this mysterious

lassitude, ceased to keep their regular ranks, and
some even settled on the beeches.

Choo Hoo himself struggled in vain against the
omen; his mighty mind refused to succumb to an
accident like this; but his host was not so bold
of thought. With desperate efforts he managed
indeed to shake off the physical torpor which en-
deavoured to master him; he shouted "Koos-
takke!" but for the first time there was no response.
The barbarians, superstitious as they were ignorant,
fell back, and lost that unity of purpose which is
the soul of an army. The very superstition and
fanaticism which had been his strength, was now
Choo Hoo's weakness. His host visibly melted
before his eyes; the vast mass dissolved; the ranks
became mixed together, without order or cohesion.
Rage overpowered him; he stormed; he raved till
his voice from the strain became inaudible. The
barbarians were cowed, and did not heed him.

The rooks, less superstitious, because more civilised, could not, nevertheless, view the appearance
of the sun without dismay, but as their elders were
accustomed to watch the sky, and to deduce from
its aspect the proper time for nesting, they were

not so over-mastered with terror as the enemy; but they were equally subjected by the mysterious desire of rest which seized upon them. They could not advance; they could scarce float in the air; some, as already observed, sought the branches of the beeches. Ah Kurroo, however, bearing up as well as he could against this strange languor, flew to and fro along the disordered ranks, begging them to stand firm, and at least close up if they could not advance, assuring them that the shadow would shortly pass, and that if they could only retain their ranks victory was certain, for the barbarians were utterly demoralised.

The drowsy rooks mechanically obeyed his orders, they closed their ranks as well as they could; they even feebly cheered him. But more than this they could not do. Above them the sun was blotted out, all but a rim of effulgent light, from which shone forth terrible and threatening flames. Some whispered that they saw the stars. Suddenly while they gazed, oppressed with awe, the woods rang with a loud cry, uttered by Kapchack.

The king, excited beyond measure, easily withstood the slumberous heaviness which the rest could

scarce sustain. He watched the efforts of the Khan
with increasing impatience and anger. Then seeing
that although the army closed up it did not move,
he lost all control of himself. He shouted his
defiance of the rebels before him, and rushed alone—
without one single attendant—across the field towards Choo Hoo. In amazement at his temerity,
the rooks watched him as if paralysed for a
moment. Choo Hoo himself could scarce face such
supernatural courage; when suddenly the rooks, as
if moved by one impulse, advanced. The clangour
of their wings resounded, a hoarse shout arose from
their throats, they strained every nerve to overtake
and assist their king.

Kapchack, wild with desperate courage, was
within twenty yards of Choo Hoo, when the dense
column of his own army passed him and crushed
into the demoralised multitude of the enemy, as a
tree overthrown by the wind crushes the bushes
beneath it. Kapchack himself whirled round and
round, and borne he knew not whither, scarce recognised whom he struck, but wreaked his vengeance
till his sinews failed him, and he was forced to
hold from sheer weariness. It is not possible to

describe the scene that now took place. The whole plain, the woods, the fields, were hidden with the hurrying mass of the fugitives, above and mixed with whom the black and terrible legions dealt destruction.

Widening out as it fled, the host of Choo Hoo was soon scattered over miles of country. None stayed to aid another; none even asked the other the best route to a place of safety; all was haste and horror. The pursuit, indeed, only ended with evening; for seven long hours the victors sated their thirst for slaughter, and would hardly have stayed even then had not the disjointed and weary fragments of Choo Hoo's army found some refuge now in a forest.

Choo Hoo himself only escaped from the ruck by his extraordinary personal strength; once free from the confused mass, his speed, in which he surpassed all the barbarians, enabled him to easily avoid capture. But as he flew his heart was dead within him, for there was no hope of retrieving this overwhelming disaster.

Meantime king Kapchack, when compelled by sheer physical weariness to fall out from the pursuit, came down and rested upon an oak. While he sat there alone and felt his strength returning, the sun began to come forth again from the shadow, and to light up the land with renewed brilliance. His attendants, who had now discovered his whereabouts, crowding round him with their congratulations, seized upon this circumstance as a fortunate omen. The dark shadow they said was past; like the sun, Kapchack had emerged to shine brighter than before. For once, indeed, the voice of flattery could not over-estimate the magnitude of this glorious victory.

It utterly destroyed the invading host, which for years had worked its way slowly into the land. It destroyed the prestige of Choo Hoo; never again would his race regard him as their invincible chief. It raised the reputation of king Kapchack to the skies. It crushed all domestic treason with one blow. If Kapchack was king before, now he was absolutely autocratic.

Where now was Ki Ki, the vain-glorious hawk who had deemed that without his aid nothing could be accomplished? Where the villanous crow, the sombre and dark designing Kauc, whose mur-

derous poniard would be thrust into his own
breast with envy? Where the cunning Weasel,
whose intrigues were swept away like spiders' webs?
Where were they all? They were utterly at Kapchack's mercy. Mercy indeed! at his *mercy*—their
instant execution was already certain. His body-
guard, crowding about him, already began the
pæan.

He set out to return to his palace, flushed with
a victory of which history furnishes no parallel.
It would have been well if he had continued in this
intention to at once return, summon his council,
and proclaim the traitors. Had he gone direct
thither he must have met Eric, the Missel-thrush,
who alone was permitted to frequent the orchard.
Eric, alarmed at seeing a stranger in the orchard,
and at the unprecedented circumstance of his ascending the ladder into the apple-tree, had started away
to find the king, and warn him that something unusual was happening, and not to return till the
coast was clear. He had not yet heard of the battle,
or rather double battle that morning, nor did he
know which way Kapchack had gone, but he considered that most probably the Woodpecker could

tell him, and therefore flew direct towards the copse to inquire.

If Kapchack had continued his flight straight to his palace he would have passed over the copse, and the Missel-thrush would have seen him and delivered his message. But as he drew near home Kapchack saw the clump of trees which belonged to Ki Ki not far distant upon his right. The fell desire of vengeance seized upon him; he turned aside, intending to kill Ki Ki with his own beak, but upon approaching nearer he saw that the trees were vacant. Ki Ki, indeed, had had notice of the victory from his retainers soaring in the air, and guessing that the king's first step would be to destroy him, had instantly fled. Kapchack, seeing that the Hawk was not there, again pursued his return journey, but meantime the Missel-thrush had passed him.

The king was now within a few hundred yards of his fortress, the dome of his palace was already visible, and the voices of his attendants rose higher and higher in their strain of victory. The Missel-thrush had seen the Woodpecker, who informed him that Kapchack had just passed, and like the wind he rushed back to the orchard. But all the speed of his wings was in vain, he could not quite overtake the monarch; he shouted, he shrieked, but the song of triumph drowned his cries. Kapchack was close to the wall of the orchard.

At the same time Bevis, not caring much about the locket or the letter, or the old gentleman (whose history he had not yet heard), while his papa spoke to, and aroused the old gentleman from his swoon, had slipped back towards the orchard gate where was an irresistible attraction. This was the sportsman's double-barrelled gun, leant there against a tree. He could scarce keep his hands off it; he walked round it; touched it; looked about to see if any one was watching, and was just on the point of taking hold of it, when the old gentleman rushed past, but seeing the gun, stopped and seized it. Finding, however, that it was not loaded, he threw it aside, and went on towards the house. In a minute he returned with the long single-barrelled gun, with which, so many years before, he had vowed to shoot his rival.

He had heard the Magpie returning, and mad with anger—since it was the Magpie's theft which had thus destroyed the happiness of his life, for

all might have been well had he had the letter—he
hastened for his gun. As he came to the orchard
gate, Kapchack, with his followers behind him, neared
the wall. The avenger looked along his gun, pulled
the trigger, and the report echoed from the empty,
hollow house. His aim was uncertain in the agony
of his mind, and even then Kapchack almost escaped,
but one single pellet, glancing from the bough of
an apple-tree, struck his head, and he fell with
darkness in his eyes.

The old gentleman rushed to the spot, he beat
the senseless body with the butt of his gun
till the stock snapped; then he jumped on it, and
stamped the dead bird into a shapeless remnant upon
the ground. As this spectacle Bevis, who, although
he was always talking of shooting and killing, could
not bear to see anything really hurt, burst out into
a passion of tears, lamenting the Magpie, and gathering up some of the feathers. Nor could they pacify
him till they found him a ripe and golden King
Pippin apple to eat.

CHAPTER VII.

PALACE SECRETS.

NEXT day Sir Bevis, so soon as ever he could get away after dinner, and without waiting for the noontide heat to diminish, set out in all haste for the copse, taking with him his cannon-stick. He was full of curiosity to know what would happen now that Kapchack was dead, who would now be king, and everything about it, all of which he knew he should learn from the Squirrel. He took his cannon-stick with him heavily loaded, and the charge rammed home well, meaning to shoot the Weasel; if the wretch would not come out when called upon to receive the due punishment of his crimes, he would bang it off into his hole in the tree, and, perhaps, some of the shot would reach the skulking vagabond.

He went up the field, reached the great oak tree, and crossed over to the corner of the wheat-field, but neither the Hare nor the dragon-fly were waiting about to conduct him, as was their duty.

He sat down on the grass to see if they would come to him, but although two dragon-flies passed over they did not stay to speak, but went on their journey. Neither of them was his guide, but they both went towards the copse. Immediately afterwards a humble-bee came along, droning and talking to himself as he flew. "Where is the Hare?" said Bevis; "and where is the dragon-fly?" "Buzz," said the humble-bee, "the usual course on occasions like the present—buzz—zz," the sound of his voice died away as he went past without replying. Three swallows swept by next at a great pace, chattering as they flew.

"Where's my dragon-fly?" said Bevis, but they were too busy to heed him. Presently a dove flew over too high to speak to, and then a missel-thrush, and soon afterwards ten rooks, after whom came a whole bevy of starlings, and behind these a train of finches. Next a thrush came along the low hedge, then two blackbirds, all so quick that Bevis could not make them understand him. A crow too appeared, but catching sight of Bevis's cannon-stick, he smelt the powder, wheeled round and went by far to the left-hand out of talking distance. Still more starlings rushed overhead, and Bevis waved his hand to them, but it was no use. Just afterwards he saw a thrush coming, so he jumped up, pointed his cannon-stick, and said he would shoot if the thrush did not stop. Much frightened, the thrush immediately perched on the hedge, and begged Bevis not to kill him, for he remembered the fate of his relation who was shot with the same cannon.

"Tell me where the Hare is, and where is my dragon-fly," said Bevis; "and why are all the people hurrying away towards the copse, and why don't they stop and tell me, and what is all this about?"

"I do not know exactly where the Hare is," said the thrush, "but I suppose she is in the copse too, and I have no doubt at all the dragon-fly is there, and I am going myself so soon as you will let me."

"Why are you all going to the copse?" said Bevis. "Is it because Kapchack is dead?"

"Yes," said the thrush, "it is because the king is dead, and there is going to be an election, that is if there is time, or if it can be managed; for it is expected that Choo Hoo will return now Kapchack is overthrown."

"When did Choo Hoo go, then?" asked Bevis, —for he had not yet heard of the battle. So the thrush told him all about it, and how strange it was that king Kapchack in the hour of victory should be slain by the very man who for so many years had protected him. The thrush said that the news had no doubt reached Choo Hoo very soon afterwards, and everybody expected that the barbarians would gather together again, and come back to take vengeance, and so, as they now had no king or leader, they were all hastening to the copse to take sanctuary from Choo Hoo. The only doubt was whether the emperor would respect the enclosure hitherto regarded by all the civilised people as a place where they could meet without danger. The barbarians knew nothing of these tacit agreements, which make communication so easy and pleasant among educated people. Still there was nothing else they could do.

"And what is going on in the copse?" said Bevis, "and who is to be king?"

"I cannot tell you," said the thrush, "I was just going to see, and if possible to vote against Ki Ki, who treacherously slew my friend and relation the ambassador, whom the king sent to Choo Hoo."

"We will go together," said Bevis, "and you can tell me some more about it as we go along. One thing is quite certain, the Weasel will never be king."

"Before I go with you," said the thrush, "you must please leave off pointing that dreadful cannon-stick at me, else I shall not be able to converse freely."

So Bevis left off pointing it, and carried his gun over his shoulder, just as he had seen his papa carry his. The thrush flew slowly along beside him, but he could not quite manage to keep at exactly the same pace; his wings would carry him faster than Bevis walked, so he stopped on the ground every now and then for Bevis to come up.

"I am sure," he said, "I hope the Weasel will not be king, and there is a rumour going about that he is disabled by some accident he has met with. But I greatly fear myself that he will be, notwith-standing what you say, for he is so cunning, and has so terrible a reputation that no one can prevail against him."

"Pooh!" said Bevis, "don't tell me such stuff and rubbish; I say the Weasel shall not be king, for I am going to shoot him as dead as any nail; after which Pan shall tear him into twenty pieces."

"But you tried to kill him once before, did you not?" said the thrush.

"You hold your tongue, this minute, you impudent thrush," said Bevis in a great rage; and he took his cannon-stick off his shoulder and looked so black that the thrush, alarmed for his safety, took advantage of a hedge being near, and slipped through it in a second.

"I'm very glad you're gone," said Bevis, calling after him, "but I'll shoot you next time I see you for leaving me without permission."

"And that will just serve him right," said a black-bird, as he hastened by, "for the thrush is the greediest bird in the world, and is always poaching about the places that belong to me.'"

Bevis was now very near the copse, and had not the least difficulty in finding the little bridge over the ditch, but he stopped before he crossed it, to listen to the noise there was inside among the trees. Whenever he had come before in the afternoon it was always so quiet, but now there was a perfect uproar of talking. Hundreds of starlings were chattering in the fir-trees, and flying round the branches with incessant motion. In the thick hedge which enclosed it there were crowds of greenfinches, goldfinches, chaffinches, yellowhammers, and sparrows, who never ceased talking. Up in the elms there were a number of rooks, who were deliberating in a solemn manner; it was indeed the rook council who had met there to consider as the safest place, the very council that Ah Kurroo so much disliked. Two or three dozen woodpigeons cowered on the lower branches of some ashes; they were the aliens who dwelt in Kapchack's kingdom. Rabbits were rushing about in all directions; dragon-flies darting up and down with messages; humble-bees droning at every corner; the Woodpecker yelled out his views in the midst of the wood; everything was in confusion.

As Bevis walked into the copse along the green track, with the tall thistles and the fern on each side of him, he caught little bits here and there of what they were saying; it was always the same, who was going to be king, and what would Choo Hoo do? How long would it be before the emperor's army could be got together again to come sweeping back and exact a dire vengeance for its defeat? Where was the Weasel? What was the last atrocity Ki Ki had committed? Had anybody heard anything more of Kauc, the crow? Had Prince Tchack-tchack arrived? Had the rooks made up their mind?—and so on, till Bevis shook his head and held his hands to his ears, so tremendous was the din.

Just then he saw his own dragon-fly and beckoned to him; the dragon-fly came at once: "What is all this"—began Bevis.

"My dear, how are you?" interrupted the dragon-fly. "I am so busy," and off he went again.

"Well I never!" said Bevis, getting excited like the rest, when the Hare came across the path, and stopped to speak to him. "What is going on?" said Bevis.

"That is just what I want to know," said the Hare. "Everybody says that somebody is going to do something, but what it is they do not themselves know. There never was such a confusion, and for aught we know, Choo Hoo may be here any minute, and there's not a single regiment in position."

"Dear me!" said Bevis, "why ever don't they begin?"

"I cannot tell you," said the Hare. "I don't

think anybody knows how : and the fact is, they
are all thinking about who shall be king, and intriguing for the sovereignty, when they should be
thinking of their country, and providing for its
defence."

"And who is to be king?" said Bevis. "The
Weasel shall not, that is certain; for I am just
this very minute going to shoot into his hole!"

"It is no use to do that," said the Hare;
"though I am very glad to hear you say that
he shall not be king. But it is no use shooting
into his hole, for he is not there, nor anywhere
in his old haunts, and we are all very suspicious
as to what he is about. I think you had better
come and see the Squirrel; he is in the raspberries,
and the Jay is there too, and there is an immense
deal of talking going on."

"So I will," said Bevis; and he followed the
Hare to the raspberries (all the fruit was now gone),
and found the Squirrel, who advanced to welcome
him, and the Jay up in the oak. Being hot with
walking in the sun, Bevis sat down on the moss
at the foot of the oak, and leaned back against
the tree whose beautiful boughs cast so pleasant a

shadow. The Hare came close to him on one side, and the Squirrel the other, and the Jay perched just overhead, and they all began to tell him the news at once. Not able to understand what they meant while they were all speaking together, Bevis held up his hands and begged them to stop a minute, and then asked the Squirrel to explain.

"So I will," said the Squirrel, "though I ought to be hiding my stores as fast as I can from the voracious host of barbarians, who will be here in a minute. But what am I to do? for I cannot get anybody to help me — everybody is thinking about himself."

"But the story—the story!" said Bevis; "tell me all about it."

"Well, since I can do nothing," said the Squirrel, "I suppose I must, though there is not a great deal to tell. You must know, then, that the news of Kapchack's death got here in half-a-minute, for the Missel-thrush came with it, and from here it was all over the country in less than an hour. Everybody knew it except Ah Kurroo Khan and the victorious legions, and Choo Hoo and the flying enemy. These were so busy, the one with slaughter, and the other with trying to escape, that they could not listen to what the swifts at once flew to tell them, but continued to fight and fly away till the evening, when the fragments of Choo Hoo's army took refuge in the forest. Even then they would not believe so extraordinary a circumstance, but regarded the account that had reached them as one of the rumours which always fly about at such times. Choo Hoo continued to go from tree to tree deeper and deeper into the forest.

" Ah Kurroo Khan, calling off his legions, since nothing further could be done, drew his victorious army back to some isolated clumps and avenues, where they intended to make their camp for the night. But in the course of an hour the rumours increased so much, and so many messengers arrived with the same intelligence and additional particulars, that Ah Kurroo Khan, dreading lest it should be true, sent out a squadron to ascertain the facts.

" Long before it could return, an envoy arrived from the council of the rooks themselves, with an order to Ah Kurroo Khan to retire at once, notwithstanding the lateness of the evening, and that the sun was sinking.

" With much disappointment (for he had hoped to continue the pursuit, and entirely exterminate the barbarians on the morrow), and not without forebodings as to his own fate, Ah Kurroo reluctantly communicated the order to his troops. The wearied legions accordingly started on their homeward journey, slowly passing over the fields which had witnessed the conquest of the morning. The sun had already sunk when their van reached the rooks' city, and Ah Kurroo came to the front to deliver the report he had prepared upon his way. As he approached the trees where the council of the rooks was sitting, in dark and ominous silence, an official stopped him, and informed him that he had been dismissed from the command, degraded from the rank he held, and the title of Khan taken from him. He was to retire to a solitary tree at some distance, and consider himself under arrest.

" Thus they punished him for daring to move without their orders (even at the direct instance of the king), and thus was he rewarded for winning the greatest battle known to history. The legions were immediately disbanded, and each individual

ordered to his home. Meantime, the news had at
last reached Choo Hoo, but neither he, nor the fugitive
host, could believe it, till there arrived some of the
aliens who had dwelt with us, and who assured the
barbarians that it was correct. Directly afterwards,
the intelligence was confirmed by the retreat of Ah
Kurroo Khan.

"All that livelong night Choo Hoo, once more
beginning to hope, flew to and fro from tree to
tree, endeavouring to animate his host afresh with
spirit for the fight; and as messengers continually
came in with fresh particulars of the confusion
in Kapchack's kingdom, he began to succeed. Early
this morning, when the sun rose, the mystic
syllables, 'Koos-takke,' resounded once more; the
forest was alive, and echoed with the clattering
of their wings, as the army drew together and
re-formed its ranks. The barbarians, easily moved
by omens, saw in the extraordinary death of Kapchack the very hand of fate. Once more they
believed in their emperor; once more Choo Hoo
advanced at their head.

"Not half-an-hour since a starling came in with
the intelligence that Choo Hoo's advanced guard

had already reached his old camp. We suppose the barbarians will halt there a little while for refreshment, and then move down upon us in a mass. Would you believe it, instead of preparing for defence, the whole state is rent with faction and intrigue! Yonder the council of the rooks, wise as they are, are indeed deliberating, having retired here for greater safety lest their discussion should be suddenly interrupted by the enemy; but the subject of this discussion is not how to defend the country, but what punishment they shall inflict upon Ah Kurroo. There is a difference of opinion. Some hold that the established penalty for his offence is to break his wings and hurl him helpless from the top of the tallest elm. Some, more merciful, are for banishment, that he be outlawed, and compelled to build his nest and roost on an isolated tree, exposed to all the insults of the crows. The older members of the council, great sticklers for tradition, maintain that the ancient and only adequate punishment is the hanging up of the offender by one leg to a dead and projecting branch, there to dangle and die of starvation, a terror to all such evil-doers.

"While they thus talk of torture the enemy is in

sight, and their own army, it is more than whispered, is discontented and angry at the reception meted out to the victorious Khan. But this, alas! is not all.

"So soon as ever Ki Ki was certain that Kapchack was really dead, he returned, and he has gathered to himself a crew of the most terrible ruffians you ever beheld. He has got about him all the scum of the earth; all the blackguards, villains, vermin, cut-throat scoundrels have rallied to his standard; as the old proverb says, 'Birds of a feather flock together.' He has taken possession of the firs, yonder, on the slope (which are the property of my friend the Jay), and which command my copse. He has pro-claimed himself king, and seeks to obtain confirma-tion of his title by terrorism. Already he has twice sent forth his murderous banditti, who, scour-ing the fields, have committed fearful havoc upon defenceless creatures. I am in dread every minute lost he should descend upon the copse itself, for he respects no law of earth or heaven.

"At the same time Kauc, the crow, has come forth in his true colours; he too has proclaimed himself king. He has taken his stand in the trees

by the Longpond—you came close by them just now
—they are scarce a quarter of a mile hence. To
our astonishment, he has got at least thrice as many
retainers as he is entered to have in the roll which
was read before Kapchack. He had reckoned, it
seems, upon the assistance of Cloctaw, of St. Paul's,
who has great influence among the jackdaws. Cloctaw, however, avoided him and came hither, and
Kauc vows he will destroy him.

"I know not which is most formidable, the
violent Ki Ki or the ruthless Kauc. The latter, I
feel sure, is only waiting till he sees an opening to
rush in and slaughter us. There is not a generous
sentiment in his breast; he would not spare the
fledgling in the nest. Between these two, one on
either hand, we are indeed in a fearful predicament;
Choo Hoo is to be preferred to them.

"Whether Raoul, the Rat, intends to strike a
blow for the throne, I know not; he is here; he
bears an evil character, but for myself I like him
far better than Kauc or Ki Ki. The Fox is, of
course, out of the question. But my great fear is
the Weasel; should he obtain the throne which of
us will be safe? By night as well as by day we

shall be decimated. His Machiavellian schemes, indeed, have thus far gone astray, and although he could arrange for everything, he could not foresee his own illness. Yet, though lying by now with a broken rib and other injuries, I have not the least doubt he is weaving new webs and preparing fresh deceptions. Thus, while the invader threatens us hourly, the kingdom of Kapchack is torn to pieces with the dissensions of those who should defend it."

"But why does not Prince Tchack-tchack take the throne and be king?" said Bevis. "He is the heir; he is Kapchack's son."

"So he ought," said the Squirrel; "but the truth is, people are weary of the rule of the magpies; nor is this young and flighty prince capable of taking up the reins of state. He is vain, and dissipated, and uncertain—no one can depend upon him. And besides, even if they could, have you not heard the extraordinary secret he has let out, like the great lout he is, and of which everybody is talking?"

"No," said Bevis; "I have heard nothing—how should I? I have only just got here. What is the secret? Tell me the secret this minute."

"To think," said the Jay, "that we should have been so long deceived. But I had my suspicions."

"I cannot say I suspected anything," said the Hare; "but I remember Kauc did make a very curious remark on one occasion; he was always looking askew into things and places that did not concern him, so that I did not much heed, especially as he had started slanders about me."

"Well," said the Jay, "the truth is, my wife—she is, you know, the most beautiful creature in the world, and quite turned the head of the late monarch —told me that she all along had her ideas; and Kapchack himself indeed told her in confidence that he was not so old as he looked, being jealous of the youth of Tchack-tchack, who objected to having his eye pecked out, and his feathers ruffled, as if he had any claims to be handsome;" and the Jay surveyed his own bright feathers with pride.

"You stupids!" said Bevis, "what is the use of talking in that way? I want to know the secret."

"There is no secret," said the Jay; "and I am not stupid. How can there be a secret, when everybody knows it?"

"Hush! hush!" said the Hare, trying to make peace; "do not let us quarrel, at all events, if all the rest do."

"No," said the Squirrel; "certainly not."

"Certainly not;" repeated the Jay.

"Well, what is it, then?" said Bevis, still frowning.

"The fact is," said the Squirrel, "Tchack-tchack has babbled out the great state secret. I myself knew a little of it previously, having overheard the Crow muttering to himself—as Ulu said, he peers into things that do not concern him. And, if you remember, Bevis, I was in a great fright one day when I nearly let it out myself. Now Prince Tchack-tchack, finding that he could not get the crown, has babbled everything in his rage, and the beautiful Jay has told us many things that prove it to be true. It now turns out that Kapchack was not Kapchack at all."

"Not Kapchack!" said Bevis. "How could Kapchack not be Kapchack, when he was Kapchack?"

"Kapchack could not be Kapchack," said the Squirrel, "because he never was Kapchack."

" Then who was Kapchack ?" said Bevis, in amazement.

"Well, he was not who he was," said the Squirrel; "and I will tell you why it was that he was not, if you will listen, and not keep interrupting and asking questions. The Reed once told you how stupid it is to ask questions; you would understand everything very well, if you did not trouble to make inquiries. The king who is just dead, and who was called Kapchack, was not Kapchack, because the real old original Kapchack died forty years ago."

" What ? " said Bevis.

" Extraordinary !" said the Jay.

" Extraordinary !" said the Hare.

" But true," said the Squirrel. " The real old original Kapchack, the cleverest, cunningest, most consummate schemer who ever lived, who built the palace in the orchard, and who played such fantastic freaks before the loving couple, who won their hearts, and stole their locket and separated them for ever (thinking that would serve his purpose best, since if they married they would forget him, and have other things to think about, while if they were apart he should be regarded as a sacred souvenir), this marvellous genius, the founder of so illustrious a family, whose dominion stretched from here to the sea—I tell you that *this* Kapchack, the real old original one, died forty years ago.

"But before he died, being so extremely cunning, he made provision for the continuation of himself in this way. He reflected that he was very old, and that a good deal of the dignity he enjoyed was due to that fact. The owner of the orchard and warden of his fortress regarded him with so much affection, because in his youth he had capered before the young lady whom he loved. It was not possible for the old gentleman to transfer this affection to a young and giddy magpie, who had not seen any of these former things. Nor, looking outside the orchard wall, was it probable that the extensive kingdom he himself enjoyed would pass under the sway of a youthful prince in its entirety.

"Some of the nobles would be nearly certain to revolt : the empire he had formed with so much labour, ingenuity, and risk, would fall to pieces, the life of one ruler not being sufficiently long to consolidate it. The old king, therefore, as he felt the years pressing heavy upon him, cast about in his mind for some means of securing his dynasty.

"After long cogitation one day he called to him his son and heir, a very handsome young fellow, much like the Tchack-tchack whom we know, and motioning him to come close, as if about to whisper in his ear, suddenly pecked out his left eye. The vain young prince suffered not only from the physical pain, but the intense mortification of knowing that his beauty was destroyed for ever. If he wanted even to look at himself in the pond, before he could see his own reflection, he had to turn his head upon one side. He bitterly upbraided his unnatural father for this cruel deed: the queen joined in the reproaches, and the palace resounded with rage and lamentation.

"Old king Kapchack the First bore all this disturbance with equanimity, sustained by the conviction that he had acted for the welfare of the royal house he had founded. After a time, when the young one-eyed prince ceased to complain, and was only sullen, he seized an opportunity when they were alone in the apple-tree, and explained to him the reason why he had done it.

"'I,' said he, 'I have founded this house, and through me you are regarded everywhere as of royal dignity; but if I were gone, the wicked and traitorous world which surrounds the throne, would certainly begin to conspire against you on account of your youth; nor would the warden of this orchard take any interest or defend you, as you were not the witness of the caresses bestowed upon him by his young lady. If you look at me, you will see that a wound, received in the wars which I waged long since, extinguished my left eye. You will also see that my tail is not, to say the least, either so glossy or so ample as of yore, and my neck and temples are somewhat bare, partly because in those wars I received divers swashing blows upon my head, and partly because of my increasing age.'

"The prince looked at him, and remarked that he certainly was a draggled old scarecrow. Not the least annoyed by this unfilial expression, the old king proceeded to show his heir how, in order for him, first, to retain the kingdom, and secondly, to keep the interest of the old gentleman owner of the orchard, it was necessary for him to present the same appearance as Kapchack himself did. 'In short,' said he, 'when I die you must be ready to take my place, and to look exactly like me.' The prince began to see the point, and even to admire the cunning of his father, but still he could not forgive the loss of his eye.

"'Ah!' said Kapchack I., 'you see I was obliged to take you upon the hop, otherwise it would never have been accomplished; no persuasion could have induced you to submit to such a deprivation, and, now I am about it, let me advise you, indeed, strictly enjoin upon you, when it becomes your turn, and you, too, are old and failing, to do the same as I did. Do not tell your son and heir what you are going to do, or depend upon it he will slip aside and avoid you; but do it first. And now, since you have already so far the same bleared aspect as myself, you will feel no difficulty in submitting to certain curtailments behind, and to the depilation of your head and neck.'

"Well, the result was, that the prince, full of ambition, and determined to rule at any price, in the end submitted to these disfigurations; the only thing he groaned over was the fear that none of the young lady magpies would now have anything to say to him.

"'My dear and most dutiful son,' said the old king, greatly pleased at the changed attitude of his heir, 'I assure you that you will not experience any loss of attention upon that score. It is in early youth indeed a very prevalent mistake for gaudy young fellows (as you appeared the other day) to imagine that it is the gloss of their feathers, the brilliance of their eyes, and the carriage of their manly forms that obtains for them the smiles and favours of the fair. But, believe me, this gratifying idea is not founded in fact; it is not the glossy feather, or the manly form, my son, it is the wealth that you possess, and even more than that, the social dignity and rank, which is already yours, that has brought a circle of charming darlings around you.

"'It is certainly somewhat mortifying to feel that it is not ourselves they care for, but merely the gratification of their own vanity. Of course you must bury this profound secret in your own breast. But if you ponder over what I have said you will

soon see how you can use this knowledge to your
own advantage. And it will at least save you from
the folly of really falling in love, than which, my
most dutiful son, there is no disease so terrible, and
so lasting in its effects, as witness that drivelling
fool who keeps this orchard for us, and surrounds
our palace as with an impregnable fortification.
Believe me, notwithstanding your now antique appearance—except at very close quarters, and without close
examination (I don't think you have quite as many
crow's-feet round your cyclopean eye as myself), it
is not possible to distinguish you from me—believe
me, in spite of this, the circle of charming darlings,
reflecting that you are the heir to the greatest crown in
the universe, will discover that you are even more
attractive than before.'

"The prince in a day or two found that the old
king was right, and recovered much of his former
spirit. As for the old king, having provided for his
dynasty, and feeling certain that his royal house
would now endure, he feasted and laughed, and
cracked the oddest jokes you ever heard. One afternoon, after spending the whole time in this way,
he recollected that he had not yet informed his heir

of one important secret, namely, the entrance to his treasure house.

"This was a chink, covered over with an excrescence of the bark, in the aged apple-tree, at the juncture of a large bough (the very bough that was lately cracked by the hurricane), and it was here that he had accumulated the spoils of the many expeditions he had undertaken, the loot of provinces and the valuable property he had appropriated nearer home, including the diamond locket. So cunningly had he chosen his treasure vault that not one of all his courtiers, not even his queens, could ever discover it, though they were all filled with the most intense desire and burning cupidity. The monarch thoroughly enjoyed the jest, for all the time they were sitting right over it, and that was, no doubt, why they could not see it, being under their feet. Well, the old king recollected that afternoon, that he had not communicated the secret to his heir, and decided that the time had come when it was necessary to do so. He therefore gave out that he felt sleepy after so much feasting, and desired his friends to leave him alone for a while, all except the missel-thrush (not the present, of course, but his ancestor).

"Accordingly they all flew away to flirt in the copse, and so soon as the court was clear the king told the missel-thrush to go and send his son to him, as he had something of importance to communicate in private. The missel-thrush did as he was bid, and in about half-an-hour the young prince approached the palace. But when he came near he saw that the king, overcome perhaps by too much feasting, had dozed off into slumber. As it was a rule in the palace that the monarch must never be awakened, the prince perched silently close by.

"Now, while he was thus sitting waiting for the king to wake up, as he watched him it occurred to him that if any one came by—as the warden of the orchard—and saw the two magpies up in the tree, he would wonder which was which. Instead of one old Kapchack, lo! there would be two antique Kapchacks.

"Thought the prince, 'The king is very clever, exceedingly clever, but it seems to me that he has overreached himself. For certainly, if it is discovered that there are two old ones about, inquiries will be made, and a difficulty will arise, and it is not at

all unlikely that one of us will be shot. It seems
to me that the old fellow has lived a little too long,
and that his wits are departing (here he gave a
quiet hop closer), and gone with his feathers, and
it is about time I succeeded to the throne. (Another
hop closer). In an empire like this, so recently
founded, the sceptre must be held in vigorous claws,
and upon the whole, as there is no one about'——
He gave a most tremendous peck upon the poor old
king's head, and Kapchack fell to the ground, out
of the tree, stone dead upon the grass.

"The prince turned his head upon one side, and
looked down upon him; then he quietly hopped into
his place, shut his eye, and dozed off to sleep.
By-and-by the courtiers ventured back by twos and
threes, and gathered on the tree, respectfully waiting
till he should awake, and nodding, and winking,
and whispering to each other about the body in
the grass. Presently his royal highness woke up,
yawned, complained that the gout grew worse as
he got older, and asked for the prince, who had been
sitting by him just now. Then looking round and
seeing that all were a little constrained in their
manner, he glanced in the same direction they did,

and exclaimed that there was his poor son and heir lying in the grass !

"With great lamentation he had the body laid out in state, and called in the court physicians to examine how the prince (for so he persisted in calling the dead monarch) came by his fate. Now, there was no disguising the fact that the deceased had been most foully murdered, for his skull was driven in by the force of the blow; but you see those were dangerous times, and with a despotic king eyeing them all the while, what could the physicians do ? They discovered that there was a small projecting branch which had been broken off half-way down the tree and which had a sharp edge, or splinter, and that this splinter precisely fitted the wound in the head. Without doubt the prince had been seized with sudden illness, had fallen and struck his head against the splinter. It was ordered that this bough should be at once removed. Kapchack raised a great lamentation, as he had lost his son and heir, and in that character the dead monarch was ceremoniously interred in the royal vaults, which are in the drain the hunted hare took refuge in under the orchard.

" And so complete was the resemblance the prince bore to his dead parent, owing to the loss of his eye and the plucking of his feathers, that for the most part the courtiers actually believed that it really was the prince they had buried, and all the common people accepted it without doubt. One or two who hinted at a suspicion when they were alone with Kapchack the Second, received promises of vast rewards to hold their tongues; and no sooner had they left his presence than he had them assassinated. Thus the dynasty was firmly consolidated, just as the dead founder had desired, though in rather a different manner to what he expected.

" But the new (or as he appeared the old) king had not been many days on the throne when he remembered the immense treasure of which his parent had been possessed. Sending every one away on one pretext and another, he searched the palace from attic to basement, peeped into all the drawers his father had used, turned over every document, sounded every wall, bored holes in the wainscot, ripped up the bark, and covered himself with dust in his furious endeavours to find it. But though he did this twenty times, though he examined every hollow tree within ten miles, and peered into everything, forcing even the Owl's ancestor to expose certain skeletons that were in his cupboard, yet could he never find it.

"And all the while the greatest difficulty he encountered was to hold his tongue; he did not dare let out that he was looking for the treasure, because, of course, everybody thought that he was Kapchack, the same who had put it away. He had to nip his tongue with his beak till it bled to compel himself by sheer pain to abstain from reviling his predecessor. But it was no good, the treasure could not be found. He gave out that all this searching was to discover an ancient deed or treaty by which he was entitled to a distant province. As the deed could not be found (having never existed), he marched his army and took the province by force. And, will you believe it, my friends, the fact is that from that time to this (till the hurricane broke the bough the other day) none of the king Kapchacks have had the least idea where their treasure was. They have lived upon credit.

"Everybody knew there was a treasure, and as time went on and new generations arose, it became magnified as the tale was handed down, till only lately, as you know, the whole world considered that Kapchack possessed wealth the like of which had never been seen. Thus it happened that as each succeeding Kapchack got farther and farther away from the reality and lost all trace of the secret, the fame of these riches increased. But to return. In course of years this Kapchack also found himself growing old, and it became his turn to prepare a son and heir for the throne by pecking out his left eye, and denuding him of his tail feathers. I need not go into further details; suffice it to say the thing was managed, and although the old fellows well knew their danger and took all sorts of precautions, the princes thus mutilated always contrived to assassinate their parents, and thus that apple-tree has been the theatre of the most awful series of tragedies the earth has ever known.

"Down to the last king Kapchack, the thing was always managed successfully, and he was the sixth who had kept up the deception. But the number six seems in some way fatal to kings, the sixth always gets into trouble, and Kapchack VI., proved very unfortunate. For in his time, as you know, Choo Hoo

arose, the kingdom was invaded, and quite half of it
taken from him. Whether he shrank from the risk
attending the initiation of Prince Tchack-tchack
(his heir), I do not know, but for some reason or other
he put it off from time to time, till the prince in fact
grew rather too old himself, and too cunning, and
getting about with disreputable companions—that
gross old villain Kauc, the crow, for one—it is just
possible that some inkling of the hereditary mutilation
in store for him was insinuated (for his own purposes)
by that vile wretch.

"Still, most likely, even if he had known of it, he
would have come in time to submit (so powerful a
motive is ambition) rather than lose the crown, had
not it happened that both he and Kapchack fell violently in love with the beautiful young jay, La Schach.
Very naturally and very excusably, being so young
and so beautiful, she was perhaps just a little capricious. Jealous to the last degree, old king Kapchack
told her the secret, and that he really was not nearly
so old as the world believed him to be—he was the sixth
of the race, and not the original antiquity. No doubt
the beauty laughed in her sleeve at him, and just for
fun told Tchack-tchack all about it, and that she

would never marry a one-eyed bird. Kapchack, full
of jealousy, bethought him that it was high time to
destroy his heir's good looks, so he attempted to peck
out his left eye in accordance with the usage of the
house.

"But Tchack-tchack having now learnt the secret,
vain of his beauty, and determined to have the lovely
jay at any cost, was alive to the trick, and eluded his
parent. This was the reason why Tchack-tchack
towards the last would never go near the palace. Thus
it happened that the hereditary practice was not resorted to, for poor old Kapchack VI. fell as you know,
in the very hour of victory. Tchack-tchack, who has
both eyes, and the most glossy tail, and a form of the
manliest beauty, is now at this minute chattering all
round the copse in a terrible rage, and quite beside
himself, because nobody will vote for him to be king,
especially since through the breaking of the bough
the vaunted treasure is at last revealed and found to
consist of a diamond locket and one silver spoon—a
hollow business you see—so that he has no money,
while the beautiful jay has just been united to our
friend here—and goodness me, here she comes in a
flutter!"

CHAPTER VIII.

THE NEW KING.

Up came the lovely young bride, full of news, and told them that the most extraordinary thing had just happened.

"Whatever is it, my love?" said her husband.

"Quick, whatever is it?" said the Squirrel.

"I can't wait," said Bevis.

"Nor I," said the Hare.

"Well," said the lovely creature—for whom an empire had been thrown away—"while the rook council was deliberating about the punishment to be awarded to Ah Kurroo, the legions, disgusted with the treatment they had received after so wonderful a victory, have risen in revolt, overthrown the government, driven the council away, taken the Khan from the tree where he was a prisoner, and proclaimed him Dictator!"

"Extraordinary!" said the Hare; "the rooks

always would have it that their's was the most perfect form of government ever known."

"No such rebellion was ever heard of before," said the Squirrel, "there is nothing like it in history; I know, for I've often slipped into the Owl's muniment room (between you and me) on the sly, and taken a peep at his ancient documents. It is most extraordinary!"

"I can't see it," said the Jay; "I don't agree with you; I am not in the least surprised. I always said they would never get on with so much caw-cawing and talking every evening; I always said——"

"Gentlemen," shouted the Woodpecker, rushing up breathless with haste, "I am sent round to tell you from the Dictator that you can now proceed to the election of a king without fear of any kind, for he will keep the enemy employed should they appear, and he will over-awe the two pretenders, Ki Ki and Kauc. Let every one say what he thinks without dread, and let there be no bribery and no intimidation. In the name of Ah Kurroo Khan!" and away he flew through the copse to make the proclamation.

Immediately afterwards the Owl, blundering in the daylight, came past and said that they had better

come on to his house, for he had just had a private interview with the Khan, and had orders to preside over
this business. So Bevis and the Squirrel, the Hare,
and the two Jays proceeded to the pollard tree; there
was no need for Bevis to hide now, because he was
recognised as a great friend of the Squirrel's, and the
enemy of the Weasel. A noisy crowd had already
collected, which was augmented every minute, and
there was a good deal of rough pushing and loud talking, not unmingled with blows. They were all there
(except the Weasel), the goldfinch, the tomtit, the
chaffinch, the thrush, the blackbird, the missel-thrush,
all of them, jays, the alien pigeons, doves, wood-
peckers, the Rat, the Mouse, the Stoat, and the Fox.

As the crowd increased, so did the uproar, till the
Owl appeared at the balcony of his mansion, and the
Woodpecker called for silence. The Owl, when he
could get a hearing, said they were all to give their
opinions and say who they would have for their king.
And that there might be less confusion he would call
upon the least of them in size, and the youngest in
age to speak first, and so on upwards to the oldest
and biggest.

"I'm the least," cried the wren, coming forward

without a moment's delay, "and I think that, after all I have seen of the ins and outs of the world, I myself should make a very good king."

"Indeed you're not the smallest," said Te-te, the tomtit; "I am the smallest, besides which you are a smuggler. Now I, on the contrary, have already rendered great services to my country, and I am used to official life."

"Yes, you spy," cried Tchink, the chaffinch; and all the assembly hissed Te-te, till he was obliged to give way, as he could not make himself heard.

"Why not have a queen?" said the goldfinch. "I should think you have had enough of kings; now, why not have me for queen? I have the richest dress of all."

"Nothing of the kind," said the yellowhammer, "I wear cloth of gold myself."

"As for that," said the Woodpecker, "I myself have no little claim on the score of colour."

"But you have no such azure as me," said the kingfisher.

"Such gaudy hues are in the worst possible taste," said the blackbird, "and very vulgar. Now, if I were chosen——"

" Well," said the thrush, " well, I never heard anything equal to the blackbird's assurance ; he who has never held the slightest appointment. Now my relation was ambassador "——

" I think," said the dove, " I should be able, if I held the position, to conciliate most parties, and make everything smooth."

" You're much too smooth for me," said Tchink. " It's my belief you're hand-in-glove with Choo Hoo, for all your tender ways—dear me ! "

" If experience," said Cloctaw, " if experience is of any value on a throne, I think I myself "——

" Experience ! " cried the Jay, in high disdain, " what is he talking of ? Poor Cloctaw has gone past his prime ; however, we must make allowance for his infirmities. You want some one with a decided opinion like myself, ladies and gentlemen ! "

" If I might speak," began one of the alien wood-pigeons, but they shouted him down.

" I don't mean to be left out of this business, I can tell you," said the Mole, suddenly thrusting his snout up through the ground, " I consider I have been too much overlooked. But no election will be valid without my vote. Now, I can tell you that

there's not a fellow living who knows more than I
do."

"Since the throne is vacant," said the Mouse,
"why should not I be nominated?"

"I do not like the way things have been managed,"
said the Rat; "there were too many fine feathers
at the court of the late king. Fur must have a
turn now—if I am elected I shall make somebody
who wears fur my prime minister." This was a
bold bid for the support of all the four-footed
creatures, and was not without its effect.

"I call that downright bribery," said the Jay.

"Listen to me a minute," said Sec, the stoat;
but as they were now all talking together no one
could address the assembly.

After a long time Bevis lost all patience, and
held up his cannon-stick, and threatened to shoot
the next one who spoke, which caused a hush.

"There's one thing *I* want to say," said Bevis,
frowning, and looking very severe, as he stamped
his foot. "I have made up my mind on one point.
Whoever you have for king you shall not have the
Weasel, for I will shoot him as dead as a nail the
first time I see him."

" Hurrah ! " cried everybody at once. " Hurrah for little Sir Bevis ! "

" Now," said Bevis, " I see the Owl wants to speak, and as he's the only sensible one among you, just be quiet and hear what he's got to say."

At this the Owl, immensely delighted, made Sir Bevis a profound bow, and begged to observe that one thing seemed to have escaped the notice of the ladies and gentlemen whom he saw around him. It was true they were all of noble blood, and many of them could claim a descent through countless generations. But they had overlooked the fact that noble as they were, there was among them one with still higher claims; one who had royal blood in his veins, whose ancestors had been kings, and kings of high renown. He alluded to the Fox.

At this the Fox, who had not hitherto spoken, and kept rather in the background, modestly bent his head, and looked the other way.

" The Fox," cried Tchink, " impossible—he's no-body."

" Certainly not," said Te-te, " a mere nonentity."

" Quite out of the question," said the goldfinch.

" Out of the running," said the Hare.

"Absurd," said the Jay; and they all raised a clamour, protesting that even to mention the Fox was to waste the public time.

"I'm not so sure of that," muttered Cloctaw. "We might do worse; I should not object." But his remark was unheeded by all save the Fox, whose quick ear caught it.

Again there was a great clamour and uproar, and not a word could be heard, and again Bevis had to lift up his cannon-stick. Just then Ah Kurroo Khan sent a starling to know if they had finished, because Choo Hoo had quitted his camp, and his outposts were not a mile off.

"In that case," said the Owl, " our best course will be stop further discussion, and to put the matter to the test of the vote at once. (Hear, hear.) Do you then all stand off a good way, so that no one shall be afraid to do as he chooses, and then come to me one at a time, beginning with the wren (as she spoke first), and let each tell me who he or she votes for, and the reason why, and then I will announce the result."

So they all stood off a good way, except Sir Bevis, who came closer to the pollard to hear what the voters said, and to see that all was done fairly. When all was ready the Owl beckoned to the wren, and the wren flew up and whispered; "I vote for the Fox because Te-te shall not have the crown."

Next came Te-te, and he said, "I vote for the Fox because the wren shall not have it."

Then Tchink, who said he voted for the Fox so that the goldfinch should not have the throne.

The goldfinch voted for the Fox that the yellow hammer should not have it, and the yellowhammer because the goldfinch should not succeed. The Jay did the same because Tchack-tchack should not have it; the dove because the pigeon should not have it: the blackbird to oust the thrush; and the thrush to stop the blackbird; the sparrow to stop the starling, and the starling to stop the sparrow; the Woodpecker to stop the kingfisher, and the kingfisher to stop the Woodpecker; and so on all through the list, all voting for the Fox in succession, to checkmate their friends' ambition, down to Cloctaw, who said he voted for the Fox because he knew he could not get the throne himself, and considered the Fox better than the others. Lastly, the Owl, seeing that Reynard had got the election (which indeed he had anticipated when he called attention to the modest Fox) also voted for him.

Then he called the Fox forward, and was about to tell him that he was duly elected, and would sit on a throne firmly fixed upon the wide base of a universal plebiscite, when Eric, the missel-thrush (who had taken no part in the proceedings, for he alone regretted Kapchack), cried out that the Fox ought to be asked to show some proof of ability before he received the crown. This was so reasonable, that every one endorsed it ; and the Missel-thrush, seeing that he had made an impression, determined to set the Fox the hardest task he could think of, and said that as it was the peculiar privilege of a monarch to protect his people, so the Fox, before he mounted the throne, ought to be called upon to devise some effectual means of repelling the onslaught of Choo Hoo.

" Hear, hear !" shouted the assembly, and cried with one voice upon the Fox to get them out of the difficulty, and save them from the barbarian horde.

The Fox was in the deepest bewilderment, but he carefully concealed his perplexity, and looked down upon the ground as if pondering profoundly, whereas he really had not got the least idea what to do. There was silence. Every one waited for the Fox.

"Ahem!" said Cloctaw, as if clearing his throat. The Fox detected his meaning, and slyly glanced towards him, when Cloctaw looked at Bevis and winked. Instantly, the Fox took the hint (afterwards claiming the idea as entirely his own), and lifting his head, said—

"Ladies and gentlemen, you have indeed set me a most difficult task—so difficult, that should I succeed in solving this problem, I hope shall obtain your complete confidence. Gentlemen, we have amongst us at this moment a visitor, and one whom we all delight to honour, the more especially as we know him to be the determined foe of that mercenary scoundrel the Weasel, who, should I be so fortunate as to obtain the crown shall, I promise you, never set foot in my palace—I allude to the friend of the Squirrel and the Hare—I allude to Sir Bevis. ('Hear, hear! Hurrah for little Sir Bevis! Three cheers more!') I see that you respond with enthusiasm to the sentiment I have expressed. Well, our friend Sir Bevis can, I think, if we call upon him in a respectful and proper manner, help us out of this difficulty.

"He carries in his hand an instrument in which the ignition of certain chemical substances causes an alarming report, and projects a shower of formidable missiles to a distance. This instrument, which I hear he constructed himself, thereby displaying unparalleled ingenuity, he calls his cannon-stick. Now if we could persuade him to become our ally, and to bang off his cannon-stick when Choo Hoo comes, I think we should should soon see the enemy in full retreat, when the noble Dictator, Ah Kurroo Khan, could pursue, and add another to his already lengthy list of brilliant achievements. I would therefore propose, with the utmost humility, that Sir Bevis be asked to receive a deputation; and I would, with your permission, nominate the Hare, the Squirrel, and Cloctaw, as the three persons best able to convey your wishes."

At this address there was a general buzz of admiration; people whispered to each other that really the Fox was extraordinarily clever, and well worthy to ascend the throne—who would have

thought that any one so retiring could have suggested so original, and yet at the same time so
practical a course? The Fox's idea was at once
adopted. Bevis went back with the Jay to his seat
on the moss under the oak, and there sat down
to receive the deputation.

Just as it was about to set out, the Fox begged
permission to say one word more, which being readily
granted, he asked if he might send a message by
the starling to Ah Kurroo Khan. The present, he
said, seemed a most favourable moment for destroying those dangerous pretenders, Ki Ki and Kauc.
Usually their brigand retainers were scattered all
over the country, miles and miles apart, and while
thus separated it would require an immense army
—larger than the state in the present exhausted
condition of the treasury could afford to pay without fresh taxes—to hunt the robbers down in their
woods and fastnesses. But they were now concen-
trated, and preparing no doubt for a raid upon the
copse.

Now if Ah Kurroo Khan were asked to fall
upon them immediately, he could destroy them in
the mass, and overthrow them without difficulty.

Might he send such a message to the Khan? The assembly applauded the Fox's foresight, and away flew the starling with the message. Ah Kurroo, only too delighted to have the opportunity of overthrowing his old enemy Kauc, and his hated rival Ki Ki, immediately gave the order to advance to his legions.

Meantime the deputation, consisting of the Hare, the Squirrel, and Cloctaw, waited upon Sir Bevis, who received them very courteously upon his seat of moss under the oak. He replied that he would shoot off his cannon-stick with the greatest pleasure, if they would show him in which direction they expected Choo Hoo to come. So the Hare, the Squirrel, and Cloctaw, with all the crowd following behind, took him to a gap in the hedge round the copse on the western side, and pointed out to him the way the enemy would come.

Indeed, Sir Bevis had hardly taken his stand and seen to the priming than the vanguard of the barbarians appeared over the tops of the trees. They were pushing on with all speed, for it seems that the outposts had reported to the emperor that there was a division in the copse, and that civil war had broken out, being deceived by the attack delivered by Ah Kurroo upon the black pretender Kauc. Up then came the mighty host in such vast and threatening numbers that the sun was darkened as it had been on the day of the eclipse, and the crowd behind Sir Bevis, overwhelmed with fear, could scarce stand their ground. But Sir Bevis, not one whit daunted, dropped upon one knee, and levelling his cannon-stick upon the other, applied his match. The fire and smoke and sound of the report shook the confidence of the front ranks of the enemy; they paused and wheeled to right and left instead of advancing.

In a minute Bevis had his cannon-stick charged again, and bang it went. The second rank now turned and fell back and threw the host into confusion; still the vast numbers behind pushed blindly on. Bevis, in a state of excitement, now prepared for a grand effort. He filled his cannon with powder nearly to the muzzle, he rammed it down tight, and fearing lest it might kick and hurt him, he fixed his weapon on the stump of an elm which had been thrown some winters since, and whose fall had made the gap in the hedge. Then he cut a long slender willow stick, slit it at one end, and inserted his match in the cleft. He could thus stand a long way back out of harm's way and ignite the priming. The report that followed was so loud the very woods rang again, the birds fluttered with fear, and even the Fox, bold as he was, shrank back from such a tremendous explosion.

Quite beside themselves with panic fear, the barbarian host turned and fled in utter confusion, nor could Choo Hoo, with all his efforts, rally them again, for having once suffered defeat in the battle of the eclipse, they had lost confidence. Ah Kurroo Khan, just as he had driven in the defenders and taken Kauc's camp (though Kauc himself, like the coward he was, escaped before the conflict began), saw the confusion and retreat of Choo Hoo's host, and without a moment's delay hurled his legions once more on the retiring barbarians. The greater number fled in every direction, each only trying to save himself; but the best of Choo Hoo's troops took refuge in their old camp.

Ah Kurroo Khan surrounded and invested the camp, but he hesitated to storm it, for he knew that it would entail heavy losses. He prepared to

blockade Choo Hoo with such strictness that he
must eventually surrender from sheer hunger. He
despatched a starling with a message, describing the
course he had taken at once to the copse, and the
starling, flying with great speed, arrived there in a
few minutes. Meantime the assembly, delighted with
the success which had attended Bevis's cannonading,
crowded round and overwhelmed him with their
thanks. Then when their excitement had somewhat
abated, they remembered that the idea had emanated
from the Fox, and it was resolved to proceed
with his coronation at once. Just then the starling
arrived from the Khan.

"Ah! yes," said Eric, the missel-thrush, who
wanted Tchack-tchack to ascend the throne of his
fathers, "it is true Choo Hoo is driven back and his
camp surrounded. But do you bear in mind that Tu
Kiu is not in it. He, they say, has gone into the west
and has already collected a larger host than even
Choo Hoo commanded, who are coming up as fast
as they can to avenge the Battle of the Eclipse.
You must also remember that Sir Bevis cannot be
always here with his cannon-stick; he is not often
here in the morning, and who can tell that some

day while he is away Tu Kiu may not appear, and while Choo Hoo makes a sortie and engages Ah Kurroo's attention, come on here and ravage the whole place, destroy all our stores, and leave us without a berry or an acorn! It seems to me that the Fox has only got us into a deeper trouble than ever, for if Choo Hoo or Tu Kiu ever does come down upon us, they will exact a still worse vengeance for the disgrace they have suffered. The Fox has only half succeeded; he must devise something more before he can claim our perfect confidence."

"Hear, hear!" shouted the assembly, "the Missel-thrush is right. The Fox must do something more!"

Now the Fox hated the Missel-thrush beyond all expression, for just as he was, as it seemed, about to grasp the object of his ambition, the Missel-thrush always suggested some new difficulty and delayed his triumph, but he suppressed his temper and said, "The Missel-thrush is a true patriot, and speaks with a view not to his own interest but to the good of his country. I myself fully admit the truth of his observations; Choo Hoo is indeed checked for a time, but there is no knowing how-soon we may hear the shout of 'Koos-takke' again. Therefore, gentlemen, I would, with all humility, submit the following suggestion.

"There can be no doubt but that this invasion has gone on year after year, because the kingdom of Kapchack had become somewhat unwieldy with numerous annexations, and could not be adequately defended. This policy of annexation which the late government carried on for so long, bore, indeed, upon the surface the false glitter of glory. We heard of provinces and principalities added to the realm, and we forgot the cost. That policy has no doubt weakened the cohesive power of the kingdom : I need not pause here to explain to an audience of the calibre I see before me the difference between progress and expansion, between colonisation and violent, uncalled for, and unjust annexation.

"What I am now about to suggest will at once reduce taxation, fill our impoverished treasury, secure peace, and I believe impart a lasting stability to the state. It will enable us one and all to enjoy the fruits of the earth. I humbly propose that a treaty be made with Choo Hoo (Oh ! oh ! from the Missel-thrush and Tchack-tchack), that upon the payment of an ample war indemnity (say a million nuts, two million acorns, and five million berries, or some trifling figure like that, not to be too exorbitant) he be permitted to withdraw (Shame! from Tchack-tchack), and that the provinces torn by force and fraud by the late government from their lawful owners, be restored to them ('Which means,' said the Missel-thrush, 'that as the lawful owners are not strong enough to protect themselves, Choo Hoo may plunder half the world as he likes'), and that peace be proclaimed. I, for my part, would far rather—if I be so fortunate as to be your king—I say I would far rather rule over a contented and prosperous people than over an empire in which the sword is never in the scabbard!"

"Hear, hear," shouted the assembly, "We have certainly selected the right person: this is truly wisdom. Let the treaty be concluded; and what a feast we will have upon the war indemnity," they said to one another.

"It is selling our honour—making a bargain and a market of our ancestors' courage," said the Missel-thrush.

"It is a vile infringement of my right," said

Tchack-tchack; "I am robbed of my inheritance, and the people of theirs, under a false pretext and sham. The country will be ruined."

"Begone," shouted the crowd, "Begone, you despicable wretches," and away flew the Missel-thrush and Tchack-tchack in utter disgust and despair.

So soon as they had gone the assembly proceeded to appoint a Commission to negociate the treaty of peace. It consisted of the Woodpecker, the Thrush, and Cloctaw: the Stoat muttered a good deal, for having been almost the only adherent of the Fox in his former lowly condition, he expected profitable employment now his friend had obtained such dignity. The Fox, however, called him aside and whispered something which satisfied him, and the Commission having received instructions proceeded at once to Ah Kurroo, who was to furnish them with a flag of truce. A company of starlings went with them to act as couriers and carry intelligence. When the Commission reached Ah Kurroo, he declined to open a truce with Choo Hoo, even for a moment, and presently, as the Commission solemnly demanded obedience in the name of the Fox, he decided to go himself to the king-elect and explain the reasons—

of a purely military character—which led him to place this obstruction in their way.

The Fox received Ah Kurroo with demonstrations of the deepest respect, congratulated him upon his achievements, and admired the disposition he had made of his forces so as to completely blockade the enemy. Ah Kurroo, much pleased with this reception, and the appreciation of his services, pointed out that Choo Hoo was now so entirely in his power, that in a few days he would have to surrender, as provisions were failing him. Long ere Tu Kiu could return with the relieving column the emperor would be a captive. Ah Kurroo begged the Fox not to throw away this glorious opportunity.

The king-elect, who had his own reasons for not desiring the Khan to appear too victorious, listened attentively, but pointed out that it was not so much himself, but the nation which demanded instant peace.

"Moreover," said he in a whisper to the Khan, "don't you see, my dear general, that if you totally destroy Choo Hoo your occupation will be gone; we shall not require an army or a general. Now as it is my intention to appoint you commander-in-chief for life ——"

"Say no more," said Ah Kurroo, "say no more;" then aloud, "Your royal highness' commands shall be immediately obeyed;" and away he flew, and gave the Commission the flag of truce.

Choo Hoo, confined in his camp with a murmuring and mutinous soldiery, short of provisions, and expecting every moment to see the enemy pouring into his midst, was beyond measure delighted when he heard that peace was proposed, indeed he could scarcely believe that any one in his senses could offer such a thing to an army which must inevitably surrender in a few hours. But when he heard that the Fox was the king-elect, he began to comprehend, for there were not wanting suspicions that it was the Fox who, when Choo Hoo was only a nameless adventurer, assisted him with advice.

The Commission, therefore, found their task easy enough so far as the main point was concerned, that there should be peace, but when they came to discuss the conditions it became a different matter. The Fox, a born diplomat, had instructed them to put forward the hardest conditions first, and if they could not force these upon Choo Hoo to gradually slacken them, little by little, till they overcame his reluctance.

At every step they sent couriers to the king-elect
with precise information of their progress.

The negociations lasted a very long time, quite
an hour, during which the couriers flew incessantly
to and fro, and Bevis, lying on his back on the moss
under the oak, tried which could screech the loudest,
himself or the Jay. Bevis would easily have won
had he been able to resist the inclination to pull the
Jay's tail, which made the latter set up such a yell
that everybody started, Bevis shouted with laughter,
and even the Fox lost his gravity.

Choo Hoo agreed to everything without much
difficulty, except the indemnity; he drew back at
that, declaring it was too many millions, and there
was even some danger of the negociations being
broken off. But the Fox was equally firm, he
insisted on it, and even added 10,000 bushels of grain
to the original demand, at which Choo Hoo nearly
choked with indignation. The object of the Fox in
requiring the grain was to secure the faithful
allegiance of all his lesser subjects, as the sparrows,
and indeed he regarded the indemnity as the most
certain means of beginning his reign at the height
of popularity, since it would be distributed among

the nation. People could not, moreover, fail to remark
the extreme disinterestedness of the king, since of
all these millions of berries, acorns, nuts, grain,
and so forth, there was not one single mouthful
for himself. Choo Hoo, as said before, full of indignation, abruptly turned away from the Commission,
and, at a loss what to do, they communicated with
the Fox.

He ordered them to inform Choo Hoo that under
certain restrictions travellers would in future be permitted access to the spring in the copse which did not
freeze in winter. The besieged emperor somewhat
relaxed the austerity of his demeanour at this; another pourparler took place, in the midst of which the
Fox told the Commission to mention (as if casually)
that among others there would be a clause re-
storing independence to all those princes and archdukes whose domains the late Kapchack had an-
nexed. Choo Hoo could scarce maintain decorum when
he heard this ; he could have shouted with delight, for
he saw in a moment that it was equivalent to ceding
half Kapchack's kingdom, since these small Powers
would never be able to defend themselves against his
hosts.

At the same moment, too, he was called aside, and informed that a private messenger had arrived from the Fox: it was the Humble-bee, who had slipped easily through the lines and conveyed a strong hint from the king-elect. The Fox said he had done the best he could for his brother, the emperor, remembering their former acquaintance; now let the emperor do his part, and between them they could rule the earth with ease. Choo Hoo having told the Humble-bee that he quite understood, and that he agreed to the Fox's offer, dismissed him, and returned to the Commission, whose labours were now coming to a close.

All the clauses having been agreed to, Ess, the Owl, as the most practised in such matters, was appointed by the Fox to draw up the document in proper form for signature. While this was being done, the king-elect proceeded to appoint his Cabinet: Sec, the Stoat, was nominated Treasurer; Ah Kurroo Khan, commander-in-chief for life; Ess, the Owl, continued chief secretary of state; Cloctaw was to be grand chamberlain; Raoul, the Rat, lieutenant-governor of the coast (along the brook and Longpond), and so on.

Next the Weasel, having failed to present himself when summoned by the Woodpecker, was attainted as

contumacious, and sentenced, with the entire approval
of the assembly, to lose all his dignities and estates;
his woods, parks, forests, and all his property were
escheated to the Crown, and were by the king handed
over to his faithful follower Sec. The Weasel (whose
whereabouts could not be discovered) was also proclaimed an outlaw, whom any one might slay without
fear of trial. It was then announced that all others
who absented themselves from the court, and were
not present when the treaty was signed, would be
treated as traitors, and receive the same punishment as the Weasel.

Immediately he heard this, Yiwy, son and heir of
Ki Ki, the hawk, who had fled, came and paid homage
to the Fox, first to save the estates from confiscation,
and secondly that he might enjoy them in his father's
place. Ki Ki was accordingly declared an outlaw.
Directly afterwards, Kauc, the crow, crept in, much
crestfallen, and craved pardon, hoping to save his
property. The assembly received him with hisses and
hoots: still the Fox kept his word, and permitted him
to retain his estates upon payment of an indemnity
for the cost of the troops employed against him under
Ah Kurroo, of 100,000 acorns. Kauc protested that

he should be ruined: but the crowd would not hear
him, and he was obliged to submit.

Then Eric, the Missel-thrush, and Prince Tchack-
tchack flew up: the prince had yielded to good
advice, and resolved to smother his resentment in order
to enjoy the immense private domains of his late
parent. The proctocols were now ready, and the Fox
had already taken the document to sign, when there
was a rush of wings, and in came six or seven of
those princes and archdukes—among them the arch-
duke of the Peewits—to whom independence was to
be restored. They loudly proclaimed their loyalty,
and begged not to be cast off: declaring that they
were quite unable to defend themselves, and should
be mercilessly plundered by the barbarian horde.
The Fox lifted his paw in amazement that there
should exist on the face of the earth any such pol-
troons as this, who preferred to pay tribute and
enjoy peace rather than endure the labour of de-
fending their own independence. The whole assembly
cried shame upon them, but the princes persisted,
and filled the court with their lamentations, till
at a sign from the king they were hustled out of
the copse.

The treaty itself filled so many pages of parchment that no one attempted to read it, the Owl certifying that it was all correct: an extract, however, divested of technical expressions, was handed about the court, and was to the following effect :—

"THE TREATY OF WINDFLOWER COPSE.

"1. The high contracting parties to this treaty are and shall be, on the one side, king Reynard CI., and on the other side, Choo Hoo, the emperor.

"2. It is declared that Kapchack being dead honour is satisfied, and further fighting superfluous.

"3. Choo Hoo agrees to pay a war indemnity of one million nuts, two million acorns, five million berries, and ten thousand bushels of grain, in ten equal instalments, the first instalment the day of the full moon next before Christmas, and the remainder at intervals of a fortnight.

4. The spring in the copse, which does not freeze in winter, is declared free and open to all travellers, not exceeding fifty in number.

5. The copse itself is hereby declared a neutral zone, wherein all councils, pourparlers, parliaments, commissions, markets, fairs, meetings, courts of justice,

and one and all and every such assembly for public or private purposes, may be and shall be held, without let or hindrance, saving only :—(*a*) Plots against His Majesty king Reynard CI.; (*b*) plots against His Imperial Majesty Choo Hoo.

6. The unjust annexations of the late king Kapchack are hereby repudiated, and all the provinces declared independent.

7. Lastly, peace is proclaimed for ever and a day, beginning to-morrow.   (Signed)

His Majesty King Reynard CI.

His Imperial Majesty the Emperor Choo Hoo.

B. (for Sir Bevis).

Sec, the Stoat (Treasurer).

Ah Kurroo Khan (Commander-in-Chief).

Ess, the Owl (Chief Secretary of State).

Cloctaw, the Jackdaw (Grand Chamberlain).

Raoul, the Rat (Lieutenant-Governor of the Coasts.)

Phu, the Starling.

Tchink, the Chaffinch.

Te-te, the Tomtit.

Ulu, the Hare.

Eric, the Missel-thrush.

Tchack-tchack, the Magpie, &c., &c., &c.

Every one in fact signed it but the Weasel, who was still lying sullenly perdue. The B was for Bevis; the Fox, who excelled in the art of paying delicate compliments, insisted upon Bevis signing next to the high contracting parties. So taking the quill, Bevis printed a good big B, a little staggering, but plain and legible. Directly this business was concluded, Ah Kurroo withdrew his legions; Choo Hoo sallied forth from the camp, and returning the way he had come, in about an hour was met by his son Tu Kiu at the head of enormous reinforcements. Delighted at the treaty, and the impunity they now enjoyed, the vast barbarian horde, divided into foraging parties of from one hundred to a thousand, spread over a tract of country thirty miles wide, rolled like a devastating tidal wave in resistless course southwards, driving the independent princes before them, plundering, ravaging, and destroying, and leaving famine behind. Part of the plunder indeed, of the provinces recently attached to Kapchack's kingdom, and now declared independent, furnished the first instalment of the war indemnity the barbarians had engaged to pay.

Meantime, in the copse, preparations were made for the coronation of the king, who had assumed, in accordance with well-known precedents, that all his ancestors, whether acknowledged or not, had reigned, and called himself king Reynard the Hundred and First. The procession having been formed, and all the ceremonies completed, Bevis banged off his cannon-stick as a salute, and the Fox, taking the crown, proceeded to put it on his head, remarking as he did so that thus they might see how when rogues fall out honest folk come by their own.

CHAPTER IX.

SIR BEVIS AND THE WIND.

SOME two or three days after peace was concluded, it happened that one morning the waggon was going up on the hills to bring down a load of straw, purchased from the very old gentleman who in his anger, shot king Kapchack. When Bevis saw the horses brought out of the stable, and learnt that they were to travel along the road that led towards the ships (though but three miles out of the sixty) nothing would do but he must go with them. As his papa and the Bailiff were on this particular occasion to accompany the waggon, Bevis had his own way as usual.

The road passed not far from the copse, and Bevis heard the Woodpecker say something, but he was too busy touching up the horses with the carter's long whip to pay any heed. If he had been permitted he would have lashed them into a sharp trot. Every now and then Bevis turned round to give the Bailiff a sly flick

with the whip; the Bailiff sat at the tail and dangled
his legs over behind, so that his broad back was a
capital thing to hit.   By-and-by, the carter left the
highway and took the waggon along a lane where
the ruts were white with chalk, and which wound
round at the foot of the downs.   Then after surmount-
ing a steep hill, where the lane had worn a deep
hollow, they found a plain with hills all round it,
and here, close to the sward, was the straw-rick from
which they were to load.

Bevis insisted upon building the load, that is
putting the straw in its place when it was thrown up;
but in three minutes he said he hated it, it was so
hot and scratchy, so out he jumped.   Then he ran
a little way up the green sward of the hill, and lying
down rolled over and over to the bottom.   Next he
wandered along the low hedge dividing the stubble
from the sward, so low that he could jump over it,
but as he could not find anything he came back, and
at last so teased and worried his papa to let him go
up to the top of the hill, that he consented, on Bevis
promising in the most solemn manner that he would
not go one single inch beyond the summit, where
there was an ancient earthwork.   Bevis promised,

and his eyes looked so clear and truthful, and his cheek so rosy and innocent, and his lips so red and pouting that no one could choose but believe him.

Away he ran thirty yards up the hill at a burst, but it soon became so steep he had to stay and climb slowly. Five minutes afterwards he began to find it very hard work indeed, though it looked so easy from below, and stopped to rest. He turned round and looked down; he could see over the waggon and the straw-rick, over the ash trees in the hedges, over the plain (all yellow with stubble) across to the hills on the other side, and there, through a gap in them, it seemed as if the land suddenly ceased, or dropped down, and beyond was a dark blue expanse which ended in the sky where the sky came down to touch it.

By his feet was a rounded boulder-stone, brown and smooth, a hard sarsen; this he tried to move, but it was so heavy that he could but just stir it. But the more difficult a thing was, or the more he was resisted, the more determined Bevis always became. He would stamp and shout with rage, rather than let a thing alone quietly. When he did this sometimes Pan, the spaniel, would look at him in amazement, and wonder why he did not leave it and go on and do something else, as the world was so big, and there were very many easy things that could be done without any trouble. That was not Bevis's idea, however, at all : he never quitted a thing till he had done it. And so he tugged and strained and struggled with the stone till he got it out of its bed and on the sloping sward.

Then he pushed and heaved at it, till it began to roll, and giving it a final thrust with his foot, away it went, at first rumbling and rolling slowly, and then faster and with a thumping, till presently it bounded and leaped ten yards at a time, and at the bottom of the hill sprang over the hedge like a hunter, and did not stop till it had gone twenty yards out into the stubble towards the straw-rick. Bevis laughed and shouted, though a little disappointed that it had not smashed the waggon, or at least jumped over it. Then, waving his hat, away he went again, now picking up a flint to fling as far down as he could, now kicking over a white round puff ball—always up, up, till he grew hot, and his breath came in quick deep pants.

But still as determined as ever, he pushed on, and presently stood on the summit, on the edge of the fosse. He looked down; the waggon seemed under his feet; the plain, the hills beyond, the blue distant valley on one side, on the other the ridge he had mounted stretched away, and beyond it still more ridges, till he could see no further. He went into the fosse, and there it seemed so pleasant that he sat down, and in a minute lay extended at full length in his favourite position, looking up at the sky. It was much more blue than he had ever seen it before, and it seemed only just over his head; the grasshoppers called in the grass at his side, and he could hear a lark sing, singing far away, but on a level with him. First he thought he would talk to the grasshopper, or call to one of the swallows, but he had now got over the effort of climbing, and he could not sit still.

Up he jumped, ran up the rampart, and then down again into the fosse. He liked the trench best, and ran along it in the hollow, picking up stray flints and throwing them as far as he could. The trench wound round the hill, and presently

when he saw a low hawthorn-bush just outside the
broad green ditch, and scrambled up to it, the
waggon was gone and the plain, for he had reached
the other side of the camp. There the top of the
hill was level and broad : a beautiful place for a
walk.

Bevis went a little way out upon it, and the
turf was so soft, and seemed to push up his foot
so, that he must go on, and when he had got a
little farther, he heard another grasshopper, and
thought he would run and catch him; but the grasshopper, who had heard of his tricks, stopped singing, and hid in a bunch, so that Bevis could not see
him.

Next he saw a little round hill—a curious little
hill—not very much higher than his own head, green
with grass and smooth. This curious little hill
greatly pleased him; he would have liked to have
had it carried down into his garden at home ; he
ran up on the top of it, and shouted at the sun, and
danced round on the tumulus. A third grasshopper
called in the grass, and Bevis ran down after him,
but he, too, was too cunning; then a glossy ball of
thistledown came up so silently, Bevis did not see it

till it touched him, and lingered a moment lovingly against his shoulder. Before he could grasp it, it was gone.

A few steps farther and he found a track crossing the hill, waggon-ruts in the turf, and ran along it a little way—only a little way, for he did not care for anything straight. Next he saw a mushroom, and gathered it, and while hunting about hither and thither for another, came upon some boulder-stones, like the one he had hurled down the slope, but very much larger, big enough to play hide-and-seek behind. He danced round these — Bevis could not walk—and after he had danced round every one, and peered under and climbed over one or two, he discovered that they were put in a circle.

" Somebody's been at play here," thought Bevis, and looking round to see who had been placing the stones in a ring, he saw a flock of rooks far off in the air, even higher up than he was on the hill, wheeling about, soaring round with outspread wings and cawing. They slipped past each other in and out, tracing a maze, and rose up, drifting away slowly as they rose; they were so happy, they danced in the sky. Bevis ran along the hill in the same direction they were going, shouting and waving his hand to them, and they cawed to him in return.

When he looked to see where he was he was now in the midst of long mounds or heaps of flints that had been dug and stacked; he jumped on them, and off again, picked up the best for throwing, and flung them as far as he could. There was a fir-copse but a little distance farther, he went to it, but the trees grew so close together he could not go through, so he walked round it, and then the ground declined so gently he did not notice he was going down hill. At the bottom there was a wood of the strangest old twisted oaks he had ever seen; not the least like the oak trees by his house at home that he knew so well.

These were short, and so very knotty that even the trunks, thick as they were, seemed all knots, and the limbs were gnarled, and shaggy with grey lichen. He threw pieces of dead stick, which he found on the ground, up at the acorns, but they were not yet ripe, so he wandered on among the oaks, tapping every one he passed to see which was hollow, till presently he had gone so far he could not see the hills for the boughs.

But just as he was thinking he would ask a bee to show him the way out (for there was not a single bird in the wood), he came to a place where the oaks were thinner, and the space between them was covered with bramble-bushes. Some of the blackberries were ripe, and his lips were soon stained with their juice. Passing on from bramble-thicket to bramble-thicket, by-and-by he shouted, and danced, and clapped his hands with joy, for there were some nuts on a hazel bough, and they were ripe he was sure, for the side towards the sun was rosy. He knew that nuts do not get brown first, but often turn red towards the south. Out came his pocket-knife, and with seven tremendous slashes, for Bevis could not do anything steadily, off came a branch with a crook. He crooked down the bough and gathered the nuts, there were eight on that bough, and on the next four, and on the next only two. But there was another stole beyond, from which, in a minute, he had twenty more, and then as he could not stay to crack them, he crammed them into his pocket and ceased to reckon.

"I will take fifty up to the Squirrel," he said to himself, "and the nut-crackers, and show him how to do it properly with some salt." So he tugged at the boughs, and dragged them down, and went on from stole to stole till he had roamed into the depths of the nut-tree wood.

Then, as he stopped a second to step over a little streamlet that oozed along at his feet, all at once he became aware how still it was. No birds sang, and no jay called; no woodpecker chuckled; there was not even a robin; nor had he seen a rabbit, or a squirrel, or a dragon-fly, or any of his friends. Already the outer rim of some of the hazel leaves was brown, while the centre of the leaf remained green, but there was not even the rustle of a leaf as it fell. The larks were not here, nor the swallows, nor the rooks; the streamlet at his feet went on without a murmur; and the breeze did not come down into the hollow. Except for a bee, whose buzz seemed quite loud as he flew by, there was not a moving thing. Bevis was alone; he had never before been so utterly alone, and he stopped humming the old tune the Brook had taught him, to listen.

He lifted his crook and struck the water; it splashed, but in a second it was still again. He

flung a dead branch into a tree, it cracked as it
hit a bough, on which the leaves rustled; then it
fell thump, and lay still and quiet. He stamped on
the ground, the grass gave no sound. He shouted
holloa! but there was no echo. His voice seemed
to slip away from him, he could not shout so loud
as he had been accustomed to. For a minute he
liked it; then he began to think it was not so
pleasant; then he wanted to get out, but he could
not see the hill, so he did not know which way to go.

So he stroked a knotted oak with his hand,
smoothing it down, and said, "Oak, oak, tell me
which way to go?" and the oak tried to speak,
but there was no wind, and he could not, but he
dropped just one leaf on the right side, and Bevis
picked it up, and as he did so, a nut-tree bough
brushed his cheek.

He kissed the bough, and said, "Nut-tree bough,
nut-tree bough, tell me the way to go." The bough
could not speak for the same reason that the oak could
not; but it bent down towards the streamlet. Bevis
dropped on one knee and lifted up a little water in the
hollow of his hand, and drank it, and asked which
way to go.

The stream could not speak because there was no stone to splash against, but it sparkled in the sunshine (as Bevis had pushed the bough aside), and looked so pleasant that he followed it a little way, and then he came to an open place with twisted old oaks, gnarled and knotted, where a blue butterfly was playing.

"Show me the way out, you beautiful creature," said Bevis.

"So I will, Bevis dear," said the butterfly. "I have just come from your waggon, and your papa and the Bailiff have been calling to you, and I think they will soon be coming to look for you. Follow me, my darling."

So Bevis followed the little blue butterfly, who danced along as straight as it was possible for him to go, for he, like Bevis, did not like too much straightness. Now the oak knew the butterfly was there, and that was why he dropped his leaf; and so did the nut-tree bough, and that was why he drooped and let the sun sparkle on the water, and the stream smiled to make Bevis follow him to where the butterfly was playing. Without pausing anywhere, but just zig-zagging on, the blue butterfly floated before Bevis, who danced after him, the nuts falling from his crammed pockets; knocking every oak as he went with his stick, asking them if they knew anything, or had anything to tell the people in the copse near his house. The oaks were bursting with things to tell him, and messages to send, but they could not speak, as there was no breeze in the hollow. He whipped the bramble bushes with his crook, but they did not mind in the least, they were so glad to see him.

He whistled to the butterfly to stop a moment while he picked a blackberry; the butterfly settled on a leaf. Then away they went again together till they left the wood behind and began to go up the hill. There the butterfly grew restless, and could scarce restrain his pace for Bevis to keep up, as they were now in the sunshine. Bevis raced after as fast as he could go up hill, but at the top the butterfly thought he saw a friend of his, and telling Bevis that somebody would come to him in a minute, away he flew. Bevis looked round, but it was all strange and new to him; there were hills all round, but there was no waggon, and no old trench or rampart; nothing but the blue sky and the great sun, which did not seem far off.

While he wondered which way to go, the Wind came along the ridge, and taking him softly by the ear pushed him gently forward and said, "Bevis, my love, I have been waiting for you ever so long; why did you not come before?"

"Because you never asked me," said Bevis.

"Oh yes, I did; I asked you twenty times in the copse. I beckoned to you out of the great oak, under which you went to sleep; and I whispered to you from the fir trees where the Squirrel played, but you were so busy, dear, so busy with Kapchack, and the war, and Choo Hoo, and the court and all the turmoil, that you did not hear me."

"You should have called louder," said Bevis.

"So I did," said the Wind. "Don't you remember I whirled the little bough against your window, and rattled the casement that night you saw the Owl go by."

"I was so sleepy," said Bevis, "I did not know what you meant; you should have kissed me."

"So I did," said the Wind. "I kissed you a hundred times out in the field, and stroked your hair, but you would not take any notice."

"I had so much to do," said Bevis; "there was the Weasel and my cannon-stick."

"But I wanted you very much," said the Wind, "because I love you, and longed for you to come and visit me."

"Well, now I am come," said Bevis. "But where do you live?"

"This is where I live, dear," said the Wind. "I live upon the hill; sometimes I go to the sea, and sometimes to the woods, and sometimes I run through the valley, but I always come back here, and you may always be sure of finding me here; and I want you to come and romp with me."

"I will come," said Bevis; "I like a romp, but are you very rough?"

"Oh no, dear; not with you."

"I am a great big boy," said Bevis; "I am eating my peck of salt very fast: I shall soon get too big to romp with you. How old are you, you jolly Wind?"

The Wind laughed and said, "I am older than all the very old things. I am as old as the Brook."

"But the Brook is very old," said Bevis. "He

told me he was older than the hills, so I do not think you are as old as he is."

"Yes I am," said the Wind; "he was always my playfellow; we were children together."

"If you are so very, very old," said Bevis, "it is no use your trying to romp with me, because I am very strong; I can carry my papa's gun on my shoulder, and I can run very fast; do you know the stupid old Bailiff can't catch me. I can go round the ricks ever so much quicker than he can."

"I can run quick," said the Wind.

"But not so quick as me," said Bevis; "now see if you can catch me."

Away he ran, and for a moment he left the Wind behind; but the Wind blew a little faster, and overtook him, and they raced along together, like two wild things, till Bevis began to pant. Then down he sat on the turf and kicked up his heels and shouted, and the Wind fanned his cheek and cooled him, and kissed his lips and stroked his hair, and caressed him and played with him, till up he jumped again and danced along, the Wind always pushing him gently.

"You are a jolly old Wind," said Bevis, "I

like you very much; but you must tell me a story, else we shall quarrel. I'm sure we shall."

"I will try," said the Wind; "but I have forgotten all my stories, because the people never come to listen to me now."

"Why don't they come?" said Bevis.

"They are too busy," said the Wind, sighing; "they are so very, very busy, just like you were with Kapchack and his treasure and the war, and all the rest of the business; they have so much to do, they have quite forsaken me."

"I will come to you," said Bevis; "do not be sorry. I will come and play with you."

"Yes, do," said the Wind; "and drink me, dear, as much as ever you can. I shall make you strong. Now drink me."

Bevis stood still and drew in a long, long breath, drinking the Wind till his chest was full and his heart beat quicker. Then he jumped and danced and shouted.

"There," said the Wind, "See, how jolly I have made you. It was I who made you dance and sing, and run along the hill just now. Come up here, my darling Sir Bevis, and drink me as often as ever you can, and the more you drink of me the happier you will be, and the longer you will live. And people will look at you and say, 'How jolly he looks? Is he not nice? I wish I was like him.' And presently they will say, 'Where does he learn all these things?'

"For you must know, Bevis my dear, that although I have forgotten my stories, yet they are all still there in my mind, and by-and-by, if you keep on drinking me I shall tell you all of them, and nobody will know how you learnt it all. For I know more than the Brook, because you see, I travel about everywhere: and I know more than the trees, indeed, all they know I taught them myself. The sun is always telling me everything, and the stars whisper to me at night: the ocean roars at me: the earth whispers to me: just you lie down, Bevis love, upon the ground and listen."

So Bevis lay down on the grass, and heard the Wind whispering in the tufts and bunches, and the Earth under him answered, and asked the Wind to stay and talk. But the Wind said, "I have got Bevis to-day: come on, Bevis," and Bevis stood up and walked along.

"Besides all these things," said the Wind, " I can remember everything that ever was. There never was anything that I cannot remember, and my mind is so clear that if you will but come up here and drink me, you will understand everything."

"Well then," said Bevis, "I will drink you— there, I have just had such a lot of you : now tell me this instant why the sun is up there, and is he very hot if you touch him, and which way does he go when he sinks beyond the wood, and who lives up there, and are they nice people, and who painted the sky ?"

The Wind laughed aloud, and said, "Bevis my darling, you have not drunk half enough of me yet, else you would never ask such silly questions as that. Why those are like the silly questions the people ask who live in the houses of the cities, and never feel me or taste me, or speak to me. And I have seen them looking through long tubes——"

"I know," said Bevis ; "they are telescopes, and you look at the sun and the stars, and they tell you all about them."

"Pooh!" said the Wind, "don't you believe such stuff and rubbish, my pet. How can they

know anything about the sun who are never out
in the sunshine, and never come up on the hills,
or go into the woods? How can they know anything about the stars who never stopped on the
hills, or on the sea all night? How can they know
anything of such things who are shut up in houses,
dear, where I cannot come in?

"Bevis, my love, if you want to know all about
the sun, and the stars, and everything, make haste
and come to me, and I will tell you, dear. In
the morning, dear, get up as quick as you can,
and drink me as I come down from the hill. In
the day go up on the hill, dear, and drink me
again, and stay there if you can till the stars
shine out, and drink still more of me.

"And by-and-by you will understand all about
the sun, and the moon, and the stars, and the Earth
which is so beautiful, Bevis. It is so beautiful,
you can hardly believe how beautiful it is. Do
not listen, dear, not for one moment, to the stuff
and rubbish they tell you down there in the houses
where they will not let me come. If they say the
Earth is not beautiful, tell them they do not speak
the truth. But it is not their fault, for they have

never seen it, and as they have never drank me their eyes are closed, and their ears shut up tight. But every evening, dear, before you get into bed, do you go to your window—the same as you did the evening the Owl went by — and lift the curtain and look up at the sky, and I shall be somewhere about, or else I shall be quiet in order that there may be no clouds, so that you may see the stars. In the morning, as I said before, rush out and drink me up.

"The more you drink of me, the more you will want, and the more I shall love you. Come up to me upon the hills, and your heart will never be heavy, but your eyes will be bright, and your step quick, and you will sing and shout ——"

"So I will," said Bevis, "I will shout. Holloa!" and he ran up on to the top of the little round hill, to which they had now returned, and danced about on it as wild as could be.

"Dance away, dear," said the Wind, much delighted, "Everybody dances who drinks me. The man in the hill there ——"

"What man?" said Bevis, "and how did he get in the hill; just tell him I want to speak to him."

"Darling," said the Wind, very quiet and softly, "he is dead, and he is in the little hill you are standing on, under your feet. At least, he was there once, but there is nothing of him there now. Still it is his place, and as he loved me, and I loved him, I come very often and sing here."

"When did he die?" said Bevis, "Did I ever see him?"

"He died just about a minute ago, dear; just before you came up the hill. If you were to ask the people who live in the houses, where they will not let me in (they carefully shut out the sun too) they would tell you he died thousands of years ago; but they are foolish, very foolish. It was hardly so long ago as yesterday. Did not the Brook tell you all about that?

"Now this man, and all his people, used to love me and drink me, as much as ever they could all day long and a great part of the night, and when they died they still wanted to be with me, and so they were all buried on the tops of the hills, and you will find these curious little mounds everywhere on the ridges, dear, where I blow along. There I come to them still, and sing through the long dry grass,

and rush over the turf, and I bring the scent of
the clover from the plain, and the bees come humming along upon me. The sun comes too, and the
rain. But I am here most; the sun only shines by
day, and the rain only comes now and then.

"But I am always here, day and night, winter
and summer. Drink me as much as you will, you
cannot drink me away; there is always just as much
of me left. As I told you, the people who were
buried in these little mounds used to drink me, and
oh! how they raced along the turf, dear, there is
nobody can run so fast now; and they leaped and
danced, and sang and shouted. I loved them as I
love you, my darling; there sit down and rest on
the thyme, dear, and I will stroke your hair and
sing to you."

So Bevis sat down on the thyme, and the Wind
began to sing, so low and sweet and so strange an
old song, that he closed his eyes and leaned on his
arm on the turf. There were no words to the song,
but Bevis understood it all, and it made him feel so
happy. The great sun smiled upon him, the great
Earth bore him in her arms gently, the Wind
caressed him, singing all the while. Now Bevis

knew what the Wind meant; he felt with his soul out to the far distant sun just as easily as he could feel with his hand to the bunch of grass beside him; he felt with his soul down through into the Earth just as easily as he could touch the sward with his fingers. Something seemed to come to him out of the sunshine and the grass.

"There never was a yesterday," whispered the Wind presently, "and there never will be to-morrow. It is all one long to-day. When the man in the hill was you were too, and he still is now you are here; but of these things you will know more when you are older, that is if you will only continue to drink me. Come, dear, let us race on again." So the two went on and came to a hawthorn bush, and Bevis, full of mischief always, tried to slip away from the Wind round the bush, but the Wind laughed and caught him.

A little further and they came to the fosse of the old camp. Bevis went down into the trench, and he and the Wind raced round along it as fast as ever they could go, till presently he ran up out of it on the hill, and there was the waggon underneath him, with the load well piled up now. There was the plain, yellow with stubble; the hills beyond it and the blue valley, just the same as he had left it.

As Bevis stood and looked down, the Wind caressed him and said, " Good-bye, darling, I am going yonder, straight across to the blue valley and the blue sky, where they meet; but I shall be back again when you come next time. Now remember, my dear, to drink me—come up here and drink me."

" Shall you be here?" said Bevis, "are you quite sure you will be here?"

" Yes," said the Wind, "I shall be quite certain to be here; I promise you, love, I will never go quite away. Promise me faithfully, too, that you will come up and drink me, and shout and race and be happy."

" I promise," said Bevis, beginning to go down the hill; " good-bye, jolly old Wind."

" Good-bye, dearest," whispered the Wind, as he went across out towards the valley. As Bevis went down the hill, a blue harebell, who had been singing farewell to summer all the morning, called to him and asked him to gather her and carry her home, as she would rather go with him than stay now autumn was near.

Bevis gathered the harebell, and ran with the flower in his hand down the hill, and as he ran the wild thyme kissed his feet and said "Come again, Bevis, come again." At the bottom of the hill the waggon was loaded now; so they lifted him up, and he rode home on the broad back of the leader.

DISTRIBUTORS
for Wordsworth Children's Classics

AUSTRALIA, BRUNEI & MALAYSIA

Reed Editions
22 Salmon Street
Port Melbourne
Vic 3207
Australia
Tel: (03) 646 6716
Fax: (03) 646 6925

GERMANY, AUSTRIA & SWITZERLAND

Swan Buch-Marketing GmbH
Goldscheuerstraße 16
D-7640 Kehl am Rhein
Germany

GREAT BRITAIN & IRELAND

Wordsworth Editions Ltd
Cumberland House
Crib Street
Ware
Hertfordshire SG12 9ET

INDIA

Om Book Service
1690 First Floor
Nai Sarak, Delhi - 110006
Tel: 3279823/3265303
Fax: 3278091

NEW ZEALAND

Whitcoulls Limited
Private Bag 92098, Auckland

SINGAPORE

Book Station
18 Leo Drive
Singapore
Tel: 4511998
Fax: 4529188

SOUTHERN AFRICA

Struik Book Distributors (Pty) Ltd
Graph Avenue
Montague Gardens
7441
P O Box 193
Maitland
7405
South Africa
Tel: (021) 551-5900
Fax: (021) 551-1124

USA, CANADA & MEXICO

Universal Sales & Marketing
230 Fifth Avenue
Suite 1212
New York, NY 10001 USA
Tel: 212-481-3500
Fax: 212-481-3534

ITALY

Magis Books
Piazza della Vittoria 1/C
42100 Reggio Emilia
Tel: 0522-452303
Fax: 0522-452845